The Girls in Green

The Girls in Green

TANUSHREE PODDER

BLOOMSBURY
NEW DELHI • LONDON • OXFORD • NEW YORK • SYDNEY

BLOOMSBURY INDIA
Bloomsbury Publishing India Pvt. Ltd
Second Floor, LSC Building No. 4, DDA Complex, Pocket C – 6 & 7,
Vasant Kunj, New Delhi, 110070

BLOOMSBURY, BLOOMSBURY INDIA and the Diana logo
are trademarks of Bloomsbury Publishing Plc

First published in India 2021
This edition published in 2021

ISBN: PB: 978-93-90252-81-7; eBook: 978-93-90252-83-1
2 4 6 8 10 9 7 5 3 1

Typeset in Manipal Technologies Limited
Printed and bound in India by Replika Press Pvt. Ltd.

MIX
Paper from responsible sources
FSC® C016779

To find out more about our authors and books visit www.bloomsbury.com and sign up for our newsletters

For the brave men and women who choose to dedicate their lives for the country

Author's Note

Many years ago, a little girl put on her father's boots and placed his beret on her little head. Then, wrapping his scarf around her neck, she stood before the mirror and saluted. A minute later, she stomped around the house. The uniform fascinated her.

Her father was in the army, and the little girl wanted to emulate him. She wanted to join the army. Alas! The army hadn't opened its doors to women. The only women allowed to join the army were doctors and nurses.

Forty-two years later, a woman sat watching a spectacular Passing out Parade at the Officers Training Academy (OTA). Tears flowed unabated as she watched her young daughter taking part in the slow march. Marching to the tune of 'Auld Lang Syne', proud and erect, they marched towards the Final Step. Yet another batch of budding army officers took their first steps towards fulfilling their dream.

The woman was the little girl, who had once wanted to join the army. She was also my classmate. I want you to write about the women officers, she said, when we met soon after the commissioning of her daughter.

Ever since I wrote *Boots Belts Berets* and *On the Double*, I have been asked why I haven't written a book about the officers, who passed out from the OTA. The response to those two books has been stupendous, and I have received dozens of emails from young men who decided to join the army after reading them.

The first time I thought of writing about women officers was when I met a smart and capable captain. 'Why haven't you written about us?' she asked.

At that time I was writing another book, so I shelved the suggestion. But it couldn't be shelved too long. The demand for a book on women officers was coming from all sides.

It was only after I saw Captain Tania Shergill leading an all men contingent at the Army Day Parade in 2020 that I knew it was time to write the book. Shergill also achieved the honour of being the first woman parade adjutant for Republic Day, 2020.

I realized that women officers had carved a special niche in the Indian Army, and were likely to achieve many more laurels in the future.

Since the passing out of the first batch of women officers in 1992, OTA has trained hundreds of young women, each one of them having gone through the same rigorous regimen as their male counterparts. They have competed against the men and won the coveted Sword of Honour, and proved themselves many times over.

Today, they serve in signals, engineers, army aviation, army air defence, electronics and mechanical engineers (EME), army service corps, army ordnance and intelligence corps. Right from carrying out mining and demining work, to manning the weapon systems in air defence, they are carrying out their duties in an efficient manner.

These girls come from diverse backgrounds and regions, but the one factor that they have in common is their zeal to serve the country. *The Girls in Green* is a tribute to these girls, who braved many challenges to reach where they are today.

Like in *Boots Belts Berets* and *On the Double*, both of which deal with the training of cadets in NDA and IMA, *The Girls in Green* is all about the extraordinary camaraderie that binds these army girls together. The bonds that are forged out of blistered feet, bruised bodies, rivulets of perspiration and broken egos last a lifetime. Personal comforts are sacrificed for the comfort of one's comrades. Individual aspirations are secondary to those of the company. Days roll into weeks and weeks morph into months as the training continues, each hour bringing fresh challenges. It is camaraderie and laughter that helps them survive.

As in the earlier books, there is enough fun and humour to keep you laughing. But there are poignant moments as well. Fun, adventure, thrill and emotions blend together to create an interesting account of the rigorous training the girls go through.

Writing any book is an all-encompassing and time-consuming job but writing a book about the army takes much more. Although it is fiction, the details have to be right, and this requires an extensive amount of research. I had to visit the OTA a couple of times and interview several officers who were kind enough to share details of training and the life in the academy. I wish to point out that I have taken the liberty of embellishing and altering some details to suit the story.

None of this would have been possible without the cooperation of the many women officers who have passed out from the elite academy. I am indebted to each one of them for their time and support.

I am thankful to my family and friends, who cheered me through the long process of research and writing.

I am sure you will enjoy this one.

PROLOGUE

THE CANNY CAT

'Girl, you have done it,' her grandfather's voice boomed into Bijli's ears, the pride in it unmistakable. 'You have been selected for the Officers Training Academy, Chennai. I have waited a long time for this day.'

'Yes!' Elated with the news, Bijli aka Billi, punched the air, and the girls in the dressing room looked at her with amusement. Her heart raced like a runaway train as she digested the news.

'It's time to go,' announced one of her teammates. There was a sudden melee as the girls poured out of the dressing room and began running towards the football ground.

'Daddu, the match is about to begin,' she said. 'I have to switch the phone off now.'

'Don't worry, Billi. Like always, you will win this match.'

Ten minutes later, she was on the field with her opponent, watching the referee as he tossed a coin in the air. Adrenaline surged through her body as she wrestled the ball away, leading it towards the goalpost, all other thoughts swept away from her mind.

Tall and muscular, she was tough as nails. Her moves struck fear in the opponents, since they could never be sure of her strategy. Fondly called Billi, she was lithe as a feline and crafty as a fox. Outwitting adversaries was her special skill.

That morning, however, distracted and indecisive, she resorted to playing a defensive game and thus provided an upper hand to the rival team.

With just two minutes for the final whistle, the match was at a nail-biting stage. Bijli stood poised with the ball, ready to kick it into the goalpost, when an opponent gave her a violent push and she fell to the ground. A cumulative protest went up and the crowd cried 'foul', forcing the referee to award her a penalty kick.

The spectators leaned forward to watch. Silence descended as Bijli prepared for the final kick. But she ran out of luck. A collective sound of disappointment went up in the air as she missed the goalpost and lost the opportunity. She had never missed a goal before; atleast not with a free kick. Yet, she had failed to score the crucial goal that would have taken her team to the semi-finals.

The football match ended in a draw. Alakhpura Eleven, the favourites for a win, ended without scoring a single goal. The only way they could reach the semi-finals was if Patiala Blues lost their next match, but that seemed near possible. The Patiala girls, led by an aggressive captain, were determined to carry the shield home.

Her dejection was compounded when Banwari Lal tried to boost her morale.

'Don't give up hope,' he consoled, grabbing her hand across the table they had occupied in a bustling café. 'Let's pray and wait for the next match.'

He was a wrestler and a national champion and had faced enough victories and defeats to understand the state of Billi's mind.

Snatching away her hand, she retaliated, 'Who says I have given up hope? I am confident of reaching the semi-final.'

Throwing him a scornful glance, she got up and walked away. Banwari was the last person she wanted to see at that moment. Six months ago, her family had found in him a suitable match for their obstinate daughter. Tall and handsome, Banwari belonged to the same caste, and his family owned several acres of farming land. Besides, his job in the Haryana Police made him a good catch.

Billi tried every possible trick to change her father's mind, but the man was just as obstinate. 'We have given you enough freedom to exercise your will. You wanted to play football, I didn't object to that. You wanted to pursue graduation, I didn't object to that either. But now I am not budging from my decision of getting you married. Banwari is a sportsman and a broad-minded chap. He will not stop you from playing football.'

'I want to study further,' she had protested, though Billi had no intention of doing so. All she wanted was to escape matrimony. 'He can wait for two more years, I am sure.'

'You can study further after marriage. I am sure Banwari will have no objection to that.'

It was futile arguing. The wedding was barely a couple of months away and Billi was desperate.

Ten months ago, an interview aired on television put her on a new path. The interviewee was the lady officer who had passed out of the Officers Training Academy with honours. She had topped the merit list and bagged the Sword of Honour. It was a rare feat. One that made an impression on Billi's mind. It was a eureka moment for the young woman, who had long been fascinated by the shining brass stars and olive green uniform. This is what she wanted to do. Bring home an award that made her parents and entire village proud. Riveted, she listened to the lady officer's experiences at the academy.

Most of her friends wanted to join the police force, but wearing the khaki wasn't her dream. She had been undecided about her plans. The one thing she didn't want to do was to marry. With the family scouting around for a suitable match, she realized that time was running out for her. Joining the army seemed the only way out for Billi.

On an impulse, she had filled up forms for the entrance examination to join the army. It was her secret. Not to be shared with anyone, except her grandfather. Subedar Major Mahavir Singh was the only one she could trust. As a child, she had sat on his lap and listened to many stories of wars and valour. A diehard soldier, the old man had wanted one of his sons to join the army, but none of them wanted to go through the rigours of army life.

He was ecstatic when she confided in him. 'I will help you in every possible manner,' he promised. Billi travelled to Gurgaon to spend her vacation with her grandfather, where the two conspired to clear the tests.

He helped her fill up the forms and provided his address for communication. He also ran her through a battery of physical tests.

Determined to succeed, she burnt the midnight oil to prepare for the tests. Her parents were surprised to note her sudden interest in books, but they refrained from commenting. The English language was a bugbear. It had always been the biggest roadblock in her path. She joined a short term course to help her overcome the handicap. To her surprise, she cleared the written examination for the army and was called for an interview. Just as Billi was wondering about the excuses she could offer for travelling to Delhi for the next round, a series of football matches came to her rescue.

She sought the help of her grandfather, who promptly invited her to stay at Gurgaon the week preceding the matches. There the two prepared for the interview, where she would be tested psychologically, physically and mentally. She had sailed through those tests with no hiccups.

Her grandfather's call was a confirmation that the sweat they had shed had been fruitful. It put to rest all the doubts in her mind.

Now that she had been selected to undergo training at the Officers Training Academy at Chennai, Billi was confused about the next step. How would she break the news to the family? More importantly, how would she travel to Chennai without their consent?

~

MISS STEEL MAGNOLIA

Shiny had just stepped out of the house when her phone began ringing.

'Guess who made it to the academy?' Aaron's voice floated down the line, and she smiled.

'That's not difficult to guess. My name's right on top of the list. You would be lucky to figure at the bottom, if at all,' she laughed.

'For once, you are right. Shiny Chacko heads the list of successful candidates, but yours truly is not too far behind. We have both made it, darling.' The delight in his voice was unmistakable.

'Congratulations to the two of us,' Shiny replied. Sailing through challenges made her happy.

'Hey Shiny, it's a big day for us. Why don't we celebrate tonight?' he suggested. 'I will pick you up at seven.'

'At your service, boss,' she gurgled happily.

No one who looked at the willowy and mild mannered girl could imagine she could be stubborn as a mule. Shiny Joseph Chacko had a mind of her own, and no one knew it better than her mother.

When she decided to pursue mechanical engineering, her dad was vehemently opposed to the idea.

'Information technology is where the future lies,' advised Joseph Chacko. 'I think you should opt for IT.'

'You are right, of course,' replied his respectful daughter. 'However, mechanical engineering is the mother of all engineering and that is where my interest lies.'

To be fair, she never argued with her parents and was polite with everyone. Yet, she managed to do whatever her heart dictated. Her friends called her Miss Steel Magnolia.

After completing B.Tech., Shiny went on to enrol for an M.Tech. in automobile engineering. An excellent basketball player and NCC cadet, the athletic Shiny was a winner all around. She will go on to get a doctorate now, her friends predicted. A month later, she demolished everyone's expectations.

'I have decided to join the army,' she declared.

But why would you want to do that, everyone wanted to know.

'I just feel like wearing the uniform,' she said.

That was not the real reason, of course. It was Shiny's boyfriend, Aaron Koshy, who had planted the idea in her mind. The two had been together since kindergarten. They grew up squabbling and fighting over toys, and competing in studies and games. The squabbles turned into affection and then love, growing with each passing year. They studied in the same college before he took up a job and she enrolled for M.Tech.

Shiny's mind was made the moment Aaron called up to announce his intention of joining the army. She wanted to be with him and enrolling in the army seemed the best way to do that. They would be together during training and get commissioned on the same day, at the same venue. Things couldn't get better than that. Also, her competitive streak had poked up its ugly head once again. It had been the same all through school. The two of them had competed for the first rank and every prize. The truth was that she had beaten him each time. Be it academics or sports, she had won all the prizes.

'I will do the same,' she declared in her characteristic gentle manner when Aaron announced his plan to join the army.

'Think again,' he said, though he knew the futility of questioning Shiny's decision. 'The entrance tests are difficult and the regimen more so. It's a tough life, really.'

With those words, Aaron had thrown down the gauntlet. She took it up with a smile. 'And you think I am not tough enough?' she countered. 'I can do anything you can do, and better.'

'Well, I can't stop you,' he teased. 'Let's see if the two of us can reach the academy.'

'I am confident of being selected, though I can't say the same for you,' she retorted.

Preparing for the OTA entrance examination had been an easy feat for the girl who had made it a habit to excel. Her boyfriend had also joined a study circle to prepare for the examination. He couldn't afford to fail. It had become a matter of honour for him.

Joseph Chacko was not surprised to hear that his brilliant daughter had been selected to undergo training at the Officers Training Academy. The news didn't bring him joy. He was sorely disappointed. Shiny was his only daughter, and he would have liked for her to find a good job and lead a stable and comfortable life. Aaron was a nice boy and Chacko approved of his daughter's choice, but he had not bargained for the two youngsters to join the army. At the same time, the astute man was aware of the futility of trying to influence their decision.

His wife, Sarah, was the one who argued with Shiny. She had tried her best to dissuade the girl but had failed. Desperate, she had reached out to Aaron's parents, asking them to discourage their son from joining the army. But the couple was proud of their son's decision and refused to intervene.

'You should be proud of your daughter, Mrs Chacko,' said Aaron's father. 'Under the circumstances, it will be better for you to support her decision. We want our children to be happy, don't we? In any case, the two of them are going to be together.'

Although disappointed with their reaction, Sarah knew they were right. She should support her daughter and pray for her happiness.

'I will miss you,' she said, helping her daughter pack her clothes in the black metal box that she had newly acquired as per the joining instructions.

'I will miss you too, Mama,' said Shiny. 'It's just a matter of six months and then I will come home for the midterm break.'

After witnessing the excitement on Shiny's face as they dropped her at the railway station, Sarah knew it would have been wrong to resist her daughter's decision.

~

THE DRAMA QUEEN

The acceptance letter arrived while Nutan was in the theatre watching her favourite star's antics on the screen. It was only after she reached home in the evening that she found the letter and read its contents. The next moment, she leapt out of the room, screaming at the top of her voice.

'I have been selected,' she announced to her large extended family, that occupied the two-storeyed house along with her.

The announcement drew several family members to the courtyard in the centre of the house. Soon, a joyous atmosphere permeated the Patil residence. Nutan had been selected to join the Officers Training Academy, and it was a reason for celebration not just for the family but for the neighbourhood as well. She would be the first girl from the village to join the army.

Nutan's father, Baburao Patil, was an ambitious man with an overworked sulky wife and three wilful daughters. He belonged to an agrarian family, where the education of girls had never been a priority. But Baburao was a progressive man. Undaunted by the lack of a son, he decided to provide his daughters with a good education so they could have impressive careers. While the elder one was the studious kind, his youngest daughter Nutan barely scraped through the examinations. Like most of her friends, the girl loved watching Bollywood movies and dreamt of living a glamorous life in the city. Her desires were restricted to fashionable clothes and exotic food.

Baburao was not a man to give up. He offered the girl an opportunity to study further in Pune, but only if she got 70 per cent in her high school examinations. Though not very good in studies, Nutan found herself being propelled by her father's ambitions. It was the temptation of journeying to Pune that drove her to perform well in her board exams.

In Pune the girl experienced a taste of freedom. Studies were pushed to the back-burner as she made friends with a few wayward girls. Together, they broke all the rules of the girls' hostel to enjoy life. Her love for movies was satisfied when she found a roommate who was as mad about movies as she was. The two of them watched a couple of movies every weekend, on a laptop. If it was not movies, she would be gallivanting around glitzy malls or dining out with her roommates.

Money was a constraint, but there were a couple of rich and generous girls who willingly loosened their purse strings for their friends. In return, Nutan regaled them with her repertoire of jokes, imitated all the lecturers, and cooked up mischievous plans. Not just that, she could parrot dramatic dialogues of her favourite hero Salman Khan and dance like Hrithik Roshan. The girl was the life of every party in and out of the hostel. She was also an outrageous flirt.

It was a chance visit to the National Defence Academy that exposed her to the glitzy and glamorous side of the army. Her friend's brother, Nitish, was training at NDA and he was looking for a girl to take to the NDA ball. Always ready for a bit of action and excitement, Nutan volunteered to be Nitish's partner. The ball changed her perspective on life. The impressionable girl decided that she would either marry an army officer or be one herself. The decision became firmer after she witnessed the Passing out Parade at NDA. For the first time, she had a goal in life.

The more she thought about the idea, the more entrenched it became. 'I will be the first girl from the village to join the army. Wouldn't that create history?' she told her sister, who dutifully relayed the information to the entire family and then to the entire clan. And soon, the news spread through the small village.

When she visited the village shortly thereafter, Nutan found herself surrounded by people wanting to know more about the steps she was taking to prepare for the entrance examination. Hopes were pinned on her, she realized.

There was no scope of backtracking.

Fully aware of her weaknesses, the girl was in a dilemma. She had never been studious, and she had been told that the entrance examination was no child's play. It would be a shame in case she failed to make the grade, and the shame wouldn't be hers alone. Her father would also suffer the humiliation of shattered hopes. Nutan loved her father too much to disappoint him. There was just one thing to do. She would have to prepare seriously for the examination.

After returning to Pune, she joined a coaching class. Her days of fun and frolic were replaced by bookish pursuits. Gone was the flighty and flirty girl she had been. Slowly and steadily, the friends vanished. She was no longer the entertaining girl they knew.

The instructors at the coaching classes did not expect her to clear the entrance exam. English had never been a strong point, nor logic or reasoning. She drew enough barbs from the boys who were attending the classes. There were very few girls in the class, and she seemed to be the most hare-brained one among them.

'Frankly speaking, you are wasting your time and money,' snarled one of the instructors, after she had failed a test. 'Why do you want to join the army, anyway?'

If anything, the ridicule strengthened her resolve. She was determined to prove the instructors wrong.

For once, the dark circles around her eyes didn't faze her, and she pored over her books every night. Her hard work began to yield results and her grades began improving. Her objective was to not only clear the entrance test but also to clear the college graduate examinations. She achieved both.

Nutan appeared for the Combined Defence Services (CDS) examination, confident of sailing through it. Shortly thereafter, when the graduation results were announced, her grades proved that the hours she had spent studying had not gone to waste.

Returning to the village after the examination, she found herself a target of heightened expectations. And then the letter arrived. Nutan had cleared the CDS entrance examination. An overjoyed Baburao threw a party to celebrate the news of his daughter's success.

~

THE SPIRITED SPRITE

Almost everyone living in the Laban neighbourhood of Shillong was aware of Lakme's fascination for the army. It had begun the day she visited her best friend Violet's house. The girl's uncle, Major Albert Diengdoh, was visiting the family. He had brought with him many tales of army life and every evening, the neighbourhood children crowded around the young officer to hear his stories of perilous adventures. Among them was the bright-eyed, eight-year-old Khasi girl called Lakmenlang Nongrum. Over the years, Albert's stories took a grip over the girl's imagination, and she decided to join the army.

While her teenaged friends read paperbacks of syrupy sweet sentimental schmaltz, Lakme aka Lucky, stocked her book rack with adventure novels whose protagonists had army backgrounds. Her friends laughed when she shared her ambition.

'Girls don't read such books,' scoffed her classmates at the Auxilium Girls School.

'Neither do they go to war,' they said.

Right from her friends and family to her teachers and classmates, everyone mocked her ambition. They had never before encountered a girl who wanted to join the army. Most girls wanted to become pop stars, fashion designers, models, film stars, microbiologists, doctors and engineers. No one spoke of joining the army.

The daughter of a wholesale grain trader from Shillong found no support for her dreams. Not even her father who usually indulged her whims and fancies. 'Our daughter is enamoured with the idea of brass buttons and uniform. She will outgrow the fantasy,' he consoled his wife, Aiti.

Lakme neither forgot nor outgrew her fantasies. All she did was relegate them to the back of her mind while she completed her graduation. An excellent crooner, she was popular for her foot-tapping numbers, and her father was sure she would take up singing professionally. She allowed them to think whatever they wanted to think, but she knew where her dreams led. Her delicate personality notwithstanding, the girl possessed a mulish nature.

Albert, a retired soldier now, was the only one who persisted in fanning the embers of her ambition. He continued to motivate and inspire the girl as she grew into an intelligent and athletic young woman, who loved climbing mountains.

'You have the focus, stamina and determination to be a soldier,' Albert told her. 'All you need is a bit of preparation.'

With his help, she found out all about the entrance examination for the hallowed institution known as the Officers Training Academy.

The two of them conspired to fill the forms and prepare for the tests. 'Wouldn't it be nice to make them all eat crow?' Albert said.

'I will make them do that,' the girl laughed.

True to her words, Lakme made the entire community eat crow the day her acceptance letter arrived. She was amazed at the turnout at home. Her parents, who had scoffed at the idea of her joining the army, were quick in heaping their blessings and grabbing a share of credit for her success.

'I was confident Lucky would sail through the tough examination,' her father declared to all and sundry.

'We have always encouraged our daughters to follow their heart,' said her mother.

It wasn't true, of course. Her vehement protests against Lakme's career choices had resulted in naught, so the wise woman had decided to go along with the flow. 'My daughter will do us proud.'

Soon, the naysayers lined up to congratulate the cheerful girl, and her parents could not stop preening. Sweets were bought and preparations for the celebrations began in earnest. It was a great day for the entire neighbourhood, for she was the first girl to qualify for the OTA.

It was party time. Since there was no time to send invitations, the Nongrum family decided to have an open house. Anyone who arrived was greeted with drinks and snacks. Parties were a great lure for people. They arrived by the dozen, and Lakme regaled the guests with lively numbers. She was in top form.

Albert's was the only sane voice that night.

'Life is not going to be parties and music. The training is tough and the routine hectic. You will have no time to relax, so enjoy all you can,' he warned.

'You have a wealth of experience. Why don't you give her some guidance about the things she can expect while training at the academy?' requested an anxious Aiti. Despite putting up a brave front, she was uneasy about sending her daughter so far away.

'Lucky is an intelligent girl. She will be able to handle everything. Besides, I am hardly in a position to give her any advice. All I can say is that she should remain calm, obey orders and think positively.'

'Keep your eyes and ears open at all times and don't get on the wrong side of the ustads,' he cautioned the girl, before taking his leave.

The days of excitement and celebrations ended, and it was time to pack.

'It seems like a list given by boarding schools,' remarked Aiti as she went through the items in 'List of Clothing Items to Be Brought by Lady Cadets'.

The list had been a part of the joining letter. 'I think there is a mistake. They have sent you a list that is meant for boys.'

'Why do you say that?' asked Lakme, smiling at her mother's puzzled expression.

'There is no mention of any women's garments.'

Lucky placed her arm around her mother's shoulders and gave her a comforting squeeze. 'Mom, your daughter is not going for a fashion show. She is joining the army.'

'I understand that. But look at this list.'

'*I...*'

Aiti read out loudly from the list:

1. White Shirt 02 Full sleeves without pocket.
2. Terry Cotton Shorts (White) 04 Two with broad loops
3. Terry Cotton Trousers (White) 01
4. Terry Cotton Trousers (Black) 02 With only one pleat and no belt loops
5. Neck Tie 01
6. Night Suit and Dressing Gown 02
7. Leather Shoes Formal (Black) 01 Pair Oxford /Brogue pattern.
8. Socks Nylon (Black) 02 Pairs
9. PT Shoes (White) 01 Pair Good quality running shoes (Adidas/Reebok plain (white) without any design could be brought).
10. White Socks Cotton (White) 03 Pairs
11. Bathroom Slippers 01 Pair
12. Undergarments 06 Sets
13. Handkerchief 06
14. Bath Towels Large (White) 02
15. Personal Toiletries 01 Set as per requirement
16. Steel Box (Size 75 x 45 x 30 cm) – Name written in white on Bottom Left Corner. Alphabet size 1.5"
17. Single Bed Sheet and Pillow (white) 02 sets
18. Lock (Medium Size) 02
19. Suitcase/Bag as required
20. Terry Cotton Half Shirt (White) 02 without pocket

'This is hilarious,' chirped Lucky's younger sister Olari, who was peeping over her mother's shoulder.

'What's so funny?' asked Lucky, frowning at the teenager.

'Who carries steel boxes these days? Not just that, they have even specified the placing and size of the letters that are to label the box.'

'Shoo! Run away,' chided Aiti. 'Don't bother your sister.'

'She's mad,' teased Olari. 'I won't be surprised if she comes running back. I am giving her one week.'

'I won't come running back, as you say. Now, run away before I box your ears.' Lucky clenched her fist threateningly.

A week later, the anxious parents drove Lucky to Guwahati, so she could catch her flight to Chennai.

An Anxious Arrival

CHENNAI RAILWAY STATION

It was a hot and humid afternoon. The overcrowded train pulled into the Chennai Central Railway Station. Restless passengers with their umpteen bags had already lined up at the train's exit, preparing to step off as soon as the train came to a halt.

Checking her hair and dress in the tiny, rusty mirror hanging in the toilet, Billi prepared to jostle her way through the aisle. The long train journey, in the company of snoring men, bawling kids and gossiping women, not to mention the terrible music blaring out of a ruffian's mobile, had been nothing short of a nightmare.

An aggressive porter insisted on taking charge of the black steel trunk lying under the seat. Grabbing it by the handle, he quoted an unrealistic amount for his services. Haggling was impossible, what with the language barrier between them, but Billi was not one to give up. What followed was a hilarious session of bargaining, with much gesticulating and sound effects, till the two of them settled on a price.

Squaring her shoulders, heartbeat accelerated, she readied herself to report to the reception committee, which was supposed to take charge of the cadets reporting for training at the Officers Training Academy.

The platform was a sea of human beings that morning. Tea vendors, newspaper sellers, toy sellers, fruit vendors and food trolleys jostled for space with rushing passengers. A cacophony of voices, punctuated by the rumble of passing trains assaulted the eardrums. Trains passed through the platforms spewing out weary passengers. Fetid air, thick with the smell of urine, stale food, cigarettes, perspiration and dirt circulated through the crowd.

The porter waited impatiently for her to take the lead, but Billi realized that she was clueless about the direction to take. There seemed to be too many platforms and foot overbridges. All around her, people were speaking an alien language, not a word of which she understood. They gesticulated or shrugged when she asked them for directions to the reception committee. The unfamiliar language made it difficult to converse with anyone. In any case, no one seemed to have the time to guide anyone. Exasperated with the situation, she looked around for help.

Just then, she spotted a smart young man striding confidently along the platform. He was accompanied by a porter carrying a black steel trunk exactly like the one she had been instructed to carry for her belongings. Confident that he was one of the cadets on his way to the Officers' Training Academy, she hurried behind him with the porter in tow. Looking back, Billi spotted a couple of girls with similar black trunks following her and the young man now had a long tail. It was obvious that the black steel trunk had become their guiding light. Thankfully, the young man seemed to know where he was going.

A few minutes later, they joined a group of young girls and boys gathered near a couple of uniformed non-commissioned officers (NCOs) at the reception centre for cadets joining the OTA. Wearing a placid expression on his round face, one of them rifled through a sheaf of papers in an unhurried manner, ticking off the names of the cadets. From time to time, he paused to stroke his moustache in a contemplative manner.

His companion, however, seemed more impatient. After subjecting the cadets to a baleful look, he ordered them to form a queue.

There was excitement in the air, and soon a few girls in the queue began whispering to each other. The whispers turned into sotto voce, and soon the decibels began rising. The girls passed comments about the young men, and soon the ripple of their giggles reached the senior NCO's ears.

'Silence!' he shouted. The order made the girls, who had closed up together for a session of note-sharing, scatter. They slithered back into the queue.

'You are here to join the army. It is not a party,' the NCO continued pompously.

By now, there were about 15 youngsters in the queue. There were more boys, of course. This was expected, since the number of Gentlemen Cadets (GCs) is about 160-200 while the intake of Lady Cadets (LCs) ranged between 35-45 per course.

'The army is a disciplined organization. Those who don't understand that, have no place in it.' The NCO was in full *josh* by then.

The warning straightened all slouching backs and stilled shuffling feet. For a while, not a person moved, nor did a gaze stray. One by one, the NCO ticked off the names from his list and directed the cadets towards a bus waiting in the parking area.

Anxiety hit Billi, as she realized that Chennai was hundreds of kilometres away from home. There had been instances when she had to travel for football competitions, but she had never been alone. The journeys undertaken with the team had been immense fun. This time around, her family didn't even know where she was.

It was her grandfather's idea. 'There is no need to tell them anything. Not until you have settled down at the academy. We don't want your father to pull you out of the training. For the moment, let them assume that you are with me in Gurgaon.'

Although uneasy with the deception, she realized the truth of his words. Her father would take the first flight to Chennai if he learnt that she had joined the academy.

Billi threw a tentative smile at the smartly dressed girl standing in front of her and received a blank look in return.

Clad in a form-fitting pair of jeans and a striped T-shirt, the girl flaunted an unmistakable air of superiority. Billi's eyes missed nothing; neither the butterfly tattoo on the back of her neck, nor her swept-up hairdo or the pale lipstick on her lips. A chunky silver bracelet clasped her right wrist, while a trendy necklace, made of beads, adorned her long neck. Her impeccable dress and accessories made the footballer aware of her own crumpled clothes and bedraggled appearance. A tad self-consciously, she smoothed the creases of her red T-shirt, which exhibited an oil stain as big as a tennis ball. The word 'Captain', printed at the back, made her cringe self-consciously.

Back home, the T-shirt had earned everyone's respect, but here, she wasn't so sure.

Riled with the girl's attitude, Billi pursed her lips in displeasure. *What the heck, we are not here for a catwalk. Bloody snob! The two of us are reporting for the same training and will soon be equals. I wonder how long her arrogance will last.* She snorted derisively.

'Did you say something?' asked the supercilious girl.

'I was just clearing my throat,' Billi smirked. On second thought, she snorted once more.

'Hi, I am Kiran from Aurangabad,' whispered a voice from the back.

Billi turned and faced a pleasant-faced girl with curly hair.

'Good morning, myself Bijli Bijarnia from Alakhpura, Bhiwani,' Billi beamed, drawing herself to her full height of five feet six inches. Blurting out this introduction was easy, especially after the innumerable rehearsals in front of a mirror. As an afterthought, she added, 'Before arriving to Chennai, I was the captain of Alakhpura Football Club. What about you? Any sport activities?'

The captaincy was the biggest achievement of Billi's life, if one discounted the struggle for a degree in commerce. The only difference between the two achievements was that she enjoyed the former, while the latter had been the mother of all pains.

'Wow! That's nice,' the girl said. 'Unfortunately, I have not been a captain of any team. I play a bit of badminton and can swim, but nothing worth mentioning.'

Billi warmed up to the girl's unassuming nature. 'I can neither play badminton nor swim. We have one pond in the village, but it's too dirty for swimming. Only the buffaloes swim in it,' she giggled.

The two of them chatted quietly while the NCO continued to call out names on his list and directed the cadets to the vehicle that was to transport them to the academy.

'Bijli Bijarnia?' Her name, at last.

'Yes, sir.' She nodded at Kiran and moved forward.

'You are Bijli Bijarnia?' The NCO subjected her to a stern look.

'Yes sir, myself Bijli…' she paused, embarrassed. She had been engrossed in conversation with Kiran and had failed to hear him announce her name.

'You may proceed to the bus,' he said finally. 'Next time, try to be alert.'

Heaving a sigh of relief, she joined the others who were making their way towards the bus. In the meantime, their signature black metal trunks had been loaded onto an army truck.

Clambering into the bus, Billi sank into the seat next to Kiran, who had extracted a big packet of potato chips from her bag and was munching busily.

'I was feeling hungry,' explained Kiran, extending the packet towards Billi, who grabbed a handful. It had been several hours since she had eaten. The food which had been served on the train had been terribly unappetizing, and after the first meal, she had survived on wafers and cold drinks.

'So, you are from Alakhpura?

'Yes, it is a small place. Not like Chennai.'

'Well, I am from Jabalpur and it's not a very big city either. But I love it.'

'Alakhpura may be small, but it is famous. It has been written about in many newspapers and magazines.'

'That's very nice. What is it famous for?'

'Haven't you heard of the Alakhpura girls' football team? Our football team has won two Subroto Cup titles. It is run with the support of the entire village, and many of the girls trained by the club have participated in the national football championship.'

'That sounds very impressive. I am sure you will do well in the academy.' There was genuine appreciation in Kiran's voice.

Meanwhile, the bus began winding its way towards the academy and everyone began chattering loudly. The ice was broken, information was shared and friends were made. Some young men, keen on making friends with the girls, were going from one end of the bus to the other, introducing themselves.

Voices began rising with excitement, and soon the bus was buzzing like a fish market on wheels.

'Has anyone in your family joined the army?' Billi asked her companion. She was keen to take the budding friendship to a new level.

'One of my uncles was in the army, but he retired a couple of years ago. What about you?'

'My grandfather served in the army, but I am the first girl in our family to join the army,' replied the Haryanvi girl, her eyes clouding with memories of the angry reactions at home.

'Why can't girls join the army?' Billi had ranted.

'We have broken all the rules to let you play football,' said her mother. 'But there is no question of your joining the army.'

'All the girls in the village play football. It's not like I am doing something against the social norm.'

'Don't argue,' thundered her father.

They refused to listen to reason. Only Daddu stood by her.

He painted a rosy picture of a world where girls were brave enough to go to war with men. 'Imagine fighting for the country, Billi,' Daddu goaded. 'You will be the pride of the town, and soon, other girls will follow your example.'

Till then, leading her team to victory in the India Women's Football Championship had been Billi's ultimate goal. That dream was suddenly replaced by a picture of herself decked in combat uniform, annihilating the enemy with a machine gun.

Now, as the bus raced towards its destination, she sighed with pleasure and sank deeper into the seat. *It will be just as Daddu predicted. I will set an example for the Alakhpura girls.*

Soon, the bus drew near the impressive portal of the academy. Engraved in shining brass letters on a black granite gateway were the words – Officers Training Academy.

The words struck a chord in everyone. Backs straightened, all chatter ceased and a feeling of pride made everyone's chests swell. They were a step closer to their dreams.

A Painful Introduction

The excited chatter in the bus came to a sudden halt. Their magnificent surroundings made the newcomers gasp with appreciation. Awestruck, Billi could barely speak.

'Wow! This is amazing!' Billi heard the wonder in her companion's voice. Unwittingly, she echoed the expression.

The bus stopped just inside the main gate of the OTA. The cadets were asked to produce their joining letters by a couple of uniformed NCOs. In their hands, they held a list of names, which they matched with the joining letters handed over by the newcomers. One by one, the cadets were given their academy numbers, by which they would be identified during their entire stay at the academy. They were also informed of the name of the company allotted to them. The company would be their home for the duration of the course, and the affiliation would exist forever. Their loyalties would remain unwavering.

While there were quite a few companies for the men, the women, owing to their small number, were accommodated in Zojila or Phillora companies.

Formalities completed, the bus wound its way through acres of neatly manicured lawns, orderly rows of plants, tall trees and beautiful structures. It was an impressive set-up. The very thought that they were going to be a part of it accelerated everyone's heartbeats. *From now on, we will be known as lady cadets (LCs)*, the Haryanvi girl reminded herself. *I am LC Bijli Bijarnia*. The very words made her chest puff with pride.

Of the seven girls who had arrived that evening, four, including Billi, had been allotted the Zojila Company. The bus dropped them off at an elegant triple-storeyed structure that was to house them during their training. The entrance of the building led to a large foyer with a grand staircase in the centre, which led to the upper floors. A long corridor, flanked by rooms on either side, ran on the left and right side of the lobby.

One side of the structure housed the Zojila Company girls, while the other was reserved for the girls from Phillora Company.

It was 6 p.m. when the exhausted girls sauntered into the main foyer.

'All I want is to take a shower and hit the bed,' said one of them.

'So do I,' seconded another.

The thought of a shower and bed was a tempting one, indeed. Just then, they ran into two smart looking LCs with their hallmark zero haircuts, dressed in the games uniform. They belonged to the senior batch.

'Those who have been allotted to the Zojila Company, stay here. Others can leave,' shouted one of them.

'Welcome to the Zalims!' greeted the other.

Zalims! A trifle confused if she had heard right, Billi wondered about the connotation of the word. But it was nice to be welcomed so warmly, so she grinned and replied, 'Thank you!'

'What is your name?'

'Myself LC Bijli Bijarnia from Alakhpura,' she said and extended her hand. Then, realizing it was impolite not to ask the other person's name, she added, 'What is your name?'

'So, you want to know my name?' the LC barked in an aggressive manner. 'I will explain who I am, but first fetch your bags from outside.'

What's her problem, Billi wondered. *All I did was ask her her name.* She shrugged her shoulders and began hauling her big black trunk, which had been dumped in front of the building by the vehicle which had ferried the cadets' luggage from the railway staton to the academy. It was left for the LCs to lug them to their rooms. *Don't they have someone to help with the heavy stuff?* She dragged the trunk by its handle. It was very challenging carrying it up the three steps that led to the lobby. All of a sudden, the box seemed to have put on weight.

Watching the others huffing and puffing even more with their metal trunks, she was thankful to Daddu for his wise advice. 'Carry the essentials only,' he had insisted. 'You won't need frills and laces, since you are not going for a fashion show,' he had said. 'Stick to the list of items provided in the joining instructions. There is no need for extra paraphernalia.'

'Quick! Hurry up, girls. You don't have the entire evening to carry the boxes inside,' shouted the senior, who seemed to have got up on the wrong side of her bed that morning.

'Who is she?' whispered Kiran.

'She is a senior,' hissed another girl in reply.

'She could be an officer,' remarked Billi doubtfully. 'I don't think an LC would order us around, even if she were a senior.'

'Silence!' This time it was the other LC. 'Zip your lips, or I will do it for you.'

Blistering under the glare of the two tormentors, the newcomers struggled with their loads. 'Let us help each other,' suggested Billi, grabbing the handle on Kiran's heavy box. The girl was perspiring with the effort of dragging it up the steps. 'Two can do the task better.'

After dumping the boxes in one corner, the four Zojila girls faced their seniors in the central lobby at the main entrance of the building.

'Stand straight,' the LC, who they learnt was the CSM (Cadet Sergeant Major), barked at her. 'Why are you swinging your arms like a pendulum? Do you have no control over them?'

'Introduce yourselves one by one. Give us your name, qualification and hobbies.'

The first one to introduce herself was a tall girl with short hair. Standing erect, arms held tight by her sides and her eyes staring at a point above the CSM's head, she spoke in a clear and crisp voice. 'My name is Koel Kukreja, and I am from Chandigarh. I did my schooling from the Army School, Panchkula, and my engineering from the Army Institute of Technology (AIT), Pune. I love to read, and I play tennis and squash.'

Impressed by Koel's military stance, the others tried to copy her.

'So you are an army brat?' The CSM's voice had a deceptive smoothness to it. Her eyes beady, she barked, 'Is your father still serving or has he retired?'

'Yes ma'am, he's still serving.' Koel continued to stare at the eighth step on the staircase, her face devoid of expression.

'What's his rank?'

'He's a Major General.'

'Well, well, Miss Smarty Pants, don't you try to pull your father's rank in the academy. We, at Zojila, don't like army brats,' the senior snorted derisively.

'You begin with a disadvantage,' quipped the other senior, who was the SUO (Senior Under Officer). 'While we make slight allowances for the others, no such tolerance is shown to an army brat.'

Noticing the malicious look in her eyes, Billi was grateful not to have a Major General for a father. Koel, however, continued to maintain an impassive expression on her face.

The second girl, Seema, belonged to a business family in Varanasi. Nervous, she stammered and faltered through her introduction.

'Is this how you always speak, or is this a one-off performance? Everyone in the academy is expected to speak clearly and loudly. Now, introduce yourself once more.'

The poor girl was made to go through the introductions half a dozen times, before they let go of her, with a warning. Glancing sideways at her, Billi noticed the moisture in Seema's eyes.

'The next time you go home, remember to drown your timidity in the Ganges. It will not serve you well at the academy,' smirked Miss Khadoos, as Billi had named the senior who was tormenting them.

Alia, the third girl, did a perfect job.

Finally, it was Billi's turn to introduce herself. Having heard the other girls and the reactions their introductions had prompted, she decided to play it safe. She would not mention Daddu or his role in her decision to join the army.

Drawing herself to her full height and, like Koel, staring at the eighth step of the staircase, she spoke in a loud voice. 'Myself Bijli Bijarnia, from Alakhpura, Haryana. I am a home science graduate. No relatives in the army.'

The two LCs exchanged amused glances.

'You are already a captain?' asked the CSM, pointing to the word printed on Billi's T-shirt.

'This is not an army rank,' the Haryanvi girl explained, the confidence she had gathered in the last five minutes crumbling away instantly. 'I am ex-captain of the Alakhpura Football Club.'

'Oh! So you play football?'

'Yes.'

'Take care you don't get kicked around.'

'Now, get started and give us 20,' shouted the CSM.

There was confusion as the girls stared at each other, trying to decipher the meaning of her words.

Did she want 20 rupees? How cheap. Billi immediately reached for the wallet in her pocket, while Kiran and Seema looked around for a clue.

Only Koel seemed to know what the LC wanted.

Without waiting for any explanation, she went down on her arms and began doing push-ups.

'The order applies to all of you, as well.' The CSM seemed determined to make them sweat. 'Come on, give us 30. It's 10 extra for the delay.'

Everyone acted immediately and began doing push-ups.

'Not good enough. You will continue doing push-ups till you have learnt to do them the right way,' sniggered the SUO.

Limbs protesting and sweat rolling off their backs, the girls continued. They must have done 50 each till, at last, satisfied with their performance, the two LCs allotted room numbers to the girls and marched away. The four girls decided to help each other carry the trunks to the rooms.

'Just give me a few minutes,' requested Billi, glad that the punishment session had ended. She hastened towards her room on the first floor. 'I will come back to take the trunk up the steps.'

Koel and Seema had been lucky to be allotted rooms on the ground floor. 'We will help you,' they promised.

Leaving them struggling with their boxes, Billi ran up the steps. Two things made her speed up her pace. One was her need to visit the washroom, and the second was the rumbling in her belly. As she scanned the numbers on the door frames, the Haryanvi girl realized that her room was at the end of the corridor.

She ran into her room and rushed towards the washroom. To her surprise, the door was bolted from inside.

'Oh, no,' she groaned. Wondering if she should rap on the door or rush into the next room, she decided on the former. *No point in taking chances. What if the next room is occupied by someone like the CSM?*

'Who's inside?' she asked cautiously, knocking repeatedly on the door. Displeasing a senior was not a good idea, she had realized.

'One minute,' came the muffled voice from inside the washroom, followed by the sound of the flush.

'This is an emergency,' Billi found herself begging. 'Can you hurry, please?'

Every second seemed to take longer than an hour, as she paced frantically from one end of the room to the other. It didn't work. Next, she crossed her legs and tried to distract herself by cursing the person inside the washroom. Finally, the door opened and a tall, lithe girl stood smiling hesitantly at her.

Billi, however, had no time to waste. Pushing the girl aside, she rushed in and latched the door. Five minutes later, she emerged from the washroom, relief writ clearly on her face. Her face wreathed in smiles, she peeped into the adjoining room and found the girl lying on a bed. The two rooms had a common washroom and were connected through a passage.

'What a relief! I am sorry for the rude behaviour,' she began. 'I desperately needed to use the washroom. Myself Bijli Bijarnia from Alakhpura.'

'LC Shiny Joseph from Kottayam,' responded the other. 'I arrived this morning.'

Wanting to ensure that she had heard right, the Haryanvi girl asked, 'Sorry, I didn't get that. What is the name of your village?'

'Kott-ay-am,' Shiny repeated, stressing on each syllable. 'Kottayam is not a village. It's a beautiful place with many lakes, where lots of movies have been shot.' The girl spoke proudly.

'Alakhpura is also a nice place. Our football team has won two Subroto Cup titles. It is run with the support of the entire village and many of the girls trained by the club have participated in the national football championship,' Billi preened.

'That sounds very impressive,' Shiny replied.

'Have you met the two LCs who are prowling around the building in games dresses? They made us do 50 push-ups,' Billi complained.

'You must have encountered the Senior Under Officer and Cadet Sergeant Major,' Shiny laughed. 'They are very important people. Don't ever cross their paths, for they can make your life miserable. Thank your stars, only two of the seniors have arrived. We didn't escape them, either.' She paused and made a face. 'We were made to execute 50 front rolls for the two seniors. It's been a sweaty welcome for all of us. You have to get used to them.'

At that moment, Billi made up her mind to be a CSM, no matter what it took.

'Will you help me bring my box to the room?' she asked Shiny.

After the box had been hauled up the steps, the footballer decided to shower and catch up on lost sleep. She had barely opened her bag and unpacked her towel and fresh clothes, when she heard the announcement.

'All first-termers come down to the centre lobby immediately.'

'Let's go,' Shiny moved towards the door.

'You go ahead,' said Billi, stepping into the washroom. 'I will have a quick shower and join you in five minutes.'

'Don't be a goof, we have to run down immediately,' Shiny said, pulling the girl by the hand. 'The shower can wait. We will be in trouble if we are late.'

'Don't you know the meaning of the word "immediately"?' an authoritative voice resounded down the corridor.

Half a dozen girls spilled out of their rooms, a couple of them in a semi-dressed state. There was a scramble and all the newcomers ran down the stairs for the fall-in, which they learnt was an order to assemble immediately, and take position in a fixed formation of two rows.

As the girls assembled in the central lobby, Billi spotted Seema, the mousy girl from Varanasi. She was running down the corridor, wearing a long wrap that flapped around her body.

Of Murgas and Rolls

They stood in silence while the CSM scrutinized them. Minutes later, a couple of girls shuffled into the group. Two more joined them, their hair dripping. The four were singled out for special treatment, to be doled out shortly.

'You think you are here for a picnic?' the CSM barked. 'Now, listen carefully. I will not repeat any of the instructions.'

After listing out quite a few dos and don'ts about the dress code and basic etiquette, she concluded by announcing that the LCs were to assemble in the anteroom at 7.30 p.m., dressed and ready to go for dinner at the Yoddha Cadets' Mess.

It was 7.15 p.m. already. With just 15 minutes left for the next fall-in, Billi's hope of having a shower dried up like a raisin in the sun. Forget a shower, she did not have enough time to unpack and change into formal clothing.

With a little help from Shiny, she finally raced into the anteroom just a minute after the appointed time. By then, half a dozen first-termers had already assembled, some of them dressed to the nines. These were the ones who had arrived in the morning and had had enough time to unpack, enjoy a bath and change into fresh clothes.

The CSM strolled in a couple of minutes later and began doling out punishments. All those who had arrived after her were made to do dozens of push-ups, and soon, they were sweating and fretting.

There were 20 first-termers in the anteroom and the CSM had been joined by a few more seniors, who were called appointments. These were senior LCs who, by virtue of their capabilities, had been assigned important designations and responsibilities. There was the Junior Under Officer (JUO), Cadet Quarter Master Sergeant (CQMS) and a few others. The CSM was the one to be dreaded as she was responsible for discipline and dished out punishments.

The CSM now gave a fresh list of dos and don'ts, even as punishments were meted out to those who didn't meet her stringent guidelines. LC Amrita was ticked off for not sitting straight, and had to remain in murga position for the next 10 minutes. Billi, having studied in a village school, was quite familiar with the punishment, which required a person to squat down on one's feet, with their knees close to the chest, after which one is required to hook their elbows behind their legs and hold their ears with their hands.

The others were going through a harrowing time. LC Vinni was punished for grinning too much. She was made to perform 20 push-ups in the corridor. LC Ruchi was awarded 20 sit-ups for whispering. By then, all the newcomers were unsure which of their acts would earn them punishments.

Just then, they heard the screeching sound of a car coming to a sudden halt. The CSM paused in the middle of her speech and raised her eyebrows. The JUO and CQMS shrugged in reply to the unspoken query. They were preparing to go out and investigate the arrival of the vehicle, when a petite and pretty girl walked into the anteroom, her high heels clicking smartly. All eyes swivelled towards her.

'Hi!' the newcomer threw a dazzling smile at the gathering.

Her greeting was met with pin-drop silence. The girls waited with bated breath for the CSM's reaction. For a moment, she seemed taken aback. Realizing something was wrong, the girl went back to the door, raised a hand and asked for permission to enter the room. There was a stunned hush.

'Welcome to the party!' said the CSM, after recovering from the girl's effrontery.

Her dazzling smile still in place, the girl walked into the anteroom and took a seat in the front row. It was obvious that she had no inkling of what awaited her.

'So, where are you coming from?' the CSM's voice was saccharine sweet.

'Sorry, my flight was delayed. Am I late?'

'Late? Oh no! You are very much in time. By the way, where is your luggage?'

'The cab driver dumped it at the entrance.'

'Never mind! Won't you introduce yourself to the girls? Give us your name, qualification and hobbies.'

Getting on her feet, the girl turned to face the others and began. 'Hi, I am Lakmenlang Nongrum from Shillong. My father is a businessman. I have graduated in law. As for hobbies, I play a bit of tennis, but my first love is mountaineering. In fact, I have done the advanced mountaineering course at the Himalayan Mountaineering Institute, Darjeeling.'

I would have liked to climb mountains, Billi mused. Unlike the robust kicking of a ball in a dusty field, mountaineering sounded quite posh. She had seen a movie in which the hero had climbed a mountain, decked out in a parka, stylish sunglasses and white snow-boots. It was easy to visualize the cute Shillong girl in that gear.

'Very impressive!' The CSM clapped her hands. 'Unfortunately, there are no mountains to climb in the academy, Madame Lah Di Dah. You will have many other things to learn.'

She paused for a moment and looked around to stare at the cadets who had giggled. Innocent faces look back at her. 'I don't want to hear any sniggering,' she barked. Turning to the newcomer, she asked, 'I didn't get your name. Can you repeat your name?'

'It's Lakmenlang! Not many people get it the first time. You can call me Lakme or Lucky,' the girl smiled.

'Like the cosmetics company?'

A couple of suppressed snorts followed the CSMs question.

'Yes.'

Turning her attention to the others, the CSM continued doling out several instructions on important matters. She instructed them to learn all about various kits and rigs, along with the nomenclature. Rig meant the different kinds of uniforms worn for different activities, and kit was the paraphernalia that went with each uniform. The number of kits and rigs were mind-boggling as were the several confusing terms like 6 Bravo, Combat Dress with Scale B, and Mufti.

It was almost 10 minutes to eight and a few rumbling stomachs declared the need for food, but the CSM had not finished her sermon. No one dared move or allow their attention to waver.

Finally, with just five minutes remaining for 8 p.m., she allotted a room to Lakme.

'Take your bags to the room,' the CSM barked at her. 'You have five minutes to change and come down.'

'Ma'am, it may be faster if we help her with the bags?' Shiny stood up and asked.

The CSM raised her eyebrows, making the girls wriggle uncomfortably in their seats. Just when everyone was expecting her to dole out some more punishments, the LC conceded.

'No one helps anyone overcome their difficulties. Considering it is quite late, I will allow it this time,' she snarled.

Five minutes later, having helped Lucky to her room, which was adjacent to the one allotted to Shiny, they joined the others to run to the mess for dinner. The entire lot of girls ran in a proper formation with two LCs in front, and the rest trying to keep in step with the leaders of the squad.

Yoddha Cadets' Mess, with its huge central chandelier, polished marble floor and portraits of mustachioed ex-army chiefs staring down from the walls, was an impressive place.

Right at the entrance of the mess was a table, laid out for a dinner with complete crockery and cutlery. The table was set in remembrance of all those soldiers who never returned from a war. They had once been cadets at OTA. A tilted chair had been placed at the table, a vase tied with red ribbon containing a single red rose was also placed on the table. An unlit candle, a slice of lemon and salt on the plate of bread presented a poignant picture. Each of the things on the table signified something important. The white napkin stood for the selflessness of the soldiers. The red rose and ribbon depicted the blood they shed for the nation, the salt symbolized the tears of those who grieve.

The Yoddha Cadets' Mess was where the GCs and LCs from different battalions and companies converged for their meals.

The CSM had instructed the LCs in the anteroom. 'You must remember that it is a place that demands decorum. It's not a place where you go berserk at the sight of food.'

Despite their hunger, the girls tried their best to behave with dignity, but all pretences vanished as food was brought to the table. Almost everyone was stuffing themselves as though it was their last meal on earth. Besides, the clock was ticking away. The time allotted for dinner was little. Suppressing the urge to use her hands, Billi struggled with the fork and spoon. With the CSM keeping a hawk's eye on her wards, it was impossible to cross the line.

The LCs had learnt their lessons quickly. The lack of time was a deterrent for any conversation. Besides, the dire consequences of trying to whisper had been illustrated by the CSM, soon after they settled into their chairs. 'I can't eat in a hurry,' Seema wailed to her companion. She was proving to be one of the slowest cadets.

Her remark drew the attention of the CSM, who walked up to the first-termer and poured water from the jug into Seema's glass. 'Drink it up!' she ordered.

Fearfully, the LC gulped the entire contents in her glass. Once again, the CSM filled it up to the rim, and ordered, 'Finish it!'

Horrified, the other LCs watched as the glass was filled the third time with an order to empty it again.

Seema burst into tears.

'That's the punishment for talking during meals,' barked the CSM.

Lesson learnt, the girls concentrated on their food.

Food had never tasted as good. Abandoning the desire to lick her fingers, Billi sighed contentedly. The chicken was one of the best she had ever tasted and the pudding that followed was delicious. Not a word was spoken as everyone concentrated on filling their stomachs.

The heaviness in their bellies slowed down the return run.

'It's cruel to make us run,' complained one of the girls. 'Running with all that food inside is unhealthy. I am ready to drop down.'

'The least they can do is to let us walk back,' Billi opined.

They found the CSM waiting in the lobby. *How had she managed to reach the company before them?* Her face thunderous, she greeted them with a volley of abuses. 'You are a disgrace to the institution. The whole lot of you ate like cannibals. Have you forgotten all about table manners? What you need is some exercise to help you with your memory.'

Her words were followed by a series of orders for push-ups, front rolling, and haunching (jumping like a frog across the corridor). Only those who have tried to exercise after a heavy meal know the torture it can be. A collective groan went up as the girls subjected their bodies to suffering.

The girls of Phillora Company were faring no better, Billi observed. They were being given similar punishments by their CSM.

Just then, a Honda Jazz, polished to perfection, glided into the portico, and a lady officer stepped out of it.

Calling for them to halt, the CSM ordered the girls to stand in a row while she rushed over to greet the officer.

'I am Major Swati Nair, your Platoon Commander,' began the smart officer. Her pleasant expression and warm smile kindled hope in the bosoms of the harried LCs. 'You have two Platoon Commanders, Major Sherawat is the other one. She will be meeting you in a while.'

With a face like that, she has to be a kind person. Should we convey our concerns to her? Such were the thoughts that ran through their minds.

Beaming, she addressed the first-termers. 'Firstly, congratulations for being selected to join the army. I know life can seem a bit tough initially, but soon you will get used to it. You must have had a busy evening, so I won't take any more of your time.'

The LCs were pleased with the mild-mannered officer. She was sure to rebuke the senior for the harsh treatment being meted out to them.

To their disappointment, Swati showed no signs of being displeased with the CSM. 'I hope all is well. Do you have any points?' she asked.

'All is fine. No points, ma'am.' The CSM threw her an ingratiating smile.

Turning to the LCs, the Platoon Commander asked, 'Does anyone have any points?'

'No ma'am,' parroted the girls, in one voice.

Billi raised her hand to make a point. But before she could speak, Shiny pulled her hand down and hissed, 'Don't be stupid.'

'So, everyone is happy.'

'Yes ma'am,' they echoed.

'See you in the morning then. Good night!' With that, Major Swati drove away.

If the girls had assumed there would be relief, they were mistaken. Punishments resumed as soon as the PC's car slithered away from the building.

The Web of Rigs

Billi was dreaming of stars and awards when a strident voice shattered the blissful silence. Turning to her side, she burrowed under the pillow and went back to sleep. Two minutes later, the voice had risen by a couple of decibels. Reluctantly, she opened one eye, and looked at the tiny alarm clock on the bedside table and yawned. Her fuddled brain suddenly realized it was an announcement.

'All first-termers double down to the ground floor centre lobby, immediately.'

What the hell! It was 5 a.m. *Sadists*! *Don't they allow anyone to sleep till a decent hour?*

Yawning and rubbing the sleep out of her eyes, she joined the flurry of feet rushing down the steps. Soon, there were 20 of them in the lobby, waiting anxiously for further orders. Looking around, Billi realized that they were an odd bunch. With unwashed faces, dishevelled hair and an assortment of outfits, they were nothing like the smart and confident girls who had arrived at the academy. A couple of girls were wearing shorts and T-shirts, a few were in pyjamas, and yet others in jeans or salwar kameez.

The CSM was nowhere to be seen and soon the girls began chattering. A few girls had arrived late at night and they were introducing themselves to the others.

Decibels rose as the tension ebbed, and soon they were in the back-slapping stage of advanced camaraderie.

It was a full 15 minutes before the CSM finally arrived. She threw a menacing glance at the lot and hurled abuses for their slovenly appearances.

'You aim to be army officers? Have you seen one like you?'

They hung their heads and listened in silence to the smartly dressed CSM. Her words drove away all lethargy.

Just then, Lucky came down the steps. She was wearing a flimsy nightdress, in pastel pink, with frills and lace. It was an infinitely sexy number. A couple of girls giggled as they saw here float gracefully towards the lobby.

'Here comes Miss Lah Di Dah. Give her a clap, girls,' barked the CSM and everyone obliged.

Blushing furiously, Lucky slid towards Billi.

'Alright girls, let's see some action.' The CSM divided the girls into three groups. The first group was ordered to do push-ups, the second to haunch and the third to start front rolling.

Anyone who has executed such exercises will realize that neither pyjamas nor nightdresses are conducive to performing these feats. Soon, Lucky realized the impracticality of sleeping in a pretty nightdress. She was ordered to change into a practical outfit and report back in three minutes. It was an impossible task. Huffing and puffing, she flew down the stairs in five minutes, which drew extra punishment.

The arrival of another LC distracted the CSM, who was debating on the next set of exercises.

Dressed in a bright blue salwar kameez, the short and plump newcomer was immediately put to task. Unaccustomed to rough exercises, the girl groaned and grunted through a series of front rolls.

It was almost 6 a.m. and the sun had begun making its presence felt. To their relief, the CSM decided it was time to give them a break.

'I want all of you here at 6.45 a.m. This time in proper outfit,' shouted the CSM.

There was a scramble as everyone rushed towards their rooms. Forty-five minutes to shower and dress, with a shared washroom between two girls is not much time, but the fear of punishment can make people do impossible things.

By 6.45 a.m., all the girls had gathered at the lobby. If they were expecting a word of appreciation from the CSM, they were in for disappointment. She went around the group, her eyes missing nothing.

'Now what!' Billi muttered below her breath.

'Alright! We get back to the warming-up exercises. Drop and give me 30,' she shouted.

Thankfully, there wasn't too much time for the exercises. Another round of push-ups and front rolls later, it was time to run to the mess for breakfast.

The dining room was a refuge for the first-termers, who sought to bury their frustration in food. Mercifully, food in the academy was good and plentiful. Since they had been allotted adjacent rooms, Billi, Shiny, Nutan (alias Nutty) and Lucky formed a foursome and decided to stick together.

The four of them were as different as chalk and cheese. Nutty, the drama queen, was a happy-go-lucky and mischievous girl with zero ambitions. Billi, on the other hand, was a go-getter and an ambitious person.

Smartphones were not allowed during training. The LCs had been instructed to bring only the basic kind of phones, which were to be deposited with the CSM and could be used only on Sundays and holidays.

'I have to call my parents,' said Lucky. 'Shillong is a long way off and they will be worried.'

'My dear Laks, didn't you call them after landing in Chennai?' asked Shiny as the girls left the mess.

'I was in a hurry, so I texted them about my arrival, but my mom will be expecting a full report from me.'

'You are right,' said Nutty. 'My mother will also be expecting a call from me. But…'

'Don't even think of it,' warned Shiny. 'If the CSM gets wind of your thoughts, she will make you execute front rolls all the way from the mess to the company.'

Billi was yet to call home. As far as her parents were concerned, she was at Daddu's place. She had decided that she had to find a way to speak to him. He would have to break the news to her parents.

Back at the company after breakfast, the LCs wondered what awaited them. The uncertainty in the routine was killing. Added to that were the whimsical punishment sessions. Rumours about the schedule were a dime a dozen. Although no one knew for sure, conjectures about haircuts, and other tasks abounded. Someone mentioned they would have to go for the allocation of kits and bikes (officially known as kit issues and bike issues).

The suspense came to a quick end when a fall-in was announced. The LCs stood in the sun, right in front of the building, the weather getting hotter by the minute. Sweat poured down their backs as they stood in *savdhan* position, while the CSM disappeared inside.

Her absence loosened tongues and soon the girls were exchanging notes on everything, right from their rooms to the weather to the cruelty of the CSM.

Fifteen minutes later, the CSM arrived. The first thing she did was to berate them for making too much noise.

'You LCs have no sense of discipline. I have the perfect method to put some discipline into you,' she declared.

Push-ups and front rolls seemed to be her favourite punishment. Soon, the cadets were rolling all over the place, the breakfast in their bellies performing acrobatics.

A couple of minutes later, a tall and smartly dressed officer, with a pair of fancy dark glasses perched on an aquiline nose, drove up on a motorcycle. The officer and the bike seemed to be made for each. The officer strode smartly towards them, and they realized the officer was a lady.

At five feet eight inches, the slim and agile Major Sherawat (lovingly called Shera by the cadets) could give Miss India a run for her money.

A year ago, when the officer was posted at the academy, she made the GCs drool and stare. A few daring ones managed to sigh and mumble under their breath. Not one to take such misdemeanour lightly, the lady officer took immediate action to halt the overactive imaginations of the testosterone-driven GCs. The punishments coupled with the denial of liberty pass did the trick. Soon, the stares ended and so did the sighs.

'Good morning, ma'am.' The CSM rushed towards the officer.

'Good morning, everybody! I am Major Meera Sherawat, your Platoon Commander.' Her commanding voice matched her personality.

With that pronouncement, she cast a shadow over their remaining happiness. The *paltus*, as Billi had named the Platoon Commanders, were tough as nails and expected their charges to be the same way. Major Swati was the gentler of the two, while Major Sherawat seemed much tougher.

After spewing some words of gyan, Major Sherawat departed on her mean machine, leaving the field clear for the CSM, who was itching to put the girls through some more action.

'Ma'am, may I make a call home?' asked one of the girls, echoing everyone's wishes.

'Are you homesick already?' barked the CSM, following up the statement with punishment. 'Get rolling some more. It will cure you of all sicknesses.'

The poor girl was made to go through a series of punishments for speaking out of turn, while the other LCs watched her in silent solidarity.

Something in their expressions must have triggered sympathy in the CSM. She announced a break and followed it up with permission. 'Alright, all of you are allowed to make one call, but keep it short.'

There was a scramble as everyone rushed to fetch their phones from the huge box where they had been placed and ran up to their rooms to make their calls.

'How are you, Daddu?' Billi asked her grandfather, who was delighted to hear her voice.

'Arre, Billi, I am so glad that you called,' he responded joyfully. 'I have been worried about you. In fact, your father called yesterday. He wanted to speak to you.'

'Did you tell Papa where I am?' she asked anxiously.

'I told him you had gone out for football practice and would speak to him later. Beti, a lie can work for some time, but it won't work forever. I will have to tell him the truth.'

'I guess so.'

'I will have to break the news the next time he calls.'

Daddu sounded a little apprehensive, Billi noted. They both knew all hell would break loose the moment her father learnt of their deceit. Then there was Banwari. He would be furious. It was all getting so complicated. She was trying to come to terms with the academy and its rules, which was tough enough. To deal with the other issues would be impossible at the moment. Drawing a deep breath, the Haryanvi lass decided to face the challenges as they occurred.

'Don't try to act smart,' Daddu advised. 'Obey orders and don't give any excuse for the seniors to punish you.'

'Yes, Daddu.' *If only he knew*, the girl sighed. The CSM needed no excuse to punish them.

The call was cut short with an announcement of a fall-in. By now, the LCs had learnt the importance of running. Minutes after they had assembled, the CSM handed over the charge to a hefty ustad. 'You will now be taken for the issue of web equipment,' she said.

'The Junior Commissioned Officers (JCOs), who are posted as instructors in the academy are known as ustads. They have enormous powers and can punish us by allotting extra duties and drills. To earn the wrath of the ustad is like committing hara-kiri,' she added.

'What is web equipment? Are we supposed to walk on the wall and roof like Spiderman?' Lucky whispered as they jogged towards the store. The girls giggled as visuals of Spiderman, jumping from wall to wall, flooded their minds.

'I hope they don't aim to turn us into Spiderwomen,' Nutty tittered.

The store was abuzz with dozens of GCs and LCs milling around, intent on collecting their web equipment. With so many GCs from various companies, there was quite a crowd.

The suspense about the equipment was finally cleared when the girls realized that the web equipment was nothing but special clothing items that were required to be worn during battle. These included belts, pouches to carry ammunition, back packs, small and big, and straps to hold them in place. Water bottles, caps, raincoats, shoes, socks, boots and a host of other things were also part of the web equipment.

They were waiting for their turn, when Billi discovered that Shiny had gone missing.

'Oh my god! Where has the girl vanished? There will be trouble if the ustad finds her missing,' she alerted Lucky and Nutty, and the three of them began scanning the crowd.

'You guys stay put, I will try to find her. Make some excuse if the ustad asks for me,' volunteered the sporting Billi, as she picked her way through the crowd towards the other end of the veranda.

She spotted Shiny in one corner. The girl was busy chatting with a GC.

'There you are,' hissed Billi. 'Do you realize what will happen if the ustad finds you missing?'

Shiny seemed quite unperturbed by the possibility of being pulled up by the ustad. 'LC Bijli Bijarnia, meet GC Aaron Koshy,' she introduced the handsome dude with a dimpled chin.

'Nice to meet you, LC BB,' responded the GC.

'Same here! I mean glad and all that,' Billi responded. Tugging at Shiny's arm, she murmured, 'We should be going.' As an afterthought, she turned to the GC and said, 'Please excuse us. We have to get back to our group.'

The two of them wound their way through the throng of cadets on the verandah.

Fortunately, the ustad had not taken a head count of his wards. It was a long and patient wait before their turn arrived and the girls were issued a set of equipment. They were told to check them and report if there were any deficiencies or damages.

'How can the same equipment fit all of us?' Lucky wondered, as she fiddled with her set. 'Shiny is at least six inches taller than me, how can we use the same stuff?'

All around her, GCs and LCs were busy trying out their equipment. Toddling up to the busy quartermaster, she began hesitantly, 'Sir, can you issue equipment in a smaller size? This seems too big for me.'

The harassed man ignored her request and continued with his task, but she didn't give up. At last, he shooed her off saying, 'In this case, one size fits everyone.'

Unconvinced by his words, Lucky grumbled, 'How can the same size fit Nutty and me? She is at least 10 kilos heavier than me.'

'Hello!' bellowed the girl in question. 'I am not bloody overweight, okay? You are underweight.' Nutty had taken to garnishing her statements with a 'bloody'. Her special pronunciation of the word 'bloody' never failed to amuse the others.'I didn't mean to be rude, Nutty,' Lucky pacified the girl. 'All I want to know is how can the same stuff fit everyone.'

While they were arguing, Billi was trying out a pair of brand new boots. 'These are a bit tight, but I will take them. Shoes are always tight in the beginning.' Dazzled with the spanking pair, she was determined to keep them.

'Don't be an idiot! Exchange that pair for one that fits better,' Shiny chided. 'Just imagine trying to perform drills in those boots. Forget drills, you will not be able to walk properly in them. What you need is a comfortable pair of boots.'

'Shoes always need breaking in. These will be comfortable after a few days of wearing,' insisted Billi mulishly.

'Have you seen the olive green socks that have been issued with the boots? They are made of thick material. The boots are not likely to fit if you wear them with those socks,' Lucky pointed out.

For once, Nutty agreed with Lucky's statement.

It was a while before the three girls managed to convince the Haryanvi girl to exchange the pair of boots for a more comfortable one.

'You are a smart cookie. It hasn't taken you long to find a guy. So, who was the dude?' Billi pounced on Shiny the moment they began walking back to the company. 'I saw you making eyes at him.'

'She's already found someone to make eyes at?' Nutty was aghast. The news didn't please her one bit. She had been confident of making a conquest before any of her friends. 'That is fast work.'

'I must say, it is,' seconded Lucky, slapping Shiny on the back. 'While we were trying out the web equipment, madam managed to trap a GC in her web.'

'Please!' Shiny protested. 'He's not a stranger.'

'What!' exclaimed Billi and Nutty.

'Aaron...'

'So that's his name?' Lucky giggled some more. 'Um, Aaron! The name does roll off the tongue pretty nicely.'

'So, who is this Aaron?' Nutty wanted to know.

'He's the reason I am here at the academy,' said Shiny shyly. 'We have known each other for years. He's my best friend.'

'Childhood romance?' Nutty tittered. 'Wow! You mean something like in *Parineeta, Devdas* and *Mohabbatein*. That's exciting.'

'Yes, you can say so,' admitted Shiny. 'Aaron decided to join the army. In fact, the two of us decided to join the army and train at the academy, so we could be together.'

'What a romantic idea!' Nutty exclaimed. 'Won't it be nice if we all managed to find the perfect guys for us, right here in the academy?

'I am not here to find a guy,' snorted Billi. 'There will be time enough for all that crap once we have been commissioned. At the moment, my heart is set on becoming a CSM.' All talk of finding guys reminded her of Banwari Lal and she had no wish to discuss the matter with her new friends.

'So, are you two planning to get married?' Lucky wanted to know, excited about the prospect of a marriage right after the training. 'I would love to attend a wedding in Kerala.'

'You will definitely be invited,' Shiny assured them. 'In fact, all of you must attend our wedding.'

Their tête-à-tête came to an abrupt end as they reached the lobby of their company and found the CSM lying in wait for them.

'Does it take so long to walk this little distance, slow coaches? I think you need a bit of energizing activity to get accelerated. Go and keep the equipment in your cabins. I want you back in two minutes,' she shouted the moment she spotted them.

Her order sent them running like headless chickens. Scampering up the stairs, they dumped their kits in Billi's cabin, which was the nearest one. Some of the equipment landed on the floor, some on the bed. There was no time to segregate things or keep them in order.

Despite hurrying, no one made it in the two minutes allowed by the CSM. Only those who had cabins on the ground floor made it by a whisker. Irrespective of the impossibility of the task, the delay in reporting was reason enough for the CSM to punish everyone.

The Cut of Despair

Forty-eight hours later, the LCs were none the worse for wear. Having learnt the hard way, they were extremely cautious about the CSM and avoided asking questions.

Much like the seven commandments in George Orwell's *Animal Farm*, Lucky had formulated an interesting one. She stuck it on the back of her door.

- Thou shall question no one. Every word uttered by the seniors is to be treated as a sacred commandment.
- Thou shall try to remain as inconspicuous as a pebble on the road.
- Thou shall keep eyes and ears open and mouth zipped tight.
- Thou facial expression shall remain unreadable. Smiling is a sin, and giggling is forbidden.
- Slacking is an unforgivable offence, and oversleeping a crime. If you wish to nap, learn the art of doing so with your eyes open.
- The CSM is always right.
- Most importantly, all LCs are equal, but some are more equal than others.

'We will survive as long as we can remember these,' she said with satisfaction as Nutty read the commandments aloud.

'Do we need tricks for survival?' Nutty asked innocently. 'Don't the same rules apply to everyone? Aren't we all equal?'

'All animals are equal, but some animals are more equal than others, I guess,' Shiny sniggered.

That was a new one for Billi. 'What do you mean by all animals are equal? We are not animals…'

'You will have to read *Animal Farm* to know that,' Lucky explained.

With the passing of days, the girls would add more points to the commandments.

It was the post lunch fall-in, and bellies tight after a sumptuous meal, the LCs were lined up before the CSM. Suppressing a yawn, Billi forced herself to listen to the senior droning. 'The Indian Army is known for its smart officers, but none of you fit the image,' she said.

It had been a busy morning, with umpteen push-ups, front rolls and jogging. Billi yearned for some shut-eye.

'Now, it's time for some essential grooming,' announced the CSM.

The dreaded moment had finally arrived. With sinking hearts, the 22 LCs heard the pronouncement.

Although everyone who joined the academy was aware that their beautiful locks of hair, tended lovingly through the years, would be chopped off, the prospect was quite daunting. The zero cut, aka katori cut, managed to eliminate all traces of femininity.

The CSM, who sported the hallmark haircut, divided the LCs into two batches.

'Report at the beauty parlour within 10 minutes,' she barked to the first batch. 'The rest of you will report for haircut after lunch. Double up, now.'

'Ma'am, where…?' One of the LCs raised her hand to ask about the location.

Her query was rewarded with 15 front rolls. After that, none of the LCs ventured to ask any questions.

Billi and her gang were the first ones to begin running towards the parlour. The four LCs had not the faintest idea where it was situated, but asking questions would attract more punishments, so they raced away without a backward look.

'But where do we go?' asked Shiny, halting at a crossing. While on their way to the mess, they had spotted a signboard pointing towards the beauty parlour. It seemed to have disappeared now.

'Where are the other LCs? Eleven of us are supposed to report at the parlour, so there should be seven more following us.'

'I don't see why you had to take off at such speed,' Nutty said, her voice laced with annoyance. 'We could have followed the others. It doesn't help to act smart.'

'I thought we could be back at the academy for a leisurely bath after the cut,' retorted Billi, who had suggested that they beat the others to the parlour.

'High hopes!' Nutty snorted.

'There's no point in squabbling,' pacified Lucky. 'Instead, let's try to find the way to the salon.'

Spotting a pair of GCs jogging towards them, Nutty was hit with a sudden inspiration. 'Let me ask them the direction to the place,' she said.

'My dear peanut, let's not do anything that would invite trouble,' Shiny shot down her suggestion. She was convinced that the girl had a brain the size of a peanut.

'Just watch me in action,' winked the irrepressible Nutty, striding towards the pair of good-looking, albeit sweaty hunks.

She shot a cute smile at one of the GCs, 'Please could you tell us the way to the beauty parlour?' She followed up the query by batting her eyelashes.

The GC, taken by her innocent, wide-eyed look, pointed towards a road. 'Follow that road and turn to the right. The parlour is at the end of that road.'

'It's so kind of you to help us. Thank you,' Nutty smiled flatteringly.

'Not an issue,' he waved off her gratitude and resumed jogging.

'See! It's quite easy to twist a GC around one's finger,' Nutty smiled triumphantly. 'All you need is an innocent expression and a little flutter of your eyelashes.'

'I hope he has given us the right directions,' Shiny remarked doubtfully as they took the route indicated by the GC. 'They had a mischievous expression on their faces.'

It was an endless road lined by shady trees.

'How far is the bloody parlour?' cursed a panting Nutty. 'We have been jogging for the past five minutes.'

'The CSM gave us 10 minutes, so it really can't be this far,' said Lucky. 'Are you sure the GC gave us the right directions?'

'Why wouldn't he?'

'Well…'

In another 100 metres, the road forked into two. 'I think we have to take the right fork from the turn ahead,' opined Shiny.

The right fork led the LCs to a vast open ground, where they found several GCs running in full combat gears. Suddenly, they realized that a trick had been played on them.

'Oh my God! That bloody GC misled us,' Nutty ranted.

'No wonder he was grinning like a Cheshire cat,' laughed Lucky, holding her sides. 'Instead of getting twisted around your fingers, he's got you panting with exertion.'

'Another lesson learnt,' Shiny sighed. 'Keep away from cute GCs. They are not trustworthy.'

'Smart alec! Well, we have 11 months to make him pay for this trick. I won't spare him.' Nutty gnashed her teeth as they sprinted back towards the crossroad.

It had been more than 10 minutes since they had left the Zojila Company.

'I can see a couple of LCs returning after the haircut,' Billi exclaimed, as she spotted two girls jogging from the opposite end of the road. At first glance, it was difficult to recognize Koel and Ananya. The girls, who had been sporting different hairstyles, now looked identical. The zero haircuts made them look more like the GCs.

'Bloody hell! That's the haircut we will get.' Nutty was aghast. 'I am not going to the parlour.'

'It's too late for theatrics,' Shiny smirked. 'You have no option, drama queen.'

'Let's get to the salon before someone sees us loitering and starts punishing us.' Billi cast an anxious look around.

The girls located the beauty parlour, which was not too far from their company. The place was teeming with lady cadets from Zojila as well as Phillora Companies. Haircuts were a matter of great importance. A little variation in the length of hair could cause great trouble, so everyone took extra care to maintain it at the optimum required length, i.e., a few millimetres.

With just a couple of beauticians (if they could be called so, since all they did was chop hair in zero cuts) and six chairs for the LCs, the parlour was the busiest place in the campus. Foot-tapping music filled the room as the beauticians got busy with their jobs. They seemed to be very proficient. Snip, snip, snip, went their scissors, keeping pace with the tune that was playing. It took them just a couple of minutes to finish one haircut.

Despite the peppy music, there was a melancholic atmosphere in the parlour.

'I feel like a sheep waiting for its fleece to be sheared,' Lucky commented with a sigh, as they waited their turns. Although shoulder length, her straight and glossy hair was worth envying. 'We will all look like unisex robots.'

'That's the idea, buddy,' replied a stoic Shiny, staring at an LC occupying the barber's chair. 'There's a thing known as fait accompli.'

'True! It helps to be philosophical about the entire process,' agreed Lucky. 'This too shall pass. The training shall be over and we will be commissioned.'

'I am not thinking that far into the future,' commented Billi. 'All I want to do is to become a CSM.' Her eyes strayed towards the tear-streaked face of Kiran, the girl she had met at the Chennai railway station, and her heart went out to the girl, whose lovely locks now lay on the floor. Giving her an encouraging smile and a thumbs up, she said, 'Don't grieve, Kiran. The style suits you.'

This was just one of the many instances where they would have to stick by each other, motivating and cheering each other on.

'Don't look now, but there is a beauty queen on the chair,' hissed Nutty. Despite her warning, Lucky's eyes strayed in that direction.

'Wow! She's beautiful! Who is she?'

'She must be from the Phillora Company. I wonder how a girl can look so beautiful with a zero haircut,' mumbled Shiny, who had also noticed her friends' object of interest.

'Next,' ordered the beautician as the beauty queen vacated the chair. Steeling herself, Shiny stepped forward. As her locks fell on the ground, she closed her eyes. Uppermost on her mind was Aaron's reaction.

On another chair, Seema was pleading with the beautician, 'Please, can you leave at least a couple of inches of my hair, just so I don't look like a boy?'

Her words brought no reaction from the scissor-happy beautician. 'This is the regulation cut, and we can't deviate from the rules. I am sorry,' replied the lady and went ahead shearing her locks in a professional manner.

Nutty, who was seated on the next chair, fondled her tresses sadly for the last time. She looked mournfully at the heap of hair lying all over the floor, feeling sorry for her waist-long hair that had been nurtured with much care by her mother. Eyes moist, she threw a pleading look at the beautician, who draped a cloth around her shoulders and went to work.

Something in Nutty's expression must have touched a chord, for the woman gave her a sympathetic look in the mirror and paused to comfort the girl, 'Don't worry, these locks will bring happiness to some women.'

Surprised, Nutty returned her stare, 'How?'

'We send your hair to an NGO that turns them into wigs, which are distributed to women who have lost their hair because of cancer. It's all for a good cause.'

True or not, the beautician's words worked wonders. Comforted by the thought of doing a good deed, Nutty relinquished her locks happily.

The next one to go on the chair was Lucky. Sighing, she closed her eyes, refusing to look at the mirror during the operation, which lasted a few seconds more than two minutes because of the thickness of her hair. When she opened her eyes, she was horrified to see her raven mane of hair reduced to nought. The famous zero cut made her look like a Khasi boy.

'Lucky, you look smart,' Shiny declared sportingly, as the girl ran a hand over her bristly head.

'Oh my God!' wailed another LC, as she looked at herself in the mirror. Her eyes brimming with tears, she chided the stylist, 'You have given me such an atrocious cut.'

In response, the wicked stylist gestured for her to occupy the chair once again. With a mischievous smile she picked up a razor, the sight of which sent the LC out of the shop, leaving everyone in stitches.

'They are bloody butchers, not barbers,' Nutty griped on their way back to the company. 'My mother will have a heart attack if she sees me now.'

'So will mine, dear coconut,' Billi confessed. From Coconut, Peanut to Doughnut, the friends had begun addressing Nutty by different names.

'Never mind, Nutty, these are small prices to pay for the eventual glory that awaits us,' Lucky consoled her friend.

‘My mother was not very happy about my decision to join the army. She feels that the army turns us into aggressive women, and that makes it difficult to find a match and adjust in a family.’

‘I am sure you will make your mother proud. You will also find a smart and handsome army officer to marry.’

‘I hope so.’

Buoyed with that thought, the four LCs walked back to the Zojila Company.

On a Darshan

It had been a hectic day with enough physical workouts and punishments. The first-termers were happy when 'lights out' was announced at 10 p.m. They needed the rest. It was too much to expect, they soon realized, as the punishments continued well after midnight, regardless of the lights out order. The *jungoos* (freshers) realized that the appointments had a right to punish them at any time they desired. By the time they finally hit the sack, every muscle and joint began making its presence felt.

The LCs had been informed that they would be taken for 'OTA Darshan' right after breakfast the next morning. A tad confused, Lucky wondered if it had to do with a trip to a temple to pray for the well-being of the soldiers guarding the borders. She decided to prioritize prayers for her own well-being, before praying for others.

The morning was pleasant enough when the first-termers ran down for the fall-in, at 4 a.m. As usual, the routine began with punishments or strengthening exercises, as the CSM called them. Soon, the pleasant morning turned into an unpleasant one.

At breakfast, Billi tucked into a two-egg omelette, half a dozen sandwiches with generous dollops of butter and two bananas, all downed with a few cups of tea. Not satisfied with the fare, she looked around cautiously.

Evading the CSM's eyes, she pocketed a couple of boiled eggs and slices of bread, just in case. Lucky, who had a small appetite, found it impossible to stuff herself. Instead, she relied on the biscuit packets she had hoarded in her room. Suppressing a burp, Billi grinned at Shiny, who was seated at the opposite side of the table. Ever since the first day at the academy, Billi had been experiencing insatiable hunger. It gnawed at her entrails and made her feel weak. Her appetite had gone up by leaps and bounds. From a strict vegetarian, she had turned into a non-vegetarian with a vengeance.

Post breakfast, the first-termers assembled before the Zojila block, and faced the fierce looking Ustad Gurnam Singh, who was to take them for the *darshan*. All of six feet two inches, a declaration of his martial race, the ustad looked down his crooked nose, his eyes, dark and smouldering, studied the first-termers critically. Spines straightened, tummies tucked in and heads went up under the effect of those eyes.

The LCs had been warned about the whimsical ways of the ustads in the academy. They could punish the cadets for the slightest infractions. A crooked beret, loose belt, overgrown hair, a pair of unpolished shoes, bad posture, anything and everything could arouse their ire. And then would come the punishments. They were known to be stricter than the Company and Platoon Commanders.

Capable of stupendous feats, ustads were the best jawans produced by the Indian Army. Their only drawback was their tenuous grasp over English. Those who succeeded in picking up a smattering of the Queen's language were assigned the job of instructing the foreign cadets.

Speaking in chaste Hindi, Ustad Gurnam Singh began by giving them a bit of gyan about the genesis of the OTA. With her inadequate knowledge of the language, Lucky struggled to keep up with the lecture.

'The academy was established in 1962, following the Indo–China conflict. The officers who passed out were known as Emergency Commissioned Officers. In 1965, Short Service Officers began to be trained for technical and non-technical streams, and in 1988, the Officers Training School was re-designated as Officers Training Academy.' Years of repeating the same lecture had made the ustad proficient in its delivery. What impressed the LCs was the passion in his voice. It was obvious that he loved the academy.

'In 1992, Lady Cadets were admitted into the OTA, and from 2008, their training was brought at par with Gentlemen Cadets and a common Merit List was prepared,' continued Ustad Gurnam Singh.

He paused, his eyes scanning the first-termers' faces. '*Koi sawal*?' he roared.

'No, sir,' came a collective response.

'First of all, we shall go to the P Hill,' the ustad announced after the initial briefing. 'Can anyone tell me what the "P" stands for?' he asked.

The word brought various images to their minds. Pleasure Hill, Peacock Hill, Picnic Hill, Platoon Hill, the replies were varied and amusing. In response to each answer, the ustad growled, '*Takreeban theek*.' The reply was meant to act as a motivator.

In the end, it was Ishita who provided the right answer. Her brother had passed out of the academy a couple of years ago and she knew that the letter stood for 'punishment'. None of the LCs had expected it to stand for something as horrendous as punishment.

'Shabaash, Cadet!' The ustad let out a rare smile and said, 'You should familiarize yourself with this area because you will be seeing it very often.'

Standing on top of a hillock named P Hill, they had a bird's eye view of the well-laid-out campus. Ustad Gurnam Singh pointed to the buildings and other facilities spread around the 700-acre campus.

'The Adyar River flows through the OTA campus,' he informed them, making a few ears cock up, but they could see nothing of a river anywhere. 'And that is the Yoddha Cadets' Mess.'

The ustad went on to point out the battalions, parade ground and main administrative buildings, before leading them down the P Hill and taking them through the rest of the campus, pointing out each landmark and narrating something interesting about it. The exercise was meant to familiarize them with the area.

From the P Hill, they went down to the swimming pool. The pool with its clear, blue waters looked inviting to the LCs, who were drenched in perspiration. From the shopping complex to the stables and the most hallowed of all, the Parmeshwaran Parade Ground, where the Passing Out Parade (POP) was held, the hefty ustad took the first-termers through all the important buildings.

On their tour, they spotted some GCs front rolling in front of their companies. Shiny gasped at the sight of her boyfriend flipping in an ungainly manner. What amused them most was the sight of a GC holding up the legs of his partner and pushing him forward, while the other moved forward on his hands.

'It's known as the wheelbarrow,' the ustad informed the LCs.

The *darshan* was not yet over. The Adyar River, which had conjured pictures of swimming, turned out to be nothing more than a nullah.

Across the Adyar River was the PT ground, with its assortment of vertical ropes, obstacle courses and playgrounds. They visited the stables with their majestic horses. 'Riding is compulsory and so is swimming,' said the ustad. 'All cadets have to pass a minimum standard before they can pass out of the academy.'

Pedalling Problems

It was their third day at the academy, and the LCs had survived the 72-hour ordeal without much damage. In the meantime, seniors had begun trickling back into the company after the end of term break.

The return of the senior LCs heralded yet more torture and trouble for the freshers. Hitherto, it had been just the CSM who had doled out punishments, but now the seniors exercised a free hand too. Their reasons for punishment were as absurd as Hitler's reasons for decimating the Jews – the first-termers' postures. The seniors said their backs were bent like those of old hags, that they were not officer material and their posture was totally unfit for a cadet. One of the most common reasons was that the *jungoos* had failed to wish them. With hardly any distinguishing features, it was very difficult for the first-termers to recognize them as seniors, but trying to tell them that would have been disastrous.

In the meantime, the second-termers continued to look down at the freshers as though they were some kind of creepy-crawlies that had just crawled out from under a boulder. Billi and her gang had already had a taste of the power wielded by the senior LCs, but some of the first-termers accepted the truth only after a series of gruelling punishments.

By the third day, the LCs had executed so many front rolls that they knew the exact number of somersaults required to traverse the corridor, lobby and the open space in front of the company.

Of the four friends, Billi had mastered the trick of front rolling. 'Take smaller steps,' she tutored her friends. 'Keep the head tucked in and legs joined together. Also, don't use your hands for support when you stand up.'

Necessity is the mother of invention. The *jungoos* soon learnt to improvise and devise various means to overcome their difficulties.

Running around the vast campus from one end to the other for meals and other activities was a big pain. The announcement that the bicycle issue was scheduled that morning, brought cheer to the LC's faces. The time saved by cycling could be utilized to rest and recoup their exhausted bodies.

After breakfast, the CSM announced a fall-in.

'You will be taken for the bike issue parade,' she said importantly.

'Bike issue parade?' Lucky wondered if they would have to parade with bicycles on their shoulders.

'Shhh!' warned Shiny. A couple of interactions with GC Aaron had brightened her. They stole a couple of minutes every day at the Yoddha Mess to update each other after a hurried meal. 'Everything is a parade out here.'

A bike was the only means of commuting for the cadets in the OTA. In fact, it was a lifeline for the time-starved LCs. The olive-green-coloured bicycles had their company's name and the bike number marked on the rear mudguard. For the cadets, the bikes seemed nothing less than Ferraris.

Along with the bikes came the responsibility of maintaining them in mint condition.

Billi thumped her bike appreciatively, saying, 'This will make our lives much easier.'

'It's been a while since I rode a bike,' Nutty confessed, handling her bike gingerly. 'You girls will have to ride behind me, not in front.'

'So, you don't crash into us, I guess,' Billi laughed. Her full-throated laughter never failed to amuse her friends.

'Well, I will take a couple of hours to get used to cycling around in a squad formation.'

In the meantime, Lucky was eyeing her contraption with fear. She didn't look very pleased with her bike.

'What's the matter, Lucky? You don't seem very happy,' Shiny asked.

'I don't want a bike,' she responded with a sigh. 'I prefer to run everywhere.'

'Are you crazy?' scolded Billi. 'You prefer to jog rather than cycle all over the academy?'

'I don't know how to ride a bicycle,' came the thunderbolt of a confession.

'What?' The three LCs looked shocked.

'YOU DON'T KNOW CYCLING?' Billi stressed on each word.

'I am from Shillong, and it's a hill station. Very few people ride cycles there.'

'Well, we will just have to do something about it. Don't let the ustad or the CSM know about your handicap,' Shiny patted the girl encouragingly. 'It's not a big challenge. All you have to do is balance yourself on the bike. Don't worry, I will help you master the art of bicycle riding.'

While the others rode their bicycles to the company, Lucky and her friends walked back with the bikes.

They found Major Sherawat waiting at the cycle stand behind the company.

'Stand in two rows with your bikes on the right,' she barked.

A shuffle ensued as the LCs formed a double line.

'How many of you can't ride? she asked. Experience had taught her that there were always a few LCs who couldn't ride a bicycle. 'Raise your hands.'

Not a single hand went up. Worried about being singled out, Lucky refrained from admitting her handicap.

'I am happy to see that there is no one who can't ride,' said Major Sherawat, walking around the LCs. She went around inspecting the bikes, and warned them to keep the machines in a shining state. 'Now park your bikes and scram.'

'We will go through a couple of riding lessons after dinner,' whispered Shiny, who had undertaken the responsibility of teaching Lucky.

That night, the two of them stole out to the cycle stand, and the lessons began in the open space behind the company. Lucky mounted the bike, while Shiny held the bike.

'Hold the handlebar tight and try to keep upright by pedalling with both your feet,' instructed Shiny. 'Are you ready?'

Lucky crossed herself, hesitated for a fraction of a second, and gripped the handle tightly. 'Yes!' she shouted loudly.

'Attagirl!' Shiny pushed the bike while Lucky tried to maintain her balance.

'Now go!' The teacher let go of the bike. Weaving from side to side, the student took off, trying not to look back.

'Keep pedalling,' shouted Shiny from the back, running as Lucky rode on.

The next minute, losing her balance, Lucky screamed and collapsed in a heap, with the cycle under her.

The scream and crash drew immediate attention. A few windows were flung open, and heads popped out trying to locate the source of the crash. Some LCs trooped out to investigate, and help came pouring in.

Having learnt of Lucky's handicap, her peers cheered and goaded the poor, bruised girl, who was in no mood to continue with the lessons. By then, a dozen LCs had gathered around the girl. The cumulative persuasion and pressure finally worked, and Lucky mounted her steed once again. This time, with the LCs whistling and cheering, she fared a tad better.

Her hands clutching the handlebar, Lucky pedalled desperately. This time, she lasted a full minute on the seat before jumping off the bike. Not one to give up, Shiny continued goading the girl, till she managed to remain on her seat for a record three minutes.

Undetected by the first-termers, the CSM watched from her window. Pleased that the LCs had learned the first lesson of camaraderie, she smiled.

It had been almost half an hour by the time the crowd dispersed and Lucky limped back to her room, feeling victorious.

'Mark my words, three lessons is all you require,' assured Shiny. 'Give yourself another day, and you will be riding with us in a squad. It's all a matter of balance.'

The gang of four gathered in Lucky's room to give her some more pep talks. It was then that they noticed her wounded elbow and knee.

'You need a tetanus shot,' said Billi, who had suffered more than her share of wounds and bruises during football matches.

'No injection,' protested the injured girl, who hated them. 'They are minor wounds which will heal on their own.'

'Aren't you a silly girl?' Nutty scolded. 'A tetanus shot is mandatory. When did you get your last shot?'

'I don't remember.'

'In that case, you must get it as soon as possible,' Shiny advised.

'I guess that will have to wait till morning. In the meantime, I will swab the wounds with an antiseptic liquid and apply a Band-Aid.'

Billi rushed off to fetch the tiny first-aid kit she had carried with her.

'Look, I can't go out of the campus to get a tetanus injection, and I don't want to tell CSM about the wounds,' wailed Lucky, as soon as Billi had gone. 'So, let's forget about it.'

Shiny's response to her appeal was a cryptic, 'We shall see.'

A Wounded Warrior

The CSM was quick to notice Lucky's injuries at the fall-in the next morning. Although the LC had taken care to remove the Band-Aid, the black and blue bruises on her elbows and knees were clearly visible.

'Report to the Medical Inspection (MI) Room, LC Lakme,' the CSM shouted.

'But ma'am…'

'No buts and ifs. Do as you are told.'

Lucky had no alternative but to limp with a thumping heart towards the MI Room. This time, she was on her own.

MI Room was a busy place. Two doctors attended to patients, mostly GCs. There were no LCs to be spotted. It wasn't a surprise. With just about 50 LCs and 400 GCs, it was unlikely that the MI Room would see too many LCs. Lucky registered her name and waited for her turn to see the doctor. There was a flutter amongst the five GCs as soon as she entered the waiting room. While the four of them looked appreciatively at the pretty, delicate looking LC, one of the GCs remained unaffected. Without a glance at her, he continued reading the newspaper. A couple of GCs shot her a hesitant smile, which she returned. Lucky was a friendly girl and these were her comrades, after all. Encouraged, the boldest among them walked up to her.

He was a lanky chap of average height and looks, but his bright smile made him look quite remarkable.

'I am GC Mishra,' he introduced himself and stuck out his hand. 'Meiktila.'

'LC Lakme,' she said, giving his hand a good shake. 'Zojila.'

'It's quite a jungle here, isn't it? Seventy-two hours later, I am still trying to figure out what is right and what isn't. The amount of *ragda* (unofficial ragging) we face is not a joke,' sighed the GC. 'Our CSM is a brute. Things are getting worse now that the seniors have trickled in. But the LCs must be having a better time.'

'Oh no!' Lucky demurred, warming up to the friendly chap. 'Our CSM is an absolute virago.' Lowering her voice conspiratorially, she added, 'I think she suffers from sadistic tendencies.'

'I think they all do.' The GC threw back his head and laughed at her words.

Soon, the three GCs in the waiting room walked up to them. An animated discussion ensued, as each one narrated his experience: the common thread in the conversation being the insensitive and cruel *ragda*.

'So, what brings you to the MI Room?' The handsome GC from Jessami Company wanted to know. His name, Lucky read from the nameplate on his uniform, was Manav Mathur.

Embarrassed to admit her inability to ride a bicycle, she hunted for an excuse. 'I...I slipped,' she blurted quickly. 'In the bathroom,' she added as an explanation, as they exchanged confused glances.

'No bones broken, I hope,' commiserated GC Mishra, a cocky-looking fellow.

'Thankfully, no.' Her eyes wandered towards the GC with the newspaper. While the other GCs in the room had gravitated towards her, that one remained aloof. His indifference puzzled her.

'Let me see.' GC Mathur took her hand and tut-tutted at the wound on her elbow. 'This one looks quite bad.'

'It's a minor one.' She quickly snatched her hand away and darted another look at the GC with the newspaper. He had lowered the newspaper to look at them. An amused smile playing on his lips, he nodded at her. Lucky blushed and turned her face.

'Next patient, go to room number two,' announced the nursing assistant, poking his head into the room.

It was GC Mathur's turn, but none of the GCs wanted to go to the room where Major Prakash Gautam waited for his patients. For some strange reason, they were keen on going to room number one, which was manned by Captain Nina Sharma.

'Why don't you go?' Mathur turned to the GC who had resumed devouring the newspaper.

'No issue,' said the GC, putting away the newspaper. 'Enjoy yourselves.'

'Bloody prig!' remarked Mathur as the GC loped away. 'That guy needs to be shown his place.'

'Is he from your company?' Lucky wanted to know. She knew that Mathur was from Jessami.

'Sadly, yes. GC Vedant Verma is a brigadier's son, so he considers himself the cat's whiskers. I am just waiting to take him down a notch or two.'

The other GCs sniggered faithfully.

Before she could react to his comments, Mathur was called to the first room. Barely did a couple of minutes pass, when she was also called to the same room.

Entering the room, she found GC Mathur in an upside-down position. His hands on the floor and legs up against the wall, he had lost all the pomposity he had exhibited in the waiting room.

'Ma'am, I am fine now. The headache has gone,' he pleaded with the doctor. His arrogance gone, the GC looked pitiable.

'You headache is due to the lack of blood flow to the brain. Remaining in the handstand position for a few minutes will speed up the flow of blood.'

'I can feel the blood flowing to the brain at a high rate, ma'am. I might faint if it flows any faster.'

'Don't worry about that. I am here to take care of you. Your ailment has to be fully cured. There may be a relapse if I let you go now,' replied the pretty doctor, who seemed popular with the GCs.

Fearfully, Lucky took in the scene. *The doctor is a raving lunatic. What is she going to do with me? What if she decides to order me to get into the same position as GC Mathur?* The thought sent a shiver down her spine.

'Alright, you can stand on your feet now,' said Captain Sharma. 'Do you think I am not aware why you have reported sick? Take this chit and report to your company commander. I shall speak to him too. Also, I don't want to see you hovering near the MI Room. Now, get lost.'

Tail tucked firmly between his legs, GC Mathur took the slip of paper and saluted the doctor. All swagger drained, he slipped out of the room without a backward glance.

Fear gripped Lucky as the GC left the room and the doctor turned to her.

'Yes, what's your problem?' asked Captain Sharma.

Deciding that no good would come out of lying, Lucky narrated the true story. Tears pricking her eyes, she ended her spiel by saying, 'Ma'am, I can't ride a bicycle.'

Her lips twitching with amusement, the doctor responded, 'What's wrong with not being able to ride a bicycle! There's always a first time.'

Relieved at not being castigated, Lucky smiled. 'Thank you, ma'am.'

'It's natural to fail a couple of times before one perfects anything in life. There's nothing to be ashamed of.' Captain Sharma smiled encouragingly. 'I will write a prescription for the pain.'

While the doctor wrote the prescription for Lucky, she called for the next patient. GC Mishra entered the room with a big smile. He winked surreptitiously at Lucky and stood waiting for the doctor to attend to him.

Without raising her eyes, the doctor asked, 'Yes GC, what's your problem?'

'Ma'am my legs are aching since yesterday,' bleated GC Mishra.

'Really? There seems to be an epidemic of headaches and leg aches in the academy,' Nina Sharma raised her eyes to look at the GC and he wilted. 'I have the perfect treatment for your legs, GC. What they need is rest. Get down on your hands and raise your legs up against the wall.'

Suppressing a chortle, Lucky hurried out of the room, but not before she had seen GC Mishra go into a headstand against the wall.

The Lure of the Sword

It was a terribly muggy morning. It was also turning out to be an action-filled morning.

After leaving the MI Room, Lucky walked towards the canteen to buy toothpaste and was walking back toward the Zojila block, when she crossed two strangers. One of them was silver-haired and had a rugged face. He was elderly and had the a bearing of a soldier. The other man was stocky and pot-bellied and seemed to be in his fifties. Clad in pristine white dhotis and kurtas, the two were standing on one side of the road and arguing.

Sure that the men had lost their way, Lucky slowed down, wondering if she could help.

'Right from her childhood, you have been spoiling her. I will no longer tolerate such irresponsible behaviour,' said the pot-bellied man, shaking his finger accusingly.

'Cool your head, Devi. Shouting or ranting will not help the situation.' The elderly man tried to pacify the other man.

'Nothing you say will change my mind. I will drag her home today.'

'I have said all I could. It's up to you, now,' the older man shrugged his shoulders. 'You are too obstinate and refuse to listen to reason, anyway.'

'Of course, I will do what I think is right. Your unconvincing arguments will not change my mind. Thank your stars that I didn't lodge a police complaint.' The paunchy fellow waved his hands in agitation.

'She is not a minor. You can't lodge a complaint against a 22-year-old for doing what she wants to do.'

'I will not listen to you anymore. She's crossed all limits this time. I am going to beat the daylights out of her. But first, I must find her.' The pot-bellied man looked around angrily. Spotting Lucky, he called out in a belligerent voice. 'Here, boy, can you tell me where the girls are staying?'

Offended, the Lucky stared back at the rude man.

'She's not a boy,' hissed the older man.

'If she's not a boy, why is her hair cut so short? And, why is she dressed like one?'

'It is the academy rule. Every cadet, girl or boy, has to wear the same uniform and get the same haircut,' the older man explained patiently.

'What a funny rule. And what kind of academy turns girls into boys? I will never allow them to do that to my daughter. It gives me one more reason to drag her away from this place.'

It was one thing to look like one, but to be addressed as a boy was the ultimate insult.

'Did you say something?' Lucky retorted in a tetchy manner.

'Don't be a fool, Devilal,' admonished the older man. Turning to Lucky, he said gently, 'Beti, can you lead us to the building where the girls are housed?'

'Are you looking for an LC?'

'Yes, we are looking for my daughter, Bijli,' snapped the pot-bellied man called Devi. 'She has run away from home. I want you to take us to her hostel.'

What an obnoxious man! Lucky was stunned to know that Billi had run away from home, and now the two men were hunting for her. The father was a boor. No wonder she had run away. In the past few days, Lucky had grown fond of the plucky and outspoken Haryanvi girl. The news that Billi had run from home to join the academy made Lucky chuckle. Her respect for her friend went up several notches.

There was no way she was going to lead Billi's family to Zojila. She didn't want them to drag her friend back to Alakhpura.

'I can't take you to the hostel,' she told the father. 'You see, I arrived yesterday night and don't know my way around the campus.'

'Don't lie to me,' roared Devilal. 'How can you not know where the girls are housed? Aren't you staying in the same hostel?'

'I am staying in the same hostel, but I have lost my way,' Lucky put on an act. 'In any case, I don't think you are allowed to visit the hostel. You have to take permission to walk around the campus.'

'That is what I was telling him,' the elderly man threw up his hands. 'This is an army academy, not a rural area college where one can strut around the campus without permission. This place has strict discipline and rules, and one can't just charge around the campus hunting for a girl. He won't listen, of course.'

'Papa, don't tell me what I can do and what I can't. I don't need anyone's permission to take my daughter home,' barked the obstinate man. 'I am going to hunt around the place till I find her.'

So, the duo were father and son. Which meant the pot-bellied man was Billi's father and the other was her grandfather. Interesting! The grandfather was definitely more refined than the boorish father.

'You can't do that, sir,' said Lucky. 'Why don't you go to the main office? They will help you.'

'Where is the office?' asked Billi's grandfather. With the sun beating down in full fury, he looked exhausted and in need of rest. 'We will be thankful if you will be kind enough to guide us to the place.'

His request set her thinking. Although she was the one to suggest that they go to the main office, Lucky realized that she needed time to warn Billi about the arrival of her father. It would be disastrous if the father-son duo landed up at the office, and Billi was summoned there before she could be warned.

After dithering for a minutes, she pointed in the direction of the cafeteria. 'I am very confused about the directions. Why don't you go to the cafeteria? They will help you to the office.'

'How is it possible that you don't know the location of the office?' Devilal asked in an obnoxious manner. 'You are telling lies.'

'I do not tell lies.' Lucky bristled at the accusation and drew herself to her full height, which, at 154.5 centimetres, wasn't very impressive.

'Well...'

'It's alright, beti,' the older man tried to appease her. 'We will go to the cafeteria.'

'Chennai is rather sultry at this time of the year, and you seem quite exhausted. You could refresh yourself with lemonade at the cafeteria, before you go to the office,' she suggested kindly.

Her suggestion drew a surly grunt from Devilal.

'That's a very good idea.' The old man smiled and folded his hands to show his gratitude. 'I will be happy to rest my tired feet for a few minutes.'

The sun beating down on her, Lucky limped her way to Zojila as soon as the two men began making their way to the cafeteria.

Once there, she found her friend front rolling along the corridor. *When will the girl learn? With her foot in the mouth disease, she was forever doing the wrong things.*

Avoiding the CSM's eyes, Lucky sidled towards Billi. It was an impossible task, of course. The hawk-eyed CSM was waiting to swoop down on the unsuspecting girls.

'There you are, LC Lakme. Does it take so long to report sick at the MI Room?' she hollered.

'Ma'am, the MI Room was very crowded...' the girl displayed a chit issued by the sympathetic doctor. It was a slip with permission for ED (excuse duty), which meant that the CSM could not punish, nor assign any chores to her.

Like a hunter deprived of a prize catch, the CSM glared at the slip of paper. 'Go to your room and remain there till you are called,' she barked.

'Thank you, ma'am,' Lucky began limping away towards the staircase, wondering how she could warn Billi about her father and grandfather's arrival at the campus.

There was just one way.

Two steps up the staircase, Lucky faltered and fell. The thud and cry brought some girls, including the CSM and Billi, running.

They helped up the hobbling girl.

'Can't you be careful?' shouted the CSM. 'The next time I find you playing the fool, it will be very unhealthy for you.' Turning to Billi, she ordered, 'Help her to the room. Get another girl to help you.'

Once they were inside the room, Lucky grabbed her friend's arm. 'They are here to take you home.'

'Who are here…'

'I ran into your father and grandfather near the canteen. Your father is determined to drag you back to Alakhpura.'

'Oh, my god!' Billi sank heavily to the floor. 'What will I do now?'

'We have to think of some way to make them go away,' Lucky spoke in a low voice. 'You don't have much time to think. They must have reached the office by now. You can expect to be summoned there, any moment.'

'Shit! Bloody hell!' Billi let out a string of profanities. She was a fast learner and the last couple of days at the academy had enlarged her vocabulary. 'I can't think of anything.'

'We, I mean the four of us, could meet and convince them,' Lucky suggested.

'My father is an obstinate man. A male chauvinist to boot, he's not likely to listen to any of you,' Billi wailed.

'There must be a way. We should consult the others.'

Soon, Shiny and Nutty were invited to share their wisdom, and the four girls put their heads together to think of a way out of the mess.

'I can't think of any solution,' said Nutty.

'You could take them around the campus. Perhaps, they will be impressed enough to discard the idea of taking you back,' Shiny opined.

'It won't work,' Billi shook her head. 'The thing is, Papa has a grudge against the army. When he was young, my grandfather had convinced him to apply to the army, but he was rejected. Since then, he has been wearing a chip on his shoulder.'

'That's unfair! He can't take out his grudge on you. He should be proud that you have been selected,' Lucky said. She refrained from mentioning how rude he had been. 'I think your father is a very unreasonable person.'

'There's nothing to do but to face the music,' sighed Billi. 'I will have to go back, but I will never forget the three of you, nor the academy. Also, I will never forgive my father for this injustice.'

'Life is bloody unfair,' Nutty remarked.

Gloom descended on the room as the three girls sat staring helplessly at their friend.

They didn't have to wait long. Billi was summoned by the adjutant a few minutes later. Hugging her friends tearfully, she pleaded, 'Wish me luck!'

The three friends nodded sadly at their friend.

'Things will be fine,' consoled Lucky as the crestfallen girl left for the adjutant's office.

There was no time for any further discussion as they heard the CSM hollering downstairs. Further punishment awaited.

The strengthening exercses continued till lunchtime. Reluctantly, the three girls joined the rest of the LCs who were jogging towards Yoddha Mess. They wondered what had happened to Billi. The girl had left for the adjutant's office a couple of hours ago.

Lunch was a quiet affair as the three friends hurried through the meal. They had little doubt that the adjutant would have to yield to Mr Devilal's threat of taking his daughter home.

'I wonder what happened to Billi,' said Shiny, as they jogged back from the mess.

'She must be preparing papers for her withdrawal from the academy,' whispered Nutty, as she jogged with the others.

'Poor girl! I feel sorry for her. To be selected and then having to give up is terrible,' said Lucky.

'I wish I had met her father,' Shiny gritted her teeth angrily. 'I would have given him a piece of my mind.'

The girls returned to Zojila after lunch, wondering if their friend had returned. To their surprise, they found her grinning like a Cheshire cat. She hugged them and performed an impromptu bhangra around the room. '*Balle! Balle!*' she shouted, hugging them by turns. 'I am not going anywhere.'

'What!' the girls cried in unison.

'It's a miracle!' exclaimed Lucky.

'After hearing all about your father's attitude, I just can't believe he changed his mind,' commented Shiny.

'I can't believe it, myself,' Billi laughed. 'The good news is that Papa and Daddu have left campus, and I am here. They will be taking the evening flight to Delhi and journeying back to Alakhpura.'

'Come on, Billi. Tell us everything, right from the beginning,' pleaded Lucky, who liked nothing better than a good story.

The three girls crowded around the Haryanvi girl on the other side of the bed, keen on hearing the story of the miraculous turnaround in Devilal's attitude.

'I covered the distance from here to the adjutant's office in the shortest time imaginable, in a greatly agitated state. I rehearsed the lines I would speak to express my anger at Papa's high-handedness. Despair and rage alternated in my mind. I couldn't believe my eyes when I reached the adjutant's office. Can any of you imagine what I saw there?' Billi tossed the question at her friends.

'Don't kill us with suspense. Just tell us what happened!' Nutty demanded.

'Well, dear coconut! Papa and Daddu were enjoying tea and biscuits with the adjutant. Not just that, Papa was guffawing at something the adjutant had said.'

'Sorry to sound rude, but I can't imagine your father guffawing,' commented Lucky.

'Well, he was in a good mood alright,' continued the footballer. 'I stood uncertainly at the door, wondering what was going on. There were two more officers in the adjutant's office.'

'There were two more officers, you said. Who were they?' Shiny wanted to know.

'One of them was a very smart lady officer called Poonam Dahiya, and the other was a smashing officer. His nameplate identified him as Samar Rathore.'

'Maybe they brought about a change in your Papa's heart,' said Lucky.

'Of course they did. It was all thanks to Major Samar Rathore, who, with his smooth and charming ways, dinned some sense into my father's brain. The lady officer also had a huge role to play in the change.' Billi smiled.

'What was your father's reaction when you entered the room?' asked Nutty. 'Considering you had run away from home to join the academy, he must have been furious.'

'Surprisingly, he didn't mention that part at all. After I sought permission to enter the office, the adjutant gave me a good dressing down. This pleased Papa. Realizing that he had an ally in the adjutant, he joined in to berate me. This lasted for a full two minutes and ended with a sermon about the importance of being honest with one's parents.'

'Didn't you point out that you were forced to run away because the parents wouldn't listen to you?' asked Shiny.

'Thank God I didn't do that. Something told me that talking back could be counterproductive. In fact, I apologized and promised not to repeat the mistake. That mellowed everyone's mood. My act of repentance brightened my father's face. He has an ego problem, you see. Any argument sets him on the warpath. Anyway, after the sermon, I was told to accompany Papa and Daddu for a tour around the campus and then take them to the cafeteria for lunch. And that was that.'

'We still don't know how the miracle happened.' Lucky sounded disappointed by the tame ending. She had been expecting fireworks.

'Like I mentioned, it was all the handiwork of Major Dahiya and Major Rathore. At the cafeteria, over a sumptuous lunch of Chinese fried rice and chicken fry, Daddu told me the whole story. The turnaround began when Papa noticed the orderly saluting the lady officer. He had never imagined a man saluting a woman. Her smart gait and brisk manner impressed him no end. "That is how people will salute our Billi when she is an officer," Daddu whispered in Papa's ears. The rest was Major Rathore's contribution. He is a very convincing and charming person. Together, the officers, assisted by Daddu, joined forces to brainwash my father. In fact, they used Chanakya's *niti* – 'Saam, Daam and Dand' – to convince him of the futility of his unwise decision. Imagine how proud you will feel once your daughter is commissioned and goes back home. Just think of the respect everyone will give her. Major Dahiya, who is also from Haryana, illustrated the point with examples from her own life. Her story made a big impression on my father. "I will take you around the academy," she promised. "And you will see everything for yourself."

'After softening him up, they warned him about the huge amount he would have to pay if he withdrew me from the academy, and also the repercussion on his reputation. "Everyone in the village will curse you for your unpatriotic behaviour," Daddu warned. That did the trick. One thing my father would not dream of jeopardizing was his reputation in Alakhpura.

'He considered every aspect and agreed that it would be unwise to take me away from the academy. Major Dahiya took us around the academy in her car, pointing out each and every detail. She spoke about Preeti Choudhary, who had won the Sword of Honour at the academy.

"Your daughter will be able to repeat the same feat," the lady officer told Papa.'

Wide-eyed, the girls listened to the story. Billi stopped to gulp down some water before continuing, 'By the time she dropped us at the cafeteria, Papa was a reformed man. He was in awe of the academy and spoke of Major Dahiya with great reverence. Satisfied by the outcome, Papa and Daddu enjoyed the lunch, while I updated them about my experiences here. Daddu had tears in the eyes as he blessed me, but Papa was so emotionally touched that he couldn't say much. All he said in a gruff voice was, "I want that sword." That's it!'

'You promised to take home the bloody Sword of Honour?' Nutty's voice went up by several notches.

'Don't you think it was too rash a promise?' Shiny said. 'I mean, it is one thing to aim for the sword but to promise…'

'Was there any other way out of the mess? At least, I couldn't think of one. For me, all that mattered was to continue with training. I will have to work harder to take the sword home,' Billi sighed.

'What if you can't take it home?' Lucky looked worried. To her, a promise was sacred. To be kept.

'It will be just too bad,' the Haryanvi lass smiled. 'Don't look worried. I am here with you, and that's what matters.'

'Yes, it's time to celebrate,' said an excited Nutty. 'Billi is here to stay. We...'

Her words were cut short by a loud command, 'First-termers report at the anteroom immediately. Immediately.'

By now, the first-termers knew the importance of the word 'immediately'. When uttered once, it meant that the order had come from the CSM. When mentioned twice it meant that one of the *paltus* had arrived, and repeated thrice was the danger level. It meant that the Company Commander (CoCo) was on a prowl.

'I want to meet this Major Rathore,' said Nutty as they trooped down the stairs. 'He must be a very smart person to be able to convince your father to drop the idea of pulling you out of the academy.'

'Oh yes, he's smart alright. In fact, he's very suave and handsome,' Billi agreed.

Of Timetables, Putti Parades, and Cabin Cupboards

Lucky was fond of sticking mementos and charts behind her door. It was a habit she had acquired during her schooling days. The LC had a beautiful handwriting and loved to write in calligraphy, and the back of the door became an unofficial exhibition panel for her expertise. Every inch of the top half displayed myriad sticky notes with various reminders. Above all was her list of commandments,

which seemed to grow every day as new points were added. Below, was a detailed timetable, which made interesting reading since she kept adding her comments to it.

0400: Wake up and punishment fall-ins

0530: Muster fall-ins

0600: PT/Drill (come, rain, hail or sunshine. Thank god for the location. No hail but plenty of sun and rivulets of perspiration).

After PT/Drill – A quick bath, provided you are not caught on the wrong foot by the CSM or a senior cadet. Getting caught means spending the time on punishments instead of in your bath.

0800: Breakfast. (Mutate into pythons and gulp down the breakfast, if you are lucky to reach the mess on time).

0915: Academics. (Olympian feat! No two classes are located together. You have to cycle in a squad of four or six to each location. Mounting and dismounting at the sight of officers, wishing seniors is vital. Failure to do so will attract punishments. The distance between classes is about 500 metres on an undulating surface. All this has to be achieved in the 10 minutes provided between classes.)

1330: Lunch break. (It entails picking up your cycle and pedaling as fast as possible to reach your company and run to the mess for lunch. The faster you reach, the more time you get to eat. Once again, you mutate into a python and gulp down the lunch in the shortest time possible, and run back to the company.)

1350: Fall-in. (Invariably followed by PT or extra drill.)

1500: *Ragda* (No patties! Sigh!)

1530: Games /Swimming

1700: Return from the ground. A quick shower, cleaning your cabin, followed by study period.

1845: Run down for fall-in

1900: Fall-in

1945: Orders followed by punishments

2000: Quick dinner (Pythons are forever hungry)

2030: Run back to company

2045: Company fall-in.

2100: Dangerous time… Anything can happen. Generally, it's some more *ragda*.

2200: Lights out.

2225: Seniors on the prowl. Yet more *ragda*.

(Note: No two days are the same. Expect the unexpected.)

The learning graph at the academy zooms upwards at a giddying rate, so much so that it seems almost vertical. In just a few days, the LCs had become used to waking up at 4.30 a.m. and had picked up the art of getting ready in less than 10 minutes and then presenting themselves for drill or PT. They were also learning the art of dodging the CSM, but it seemed impossible to know when or where she was lurking. Fortunate were the ones who could escape her attention for a few hours.

True to Lucky's postscript, the unexpected happened the very next day. Seniors had been trickling into the academy since the previous day. Wary, the first-termers watched out for them, taking care to keep out of their way. Rumours about punishments being meted out by senior LCs abounded in the academy, and no one wanted to add to the misery.

Chatting animatedly, the gang of four were walking towards Zojila Company, eager for a bath after a hectic session of physicals, when Koel raced past them, along with Deepa Chavan huffing and puffing in tow. The girl did not seem to be in her best physical form. 'Come on, hurry up,' spurred Koel. 'We can have a nice shower.'

'There they go,' Nutty chuckled. 'I mean the general's daughter and her *chamchi*.'

'You mean *chamcha*, don't you? Isn't a spoon called a *chamcha* in Hindi? Anyway, I don't see her carrying a spoon,' Lucky wanted to know. Her grasp of Hindi was rudimentary, at best.

'You are so funny,' Billi laughed. 'A *chamchi* in this case means a bootlicker.'

'Well, why would anyone want to lick Koel's boots?' Lucky was puzzled.

'The Chyawanprash is an opportunist,' replied Nutty. She was a master at giving absurd nicknames to all her opponents. So Koel was honoured with the moniker of

Cockroach, and Deepa Chavan became Chyawanprash. 'The moment she heard that Cockroach's father is a general, she latched on to the girl and has stuck to her like a leech.'

'Now, who are Cockroach and Chyawanprash?' Lucky wanted to know.

'Those are the epithets given by our brilliant friend, Miss Peanut,' Shiny sniggered.

'Peanut! Well, I will be damned,' Billi burst into laughter.

'No, she's a sweet doughnut,' Lucky said with a wink. 'She's got a hole where her brain ought to be.'

'Look, you may call me Peanut or Doughnut, whatever you want,' Nutty responded forgivingly. 'The fact remains that Cockroach is a pest and needs to be squashed.'

'Have you noticed the expression on Koel's face? That girl's mouth is set in a perpetual sneer. She seems to think of everyone around her as an idiot,' Billi said a bit waspishly. She had taken an instant dislike to the general's daughter.

'Very true!' agreed Shiny. 'She has a supercilious attitude.'

A funny sight greeted their eyes, on reaching the company. Cockroach and Chyawanprash were rolling in the long corridor that ran along the rooms. Like huge balls of human limbs, they moved down the passageway, their rolls accompanied by silent curses and muted groans.

'What are you staring at? Come and join your friends on the floor,' ordered an authoritative voice. Turning, Billi spotted the two tormentors.

'But…' Nutty's protest was cut off with a stern look from them.

'And you will do 10 extra,' commanded one of the senior LCs. The four of them began rolling without further ado. None of them knew why they were being asked to roll nor did they dare to ask. At least the punishers were fair. It didn't matter to them if one was a general's daughter or a cobbler's. Everyone got an equal share. The academy was a great leveller.

'Next time, don't forget to salute your seniors,' said one of the tormentors.

It was only then that the first-termers realized that the punishment had been given for not having saluted the seniors. Thankfully, the two disappeared after issuing their warning.

'Whew! I didn't know we were supposed to salute the seniors,' said Shiny, rubbing her sore elbows.

'I guess it's time to begin saluting everyone in sight,' giggled Lucky.

To the list of commandments pasted on her door, she added another point:

- When in doubt, salute and front roll

The same evening, after another session of rolling, they dusted themselves and made a beeline for their rooms, intending to bathe before dinner. All plans of cooling off were put aside as a couple of seniors made an appearance and began raining abuses on the *jungoos*.

'Get off your arses,' shouted one of them. 'It is time for *putti* parade.'

Even as they wondered what those words meant, orders were issued at a rapid-fire rate. They were told to change into full combat dress.

'And you get a full 60 seconds to report to the upper floor,' the senior bellowed, her foghorn voice echoing down the corridor. 'Those who get here in less than two minutes will be free to go back to their rooms.'

Suddenly it seemed as though a war had broken out. Driven by the promise of freedom, the girls ducked into their rooms and struggled to get out of their sticky, sweaty games dresses and don full battle gear, which included belts, boots and a camouflage cap.

Pleased as punch, Lucky emerged from her room in the allotted time. She ran up the stairs and presented herself before the seniors. The grin was promptly wiped out, and she found herself rolling down the corridor. Obsessed with the idea of keeping time, she had forgotten to put on the mandatory back pack and the pair of front pouches.

As expected, none of the others could finish in the given time, and everyone found themselves rolling. The seniors pointed out a dozen mistakes – untied laces, wrong socks or boots, missing paraphernalia or taking too much time to change. They had barely straightened, when they were ordered to change into games dresses in 30 seconds.

It was an impossible task, given that reaching their rooms would take at least ten seconds. There was a melee as the first-termers ran down the stairs to their rooms. Changing from combat dresses into white shorts, shirts, white shoes and socks seemed to take ages. The laces eluded their trembling fingers, or the buttons refused to oblige. When they ran back to the second floor, the displeased seniors let loose another volley of abuses.

'Give us 50,' commanded the senior with a foghorn voice.

By then, the *jungoos* had realized the futility of the exercise. No matter how much they hurried, they would never make it in the stipulated time.

Once again, they were ordered to return in 6 Bravo, which was a formal dress with a cummerbund worn during mess functions. They were given 30 seconds. Once again, the hectic rushing ended in push-ups and front rolls. They kept rolling till the entire world began spinning before their eyes. There was no better way to prove Copernicus' theory of heliocentrism. Billi was tempted to tell the tormentors that they could skip the orders and keep them rolling all day.

From 6 Bravo to games rigs and then muftis, the *Putti* parade (interspersed with punishments), continued for the next half hour.

The only positive outcome of the exercise was that the LCs picked up the art of changing in record time. They were not likely to forget the details of each rig, either. Also, they had become experts at kissing Mother Earth. Another thing that they realized from the experience was that the *putti* parade was one of the favourite punishments of the seniors. This was one parade that needed to be mastered if one was to escape their ire.

Mastering the game of swift changing wasn't enough, the first-termers soon learned. There was a deadlier punishment awaiting them. It was known as cabin cupboard parade.

The confusing words were thrown at them just after they had finished a round of *putti* parade. In a hurry to complete the task of changing into different rigs in the stipulated time, they had tossed their socks, shirts, trousers and other paraphernalia all around their beds and the floor.

'Couldn't be a punishment I am sure,' remarked the ever-optimistic Lucky.

She couldn't have been farther from the truth. Put simply, the words cabin cupboard meant organizing their rooms to a set layout. First, they were taken to a room and shown a demo layout.

'There should be no deviation,' said a senior with a rasping voice. All that screaming and shouting at the juniors must have done the trick. Whatever the reason, the rasping voice was impossible to ignore.

'Everything should be placed just as displayed. You don't have the liberty to exercise your interior decoration talents.'

'Don't try any tricks, because we know them all,' warned another senior. 'You have 15 minutes to set your rooms. Don't forget that all items in the cabin must be cleaned and folded before they are put in the black steel trunk. There should not be a speck of dust around.'

'Great expectations!' muttered Shiny.

She stared ruefully at her room, which looked as though a tornado had swept through it. Clothes were strewn all over the place, shoes flung along the walls, their laces knotted; berets, belts and socks occupied a major part of the floor and bed. There was no way she could create a semblance of order in the given time.

Stop working and stand outside your room, an announcement echoed down the corridor. The announcement made the girls dart out of their rooms. Much like the Jews during the midnight visits of the Gestapo, they stood waiting for their fates to be decided.

The two seniors began their inspection. Their entry into the first cabin was followed by loud shouting, banging, and the next instant everything came flying out of the room and landed in the corridor. Seconds later, a crestfallen Nutty emerged from the cabin looking numb with disbelief. In two minutes flat, the seniors had demolished her labour of 15 minutes. They did this to everyone's rooms.

'Morons, get your act together! The next inspection will take place in half an hour.'

If ever there were an award for torture, the seniors were sure to bag it.

A hectic 30 minutes later, Lucky stepped back to admire her neat cabin. Every object in the room was in the right place, neatly arranged. *This time, the Gestapo won't be able to find any fault*, she thought smugly.

The bullies entered her room and threw Lucky a blistering glance, after which they went on to inspect shoelaces, mosquito net poles and peeped under the bed.

'The shoes laces are twisted, and look at all this dust,' the senior with the raspy voice announced, after running her finger on the mosquito net poles. The temperature in the room had dipped by at least 10 degrees and Lucky shivered.

'You call this cleaning?'

Grinning rather unpleasantly, she displayed her grimy finger and wiped it across Lucky's face. 'The next time I will make you lick it clean.'

Nothing seemed to be right with the cabin, as far as the tyrants were concerned. The clothes were not folded properly, the shoes not lined up properly. The bed, chair and tables were not properly aligned.

It was the same story in each of the cabins they inspected.

Each time, the LCs were punished and reassigned the same task, to be completed in progressively shorter periods.

By the end of the hour, exhausted by the ordeal, the *jungoos* were happy to front roll rather than do up their cabins.

The seniors had arrived and how!

Enter the CoCo

That evening, after being ordered to assemble in the anteroom, the LCs raced down the corridor, wondering if they were likely to face another round of punishments.

They were surprised to find not only the CSM and JUO, but the two Platoon Commanders (*paltus*) present in the anteroom.

'This looks serious,' Nutty declared. 'I hope they are not planning another offensive against the first-termers.'

Alerted by the deep thrum of a motorcycle engine, the CSM and the *paltus* rushed towards the door. Minutes later, they reappeared with a dreamboat of a man. Although he was a little less than six feet, his looks made up for the lack of inches in height. In short, he had all the traits of a heart-throb.

It was none other than the officer who had persuaded Billi's father to change his mind. 'Oh my God!' groaned Nutty, her eyes widened. She was staring at the smart hunk striding into the anteroom. She gasped.

There was a sharp intake of breath as the LCs stared at the vision. Billi sighed. A pair of dark dancing eyes met widened ones with much amusement. Under a thick mop of cropped hair was an angular face with prominent cheekbones, that ended in a chin with a deep cleft. The pair of faded blue jeans topped by a fitted T-shirt promised a toned body.

'Good evening!' His rich baritone rang across the hushed hall. Pausing to smile, he continued, 'Welcome to the academy. I am your Company Commander Major Samar Rathore.'

'It's not fair,' whispered Nutty. 'No one has the right to look so good.'

'You are some of the best. I am sure you know that already. Each year thousands of young men and women appear for the selection exams, and only some manage to clear them. To be selected for the academy is an honour. At first your training may appear tough, but you will find it easier to cope with the demands of the profession after the first month. It is all about tuning your body and mind to the task at hand.' He went on to motivate and advise the LCs in a friendly manner.

'Anything which is short is sweet, and therefore I shall not take too long.' He paused meaningfully, before asking, 'I hope you girls are having a wonderful time?'

There was slight hesitation as the LCs wondered if they could complain about the harsh punishments, but they wilted under the CSM's stern look.

'I can assure you that everything that is happening now is meant for your good,' he continued, as if he had read their minds. 'You may not realize it today, but the exercises are meant to toughen you. Having said that, let me inform you that you are going through the "honeymoon period" right now, and things will get tougher as days pass.'

Confused by the term 'honeymoon period', the LCs looked at him for an explanation.

'I can see that you are wondering about this so called "honeymoon period". Well, the academy is generous enough to allow a month's time to the first-termers, before their nose is put to the grindstone.' The killer smile back on his face, he continued, 'The period allows you to acquaint yourself with rules and regulations, learn the basics of using the correct rigs and get used to a disciplined life and routine. You learn how to move around in squads while walking or cycling. It's also meant to reduce the number of cadets fleeing the academy just after joining it. Yes, don't look so shocked. Many cadets find it difficult to adjust to the demands of the training and take the easy way out by quitting. Isn't that right, Sasha?' The CoCo cast a mischievous smile in the LC's direction. He had heard rumours about her wanting to leave the academy.

She blushed and lowered her head.

'My advice is that you do your best to adjust. In life, there are many situations that don't please us. Running away is never the solution. Complaining about hardships is also not a solution. One has to face up to them.'

At his words, the complaints rearing in their heads shrivelled and dried up. The CoCo wasn't on their side, the LCs realized. His lenient words and killer smiles were a trick to win them over. Like deflated balloons, their determination to complain sagged after the handsome officer's lecture.

They wanted to complain about the CSM and the *paltus*, who excelled in nitpicking and punishing them for the smallest of errors. The first-termers were convinced that the CSM was a lunatic. There were times when she made them execute front rolls without assigning any reason.

Despite the sermon, Sadhna aka Saddie, couldn't resist the urge to squeal. She was determined to point out the high-handed behaviour of the senior. *No better time than now.*

A defiant look on her face, she raised her hand. All heads turned to her in surprise. Snitching was a blasphemy, for which all the first-termers of Zojila would have to pay.

'Yes, LC Sadhna, what is it that you wish to say?' CoCo prodded the LC.

Having realized that the impulsive action could lead to trouble, Saddie hesitated for a couple of minutes while the CoCo waited patiently for her to make up her mind.

Drawing a deep breath, she blurted, 'Sir, we hardly get any time to rest, we are doing bends, stretches and front rolls all the time.'

'Is that so? It's really unfair.'

The LCs looked pleased.

'Well, we will have to change that,' he smiled. Turning to Major Sherawat, he said, 'Please give them cream rolls. It will be a change for them.'

What they missed was the wink he gave Major Sherawat.

Minutes later, he drove off on his bike. As pleased as punch, the LCs waited for the promised cream rolls. Only Ishita continued to wear an anxious look.

'Now, for the cream rolls,' said Major Sherawat after seeing the CoCo off. 'You shall all have cream rolls for the next 15 minutes. I hope you like it.'

The LCs had assembled at the ground in front of the building. With a wicked gleam in her eyes, the CSM explained what a cream roll was.

'A cream roll is a front roll followed by a back roll,' she said. 'You can have as many of them as you want.'

Saddie felt the heat of anger directed against her. The entire lot of LCs were bearing the brunt of her complaint.

The next 15 minutes saw the LCs executing cream rolls on the ground. While they excelled in the art of frontrolling, the back rolls proved to be more difficult to execute, and the combination of the two rolls was nothing short of torture. There were loud grunts and sighs.

If this was the honeymoon period, they couldn't imagine what awaited them after.

'You need more practice doing back rolls,' the CSM declared after watching them struggle with the exercise.

No sooner had the CSM left, than the LCs gathered around Saddie.

'When will you learn?' demanded Sasha. 'There is no one to whom we can address our complaints.' The bitterness in her tone surprised no one. The girl was a pain in the arse.

'We don't need to draw more punishments. We have enough and more without complaining,' said Cockroach. 'Henceforth, please zip your lips.'

'Yes, it is best to bear the punishments than to complain,' agreed Chyawanprash.

In a unanimous vote, the first-termers of Zojila vowed not to snitch again.

I Just Wanna Go Home

By the end of the fourth day, it was easy to distinguish the laggards from the self-starters. While most first-termers were slowly getting used to the routine and punishments, some found it impossible to keep the pace. They cried, complained and grumbled more than the others. Of them, some tried hard to catch up, but some gave up. The first one to give up was a girl called Ruby, who left the academy on the second day.

Next was Natasha Sharma, aka Sasha, from Delhi. The LC could not keep up with the demands of the training. It was difficult enough for her to get up early and follow the routine, but the front rolls and haunches were simply unbearable.

A malingerer, she invented fresh excuses to avoid exercises. It had been severe stomach cramps the first day, toothache the next. However, it was not easy to fool the CSM, who was conversant with every excuse that could be offered by a fresher. As a result, Sasha found herself singled out for extra punishments every day. By now, everyone was aware of the girl's disinterest.

The LCs were fed up of her whining. 'I am going home,' she declared a dozen times every day. 'I don't want this shitty training.'

That fateful morning, the alarm went off at 3.30 a.m. as usual. They had half an hour to get ready and run down for the fall-in. Her roommate, Brinda, emerged from the bathroom and found Sasha sleeping with her head burrowed under her pillow to escape disturbance. It was Brinda's responsibility to wake her up every morning.

'Get up you lazy bum, or we'll be late for the fall-in, and you know what happens if one is late for anything,' Brinda shook her friend.

'Stop shaking me up,' protested Sasha. 'I am not getting up at this unearthly hour.'

'Enough of your nonsense,' retorted Brinda. 'It's become a daily affair. Firstly, it's not my responsibility to wake you up every morning. Secondly, I have no intention of starting my day listening to your grumbling. Thirdly, you opted to join the academy, so you have no one else to blame. Grow up and take charge of your life.'

Her rebuke made Sasha sit up on the bed and begin ranting. 'This place is shit. I am sure it is going to be a repeat of yesterday. The CSM will rant and rave and punish us. I am fed up.' Saying this, she entered the bathroom to get ready for the day.

'If it is a repeat of yesterday, I am quitting,' Sasha said as they doubled down in their white PT dress for the fall-in. She had mulled over her miseries for a long time, the previous night.

'Cheer up! Once you stop grumbling and start looking at the positive side, you will realize it's all for our good,' Brinda tried to pump some gyan into her.

The morning began, as usual, with a lecture by the CSM, after which the JUO handed them a few forms to complete their documentation. Once the forms were filled and handed over to the JUO, the CSM took over from her.

'LC Mehra, why are you yawning?' she shouted. The LC, who had opened her mouth to yawn, shut it immediately.

'Why are you dancing, LC Rawat? For the last three minutes, you have been switching your weight from one leg to the other. Has your bottom grown too heavy due to inactivity?' The CSM continued to pick on the *jungoos*.

'Lazy bums, get down on your hands and give me 20,' the CSM shouted.

Groans suppressed, the LCs got down on their hands and began executing front rolls.

Sasha continued standing.

'LC Sharma, are you hard of hearing?'

'No, I am not.' The CSM noted that she did not add the customary 'ma'am' to the statement. Gleefully, the others noted it too.

Taken aback, the CSM was too outraged to speak for a moment and then she went into full throttle mode. 'Is it another of your excuses or are you trying to take *panga* with me?'

No one had ever dared to misbehave or disobey a CSM in the academy. Sasha's defiance in the presence of the freshers added insult to injury.

'How dare you defy my orders? I will fix you. You are unfit to be here,' the CSM fumed.

'Yes, you are absolutely right. I have realized that I am unfit to be in this academy. So, I have decided to quit training and go home.' Saying this, Sasha turned and began climbing the stairs with as much dignity as she could muster, while the first-termers gaped in silence.

There was a stunned silence as the LCs wondered at their course-mate's fate. What would the CSM do, now that one of them had declared war? At a loss, the CSM directed Brinda to run up to her room and din some sense into her roommate's head.

'Look, Sasha…' the girl began earnestly, only to be cut off by her adamant roommate.

'Don't preach, Bee. Nothing you say will change my mind. I am sick and tired of this place.'

'But…'

'This place is worse than hell. I gave up a nice job to join the army. It was a foolish decision. I am not made for the army.'

'None of us is made for the army,' Brinda tried once again. 'We are here to train for it.'

'You won't understand.'

'Try me.'

'I really don't have the patience to make anyone understand my problem. Please leave me alone, Bee.'

Meanwhile, the CSM and the JUO had also arrived.

'What will your parents, relatives and friends say? They have already given you a warm send-off and expect to see you return as an officer. You will be letting all of them down. They will have no face to show to anyone,' the JUO tried to persuade the LC.

Sasha remained seated on the bed, refusing to be baited into an argument.

'Things will settle down, this will not go on forever,' Brinda consoled. 'The training is intended to toughen you, both physically and mentally.'

'I am quite strong, both physically and mentally,' countered Sasha.

'In that case, you should have no difficulties coping with the demands of the training,' argued Brinda.

The entry of Major Sherawat at that moment put an end to the discussions and arguments. Having heard of the incident, Major Sherawat had decided to try her persuasive powers on the girl.

The first thing she did was send the others out of the room. After that, she sat down near the recalcitrant LC and placed a hand on the girl's shoulders.

'I can understand what is going on in your mind,' she began her pitch in a motherly tone.

'No, you don't,' retorted Sasha. She was fed up of hearing the lectures. Everyone was trying to convince her against leaving. 'No one can understand what I am feeling.'

'That's what you think,' continued Sherawat patiently. 'Nine years ago, I felt the same way. I can still recall the day I made up my mind to leave the academy. Like you, I had declared war on my CSM.'

Sasha looked at the woman in disbelief. *It's just a story. She has fabricated the yarn to make me change my mind.*

'It's not a fabricated story,' the *paltu* smiled. She had read the girl's mind. 'The decision to join the army was not mine. It was forced upon me by my father, who was an army officer. From the very first day, I hated everything about the academy and wanted to run away. The tough regimen, *ragda*, everything irked me. Back home, girls were enjoying an unfettered life, I knew, while I was pushing myself to the very edge of a physical and mental precipice.'

Sasha leaned forward and cupped her chin in her hands, listening carefully. The earnest tone in Major Sherawat's voice had convinced her about the veracity of the story.

'I clearly remember that fateful evening when I declared that I had had enough of the academy and wanted to leave. At that moment, all I wanted was to run away.'

'Did you run away?'

'I didn't. Our CSM was like a coconut, with a hard exterior and a soft heart. She sat with me for a long while, listening to my vitriolic outpour. Not a word did she utter as I cursed her. At last, having exhausted myself, I turned to her and demanded – "Won't you say something?" She smiled and said, "No." That night, I couldn't sleep a wink. I thought of the friends I had made, the camaraderie between us and the sense of achievement I felt when completing a task. I couldn't abandon it all on a whim. I stayed. Not just that, I also won a silver medal.'

Major Sherawat's narration was interrupted by the company commander's arrival. He had hurried to Zojila the moment the news reached him. This was the second instance of a first-termer wanting to quit the academy. Every year, a few cadets, both GCs and LCs, invariably left the academy. This didn't reflect very well on the company commanders. Major Rathore was due for promotion and had no wish to allow such instances to mar his chances.

The LC had to be stopped from leaving. A mature man, he knew the dangers of trying to play the good cop, bad cop game. It simply didn't work on distraught cadets.

After knocking on the door, he entered the room. Major Sherawat hurriedly got on her feet and greeted him.

'What's going on?' he demanded.

'LC Sharma wants to go home,' she replied.

'Is that so? It's a pity we will be losing an intelligent cadet like her.'

Sasha, who had been feeling quite important with everyone trying to persuade her to stay, was taken aback. *Isn't he going to try his persuasive powers on me?*

'I don't believe in holding anyone against their wish. If you want to leave, you should leave.'

The LC's surprise knew no end. She had been looking forward to a session of coaxing with the handsome and charming CoCo.

'I will neither hold you back, nor waste my time trying to convince you. All I am going to do is to tell you a few things that may help you in life. Take it as a sermon or discard it, if you think it is useless,' he said.

'The Indian Army is one of the best in the world, and the honour has not come easy,' he began. 'It has been earned by the exemplary conduct of the men and women in the army. I am proud of my profession, let me confess. Officers have to lead by example. Why will your troops follow you, if you don't have any leadership qualities? Will they follow the orders of a slovenly officer who doesn't have the right posture, discipline or OLQ (Officer Like Qualities)? Don't forget, here in the academy, we are grooming leaders, not shirkers. You have to lead from the front. By virtue of being selected for entry, you have proved yourself to be better than the thousands of hopefuls who appeared for the test. You have the requisite qualities in you.'

The CoCo paused for a minute to study the reactions on Sasha's face. Finding none, he continued, 'Do you know what we are taught at the IMA (Indian Military

Academy)? The first few sentences you see on entering the Chetwode Hall of the IMA are the motto for every army officer. Eventually, the motto gets engraved in the minds of every cadet who passes through the academy.'

Sasha raised her eyebrows. Without waiting for an answer, the CoCo recited, 'The safety, honour and welfare of your country come first, always and every time. Second, the honour, welfare and comfort of the men you command come next. Third, your own ease, comfort and safety come last, always and every time.'

The LC lowered her head.

'You are quitting because of the punishments and the tough routine you are being made to follow. These are meant to make you give up old habits and to toughen you for the role you have to undertake. They are meant to break the sense of self, the ego. Eleven months later, when you are commissioned and have to leave the academy, you will not want to leave. You will want to live this life forever. Why 11 months, six months later, when you are senior-termers, you will be ordering the first-termers around. Not because you want to bully them, but because you have learnt the value of training. You will be sharing your experience with them and advising them to toughen up. I will not promise you a punishment-free training, or an easy time. It will be tough; as tough as can be. I have put forth my arguments, now it is for you to decide whether you want to continue or quit.'

With that, Major Rathore marched out of the room. There was silence for a while. The CSM and JUO, moved by his words, looked at the LC for a response.

'So?' Major Sherawat asked. 'I hope you have changed your mind.'

'No, ma'am, I haven't,' Sasha's voice wavered uncertainly. 'I will leave tomorrow.'

This time, it was the *paltu*'s turn to look puzzled.

That night, as Sasha packed her belongings dispiritedly, the gang of four visited the girl. The power of psychological persuasion had been amply proved after Billi's dogged father had changed his mind. The four girls were determined to try it on Sasha.

'Let me help you,' offered Billi.

The story of her father's visit to the academy had already spread through the company, with embellishments.

'Was it your decision to join the academy?' Lucky asked sweetly.

'Yes,' Sasha looked suspiciously at her. 'If you guys are here to make me change my mind, please leave the room. I can manage my own packing.'

'Heaven forbid! Why should we want to change your mind?' Shiny pretended to be shocked with the suggestion. 'You have every right to withdraw from the academy.'

The four LCs continued handing the clothes and folding them in silence.

'You are quite a lucky girl, Sasha,' Nutty began. 'Speaking of myself, the people in my village have reposed such faith in my ability that I can't think of going back without completing the training. No matter how tough the training, I will just have to stick around and complete it.'

'Same with me,' said Lucky. 'My parents were not in favour of my decision to join the academy. I can't go back. Also, the thought of the humiliation my parents would have to face keeps me from quitting. Failing is not viewed with favour in our country.'

'Shut up!' Sasha shouted. The next moment she dissolved into tears. 'Please leave me alone.'

It was the longest night Sasha had spent in a long time. Every word spoken by Paltu, CoCo and the gang of four resonated through her brain, amplifying the shame of quitting.

The next morning, all the first-termers were surprised to see her at the early morning fall-in. Dressed smartly in her PT uniform, Sasha grinned sheepishly at them.

'Don't look so surprised,' she said. 'A girl is allowed to change her mind. Isn't she?'

A Brief Reprieve

It was their first holiday, and the gang of four had been dreaming about the day. Shiny had set up a rendezvous with her boyfriend at the cafeteria, Billi wanted to eat as much as she could. 'I want a change of taste,' she declared.

Nutty's agenda included eyeing some smart GCs, while Lucky planned to buy packets of potato wafers, to which she was addicted. Everyone wanted to get away as soon as possible.

However, the CSM had other plans for them. Just as the first-termers were preparing to step out, she decided that they couldn't be allowed to leave without the mandatory workout of some front rolling and sit-ups.

That done, the dishevelled lot were allowed to take their phones from the carton laid out in the lobby. Soon, the lobby and adjacent areas were echoing with the excited chatter of the LCs.

Billi spoke to her parents as well as Daddu for a long time. Just as she was walking towards the carton to deposit her phone, it rang once again. It was a call from Banwari.

Skipping the details of punishments, Lucky updated her parents on the goings-on in the company. The girl had no intention of upsetting her parents. She spoke of the sumptuous meals, Yoddha Cadets' Mess, the beautiful campus, smart instructors, and the camaraderie between the cadets. She also told them about her cycling experience.

'Your descriptions make me keen on visiting the OTA. Don't worry, we will all be there for your POP,' promised her father.

Engrossed in their calls, the girls forgot all about their plans. Not just that, Lucky went for a shower and missed her breakfast.

An hour later, when the girls arrived at the cafeteria, they found it packed with cadets.

The café, with its varied fare, attracted the cadets in droves. Although the food wasn't something to write home about, it offered them a chance to get away from the punishments and catch up with friends. The sexagenarian owner, Mr Fernandes, a fatherly figure, had seen generations of cadets pass out of the academy. He was a kind man, with an incredible memory. Always ready to lend an ear to the complaints or offer advice, Papa Ferdy, as he was fondly known, not only possessed a kind but also a romantic heart. He fed both the body and souls of the cadets. Many were the romances that blossomed in the friendly atmosphere of his café.

Almost all the tables had been taken when the girls entered the café. Thankfully, Aaron, having reached the cafeteria quite early, had managed to grab a table. With him were two of his friends, including the cocky GC Manav Mathur, and his buddy GC Kale.

Shiny's boyfriend glanced pointedly at his wristwatch, but before Shiny could open her mouth, Nutty jumped up in her defence. 'Sorry, we are late,' she tittered. 'The CSM thought we were looking too smart, so we had to roll in the dust before leaving for the cafeteria.'

The apology was followed by a round of introductions. The ever-gallant GC Mathur, who was quite affluent by GC standards, ordered a round of drinks for the seven of them.

'I hate the guts of the CSM,' Billi ranted. The girls knew that she nursed the ambition of holding the appointment. 'Just wait till I become one.'

'The LCs have no idea about our CSM,' Mathur slapped the back of Kale, who was drinking his cola at a rapid speed. The thwack resulted in making Kale cough violently, and everyone joined in in thumping his back. Once their buddy had recovered, Mathur continued, 'So what was I saying?'

Kale, having finished the cola, reminded him, 'You were telling them about our CSM. By the way, are we not ordering anything else?' he asked timidly.

The guy was a glutton and a sponge too. Never the one to pay for anything, he was bent upon tucking in as much food as he could. Besides, Mathur's burst of generosity was not likely to last long. The presence of girls was making him more charitable than usual.

'Oh yes, the LCs think that their CSM is tough,' Mathur laughed raucously. 'You should meet our CSM. The guy is the reincarnation of the devil. Nothing escapes his eyes.'

'That's what you think,' Lucky couldn't help sniggering. 'Wait till you meet Miss Khadoos.'

'Miss Khadoos,' Mathur broke into another round of laughter. 'I like that. Hey guys, we should also find an appropriate name for our CSM,' he suggested.

'How about Mogambo or Gabbar Singh?' Nutty offered. She had already taken a shine to the exuberant GC.

'Yes, that suggestion is worth considering,' said the pompous ass. All through the conversation, Mathur had been eyeing Lucky, much to her discomfiture. 'Let's have some chicken cutlets. I have heard that they make it well,' he said, beckoning the harassed waiter. 'Bring us 10 cutlets,' he ordered.

'Aaron, I am speaking to you,' Shiny remarked. She had caught her boyfriend staring at the pretty LC seated at the far end of the cafeteria. It was the beauty queen she had seen at the beauty parlour.

'Sorry, Shiny.'

'You have been staring at her for the past five minutes, while I was talking.'

'We saw her at the parlour, but who's she?' asked Nutty, who had also noticed where Aaron had been looking. Not just Aaron, but almost every GC in the café was staring at the LC.

'Don't you know her?' Mathur sat back and toyed with a spoon. 'I am surprised you haven't met her. She's in the Phillora Company. Urvashi, aka Urvi, is an ex-beauty queen from Chandigarh, an *apsara* who walks on earth.'

'It's obvious that you know more about the LCs than we do,' Billi's voice was tinged with sarcasm.

'Well, I happen to be a well-informed person,' smirked the GC. 'You can ask me about anything.'

'Thank you!' scoffed Shiny, turned off by Mathur's brash behaviour. 'You are very kind. Now we know whom to consult in case of queries.'

Aaron, who knew her well enough to read between the lines, found it difficult to suppress a snort.

The chicken cutlets, served with a generous portion of ketchup and salad, turned out to be as delicious as Mathur had promised. Even before the others could react, Kale quickly grabbed a couple of cutlets. Placing them on a napkin, he began devouring them as fast as he could.

'Easy, buddy!' exclaimed Aaron, swatting at Kale's grasping hand as he reached for another cutlet. 'Leave something for the ladies.' Shifting the plate away from Kale's reach, he proceeded to cut the last of the cutlets into four pieces. Like a true gentleman, he pushed the plate towards the girls.

'Thank you, Aaron,' said Lucky, picking up a piece of cutlet.

Just then, her eyes widened at the sight of GC Vedanta Verma, who had entered the café. His eyes alighted on the beauty queen and he made a beeline for her table. He took a seat at the table and scanned the room. GC Verma's eyes met hers, and he raised a hand in acknowledgement. Thereafter, he had eyes for no one else other than LC Urvashi. The two of them chatted in a familiar manner, breaking into laughter every few minutes.

'Lucky bastard!' remarked Mathur. 'I don't know what she sees in him, though. There are much better looking and smarter GCs waiting to grab her hand.'

'Why don't you stop yapping for a while?' Billi snarled. For the past half hour, she had listened to the prick. His prattle was getting quite unbearable, and she had reached the end of her tether. 'Give your mouth a little rest?' Leaving him gaping, she got up and wandered around the café, studying the menu and the assortment of pastries in the glass-topped showcase.

She sauntered towards Papa Ferdy and asked if he could include aloo parathas in the menu. Ferdy, who was used to the demands of the cadets, promised to include the fare in the menu. 'Why don't you try our grilled sandwiches? They are very nice,' he offered.

'Actually, it's aloo parathas I want. My mother makes the best stuffed parathas in the world,' she smiled and explained. 'You see, I am feeling homesick and aloo parathas are my comfort food.'

'Next Sunday, I promise, you shall have your aloo parathas, even if I have to bully my wife into making them,' assured the kind man.

Satisfied with his promise, Billi asked for a grilled sandwich.

At the table, embarrassed after Billi's dressing-down, Mathur remained silent for a few minutes, and then he covered up what had happened with a guffaw, 'That girl has a good sense of humour. I appreciate her bluntness.'

Instead of being impressed by his high-spiritedness, the girls were beginning to get bored of him. Lucky's eyes were riveted on the taciturn GC seated at the far table. She found him fascinating.

Mathur, who noticed her interest in the couple, bellowed loudly, 'I guess you are attracted to GC Vedant Verma. Here's some free advice from Uncle Mathur,' lowering his voice, he leaned towards her and said, 'Don't waste your time over him. That guy is a misogynist.'

'You are mistaken,' Lucky snapped, embarrassed at being caught staring at GC Verma. 'A misogynist doesn't have a girlfriend.'

'Well, it's your funeral. I have done my bit.' Sighing dramatically, he continued, 'Just look around. There is a nice, amenable GC sitting next to you.'

'Forget it!' Lucky swatted the hand he extended towards her. 'I…'

'Can we order some grilled sandwiches?' Kale interposed, eyeing Billi's grilled sandwich.

'Go ahead and order some, but pay for them this time.' Mathur doused his buddy's enthusiasm. 'Don't look so shocked. Didn't I pay for the drinks and a platter of cutlets?'

That put an end to Kale's overtures.

'Never mind, I will order a few sandwiches,' offered Aaron, who had been conferring in a low voice with his girlfriend. 'But only if you promise to share them equally with the others.'

'He can have my share,' said Lucky. She had noticed the disappointed look on Kale's face.

Over the grilled sandwiches, and a second round of drinks ordered by Lucky, they vented their frustrations and discussed their aspirations.

'Let's change the topic. The complaints will not help us. Instead, let's gear up and face our challenges,' said Billi, who had grown bored of grumbling. 'I don't think it's so difficult. Hundreds of cadets have gone through all this and survived. So shall we.'

'Well said!' Aaron clapped.

'Yes, let's look at the bright side,' seconded Lucky, with her typical sunny attitude. 'Let's plan our next holiday.'

'Movies for everybody,' declared Mathur. 'I will pay for the tickets. As for lunch, we can go dutch.'

'Talking of lunch, isn't it time to jog to the Yoddha Mess?' Kale reminded them. 'They have Chinese cuisine today, and I love it.'

'Is there any cuisine you don't love?' asked Mathur. 'You should see the amount of food he can tuck in. Half a dozen parathas are nothing.'

'That's not fair, Mathur. A chap needs nourishment. Think of the calories we burn with all the front rolling and flipping.' The good-natured Kale grinned bashfully at everyone.

'You are a tapeworm,' commented Aaron as the seven of them jogged towards the mess.

Billi had been behaving in a moody manner since morning. It was only after lunch, when the girls were jogging back to the company that Nutty found an opportunity to speak to her.

'Why are you in a glum mood?' she asked. 'It's been quite a nice day.'

'True! With hardly any punishments, good food and nice conversation, it's been nice so far,' agreed Lucky.

'Come on, speak up,' urged Shiny. 'It's obvious that something is bugging you.'

'It's Banwari!' Billi burst out. 'He called this morning and blasted me for running away from Alakhpura.'

'And what did you say to him?' asked Nutty.

'I let him have an earful. First, I told him to go to hell. Not just that, I informed him that our engagement is over. As far as I am concerned, he doesn't matter to me. Not that he ever did.'

'In that case, why are you looking so glum?' Lucky wanted to know. 'You ended the matter, and that's it. You are a free girl now.'

'It's not that easy. He will complain to everybody in the village, and my father is likely to come down to the academy once again.'

'He won't!'

'Speak to your grandfather,' suggested Nutty. 'Let him handle your father.'

'Cheer up, Billi!' Shiny thumped her friend's back. 'Take my word. It's all for the best. I can bet that your father will not come here before the POP. At most, he will blast you over the phone, and that can only happen next week. By then, the dust would have settled.'

Her words brought a smile to Billi's face.

'What would I do without friends like you!' she said and stopped to hug each one of them.

LEARNING THE ROPES

That morning, after the fall-in, when the Zojila LCs were told to report for PT, they were clueless about the troubles that awaited them at the grounds.

Dressed in spotless white outfits and shoes, they reached the ground expecting to be taken through some simple exercises. By then, they had learnt to execute dozens of front rolls, cream rolls, and push-ups. The thought of exercises didn't faze them anymore. The muscles, which had earlier

protested and groaned, had become obliging. The joints that had been inflexible and adamant had turned pliant. Each night, they went to bed feeling like train wrecks, each morning they sprang up fresh and ready to face the day. They prided themselves for their achievements, berated themselves for their failures.

It was a pleasant morning, the energy levels were high and the PT ground seemed inviting. The huge field was fringed with a variety of ropes and obstacles. Undeterred, the LCs looked forward to an enjoyable session of warming up. The ropes and obstacles would come later, they mused.

However, Ustad Sultan Singh, their PT instructor, turned out to be absolutely unlike the lackadaisical PT instructors in their schools. The ustad, a towering man with a handlebar moustache, craggy face, barrel chest, and the loudest voice they had ever heard, managed to strike terror in the first-termers on the very first day of PT. Every command was an ear-splitting experience, every look a smouldering fire.

While all the cadets knew that they were expected to perform incredible feats, they thought those would come much later.

The PT period began with some warm-up exercises. They ran along the perimeter for a distance, jogged for a few minutes and stretched themselves to loosen stiff muscles. It seemed easy enough.

After the initial warm-up exercises, the squad was made to line up in front of the vertical ropes. A bit apprehensive, Nutty slithered towards the end.

Wondering if they were being taken through a demonstration of his skills, the LCs watched as the ustad took them through the technique of gripping the rope and then climbing up the rope in slow motion. He made it look simple and effortless.

'Grip the rope firmly with both hands,' he instructed. 'Wrap your feet around it, and then reach for a higher level with the right hand. Follow it up by gripping the rope at the same level with the left hand. Now pull your body up. Continue the same actions.'

Having finished the demo, the ustad ordered them to line up and repeat the feat. 'It's not difficult,' he told the hesitating LCs.

He won't expect us to climb ropes in the very first PT class, Nutty assumed. *This is madness.* She crept farther from the rope.

The ustad, however, exhibited no intention of letting go. With a menacing gleam in his eyes, he beckoned, 'First two in the line,' he barked. 'Climb *karega*.'

Get real, man! We are not magicians performing rope tricks. Shiny was indignant.

Anxiety etched on their faces, and hearts palpitating, Billi and Cockroach steeled themselves for the ordeal.

'Up,' shouted PT Ustad, as they loitered near the ropes. The two of them grasped the ropes, which were much rougher than they had imagined. Trying to emulate the ustad's example, Billi gripped the rope with both her hands and pushed her unwilling body upwards. She went up by a couple of inches only to find herself slipping down.

'Go up!' the ustad commanded.

Lips clenched, she hauled her body up by a few more inches, but holding on to the rope with clammy hands was proving to be a challenge. All her life, she had prided herself on possessing an athletic body, but now the same body felt heavier than ever before. It would be humiliating if she failed to haul herself up even a few feet above the ground, she decided.

Stunned, the others watched as the two LCs struggled with the challenge. Cockroach, who had shimmied up a few metres, looked down triumphantly. All she had wanted to do was to prove her superiority to the LCs. While Billi was struggling at two metres above the ground, she had managed to go up to the top of the six metre rope, thanks to her brother's efforts. Her brother had passed out of the academy a couple of years back and had spent his annual leave training his ambitious sister. The rope had seemed easy to climb, and she had done well till she looked down derisively at the other LCs. She froze. Hit by a dizzy spell, she felt paralysed and could neither move up nor down.

With a determined last-ditch effort, Billi managed to haul herself up another few metres. Her shoulders felt as though they would leave their joints, and her palms were beginning to blister with the effort of hauling her body up. Using sheer willpower, she had climbed up that much, but now the same willpower seemed to desert her.

'Very good, cadet,' the ustad shouted encouragingly. 'Go up!'

Having exhausted all her energy, Billi paused for some rest and found herself slipping down the rope. Surprised by the change in situation, the ustad shouted once again, '*Neeche nahin, upar jao*.'

In the meantime, Cockroach was facing a different kind of problem. Having reached the top, she could not descend.

Ustad Sultan Singh had handled more situations than he could remember. Each and every batch of cadets went through the same issues in the beginning. Fear was at the root of the problem, and he had mastered the techniques to make them shed fear. By the end of the fortnight, he could make them shimmy up the ropes like monkeys.

Stepping forward, he grabbed the bottom end of both the ropes, and began to shake them violently. There was a loud gasp as the LCs watched the rope swaying dangerously.

Didn't he realize that his actions would make the two girls fall and break their bones?

Surprisingly, it produced the desired effect. The ustad's actions brought desperate screams from Billi and Cockroach. 'Sir, please, I will fall,' shouted Cockroach.

'Then come down,' he shouted back.

There was only one way to escape the situation. Closing her eyes, and muttering fervent prayers, Cockroach slid down the rope and hit the ground. Billi, who found herself following suit, found her rope being shaken violently by the unforgiving ustad.

'LC, *upar jao*,' he shouted, continuing to tug at the rope.

Desperate, she willed herself to climb further and further till he stopped jerking the rope. '*Shabash!*' came the approval. A minute later, he ordered, '*Ab neeche ayega*!'

One by one, everyone went up the rope, with the unrelenting ustad goading them to go higher and higher. There was no escape. The carrot at the end of the stick was rather satisfying. The LCs knew they would never forget their first climb.

...and the first drill.

To their surprise and delight, the LCs found themselves under the wings of capable seniors. These guardian angels, known as overstudies, were assigned to help the first-termers cope with the hazards of training. They would henceforth supervise the newly minted cadets, instruct them on etiquette and help them achieve their aims. On their frail shoulders rested the onerous responsibility of moulding the greenhorns into smart cadets. An overstudy was supposed to guide her charge and help her settle down. She was to tutor the first-termer about the expectations, norms, privileges, and infinite-plus-one traditions of the company. Like a mother hen, she was expected to protect her ward. She was the senior who occupied the room right across the corridor and so she could keep an eye on the first-termer under her charge.

In short, an overstudy was a wet nurse to a junior. Right from teaching the understudy to shine their buttons, to eating with a fork and knife, it was all the responsibility of the overstudy. Even an itsy-bitsy mistake, like a truant loose thread waving from the uniform of the *jungoo*, was enough to invite trouble for the overstudy. They were put in the line of fire for every error committed by their charges.

Little wonder, most seniors were not happy with their portfolios. This was especially true when the charge was someone like Nutty, who was an ace at erring.

The day after the overstudies were assigned their juniors, the four friends got together to discuss the matter. It was a balanced discussion, with two of them praising their overstudies and two criticizing theirs.

To Nutty's chagrin, she was assigned a senior called Dipti Duggal. Although everyone called her DD, Nutty referred to her as Didi. Didi was an expert at *dadagiri*. She criticized, harangued and punished Nutty for every petty act. Not just that, she kept a strict watch on her ward, much to the Jalna girl's annoyance. Worse, she had forbidden Nutty to use cuss words. Not that it cured the girl of her habit. Her habit of bloody-ing everything wasn't easy to quit. 'I am not a bloody two-year-old,' she raged. 'One of these days, I am going to turn the tables on bloody Didi.'

Lucky, with her petite physique and gentle smile, brought out the protective instincts in her overstudy, an Amazonian Sikhni called Jagjit Grewal. Some called her Juggy, and some Grewal. But Lucky called her the Grey Wall. Soon, the Grey Wall became the Wall, a wall with a large shadow, under which she felt secure. The Wall took great care of her charge, tutoring and counselling her on each and every aspect of the training. 'I am sure the Wall trained with Geeta Phogat,' Lucky told the others. 'She has the muscles of a bodybuilder.'

'You are really lucky,' said Nutty. 'The Wall is shielding you against the seniors. No one wants to take *panga* with her.'

For easy-going Shiny, her overstudy, Roshni Sharma, was a true angel. Ever accommodating, generous and patient, Rosh was the epitome of a guardian angel. 'Ask and you shall receive' being the watchword. Like a true guardian angel, invited or not, Rosh was sure to show up during the pivotal moments in Shiny's life, as well as all the little moments in between. 'Roshni and Shiny are synonymous,' the happy girl told her friends. 'I couldn't have wished for a better overstudy.' The two of them got along like a house on fire.

'Mine is a big snob,' Billi declared. She had no love lost for her overstudy, Jyoti Thakral aka Joe. 'She barely speaks to me, except to order me around or send me on errands.'

The truth was that Joe, just like her charge, was an ambitious girl, who had set her heart upon winning the Sword. She had little time and patience for the aggressive and outspoken junior.

'I wish we could choose our overstudy,' Nutty sighed. 'It would be so nice if we could have a GC as our overstudy.' Her imagination was going haywire.

'Half of us would be pregnant by the time we passed out. At least, you would be,' Lucky laughed. 'Just imagine a heavily pregnant Nutty waddling around like a duck, during the POP.'

No matter what the juniors felt, the overstudies were to prove a big boon in the coming days.

Mother of All Pain

Lucky grimaced at the big leather boots that lay near her bed. They looked more like a torture contraption than boots. The damn things came with metal strips, 13 nails in the front half of the sole, and a heel adorned with a horseshoe. Of all the shoes she had encountered in the 20 plus years of her life, this was by far the most bizarre. Wondering if the horseshoe was placed for good luck, she tightened the polished-to-perfection black leather belt of her uniform. From what she had heard on the grapevine, she would need all the luck the horseshoe on her boots could bring.

The boots weighed a kilo and a half, but the drill that awaited them was worse. It was the mother of all pains, was the consensus.

Nutty struggled with the shoelaces of her heavy, ankle-length boots. '*Saala*,' she cursed, trying to tighten the laces through the dozen eyelets before passing it through the loop at the back and tying them around. Feat performed, she stood up and stretched. It was going to be a long day. One that was likely to turn out to be more gruelling than the previous one.

For Shiny, it was just another ordeal that had to be faced before wearing the stars on her lapels. She didn't like marching. At school, she had successfully managed to avoid participating in the parades, but now it was mandatory, and from what she had heard, the damn thing was a regular pain. One had to pass the drill test to obtain an out pass, without which one could not go out of the academy. Every cadet worth his or her salt gave extra attention to the exercise. Added to that were the terrifying stories of authoritarian drill ustads. All said, she wasn't looking forward to her first drill.

The only person who seemed excited about the drill was Billi. She had several accomplishments to her credit, right from being a senior NCC cadet, to being the flag-bearer of her school, to having taken part in the Republic Day parade with the hand-picked squad of NCC cadets. This was one area where she was confident of beating everyone.

A day earlier, the four friends had gone through the painstaking task of shaping their newly issued berets to their heads. It required a lot of skill and patience to shape it to perfection. Working under Shiny's instructions, who had in turn been instructed by Aaron, they soaked the brand new berets in hot water for a few minutes. Once they were soaking wet, they wrung out the excess water and placed the wet beret on their heads as per Aaron's directive. The guy was proving to be a boon for the girls. A keen cadet, he tried to maintain a lead over the other cadets and never hesitated in sharing his newly acquired tricks and tips with his heartthrob.

Although it sounded easy, shaping the beret to fit the contours of one's head required practice as well as expertise. Fortunately, Lucky was gifted with both.

The result of the task was a perfectly shaped beret on her head, along with a runny nose and a headache. Sitting for a long time with the wet beret on her head had done its bit.

It was still dark when the LCs set out for the parade ground. Unlike on the other days, none of them chattered. Anxiety had sealed their mouths. Apart from Zojila and Phillora, a company of GCs had lined up on the ground.

Suddenly, a huge figure detached itself from the shadows and stood before the cadets. His uniform was laden with several medals. The imposing soldier with a fearsome moustache turned out to be the dreaded drill ustad, Havaldar Satyaprakash Yadav, called Sappy by the cadets. It was a misnomer. For the ustad was anything but sappy.

Confidence oozing, Billi greeted the ustad, 'Good morning, ustad.'

A loud grunt emerged from under the moustache.

A dress inspection began in earnest. Sappy marched up to Billi, who was the first one in the line, and stared at her beret. It seemed to meet his stringent criteria, so he switched his attention to the tightness of her belt, the sharpness of the trouser crease and the polishing of the brass work and boots.

It was agonizing to stand still while the inspection went on, but she didn't dare fidget. To earn the wrath of the ustad was to commit suicide, for he wielded substantial powers. Punishing the cadets by allotting extra duties and drills was a habit with the ustads.

'Left foot up,' the ustad commanded. He proceeded to inspect the soles of Billi's drill boots. 'Left foot down. Right foot up,' he barked. The process was repeated.

Luckily, all the nails and the horseshoe stuck on the sole were intact. He went around her, trying to find a reason to holler. It took all of four minutes for Sappy to complete his inspection.

Finally, satisfied with her get-up, he grunted and moved to the next cadet. Grunting was Sappy's way of showing approval, albeit grudgingly.

Across the ground, however, the Phillora girls were having a bad time. Their ustad, having got up from the wrong side of the bed, was shouting in an irritated manner.

'Loose belt,' his voice boomed across the ground.

Not to be outdone, Sappy shouted in an equally loud voice, 'Small head, big beret.' He had picked on Saddie, who had not shaped her beret to perfection, and it slouched tiredly on her head.

'Loose lace,' came the voice from the other end.

It seemed like a contest between the two ustads. While one seemed to find everything loose, the other was bent upon finding as many faults as possible.

'Loose screw,' Lucky mumbled under her breath. She had been sniffling all through the night and now fever was making her body weak. Yet, the poor girl soldiered on.

Billi, who had turned her head to see the goings-on at the Phillora end, was immediately hauled up for the crime.

'Nonsense lady cadet, look front,' Sappy yelled in an eardrum-splitting decibel. 'No discipline.'

Although the ustads at the academy were some of the best jawans and were excellent in their respective fields, their tenuous grasp of English was the butt of many jokes.

Sappy marched to the rear of the row and several LCs were categorized as 'nonsense'. The LCs realized it was one of his favourite words. Anything that didn't meet his approval was 'nonsense'. A similar scene was being enacted at the Phillora end, which was full of nonsense cadets. It offered some consolation to the Zojila girls. According to the two ustads, almost all the lady cadets were nonsense and useless, since many of them had been hauled up for loose belts and berets. Some were nonsense because of twisted boot laces, some for scruffy boots, and some for their slouching posture. A couple of LCs were nonsense for no reason other than looking the ustad in the eye. It was the biggest crime of all.

Lucky, with her constant sniffling, drew a barrage of nonsenses, with Saddie in close contest.

The drill began in full earnest, once the inspection was over.

'*Tez Chal* (Quick March),' hollered Sappy. The command was followed by an order to *Tham* (Halt).

Diligently, the girls continued to march.

Right turn, left turn and about turn, they marched like automatons, terrified of being singled out by the hawk-eyed ustad.

Their efforts were rewarded by the words – shocking and nonsense. The ustad demonstrated the correct way of marching, his legs going high up and then coming down with force, so the boots hit the ground in a fierce manner.

In a few minutes, the entire lot of LCs were banging their feet on the parade ground, the nails on their boots hitting the ground to generate as much sound as possible. No matter how hard they tried, the ustad continued to remain dissatisfied with their performances.

'High! High!' he bellowed in his foghorn voice. 'Foot *upar utha*.'

Just then an aircraft flew over them. It lowered its landing gear to land on the runway just beyond the academy.

'Nonsense cadets. *Udhar kya dekh raha hai.* What are you staring at?' he shouted.

'Bang your feet harder till the aircraft begins to wobble,' he shouted louder, trying to drown out the noise of the aircraft.

'He's a raving lunatic,' muttered Lucky breathlessly, as she jumped up and banged her feet on the ground. Both the ustads, competing with each other, continued shouting like mad men.

Turning right, turning left, executing about turns, the cadets continued to bang their feet on the ground. By now, every muscle in their bodies had begun a protest march, with knees and ankles joining forces. Their heads were beginning to ache with all that foot-banging. But, there was no let-up in the ustad's *josh*. No matter how hard the girls tried, there was no pleasing the ustad. The LCs prayed for the drill period to end.

Sapped of energy, they were finally allowed to leave the ground, but not before they were warned to perform better the next time.

The moaning sounds that floated down the corridors of the company after lights out that night were a testimony to the drill ustad's efficiency. Disturbed by the loud groans emanating from the neighbouring room, Lucky hobbled towards it. Her legs propped up on a pillow, Nutty lay on the bed, cursing and moaning.

'Shhhh! Calm down!' Lucky hissed. 'You will bring the CSM here with all that moaning.'

'I can't help it,' retorted Nutty. Pointing at her feet, she continued, 'I have bloody blisters on my feet. How will I wear shoes tomorrow?'

'Can't you hear the moaning? You are not the only one suffering.'

'Bloody ustads are sadists. This is inhuman. I am done with the training.'

'Do you have some soothing lotion?' asked Lucky, ignoring her friend's complaints. 'Apply it to the blisters and go to sleep. You will be alright.'

'What sort of drill is this? All that the crazy guys want us to do is jump high and bang our feet. This is no drill.'

'It's not a good idea, I agree. But, just like punishments, we have to endure it.'

'The crazy chap says the sound should be loud enough to surprise the pilot in the aircrafts. Isn't that a sign of madness?'

'Egoistic seniors, moody officers, moodier ustads and killing weather, what else can one want?' said Lucky cynically. She had tried to find the silver lining in the dark clouds, but had failed miserably.

'If this is the bloody honeymoon phase, I don't even want to imagine what the post-honeymoon life will look like,' grumbled Nutty.

'Let's cross the bridge when we come to it,' said Lucky.

At the Movies

Nutty was a movie freak. Never one to miss any movie, the poor girl had been sentenced to a period of abstinence at the academy. It rankled her, till the day she learnt there was a movie hall in the campus, where movies were screened twice a week. The best part was that like every other parade, cadets had to compulsorily attend the movie parade at the Chanakya Auditorium.

Movie days were very popular with the hassled cadets. Everyone looked forward to a few hours of respite. For the sleep-deprived cadets, it was an opportunity to catch a blissful 40 winks in the safety of the dark and cool atmosphere. It was usual for the dialogues in the movie to be punctuated by the sound of snores. No one grudged them the nap during the movie, but what happened thereafter was a different matter altogether. Every bit of enjoyment should come with payback, the appointments believed.

The rules were strict. No hooting or whistling was allowed, not even when the sexy heroine gyrated to a hot number. Boys being boys, laboured under the false impression that mischief would go undetected in a crowd. A GC would let out a whistle under the cover of darkness. No mischief remained punishment free in the academy. After the end of the movie, the entire lot of cadets had to pay for that single act of recklessness. Every GC was made to roll all the way to the mess, which was quite a distance away. The LCs, however, were a sedate lot. They were content in giggling or sleeping, with no intentions of attracting attention. In any case, it was doubly risky for them to commit mischief, since their small number made it easier to single out the offender.

There was much hullabaloo on the first movie day, with Madame Nutty going total nuts. The fact that GCs and LCs sat in different areas didn't seem to matter to the girl, who was intent on catching a few eyes.

'Just think of all the boys who will be there,' she said, her bright eyes alive with excitement. 'Girls, I just can't wait to reach the auditorium.'

She dressed carefully in her mufti, debating if she should risk a dab of perfume. Better sense prevailed. The CSM was like a sniffer dog. Nothing escaped her twitching, long nose.

'Watch out!' warned Shiny. 'We will be surrounded by wardens.'

'What a damper you are! Think of your boyfriend. Aaron will be there, too.'

'I know he will be there, but I am not risking my neck to meet him,' retorted the cautious Shiny. 'Don't we have enough trouble on our hands?'

'I feel it is madness to go an hour before the show,' said Lucky. 'The theatre is not even a kilometre away. Are we allowed to carry potato chips inside?'

'Don't even think of it,' Shiny cautioned. 'Where will you hide it? In any case, there might be a refreshment counter in the theatre.'

'We don't know that, do we?' countered Lucky, who loved chips as much as she loved her mother's *tungrymbai*.

Most LCs had taken pains with their looks. It was their first outing, after all. Some of them had risked a dab of natural lipstick or a faint line of kohl.

It didn't take them long to realize the folly of it all. A team of appointments stood outside the entrance, carrying out dress check.

One by one, the girls were checked, and some of them were pulled aside. Saddie's trousers were creased and grimy. Seema was pulled aside because only one lace of her shoes was visible beneath her trousers, instead of the mandatory two. She tried to adjust the trousers so two laces were now visible, but the senior was not convinced. Dirty collars, unpolished shoes, wrong socks, un-ironed dresses, lipstick, kohls, perfumes, there were reasons galore. The offenders found themselves ordered to remain in *murga* position. Lucky, who had not been able to resist carrying a packet of chips, found herself joining the *murga* gang, while the rest of the first-termers entered the hall.

A similar thing was happening at another part of the hall, where the GCs were being checked by their appointments. Soon, half the cadets were squatting in *murga* position outside the hall.

Their ordeal came to an end just five minutes before the movie was to start, when the *murga* gang was let off with a warning and told to rush to their seats in a disciplined manner. The seating plan was fixed. The balcony was reserved for the officers and the families of the officers posted at OTA, while the lesser mortals called GCs and LCs sat down below. The juniors sat in the front rows while the senior cadets sat behind them. The LCs sat separately, away from the boys.

The LCs were herded to their seats by the watchful appointments, with strict warnings against any misconduct. Despite craning her neck, Nutty failed to catch the attention of any of the GCs sitting across the aisle. The poor chaps stared at the screen, not daring to allow their glances to stray towards the area where the LCs were seated.

'It's such a disappointment,' grumbled Nutty, who had been looking forward to fluttering her eyelashes at some GCs. 'The guys are not even looking this way.'

Just then, she felt a hard knock on her head. It had come from the back.

'Ouch!' She rubbed the spot and winced. The message was loud and clear, juniors were not supposed to talk or look around. The seniors sitting behind them were on the watch.

'Focus your eyes on the screen,' the warning followed the knock. 'Or I will be forced to focus it for you.'

Not a word was exchanged after the warning. The realization that the CSM had eyes that could bore through the darkness kept Nutty in check, although her deep sighs continued to assail her companions.

The movie screened that day was *Manikarnika*, and the cadets were soon engrossed in the action unravelling before them. Impressed by the rani's horse-riding and sword-wielding skills, Nutty forgot all about the GCs.

Those who were desperate for some shut-eye began snoring soon after the movie began. The perception that ladies do not snore was laid to rest inside the theatre.

Some LCs were certainly capable of beating the GCs at the game.

During the interval, just as Shiny had predicted, there was a refreshment counter and a well-stocked one too. The tantalizing smell of piping hot snacks lured the cadets in droves. Lucky, who was determined to buy a packet of chips, was disappointed to observe that the seniors were given the first chance to line up at the counter. Only after they finished were the juniors allowed to line up. Also, they were ordered to enter the hall before the seniors. As a result, the juniors were either unable to buy the refreshments, or they had to dump half-eaten snacks and drinks in the dustbin and rush to the hall before the seniors.

The juniors who had visited the washroom found no time to buy anything at all.

But some people never learn. Excited by Rani Laxmibai's stunts, one of the cadets couldn't resist yelling. All of a sudden, he shouted 'Yeeha!' Loud and clear, it echoed in the hall. All heads turned in the direction of the errant GC. The poor sod was so engrossed in the movie, that he forgot that he was sitting in the Chanakya Theatre inside the OTA. To make things worse, he followed up the yell with a whistle, not unlike the ones one normally hears in theatres when the heroine is swept off her feet by the hero. Such behaviour was not condoned at the academy.

The cadets realized it the hard way, as they were made to front roll all the way to the mess for dinner. It was clear that it is never about individual punishments, but a cumulative one, where everyone shares the blame for misconduct.

'Why should all the GCs suffer punishment, just because one of them was stupid enough to whistle? I don't think it's fair,' said Nutty as they walked out of the auditorium.

'It's an important lesson, Peanut. Comradeship is all about shared experiences. The cadets do not become brothers due to blood ties; they are bonded together because of common joys and sufferings. As they say, nothing can bind people together, than calloused hands, blistered feet and broken egos,' said Shiny.

For those that went punishment free, the excellent dinner after the movie was the topping on their cake.

And the cadets who rolled all the way to the mess and shed gallons of sweat, sank their frustration in heaps of rice and chicken curry, and found their salvation in the delicious dessert.

Sated, the gang of four jogged back to the company, their discussions revolving around Kangana Ranaut's sword-fighting and riding skills.

'I am impressed by that woman,' Lucky remarked. 'She must have trained and practiced for hours to attain her expertise in handling the reins and riding on rough terrains.'

'It's a part of their job,' Billi countered. 'Don't forget they are paid an astronomical amount of money.'

'That's true! Yet, one has to be sincere to make the effort. She could have easily used a double.'

'How do you know it wasn't her double who was riding and sword-fighting?'

'I don't think it is such a difficult thing to learn riding. Give me a month and I will be riding better than her,' boasted Nutty.

Her comment drew amused titters from her friends.

'Before you know, Nutty will be a famous Bollywood star,' Shiny joked.

The very next day, her friends were tickled to find an aim card stuck on Nutty's door. Aim cards were popular among the cadets. They stuck the card on the cabin's door, listing out the goals they hoped to achieve each month. Along with a couple of other aims, she had written – 'Become an excellent rider.'

Little did she know that the opportunity to prove herself would arrive very soon.

Charger Capers

A couple of weeks had flown by. New subjects and training activities were being introduced to the LCs in a gradual manner. The weekly training schedules were distributed and displayed on the noticeboard of each company every Saturday. Billi was ordered to pin the training programme on the board after lunch that day. While doing so, she discovered that riding had been added to the schedule for the week.

Excited, she shared the news with the others. 'We have riding class on Wednesday morning.'

'Why are you so excited? It's part of the curriculum,' Nutty remarked coolly.

No one had forgotten the aim that stared at them from Nutty's aim card on the door.

'There will be no PT or drill on Wednesday. Instead, we will be riding for almost an hour. Isn't that good news?' Billi asked.

The LCs were fed up with banging their feet during drills.

'I agree. It will provide some respite from the endless rope-climbing and hurtling along obstacles,' said Lucky, who hated the two activities. 'All that banging of shoes gives me intense headaches.'

'Hope you haven't forgotten our friend Nutty's determination to beat Kangana Ranaut at riding,' Shiny sniggered.

'She will beat her hollow,' added Billi. 'Our friend is a superstar.'

'Don't you dare pull her leg,' Lucky warned.

'It's alright!' Nutty laughed good-naturedly. 'Let them have some laughs at my expense. I only wish someone had pulled my legs when I was a child. I might have been three inches taller.'

Further discussion about riding had to wait till after dinner, as they had to rush for the evening games.

It was only after lights out that the girls crept into Lucky's room to exchange notes on everything under the sun. Gathering like this was a risky proposition as Major Sherawat had a habit of pussyfooting around the building at night, pouncing on unsuspecting cadets. She inspected drawers, lockers and satchels and confiscated whatever she felt was prohibited. Hiding perfume, phones, cigarettes, even chewing gum, was considered an unforgivable crime. Her list of banned items was long. The cadets wondered whether even breathing freely was in the list of prohibited items.

Surprisingly, Major Sherawat remained conspicuously absent on the days when the seniors took to punishing the first-termers after the lights out order. It was a frequent affair. From *putti* parade to front rolls to sit-ups and push-ups, the first-termers had a liberal dose of punishment almost every night.

That night had been a rare, peaceful one. After making sure that neither the *paltu*, nor any of the seniors were prowling around the corridor, Shiny and Billi stole into

Lucky's room. Nutty, who shared a washroom with Lucky, was already there.

'Do you think all this hardship is worth the commission?' Nutty was the first one to broach the topic. 'I am getting quite fed up of the seniors. The bloody sadists think it's their prerogative to torture us day and night.'

'Have faith!' Lucky counselled. 'The entire training is just 42 weeks long, of which we have passed two, and then there are the mid-term breaks and a term break too. Before you realize it, we will be marching for the POP.'

'That's true! In many ways, the worst is over,' seconded Shiny.

'I hadn't imagined it would be so tough,' sighed Nutty.

'Well, think of my plight. I joined the academy to be near Aaron, and now we rarely find the time to talk. All we can do is steal a few minutes at the mess or cafeteria. Even in those few minutes, we end up arguing about the superiority of our respective companies.'

'That's sad. You shouldn't talk about training to him,' advised Lucky. 'He's a competitor, after all. Just as you want us to win every competition, he would want his company to win, too.'

'You are right. It's no point arguing when we have so little time. At this rate, we will end our relationship before the training is over.'

'I miss football,' Billi stated. 'Playing football gave me a high. The cheering of the crowd always pumped up my adrenaline.'

'You won't have to wait for long. There are quite a few competitions in the academy, so there will be a lot of cheering when you play,' Lucky soothed her friend.

'It's not the same. No matter how well I perform, there's no word of appreciation from the ustads.'

'They want to push us to do our best. Anyway, I am looking forward to my first riding experience,' said Lucky, changing the topic.

'Has any one of you done any riding?' asked Nutty.

'Just once,' said Billi.

'Oh! When?'

'It was during my uncle's wedding. I was just a kid. Fascinated by the horse, I wanted to sit on it, so they indulged me for a few minutes.'

'You were not scared? I mean, horses are big animals.' Nutty's eyes were round with wonder.

'I read somewhere that the ones used during weddings are not horses,' Shiny broke the spell. 'They are mares, and old ones at that.'

'Unfortunately, the ones we will have to ride are not docile mares but wilful ones that canter and gallop, and even throw down their riders,' tittered Lucky.

'We better be careful,' warned Shiny. 'Aaron was telling me that a couple of GCs fell down and broke their limbs.'

'Don't assume that riding a horse is as easy as they show in the movies. We are not Kangana Ranaut, nor are we riding docile wedding mares,' added Billi.

'Are you trying to scare me?' Nutty challenged. 'Well, I am not afraid.'

'I just shared what Aaron told me. Why don't you ask your overstudy, if you don't believe me?'

'Okay, I will speak to my overstudy and find out if there is any method to the madness,' said Nutty. 'Having said that, let me tell you I am not scared.'

'Of course you are not scared,' echoed her friends. They knew it was her fear of riding that made her insist on her fearlessness.

Nutty's overstudy, Dipti Duggal, had several tips to offer. Having had a nasty fall during her first lesson, she cautioned against choosing a moody horse.

'So, which of the horses do you think I should choose?' asked Nutty, trying to understand the behaviour patterns of horses.

'I would opt for either Shabnam or Tota. Those two are fat and slow. Not just that, they often refuse to run, so there is no danger of falling. Don't make the mistake of going for Baaz or Toofan. Those two are moody and dangerous,' advised Manjeet.

Once she had the names of the slow and safe horses, Nutty strutted around confidently. She was no worse a rider than Kangana, she decided to prove to her friends.

Wednesday morning saw the LCs at the stables, looking smart in their riding breeches and riding helmets. Fear, bravado and uncertainty filled the girls. Running through their minds were a medley of thoughts that ranged from maudlin to morbid. Only a couple of them, who were army officers' daughters, had had the advantage of handling a horse.

'Do we have to go through this?' whispered Lucky. All her resolutions of putting up a brave front vanished at the sight of the huge, handsome beasts in the stable. She could almost see the evil grins on some of them. 'Can't we opt for some other activity? After all, who rides horses to wars these days?'

The class began in earnest, with the ustad introducing the LCs to a serious looking horse called Tota. To be named a parrot couldn't have been a pleasant experience for a horse. Patting the animal lovingly, he detailed the physical characteristics of the horse, just as he had done during the introduction to rifles. The white and magnificent horse wore a benign expression on its face as it began studying the LCs. It appeared to be worrying about its fate, what with its reins in the hands of novices.

'I wish I had some sugar cubes or carrots to feed the horses,' whispered Lucky. In school, she had read *Black Beauty, National Velvet, Black Stallion* and *Sea Biscuit*. In all those stories, horses were gentle creatures that loved their owners. Be it Sea Biscuit or Merrylegs, they had all been kind and friendly souls. Also, they loved sugar cubes.

The ustad demonstrated how to mount and dismount a horse with one jump and a swing of the legs. The entire exercise seemed quite simple.

'You have to gain the horse's confidence, first. It should treat you like a friend and not like a foe,' instructed the tall and thick-built ustad, who sported an impressive, twirling moustache. Most of the ustads wore moustaches in a variety of styles. It added to their gravitas.

'Pat your horse a couple of times before you mount it,' he instructed, patting Tota on its rump.

When it came to the selection of horses, to her dismay, Nutty found there was fierce competition for Shabnam and Tota. Their reputation of being easy-going had spread through the companies, and almost every LC was clamouring for one of the two horses. In the end, it was Lakme who managed to grab Tota's reins. In the meantime, Shabnam had been claimed by Saddie.

With both the horses gone, Billi chose Baaz, and Nutty was forced to opt for Pawan.

'Cadets mount,' barked the ustad. The LCs tried to swing their legs and mount their horses in the manner he had demonstrated.

The exercise turned out to be tougher than they had thought. Most LCs failed to mount in one move, as instructed by the ustad. Billi, with her inborn athletic traits, was the only one who could manage the task. In a single fluid move, she mounted Baaz, drawing the ustad's appreciation.

Lucky patted Tota and stared fearfully at him, and Tota returned the stare. The horse's bright and big eyes looked kind and gentle. Having gone through the experience innumerable times, the horse seemed to understand her predicament.

'Cadets mount,' said the exasperated ustad, who had been watching her. She patted the horse once more, and tried to mount but failed. Although Tota continued to remain cooperative and remained stock still, she struggled. It was only after several trials and rebukes that she finally managed to mount the horse.

Nutty patted her charger a few times and then some more. 'Please be kind,' she whispered. 'It is my bloody first time. Don't toss me to the ground.'

The benign horse seemed to understand her fear and neighed sympathetically. Encouraged by the response, she mounted it on her second attempt.

'Cadets, dismount!' commanded the ustad.

Everyone hastened to dismount. By now, a bit more confident with their horses, the LCs managed to complete the feat in two or three attempts. Only a few were successful in dismounting the first time.

Once the process of mounting and dismounting had been completed, the ustad decided to put the LCs through a simple lesson. Astride his horse, he led the cadets in a single file into an enclosure, and then slowly along the periphery. Well trained, the horses seemed to know their job very well, and all that the cadets had to do was to sit erect and hold the reins gently.

The exercise was meant for the horse and the rider to get used to each other. All of a sudden, the ustad shouted out a command, which only the horses seemed to understand. The girls were surprised as their chargers picked up speed and began trotting. By now, used to their horses, the LCs began enjoying the exercise. Riding didn't seem to be daunting any more.

After a couple of rounds, satisfied with the progress of his cadets, the ustad shouted – '*Chaal badal.*' Change the pace. It was an indication for the horses to begin cantering.

Lucky was having trouble trying to grip Tota with her knees. The horse was too fat. She found it difficult to keep time with the horse's trots. Exhausted with the effort of keeping pace with Tota's movement, she wished the class would end fast.

On the other hand, Billi found herself enjoying the ride. Baaz and Billi seemed to be made for each other, as they went through the paces in a synchronized manner.

Nutty, who was comfortable on her steed, turned out to be the most enthusiastic rider of all. Charged with the images of Kangana Ranaut's feats on her horse, she decided to beat the other LCs. Pawan was moving at a sedate pace, following the ustad's orders, which didn't satisfy Nutty's adventurous streak.

Egging her charger with her heels, she bid the horse to go a little faster. Essentially a show-jumping horse, he was trained to obey the rider's urging. Pawan understood the girl's wish to speed up. It broke ranks, took a huge leap over the wooden enclosure, and after throwing Nutty to the ground, it took off at a great speed and disappeared. She lay groaning on the ground, her body spread-eagled.

Blowing a whistle to indicate the end of class, the ustad rushed towards Nutty. Pawan, who had also heard the whistle, returned sheepishly to the stables. There was frantic activity as the cadets followed the ustad, and an ambulance, which is always on standby for such accidents during riding classes, immediately transported Nutty to the hospital.

Crushing on an Intern

When the three friends visited Nutty on the very next Sunday, they found her beaming with excitement. It was her fourth day in the hospital. The first 24 hours had been crucial, since the doctors had kept her under observation for any signs of a head injury. In those four days, her bruises, and sprained ankle, had been taken care of. As she did not have any broken bones, the girl had been declared fit to leave in another day.

'You are one helluva resilient girl,' Lucky complimented her cheerful friend, who was allowed to limp, with some help, to the lawn in front of the ward. 'I feared you would have suffered some broken bones.'

Seated in a bench under a huge ficus tree, the four friends shared the chocolates and chips they had brought for Nutty.

'True!' seconded Shiny, helping herself to some salted peanuts. 'Your dazed eyes after you fell to the ground had me worried.'

'The lucky gal got some well-deserved rest,' said Billi, who had been declared the best first-time rider by the pleased ustad. He had had very low expectations from a lady cadet.

'It was her wish to ride like Kangana that did the harm,' Lucky deduced. 'What she forgot was that she's not a film star.'

'Did you know she used a prop for those scenes?' tittered Shiny. 'She was riding a dummy horse and pretending to be riding an actual horse.'

'Don't tell me that!' Nutty said irritably. 'You are trying to console me.'

'Trust me!' Shiny fiddled with her phone. Seconds later, having found the clip, she handed it to her friend. 'Here, you can see for yourself.'

'It has gone viral after the release of the movie,' informed Billi, as she watched Nutty's expression change.

For once, the star-struck girl was at a loss for words. 'This is cheating,' she spat out, after watching the dummy mechanical horse.

'It's only the foolish who get taken by the daring feats performed by film stars. Darling! That's why it's known as show biz – all show and no know,' Billi sneered. 'You thought it was real and went on to risk your pretty neck.'

'Don't worry! We will be riders before we pass out,' Lucky consoled their distraught friend. 'Henceforth, learn to distinguish between bravery and bravado. The line between the two is very thin, but remember bravery pays, bravado doesn't.'

'Have you girls finished your sermons?' retorted Nutty. 'If you have, I will tell you something interesting.'

'We are done with the sermons,' Shiny raised her hands in surrender. 'Now, tell us the interesting news.'

'I don't want to go back to the academy,' declared the injured friend.

'Given a chance, none of us would,' said Lucky. 'No getting up at the crack of the dawn, only to front roll till your spine feels unhinged, no PT or drill, no seniors baying for your blood, it must be quite cushy lying in a hospital bed.'

'You forgot to mention the hollering ustads, cruel *paltus*, and the sadist CSM,' reminded Billi.

'I would willingly fall off a horse if I could avoid all the punishments,' Shiny sighed. 'I could ask Aaron to visit me at the hospital. We could sit on this bench and chat to our hearts' content.'

'It is not just the training and punishments, I have a stronger reason to stay here,' confided Nutty, snatching the packet of chips from Lucky's possessive hands. 'There's a handsome intern on night duty.'

'What!' Billi shouted. 'You are making eyes at an intern?'

'He has Shashi Kapoor's dimples and a twinkle-eyed smile, Hrithik's physique, Amitabh's baritone and…'

'Oh my God! You mean he's a heady cocktail,' laughed Billi. 'You are such a dreamer, Nutty. I am not surprised. With film stars crowding your pea-size brain, you hardly have a choice.'

'Laugh as much as you want, but the fact is that I have fallen for him. For all you know, he might be attracted to me. He wouldn't be able to confess, of course. What with his duties and responsibilities, but I can wait. We have many more months at the academy before we are commissioned, and he's not going anywhere in a hurry. However, we need to spend time together for the sparks to flare. Therefore, I am not going to leave the hospital.' Nutty finished her spiel and gave them a defiant look.

'You are nuts!' Shiny exploded. 'Do you realize the implication of your words?'

'You are fit to be sent back on Monday.' Lucky took one look at her friend's determined face and pleaded, 'Please don't try any tricks. They are likely to backfire.'

'I have already thought of a plan. When the intern comes for night duty, I will pretend to be in great pain.'

'Look darling!' Lucky implored. 'You have been falling in love with every handsome hunk that crosses your path. This is no different. Hospital romances are quite common. There are umpteen cases of patients falling in love with doctors.'

'This is not one of those cases. I am convinced it is genuine love.'

The four friends had often brooded over their love lives or the lack of it. Shiny was the only one with a steady boyfriend. Unfortunately, the two rarely found the opportunity to spend time together. Lucky, with her exotic and delicate features, found herself attracting a lot of attention from the male species, some welcome, most of it not. Her fragile looks brought out the protective instinct in them. Even the ustads handled her with kid gloves.

As far as Billi was concerned, she was a tough nut. The strong-minded girl was determined to bag the appointment of CSM, and to carry the Sword of Honour home. Propelled by these two objectives, she pushed herself beyond the limits of her physical capacity. In the few weeks at the academy, the girl realized that there are no limits. One could push oneself to any extent, provided one had the willpower to do so. She threw all ideas of love and romance out of the window and concentrated on her goal. Thankfully, after the initial days at the academy, Banwari had stopped bothering her with phone calls.

She had bought a new sim card and warned her family against sharing the number with the jilted guy. For once, they agreed to stand by her. The tantalizing image of the Sword of Honour displayed in a prominent spot in the house made her father toe the line.

Intimidated by her foul language, the GCs kept out of her way. Also, they found her too aggressive and blunt to fit the image of a pliable girlfriend.

Nutty was the total antithesis. An incurable romantic, she was the kind of girl who shed buckets of tears while watching movies, swooned over good-looking GCs, and dreamed of romance even when she was front rolling. One of her objectives for enrolling in the academy was to find a smart life partner. In the last few weeks, she had been attracted to at least half a dozen GCs or instructors. The friends were privy to her secret crushes, which invariably ended in heartbreak. But the girl never gave up. All the advice doled out by her friends had done nothing to change her attitude.

'Don't be a fool,' warned Billi. 'All he has to do is complain against you. Can you imagine the outcome if CoCo or any of the two *paltus* learns of your crush?'

'Get yourself discharged and return to the academy. If the intern is interested in you, he will find some way to contact you,' Lucky advised.

Nutty was not ready to heed any warnings or advice. Half an hour later, the three girls returned to the academy having been unable to convince their friend.

It was Monday afternoon. Lucky returned to her room after lunch to find an ebullient Nutty idling on her bed.

She was flipping through the latest issue of a gossipy movie magazine.

'Hey there!'

'So, your tricks didn't work?' Lucky asked as she flopped onto the bed. 'You have been discharged from the hospital.'

'You will never guess what happened.' Nutty sat up and smiled secretively.

'I think I should call Billi and Shiny. They might be better at the guessing game.'

'Yes, three heads are better than one,' agreed Nutty. 'Besides, I won't have to repeat the story.'

Five minutes later, after the girls had huddled on the bed, she declared triumphantly, 'I now have his phone number.'

'You mean he gave you his number?' Lucky sounded incredulous.

'I can't believe this,' Billi thumped her forehead. 'You went and asked for his phone number? Where's your sense of self respect?'

'Perhaps it's not his number,' Shiny giggled. 'He may have given it to fool you.'

'Shut up!' Nutty scolded. 'He didn't give it to me. I have managed to get it out of him.'

'You tricked him into giving you his number?' Billi was outraged.

'By the way, his name is Kartik Iyer. How does it matter how I got the number?' Nutty asked peevishly.

'He's South Indian?' Lucky asked. Her mind filled with images of a fat and domesticated Nutty grinding batter for idlis, a pair of bawling kids with runny noses by her side.

'It doesn't matter which state he is from. I love him and that's what matters.'

'So, how did you get his phone number?' Shiny wanted to know.

'Last night, when he was on duty, I asked him if I could use his phone to make a call.' Nutty's eyes took on a dreamy haze.

'You did what?' Billi sounded doubly outraged.

'I told him I was feeling homesick and wanted to call my mother, but my phone was locked up in the CSM's room.'

'And he gave you his phone?' Lucky asked.

'No gentleman can refuse a request like that, especially when it comes from a young and pretty girl.'

'Oh, sure!'

'Well, he handed over his phone with a warning to keep

the call short. All I did was ring my phone from his. So, I now have his number on my phone.' The girl thumbed her nose at them.

'Of all the bloody...' Billi let out a few expletives.

'You seriously think he will entertain any calls from you?' Shiny asked.

'Why wouldn't he?' retorted Nutty.

'Look, just forget about Kartik Iyer,' suggested Lucky. 'Concentrate on getting your foot better, so you can finish the training.'

'That's sane advice,' seconded Shiny. 'You better catch up, if you don't want to be relegated.'

'I think you guys are jealous,' declared Nutty.

'Why would we be jealous? Keep your medico with you. I have no interest in your Kartik Iyer or anyone else, for that matter,' barked Billi.

'She's right,' said Lucky. 'I have no interest in him, either.'

'You are so mean.' Nutty burst into tears.

Contrite, the three girls tried to console their friend. It was futile to din sense into the stupid girl's brain, they knew. They had no choice but to see her making a fool of herself once more.

Dunking Doughnut

The gang of four managed to sneak into each other's rooms at odd times despite all the rules. Staying in adjacent rooms helped, of course. They made it a practice to get together after the lights were out, and the punishments had ceased. It wasn't often that they managed to do so. Either they were dog-tired and hit the sack, or an overstudy was on alert.

Soon, there were no secrets between them. They swapped stories of their crushes, failures and victories. Conducted in low voices in the dark, the cribbing sessions provided a promise of solidarity and support, which gave them the strength to face the next day.

As the days and weeks passed by, the training started to pick up pace. The day began with drill or PT followed by indoor classes. As the days passed by, new elements were introduced. The latest was a 10-kilometre run every day. Tanned and blistered, feeling like chickens on a rotisserie, they continued to run. Life was an action movie, playing on fast forward. Their lessons had come the hard way. Punishments teach you much more than sermons can, and faster, the four friends realized. Soon, they found themselves hurtling like comets from one part of the campus to the other, changing rigs at supersonic speed, stuffing food in their bellies as though there was no tomorrow, and sleeping with their eyes open in theory classes.

While going to the mess for dinner one night, the girls found Nutty missing. Worried, they rushed to Nutty's room.

They found her lying on her bed, groaning. Her eyes were bloodshot like those of a drunkard, and she was in a tetchy mood.

'Are you unwell?' asked Lucky, checking the girl's forehead for fever. 'You didn't come down for dinner.'

'Come on, get up!' exhorted Billi. 'We will be late.'

'I am not going for dinner,' said Nutty.

The statement was rather unusual for a person who could gorge on food like a python. Not once had she foregone a meal.

'Look at my bloody stomach,' Nutty pointed at her distended belly.

'That's the normal size of your belly after a meal,' commented Shiny. 'What did you eat? You look like a pregnant cow.'

The girls tittered at the comment.

'Yes, I am bloody pregnant,' shouted Nutty. 'My bloody belly is full of water. Have you ever seen anyone pregnant with water?'

It was the swimming lesson. It had managed to separate the swimmers from the sinkers. While Shiny was a good swimmer, Billi and Lucky barely managed to keep themselves afloat.

Swallowing pool water was common for the sinkers and they soon realized that they would not die of dehydration, at least not in the near future. Some of the girls, Cockroach for one, preened around in their swimming costumes confidently.

Nutty was definitely a sinker. She was scared of water.

While the girls splashed bravely around the shallow end of the pool, she stood gaping at the water, unwilling to join them.

During the first lesson, the first-termers were taken through some warm-up exercises. They were made to jog along the perimeter of the pool to gain confidence. After which the ustad tried to teach them the technique of keeping afloat and then propelling themselves forward. He also introduced them to the art of holding one's breath under water.

'Put your head under water and count till ten,' instructed the ustad, who was an ace swimmer from Bengal.

A few girls managed to count till five and a few till two. Nutty, however, refused to oblige.

'Jump into the water, cadet,' shouted the irate ustad. He was a national level swimmer, who had represented India in the Asian Games and brought back a gold medal. An accomplished trainer, he had dealt with many sinkers and changed them into swimmers within a couple of weeks. He might have been an ace swimmer and trainer, but teaching Nutty to swim was definitely a double-dog-dare.

Jutting her chin out, she continued to disobey his orders, till someone pushed her into the pool and she fell heavily into the water.

She emerged spluttering and coughing to find the ustad glowering at her.

'Into the water,' he shouted, as she tried to clamber out of the pool.

An incensed Nutty flapped her arms wildy and, splashed her legs around to keep herself from sinking inelegantly to the bottom of the pool. Poor Nutty found herself unable to breathe through the nose, so she opened the mouth to do so, and the chlorinated pool water entered her stomach. She coughed and spluttered, and swallowed some more water. She also managed to land a few solid kicks on another LC, who was trying to help her. By the time the ustad allowed them to emerge from the pool, Nutty had swallowed a couple of gallons of pool water.

'That bloody Bengali ustad! He's a fish flea!' she now cribbed to her friends. No one reminded her that fish don't have fleas. By now, they were used to her habit of assigning strange monikers. They also knew she meant water flea. 'I told him I was afraid of water. Arre! Where I come from, there's not enough bloody water to drink, forget swimming. Bengalis can swim because they eat bloody fish. I was a bloody vegetarian till I joined the bloody academy.'

The impressive number of bloodys punctuating Nutty's speech was a clear indication of her state of mind.

'That bloody ustad,' Lucky tried to maintain an impassive expression while the others giggled. 'Don't worry, we will teach him a bloody lesson, soon,' she promised.

'Come on, Nutty. Just eat something, maybe the dessert.' Shiny tried to pull the girl from the bed.

'Eat! Are you mad? There is no bloody space for my diaphragm to move. I wish I could drown the bloody ustad. I hope he gets posted out soon.'

'Don't be a goof!' scolded Billi. 'Ustad Roy has managed to turn sinkers into swimmers. Just you wait! He will turn you into a fish.'

'My bloody foot!'

'Nutty, you are a cute doughnut!' exclaimed Lucky, hugging the angry girl.

'Dunking the Doughnut, wouldn't that make an apt title for Nutty's first swimming lesson,' laughed Shiny.

'Get out!' Nutty picked up a pillow and threw it at the girls.

In the end, the three girls had to abandon the idea of dragging Nutty to the mess for dinner. Lucky left a packet of chips in the girl's room, just in case…

Without Nutty to regale them with amusing acts, food didn't taste as good, nor did the dessert. To make things worse, the dessert served that evening was trifle pudding, one of Nutty's favourite desserts.

The three girls ran into Aaron and Kale as soon as they exited the mess.

'Hey there,' Aaron greeted them enthusiastically. It was a huge risk. If spotted by a senior, the GCs would draw a string of punishments for talking to the LCs. For once, he didn't seem to care.

'Hi,' Lucky dimpled, while Shiny looked fearfully around.

'We shouldn't be loitering here,' she warned. 'I can't take another round of punishments tonight.'

'Don't worry! I am keeping a watch,' said Billi, her eyes scanning the area for seniors, both LCs and GCs.

'I just wanted to give you some good news,' said Aaron.

The word 'good news' sounded like music to the LCs ears. The one thing missing from their lives was good news.

'What is it?' they asked eagerly.

'The seniors will soon be off our backs.'

'You are fibbing.' The enthusiasm drained away from Shiny's voice.

Her words dampened the heightened hopes in Billi's heart, but Lucky was unwilling to accept defeat. 'Tell us the news and then we will decide if it is good,' she said.

'Well, according to the schedule, they will soon be going away for a camp. The best part is that they will be away for not just a few hours but a few days.'

His statement brought back the twinkle in Shiny's eyes. 'Is that true, Aaron? You are not fooling us?'

'Why should I fool you?'

'Wow! I am already feeling unburdened,' Lucky shrugged her shoulders dramatically. 'Just imagine the freedom… Freedom from punishments, freedom to smile and celebrate,' she trilled.

'Now we better scram before we are caught,' warned Billi. Her eyes had detected some movement.

'It's just a matter of a few days,' assured Aaron. 'Then we can stand here and chat for as long as we want.'

'Good night and thank you, Aaron,' warbled Lucky, and the girls turned to go.

'Hey!' Aaron called. 'I forgot to tell you another thing.'

They walked back to him.

'Quick!' Billi warned. 'The seniors are coming.'

'Who's there?' They heard a voice, followed by a holler. 'Stop!'

'Let's vamoose!' shouted Shiny.

'Do well in the drill test. You will get an out pass if you clear the test,' Aaron shouted before melting silently into the darkness.

'You bet we will,' Shiny shouted back. Her comment drew a clatter of running feet.

'Why are you loitering around?' demanded a GC. To make things worse, he was an appointment.

Getting caught by an appointment topped the list of things-not-to-do. Fortunately for them, it was a GC from a different company. It was an unwritten code of conduct that appointments from other companies did not punish first-termers not belonging to their companies. Instead, they complained to their counterparts in the guilty cadet's company. Rare was a cadet who dared to take *panga* with an appointment.

'We are leaving, sir,' Lucky said, putting on her most innocent expression. It rarely failed to work.

'Get moving before I report you to your CSM. Get lost!'

For once, even the fear of punishment couldn't dampen their spirits. Warmed by the promise of good times, the LCs went back to their company.

'Let's give the good news to Nutty,' suggested Lucky. 'It will perk her up.'

'Bloody hell!' Her distended belly notwithstanding, Nutty whooped and did a quick tango around the room. She followed it up with the actions of uncorking an imaginary champagne bottle. 'Let's do a countdown, just like the DLTGH (Days Left to Go Home).'

A Crucial Test, and Then Some

The dreaded Drill Square Test (DST) was at their doorstep. Passing it was of the greatest importance. The programme for the week notified them that the DST was scheduled for Friday. It gave them exactly one week to pull up their socks. There was consternation among the ones who had failed to please the ustad, while the ones who were good in drills feared for their pals. Everyone knew it was impossible to dream of leaving the four walls of the campus without clearing the test.

Worse, very few first-termers were known to clear the test in the first attempt.

'We can't afford to fail,' Billi told her friends. She was supremely confident of herself, but Lucky and Nutty's performances were far from satisfactory.

Lucky, with her delicate frame, couldn't bang her feet hard enough, and Nutty was a malingerer, who excelled in inventing excuses to avoid difficult tasks.

'Out passes are given only to the ones who pass the DST,' Shiny reiterated. 'The four of us have to pass.'

'All you have to do is to bang your feet till Sappy is satisfied. That isn't so difficult, right?' Billi tutored Lucky. 'Make sure the ground quivers under your feet.'

'My brain wobbles, and my joints rattle,' complained Nutty. 'Nothing I do pleases Sappy.'

‘The only way to pass is to spend all our free time on the drill ground.’

‘We don’t have any free time,’ cribbed the Jalna girl.

‘Where there’s a will, there’s a way,’ Shiny chanted.

‘Let’s alter that a bit,’ suggested Lucky. ‘In our case, it’s where there’s a whip, there’s a way.’

So, preparations for the DST began in earnest. It was not an easy test to pass since there were quite a few elements that one had to master. The first part was the turnout (the drill uniform), which was considered one of the toughest to clear. The ustad never failed to find some fault with the rig. Either the creases on their trousers were not sharp enough, or their shoes and brass works were not polished to perfection. Sappy checked each cadet’s rig with surgical precision. He was capable of detecting hundreds of little flaws. Four buttons showing above the belt, instead of the regulation three, the shirt and the trousers not perfectly aligned, or the belt not tight enough. Even the tiniest of threads peeping from the seam of the uniform was considered an unforgivable offence. If these were not to be faulted, there were the 13 nails on the soles of their shoes. Heaven forbid that a single nail went missing.

As a result, only 50 percent of the first-termers made it to the second stage, which comprised marching, turning, saluting and other drill movements. What mattered most was how hard the cadet stamped their feet on the ground. The force of stamping was judged by the level of sound produced by the LC. The higher the decibels, the more the ustad’s satisfaction.

All that Lucky gained with the repeated stamping of her feet were a couple of blisters on her heels. Nutty, who had managed to rope in the help of her overstudy, tried her best to make the earth vibrate, only to fail miserably at creating the right impact.

Billi, her mind set on the Sword, turned out an impressive performance during the practice session. Shiny fared just a little above average. The two of them were sure to clear the test.

'I can't do it,' wailed Lucky, after a brave attempt at creating noise with her blistered foot. She had already given up the idea of passing the DST. 'I have accepted the idea of failing.'

'No matter how hard I try, it's far from satisfying.' Nutty back-pedalled. 'What's the point of making all this effort? I won't pass.'

Notwithstanding their doubts, the four friends began preparing their dresses for the test. Their dresses were checked for the tiniest of dirt spots, which is what the ustad would be hunting for. All he wanted was an excuse to fail an LC. Standards were very high, the overstudies warned their juniors. The boots, belts and berets were subjected to scrutiny. They polished their boots, belts and buckles to perfection, shaped their berets to fit their heads, and went through another haircut, just in case. It was better to err on the positive side, which meant an even shorter buzz cut. Nails were trimmed and belts tightened. Anxiety over the DST overshadowed the preparations for the other tests, which were soon to follow. The liberty clause was overwhelming. So zealous were the preparations that a few uniforms got burnt, shoe brushes lost most of their bristles, and those who practiced banging their feet a bit too much lost their sleep as their overworked calf and thigh muscles began aching.

'I could not sleep the whole night,' Nutty cribbed a day before the test. The girls were returning from the mess after breakfast, when Nutty's overstudy, intent on getting her to practice one more time, waylaid the girl.

Nothing she said could deter the strict overstudy, who wanted her charge to clear the DST in the first attempt. For the seniors, it was a matter of pride if an understudy performed well, while the underperformance of the charge drew brickbats from the *paltu*.

When excuses didn't work, Nutty decided to report sick, but her idea was condemned by her friends.

'The doctor is sure to debar you from appearing for the test,' Billi scolded. 'All your hard work will go waste.'

'Not just that, you won't get an out pass,' informed Shiny. 'And you won't be able to go out of the academy on Sunday.'

'The two of you are good at drills,' pouted Nutty. 'Shiny has to prove herself equal to her boyfriend and Billi has promised to take the Sword home, but I neither have a boyfriend nor do I have ambitions of winning the Sword.'

'Yet you have to pass the test to be commissioned,' reminded Lucky, who had been stamping her feet despite the blisters.

Finally, it was D-day. The ground was bustling with activity as both the Zojila and Phillora girls lined up to take the DST together. The CSMs and *paltus* of the respective companies had spent considerable time and energy on the first-termers, telling them about the importance of passing the test. They had also warned them of the shame the company would face if the LCs of the opposing company were to surge ahead. It drove a wedge of rivalry between the two companies, who had hitherto not been in competition with each other.

Not many LCs had slept well in their anxiety over getting through the test. As expected, the test began with the dress inspections. The LCs had adhered to a very high standard, and they were sure to clear the first part of the test. With bated breath they waited for the ustad to declare them fit for the next stage.

Dress inspection carried on for a long time, and by the time it ended, almost half the LCs had lost the battle, most of them clueless about the cause of elimination. Of the 40, only 12 remained in the reckoning.

Only the sassy Saddie dared to ask the ustad for a reason and found herself running all around the parade ground until the tests ended.

Just as the girls who had been approved for the drill test drew a sigh of relief, they noticed the adjutant. Mounted on a white charger, he cantered around, supervising the tests. It was a solemn occasion, even the horse realized. The animal's haughty demeanour came from the realization that his was an important role in the drama.

The adjutant turned out to be a bigger devil than the ustad. He inspected the uniforms again, before commanding the 12 cadets approved by the ustad to perform the drill. From the lucky dozen, he weeded out some more. When the results were announced, only eight LCs had made the mark, Billi and Shiny amongst them.

It was a damper of a night as the first-termers licked their wounds after the callous cuts dealt by the adjutant. The gang of four gathered in Shiny's room after the lights were out, dissecting the morning's event.

'I am so happy that you got through,' said Lucky, shaking Billi and Shiny's hands. She had not expected to pass, so her level of disappointment was low. 'It is an impressive achievement to make it through the DST in the first attempt. I had no doubt that the two of you would pass.'

'Thank you, Lucky,' said Shiny. 'I wish all of us had got through.'

'The ustad is a bloody mean guy,' declared Nutty, her hopes of going out of the academy dashed against the will of Sappy. 'The bloody adjutant is meaner. It's our first attempt, and we worked so hard to clear the test. How would it have hurt them to pass us? Can you imagine only eight out of 40 bloody LCs making the grade? It's a dismal result, to say the least. Passing us would have motivated us to do better.'

'I don't think so, Nutty!' Billi butted into the conversation. 'It will make everyone work harder now.'

'I had set my heart on going out this bloody weekend,' sulked the girl. 'Now the two of you will have to leave us when you go out on bloody liberty.'

'We are not going anywhere,' professed Shiny. 'Either the four of us go together or no one goes out.'

That statement managed to take away a bit of Nutty's bitterness. 'That's very magnanimous of you,' she said. 'Considering that Aaron has passed and will be going out, don't you would want to bloody meet him?'

'I do want to meet him. But we can do that at the cafeteria this weekend.'

'Yes, just like the last time.' The anticipation of repeating that day's fun made Nutty happy. 'We can go out after passing the bloody DST.'

'But you have to work harder at passing the next time,' reminded Billi. 'Passing the DST is mandatory.'

'I would have worked harder if the damn blisters had not hindered my stamping,' Lucky winced as she touched her sore foot.

'To be honest, you have been a very brave girl,' complimented Shiny. 'I couldn't have practiced for drill with blisters on my feet.'

'You will have to dig your heels a little deeper, march a little straighter and hope for the best,' Billi advised. 'I will help you practice harder and you will clear it the next time.'

Dinner Night is a very solemn occasion, one that offers the cadets a glimpse into their future as officers. In short, it is a formal dinner that requires the cadets to display their dining etiquette, taught to them during their training in the academy. The dinner would be their first exposure to the army culture that has existed from the British days. The protocol that the cadets imbibed had to be followed on this special night, hosted during the visit of a very senior officer or VIP.

Although it was just a rehearsal, there was a buzz around the campus as excited cadets prepared for the dinner.

Dressing up in the ceremonial uniform of white shirts with the dazzling company tabs on their collars, black trousers, and a red and black striped waistband, along with a peaked cap, never failed to give the cadets a high. The uniform had a magical effect on everyone. It straightened postures and made everyone feel just a bit smarter. With their additional shoulder tabs, the appointments looked most impressive.

'Why is it called a dinner night?' Nutty asked a relevant question as they made their way towards the mess.

'Dinners are always held at night, so it is called a dinner night,' explained Lucky patiently. 'Not every dinner is known as dinner night. Only the ones hosted to honour a

VIP or one held on a special occasion are known as dinner night.'

'So if a lunch is hosted for a VIP, it should be called lunch noon, or noon lunch,' Nutty pointed out.

This time, no one responded to her silly idea.

'A dinner night also means that the menu will be special,' said Billi, who was looking forward to good food.

'That's good news,' remarked Nutty, rubbing her hands in anticipation. 'I am going to bloody hog like nobody's business.'

'Unfortunately, my dear Doughnut, you will not have the freedom to do so,' Lucky informed her gleefully. 'Don't you recall the warnings issued by the Reichsführer?'

The *paltu*, Major Sherawat, had devoted an entire half hour to issue warnings and instructions about the forthcoming event. No use of hands while eating, no pigging, no spilling, no whispering or laughing, no elbows on the table, no rushing, no scraping of chairs, the list of no's was a long one. She ended the lecture with a stern warning, 'You will eat as long as the band plays, and stop as soon as the music stops. Don't make mistakes. I will be watching.'

The LCs entered the dining hall and stood transfixed. The place looked magical under the light thrown by the chandeliers. The silverware and crockery were laid out to perfection, with name cards placed on each plate. Anxiously, they watched the umpteen sets of spoons, forks, knives and glasses that were enough to confound even seasoned diplomats. They were expected to handle them without displaying any discomfort. Although the cadets had been instructed on table manners, they felt daunted by the formal setting.

Everything had a royal touch, and the place looked like a scene straight out of a British period movie, with the officers and cadets dressed in their ceremonial uniforms.

There was either a company commander or a *paltu* on every table. The CoCo arrived looked like a hero in his attire, accompanied by his elegant and pretty wife.

Attired in their regalia, a band provided live music. Everybody had been instructed to ape the officer seated at their table. The appointments had been placed strategically with a company commander. Billi found herself placed next to CoCo while Shiny had been assigned a place at another table. To her misfortune, Major Sherawat was to occupy the chair next to her.

Everything happened in a synchronized manner. The moment CoCo and the *paltu* pulled their chairs out and sat down, so did the LCs. Those who dragged their chairs and produced a scratchy sound found themselves under the glare of the officer.

The band stopped playing and the liveried mess staff proceeded to serve the dishes. The CoCos and *paltus* were served first and then the cadets. The officers picked up a single piece of cutlet daintily, and the rest of the diners followed suit. Much as she was tempted to do so, Nutty refrained from picking another piece of cutlet, cursing the dinner night and the dining etiquette that came with it. No one was supposed to start eating until everyone had been served.

Much to Nutty's chagrin, the officers displayed no inclination to get on with the meal. Hungry and impatient, she waited as CoCo looked around to check if everyone at his table had been served. Then, he picked up his fork, and he began pecking at the food. The cadets followed suit, pecking at the cutlet and dinner roll.

To their annoyance, the band suddenly stopped playing. It seemed to be a cue for the officers to stop eating, for they put down their forks and knives. Nutty, who had been relishing the first course, found herself eyeing it unhappily. It was a pity to leave the half-eaten delicious cutlet. Surreptitiously, she eyed the CoCo, and gobbled the rest of the food without anyone noticing. Those who had been eating slowly watched sadly as the waiters removed their plates.

The bloody band was the mischief-maker, Nutty realized. The officers had to keep time with the band, thus fomenting trouble for the cadets.

Each course of the dinner was special and delicious, the cooks having surpassed themselves. Yet, no one could enjoy the food as they had to stop eating the moment the music stopped.

The dinner ended, leaving a hungry lot of cadets to crib about dinner night. The gang of four made their way back to their rooms, their stomachs rumbling with hunger.

'They bloody give you no time to eat,' complained Nutty, pacing around the room. 'I want to bloody give the band master a piece of my mind.'

'Oh no! Please don't do that, Peanut,' begged Shiny. 'You will be left with no brains if you give a piece of it to the band master.'

'The CoCo and Shera must have eaten before reaching the mess for dinner night,' Nutty continued grumbling. She was in no mood for jokes. 'I have to eat something or I will not last the bloody night.'

'Here, take some,' Lucky offered a packet of her favourite wafers. She hoarded them by the dozen.

'There should be no PT, drills or outdoor activities on dinner night days,' Nutty declared, chomping busily on the wafers.

'Imagine my plight!' complained Billi, who had been sitting next to CoCo. 'I had to maintain a ramrod posture though the dinner and now my back is aching.'

'I am still hungry,' declared Nutty after having gone through an entire packet of wafers. 'Do you have those delicious biscuits you bought last time,' she asked Lucky.

'You finished the entire lot yesterday,' said Lucky. 'Let's have some cookies,' she said, taking out a packet from her cupboard.

Once the cookies were over, they gathered the eatables everyone possessed. Billi brought some laddoos from her room, Shiny added her biscuits and chips to the lot. Only Nutty had nothing left in her cupboard.

'The bloody mice are not giving up,' complained Nutty, after they had devoured the goodies. 'They are bloody holding an obstacle race around my stomach.'

'Just tank up with two glasses of water and go to sleep,' Shiny suggested.

'... And the rats? What about them?'

'They will get drowned, and you can sleep in peace.'

'Just like our Bengali swimming instructors, the bloody mice in my stomach are good swimmers,' Nutty whined.

In the end, they drowned their hunger in jugs of water, just as Shiny had suggested.

Testing Times

Excitement grew in an inverse proportion to the approach of the midterm break. Two breaks of a week each, placed strategically between the terms, were an occasion to look forward to. Plans were being made, and dreams revved up. But first, there were the midterm tests to be cleared. Days flew by and the LCs were left with just a few days to prepare. Rumours abounded. According to the grapevine, first-termers who did not fare well in the tests would be stopped from going on midterm break. Major Sherawat had reinforced the gossip with a stern warning.

The mood in the academy seemed to undergo a sudden change. The campus, which usually pulsated with activity, now seemed very quiet. Cadets who spent their days running and cycling around suddenly vanished into the confines of their rooms. Merriment and fun were put on the back-burner. Food was gobbled faster, some of it pocketed to be consumed later. Noses buried in books, the studious cadets studied with the help of a torch, beyond the witching hour. The seniors turned accommodating. Punishments ceased for a while, and peace prevailed.

The gang of four decided to study together.

'I am itching for a fag,' said Lucky. Surprised, the others turned to her. 'Don't look so shocked. I have been smoking since I was 16, especially during examinations. It clears my brain.'

'You bloody smoke?' Nutty was awestruck. She had an unadulterated admiration for girls who broke the rules.

'It's nothing to be surprised about. Many girls in the North East love to smoke. By the way, I also drink,' Lucky winked.

'Bloody hell!' exclaimed Nutty. 'It must be awful to not smoke or drink.'

'I am not an addict,' clarified her friend. 'Like I said, a ciggy helps me think.'

'Girls!' Billi clapped her hands. 'Can we get back to studying?'

'We have to get hold of PCK,' said Shiny, who had been briefed by Aaron.

'What the fuck is PCK?' asked Billi.

'It's short for previous course knowledge. Notes from the previous course, something like solved question papers. As per Aaron, possessing them is the secret to doing well in the exams.'

'How will we lay our hands on the bloody PCK?' asked Nutty eagerly. She was not the studious kind, and tests had a depressing effect on her.

'Aaron has promised to pass us a copy, if he's able to get hold of them.'

'There's hardly any time left for the tests. When and how will he give us the bloody PCK?'

'According to Aaron, those with links to senior cadets or with siblings who have passed out of the OTA can get them. The owners of PCKs guard them with their lives. No one shares them.'

'Bloody hell!' Nutty exploded. 'We don't have siblings who passed out from OTA.'

'Cockroach has them,' said Billi. 'I heard her whispering to her *chamchi*.'

Cockroach was Billi's closest competitor for the Sword. Ever since she passed the DST, Cockroach had been strutting around like a peacock in the rain. With PCK in her possession, she was likely to beat Billi in the race to the top.

'That snob will never share the bloody PCK with us,' said Nutty. 'I will have to steal it from her.'

Her friends were astounded with the announcement.

'Don't be stupid!' Shiny rebuked. 'You can't go around stealing stuff.'

'We still have a couple of days. Let's study harder, that's all,' Billi ended.

'How hard can you study?' Nutty demanded. 'Didn't we practice hard for the bloody DST? What was the result of stamping our bloody feet on the ground and limping around for hours? We failed. No sir, I don't think studying harder will help. I will get the PCK.' She jutted her chin out in her characteristic manner.

She got up to go, challenging the others to stop her. No one did. If she was bent on digging her own grave, no one could stop her.

Tiptoeing across the darkened and deserted corridor, Nutty peeped into Cockroach's room. There, bent over photocopies of hand-written notes, the girl, along with her *chamchi*, were intently scrutinizing a small booklet. There were a few more booklets lying around. Wondering how she could steal the booklets, Nutty hovered near the door. It was impossible to lay hands on the PCK.

Frustrated, she stole back to the room.

'What? No PCK?' exclaimed Shiny.

'It's not possible to steal them till the bloody cockroach goes to sleep,' sighed Nutty. For the past few weeks, she had been picking up exotic words to describe people. One of her favourite words was jackass. It was only when she began using it for the CSM that Lucky told her its meaning. Since then, the girl had unleashed her creativity and added a gamut of animals and pests to her vocabulary. Cockroach, toad, rat, head louse, bedbug, flea and dust mite soon became her favourite nomenclature. She had a name for the LCs as well as each of the instructors. No one could fault the girl for deficiency of imagination. The girl was an incorrigible clown.

'Instead of wasting your time cooking up senseless plans, why don't you start studying?' advised Billi.

An hour later, the girls departed. Nutty's mind was in a whirl as she went to bed that night. She would steal the bloody PCK when the bloody roach went to sleep, she decided.

It was past midnight, but the bloody cockroach hadn't gone to bed. Twice, Nutty peeped into Cockroach's room, hoping to hear the girl snoring, twice she returned disappointed. Despite her best attempt to keep awake, the Jalna girl fell asleep.

The gang found Nutty in a foul mood the next morning. 'That bloody jackass! She didn't go to sleep last night.'

'Darling! You were snoring when she went to sleep,' Shiny burst out in laughter.

'Whatever!'

The hours flitted away on impatient wings, as the girls pored over their notes. Just before lunch time, Nutty had left for her room pleading a headache. When she didn't come down for lunch, the gang rushed to her room.

They found her groaning on her bed. 'I am not going to the mess for lunch,' she said. 'I have a terrible stomach ache.'

'Can't you decide if it's a headache or a stomach ache?' scolded Billi. 'Stop making excuses and get up.'

'I am not making excuses. I really have a stomach ache, and a bad one.'

Concerned, Lucky offered to bring her some aloo parathas and eggs from the mess. Very often, when an LC wasn't able to make it for a meal on time, her friends would bring back a couple of parathas, eggs and fruits for her. Most of them had mastered the art of packing a few stuffed parathas in their pockets without anyone noticing. After the very first day, they had begun carrying a plastic bag in their pockets for this purpose.

'Thank you, Lucky. That will be very nice.' Nutty followed up the statement with another groan.

'You must report sick,' suggested Billi as the girls turned to leave.

Once the LCs had left for the mess, Nutty rushed into Cockroach's room and began hunting for the PCKs till she located them under the mattress. There were quite a few of them, some of them were hand-written notes, and some photocopies. There were different booklets for different subjects. Thrusting them into her voluminous pockets, she ran down the stairs. She had very little time to carry out her plan.

Undeterred, Nutty rushed to the bike stand, grabbed the bike and pedalled furiously towards the shopping complex to get the booklets photocopied.

Shiny had not been convinced by her friend's excuse. Knowing Nutty, she could guess what was going on in the girl's mind. 'She must be planning to steal the PCKs while Cockroach is in the mess for lunch,' she told the others as they stepped out of the dining room.

'She's an idiot. Cockroach will finish her meal and rush back to the room before Nutty can get them copied,' Billi burst out. 'That girl's stupidity knows no bounds.'

'We will have to detain Cockroach and Chyawanprash on some pretext,' said Lucky. 'It will be terrible if Nutty is caught with the PCKs.'

'I refuse to collaborate for her rotten plans,' Billi raised her hands in exasperation.

'One last time, please,' exhorted Lucky. 'I will make sure Nutty doesn't get into mischief again.'

'You have high hopes,' snorted Billi. 'That girl is incorrigible. She will never give up her stupid ideas. Not just that, she will drag us into trouble.'

'Instead of wasting time, let's think of some way to detain Cockroach.'

'How will we detain her?' asked Lucky as they made their way toward the bike stand.

Just then, Shiny spotted Cockroach coming out of the mess. 'Quick, take out a pin and puncture her tyres,' she ordered.

Billi and Lucky worked fast, and a couple of seconds was all it took to puncture both the tyres of the LCs bike.

'Hey, there you are,' Shiny hailed Cockroach, who had just reached the bike stand. 'Paltu is looking for you.'

'Which *paltu*?' asked the surprised girl, wondering if she had done something wrong.

'Shera is hunting for you,' said Billi. 'She asked us to convey the message to you.'

'Where is she?' asked Cockroach, anxiety clouding her face.

'She's waiting for you at the Battalion Office,' informed Shiny. 'You better double up. She looked furious.'

'Oh no!' groaned the LC as she inspected the punctured tyres. 'I have flat tyres.'

'Leave the bike here and run,' Billi urged. 'Don't keep her waiting.'

Cockroach took off on the double, leaving the girls holding their sides.

'I just hope Nutty is able to put the PCKs back in the bloody roach's room before she returns,' laughed Shiny.

'Not just that, we have to prepare for a nuke. Cockroach will not spare us for deceiving her,' said Lucky.

'Should we pedal to the shopping complex to warn Nutty?' asked Lucky. Her pockets were bulging with the food she had stashed for her friend, and she was keen on handing it over.

'Let's split forces,' suggested Billi. 'You go after your beloved Doughnut, while we go to the company. Someone has to handle things if they get out of control.'

A worried Lucky pedalled frantically towards the shopping complex. Once there, she found her Doughnut munching salted peanuts, a tetra pack of orange juice lying by her side. The photostat machine was working speedily over the PCKs, while Nutty flirted with the young shopkeeper.

'There you are,' exclaimed Lucky. 'Have you finished?'

'There's a lot of stuff to be photocopied, but Rocky promises to finish the job in a few more minutes,' Nutty informed her airily, biting into the paratha and paneer roll Lucky had brought for her. 'Umm! This is quite nice. Thanks pal!'

'I have the fastest machine in town. It can print 120 copies a minute,' boasted the long-haired apish looking young man. 'The fastest one in the world is a Japanese brand called Orphis. It's capable of doing 150 per minute…'

'Just tell me how long it is going to take,' harangued Lucky, who was least interested in the data about photocopiers. Her aim was to drag Nutty back to the company before all hell broke loose.

'Cool it!' admonished Nutty, who was enjoying Rocky's company. Not only had he offered her the juice and salted peanuts, he had proven to be a movie buff like her. Pleased by her attention, he also promised to lend her his stack of film magazines.

'How long will it take to photocopy the entire lot?' Lucky repeated her question. She was exasperated by Nutty's attitude. Flirting with shopkeepers was not something she approved of.

'A couple of minutes more,' said the fellow flippantly. 'Why don't you sit down? I will fetch a soft drink for you.'

'Thanks, but I don't want anything.'

Undeterred by Lucky, the pest continued to chat. 'The training must be tough for women.' Noticing the unyielding look on her face, he stammered, 'I mean, what with all the punishments and high pressure routine.'

'Look buddy, you don't have to bother about us. Just do the job,' Lucky drew herself straight and hissed in her harshest voice.

'Relax!' said Nutty. 'Rocky is trying to bloody help us.'

'Let's be clear. We are here for business and not for help.'

There was silence for a while, as the fellow retrieved and arranged the photocopies and stapled them together.

'You didn't have to be so bloody rough with the chap,' chided Nutty as the two of them began pedalling towards the company. 'He was giving my job a priority.'

'I have no intention of consorting with the likes of him,' snapped her friend. 'First, you put us all in trouble with your silly plans and then you go and flirt with a shopkeeper.'

For once, Nutty kept her trap shut.

At the Battalion Office, Cockroach hunted for the *paltu*, but Shera was missing. Perplexed, she waited. After her stellar performances in PT, riding, swimming and drills, she was sure of bagging an appointment and didn't want anything to go wrong. Perhaps Paltu was calling her to give some good news. It wouldn't do to displease her at this juncture.

She continued to wait. Five minutes passed and then 10, but there was no sign of Shera. By then, she had begun wondering if the gang of four had been playing a trick on her. At the same time, if Paltu had truly been looking for her, it would be hara-kiri to leave without seeing her. She decided to wait for another five minutes.

Fifteen minutes later, when Paltu didn't arrive, Cockroach decided to go back to the company and confront the pranksters. She jogged back, her mood plummeting faster than the weather on an icy night.

Nutty had barely managed to put the PCKs back in Cockroach's room and rush down when the girl arrived. The gang was waiting for her in the lobby.

'What do you mean by sending me on a wild goose chase?' Cockroach barked at them. 'I am going to complain to Major Shera.'

'Wild goose chase?' asked Nutty, her face a mask of innocence. 'Bloody Cockroach,' she muttered under her breath.

'Shera was not in the Battalion Office. I waited for her for a full 15 minutes,' shouted the exasperated general's daughter. 'You are a bunch of idiots.'

'Cool it!' admonished Billi. 'Who are you calling an idiot? Shera said she wanted to see the tall girl who had cleared the DST and performed well in all physicals. We assumed she was asking for you.'

'Yes, we acted in good faith,' Lucky supported her friend.

'Be reasonable,' said Shiny. 'Whom does the description fit? It fits you to a T. We are sorry if she didn't mean you. At the same time, I fail to understand whom she could mean.'

Cockroach looked unsure. Either the girls were telling the truth or pulling a fast one. Other than asking Paltu, there was no way of knowing, and there was no way she was going to ask Shera. Cursing the lot, she retreated to her room, leaving the gang of four sniggering behind her.

'You monkey! You have bought us a ticket to fame,' said Shiny once they were back in her room. 'With those PCKs, no one can stop us from doing well in the tests.'

'Congratulations on carrying out the perfect coup!' Lucky remarked.

'All I want is to wipe that smug expression from the bloody Cockroach's face,' Nutty gritted her teeth. 'She called us idiots.'

'Don't worry, Coconut! We'll leave her panting far behind,' Billi thumped the irate girl's back.

'Just possessing the PCKs is not enough,' counselled Shiny. 'We have to start cramming them.'

Rejuvenated with the study material, the girls began swotting. For the next two days, the girls pored over the notes, fortifying themselves with chocolates.

'I am going to carry chits,' declared Nutty, who had the memory of a goldfish. 'I can't bloody remember anything.'

Her idea was shot down by the gang. 'You will do nothing of the kind. Cheating is not an Officer Like Quality (OLQ). Besides, you will be thrown out of the academy if the instructor finds you cheating,' reprimanded Shiny.

Once the tests were over, the gang waited with bated breath. The results would decide the appointments and other matters. Prayers were sent up for divine intervention, and fingers and toes remained crossed till the results were declared.

Not everyone was surprised when the results were announced. Shiny had beaten everyone in academics, her marks giving her a big lead over Cockroach. She had performed well in the outdoor activities too. Billi had fared well in the physicals, but had not fared too well in academics. Cockroach had beaten Billi in academics and found herself in the second spot. As for Lucky, she was somewhere in the middle with Nutty following at her heels.

Once the results had been announced, all the LCs knew where they stood in the order of merit. Those up on the list were eyed with envy, while those at the bottom of the list were quite demoralized and knew that getting out of the rut would require a Herculean effort. Some of them decided to work harder, but a few gave up and decided to enjoy life. In the end, we all will be the same, and pass out as lieutenants, they consoled themselves.

Soon after the results were announced, Shiny bagged the coveted rank of Corporal. The cockroach had to be content with the rank of Lance Corporal, leaving Billi high and dry.

'I will never be a CSM,' she wailed.

'You will do better by being appointed as the Senior Under Officer (SUO),' Shiny thumped her friend's sagging shoulders. 'With a little more work, you will beat Cockroach to the post.'

Nutty Makes a Call

Come Sunday and several girls who cleared the DST, including Cockroach, were given out passes. Although Shiny and Billi were eligible for the pass, they decided to stick around with Lucky and Nutty.

'Don't look so disheartened. We will celebrate in the cafeteria,' Shiny thumped Nutty's back. The girl had been cursing the lucky ones, who were dressed in smart muftis and were preparing to leave for a day's outing.

'Shall we have American chop suey?' said the Jalna girl, who had taken a sudden fancy to the dish. The gang was aware that her choices were changing faster than Chennai's weather. Lately, she had developed a taste for exotic dishes like manchow and lung fung soup. They were not sure if the girl's choices were dictated by the need to keep up with the trends. Most of the time, though, none of Nutty's preferred dishes were available at Papa Ferdy's cafeteria.

The menu at the cafeteria boasted some exotic stuff, but they were nothing like authentic Thai or Chinese cuisine. They all tasted the same, since the café employed a Tamil cook, who was partial to tamarind, curry leaves and coconut. Even the lung fung soup was prepared with a generous dash of tamarind and curry leaves, with only the sprinkling of coconut missing. Thankfully, Nutty, who had never tasted the dishes before, knew no better.

'Yes, my dear Peanut, we'll have everything you want, and some more,' Shiny assured her friend.

And so it was decided that the gang would meet Aaron and his pals at the cafeteria for lunch, after everyone had made the mandatory calls home. Since they were allowed to use their phones for a limited time on Sunday mornings, their families waited eagerly for an entire week to hear from the cadets.

The calls often elicited questions that required diplomatic replies. Lucky's mother wanted to know if she had worn the lovely dresses she had packed for her. Shiny's father was keen on knowing if Aaron and she had discussed wedding plans.

Nutty's parents had found a suitable boy for her and wanted to know the date of her arrival, so the boy's family could meet her. Billi's father was keen on knowing how far she had progressed in securing the coveted Sword. Her mother, on the other hand, took great pains to inform her about the weddings of all the young girls in Alakhpura. 'You are the only one left on the shelf,' she sighed. 'Banwari is still waiting for the green signal from you.'

None of the girls had positive replies to these queries, so they invented convincing excuses. We are not allowed to keep smartphones, Lucky told her mother. Shiny said she was in the process of finalizing the wedding plans. As for Nutty, who had no wish to tie the knot with a person of her parents' choice, she told them that the cadets were not allowed to go home until the POP.

Not wanting to sadden their parents, they did not tell them about the tough life they led at the academy.

Instead, they painted imaginary pictures of their lives. In those pictures, life was a ball. They were eating the best food, having a rollicking time and doing very well in the academy.

The calls over, everyone placed the phones in the cardboard carton that would later be placed in the CSM's room. Minutes later, they were cycling towards the cafeteria.

Aaron and Kale had already grabbed a table and were enjoying soft drinks and French fries. The first few minutes were spent in dissecting the results. Like Shiny, Aaron had scored above everyone in the academics part of the examination, but Vedant Verma had beaten him in overall performance. As a result, Verma had been appointed the Corporal and Aaron was left with the rank of Lance Corporal.

'I think the ustads as well as instructors are a partial lot,' Nutty sympathized with Aaron. 'I have seen them ignore major faults in their favourite cadets, but punish the rest of us for the tiniest slip-ups.'

'I don't agree with your remark,' said Billi. 'They are an impartial lot. Even the CSM has no favourites.'

Not interested in any of the appointments, the unambitious Kale pulled the fries closer and grabbed a handful. Content in passing through the academy without flying colours, he was keen on making the best of the situation.

Like most first-termers, the gang kept their interest confined to the Zojila Company and their platoon. They were not interested in the performance of the Phillora Company or the other Zojila Platoon.

'That's a very parochial way of looking things,' said Aaron. 'You will have to gird up for the competitions. Not only will you have to beat the other platoon, you will also have to beat the Phillora LCs for every honour and every prize.'

'Thanks for adding to our worries, Aaron,' exploded his girlfriend. 'I guess the GCs have already girded up their loins to compete for the top honours.'

'We certainly have done the spadework,' Aaron said pompously. The couple had been having tiffs every time they met. The equation had shifted ever since he had begun displaying the macho side of his personality. The lovers were more in competition with each other than with the others in their respective companies. 'You've got to think of the bigger picture,' he said.

'Oh! Really?' Shiny's voice dripped acid.

'Yes, really,' Aaron was quick to bite the bait. 'It's a competition. You can't be thinking of your platoon only. You have to think of the entire company as well as the battalion, know their strengths and weaknesses, and prepare accordingly.'

He was right, but Shiny was in no mood for a sermon.

'I am hungry,' Nutty piped in, trying to defuse the tension. 'Shall we talk of food instead of competitions?'

'Yes, please, let's order food,' Kale supported Nutty's decision. He had polished off the fries and was looking forward to satisfying the mice that were creating a din in his cavernous stomach.

'I agree. Stress is not good for digestion. We can discuss the stressful stuff after we've eaten,' said Lucky. No one wanted the discussion to escalate into a hostile situation between the lovers.

Papa Ferdy was summoned and the gang pored over the menu. 'Do you have manchow or American chop suey?' asked Nutty, who had been craving the dishes.

'Alas! No, my lady!' Ferdy pulled a long face and rolled his eyes dramatically. 'However, I can offer you the best chicken noodles on this side of the continent. I will suggest sweet corn soup to go with it.'

'What about rajma rice?' Billi demanded. On their last visit to the cafeteria, Papa Ferdy had made the mistake of promising to prepare rajma and rice for her.

'It was served last Sunday. Unfortunately, you didn't come last week,' said the man with a glib tongue. He was used to the ways of whimsical cadets. 'You will love the mutton biryani the chef has prepared this morning.' Ferdy insisted on referring to his cook as a chef. The word had an inspiring effect on the cook, he felt.

A round of discussion later, they ordered everything suggested by Ferdy, so there was chicken noodles and sweet corn soup, as well as mutton biryani. As a concession, the sly owner had agreed to send some fries on the house. He knew the cadets were a hungry lot and this particular gang regularly haunted his café.

'Where's Mathur?' asked Lucky. She didn't want her appetite to be spoilt by the guy's presence. 'Has he gone out on liberty?'

Kale's crestfallen expression hadn't escaped her attention.

'No, he's been punished by the CSM. That guy is forever looking for trouble. Guys like him will never improve,' Aaron waved his fork dismissively.

Relieved, Lucky began pecking at her food.

‘I am missing him,’ said Kale, who had been looking forward to a feast like the last time. He had served himself a generous portion of the biryani and was intent upon finishing it as fast as possible, so he could enjoy the chicken noodles. ‘He is the most generous chap around.’

‘I am sure none of the girls are missing the chap,’ Aaron laughed. ‘He has a knack of turning them off.’

‘Alright, I will order a round of chicken tikkas for everyone,’ offered Lucky. ‘I think Kale will not miss Mathur if there is a platter of tikkas before him.’

Her eyes strayed towards the entrance, just as GC Verma entered the café. The guy made her heart beat faster, and butterflies crowded in her stomach. Just then Lucky’s eyes fell on the beauty queen, who was accompanying him, and she lost her appetite.

Verma led his companion towards a table, and the two of them were soon lost in hushed conversation.

‘Thank god Mathur is not here,’ commented Kale, his eyes settling on the couple. ‘He hates the guts of that cadet.’

‘I am sure most GCs hate Verma’s guts, not because of any other reason but his beautiful companion,’ said Shiny. She had not failed to notice Lucky’s reactions.

‘There’s nothing to hate him for. The girl is not available. It is as simple as that,’ Aaron expressed his opinion. ‘One should take it with good grace, rather than hating the guy who is successful at winning the heart of a girl.’

‘The world is not as simple as you make it sound,’ sighed Lucky, the green serpent of jealousy wrapped firmly around her little heart.

‘Why the long sigh?’ Billi laughed. ‘Don’t tell me you have taken a shine to the chap?’

The blush that flooded Lucky's face was a giveaway, although she was quick to object. 'Nothing of that sort. I will leave all the crushes for Nutty, since I have no time for romance.'

'Thou doth protest too much,' chanted Shiny, teasing the girl who was trying not to look at the GC.

'Speaking of romances, did you know that one of your *paltus*, Major Swati, has recently been married to an instructor?' Aaron informed the girls. 'Obviously, a lot of romances have been going on in the campus.'

'No wonder Major Swati has been missing for the past few weeks,' said Nutty. 'I am keen to meet the man who won her heart.'

'It won't be long before you are punished by him,' Aaron laughed.

'I am sure a honeymooning officer won't be cruel,' Nutty retorted.

'Now that the midterm break is around the corner, have you guys done some planning?' Kale began taking an interest in the conversation now that he had polished off everything on his plate. Just then the waiter brought the tikkas, and he pounced on them.

'Thanks for reminding us,' said Lucky. 'We have been tossing around a few ideas, but nothing concrete so far.'

'Kale is banking on Mathur's generosity once again,' Aaron slapped the GC on his back, making Kale choke on the last bit of tikka that he was chewing.

It was an enjoyable morning, with heaps of flirting, sprinkled with banter, airing of grievances and lots of food and laughter. But Nutty was far from satisfied. Her mind was brewing mischief.

~

Post dinner, just when the girls settled down in Billi's room for a chat, Nutty took out a phone from her pocket and announced, 'Girls, brace yourselves for a rollicking ride.'

'Where did you get that phone from?' screeched Billi, trying to snatch it from her hand.

'Didn't you once say "where there is a will, there is a way"?' demanded the irrepressible girl as she swatted away Billi's hand.

Horrified, the three friends watched Nutty as she extracted the sim card from the phone and replaced it with another one, before activating the phone.

'What are you doing?' hissed Lucky. 'There'll be hell to pay if the CSM learns that you have brought a phone to your room.'

'She'll not know,' Nutty smiled complacently.

'Did you know that she counts the number of phones in the carton before carrying it back to her room?' asked Shiny. 'If she finds one missing…'

'No worries!' Nutty chuckled in her typical way. 'There won't be a single phone missing from the carton.'

'I don't understand…'

'Elementary, my dear Watson! My phone cover, with the name and number, is in the carton,' Nutty reassured her friends.

'In that case, where has this one come from? Have you been hiding it in your room, you crazy girl?' Billi asked shrilly.

'Shhh! Not so loud. We don't want the CSM to come running,' Nutty warned. 'Let me explain. I have brought only the phone to the room. I inserted a used bar of soap into the phone cover lying in the carton. It's a dummy.'

'There's soap in the carton?' Lucky was aghast at the audacity of the girl.

'Why are you looking so shocked? The CSM doesn't have the time to check each and every phone cover to see if there is a phone in it. Besides, I have secured it with a rubber band.'

'Alright, Madam Smarty, what do you intend doing with the phone?' Shiny asked after a resigned sigh. The girl was a habitual rule-breaker and too high-spirited to be tamed. She managed to go from one shenanigan to another without any remorse. Punishments couldn't dampen her spirit, nor could fear of relegation.

'I am going to make an important call,' announced Nutty.

'Didn't you speak to your parents in the morning?' asked Lucky.

'This is not a call to the parents. I am about to call Captain Kartik Iyer.'

'NO!' Lucky shrieked. 'Please, don't. Someone stop this girl. She's gone crazy.'

'Shhh! You will bring the overstudy here with all that screeching.' Nutty clamped her hand on Lucky's mouth. 'Look, there's nothing to be alarmed about. All I want is to make a call.'

Realizing that the girl was bent upon committing suicide and getting them killed too, the gang waited for her next step.

'I will put the phone on speaker mode, so please keep quiet,' said Nutty, punching in the doctor's number on the phone.

There was silence as the girls waited for his response, their hearts beating erratically.

'Hello! Iyer here,' Captain Kartik's pleasant voice covered the short distance between the Military Hospital and the academy.

'Hi Doc,' Nutty warbled. 'How are you?'

'Who's speaking?' the captain's voice turned wary.

'I am calling from the OTA,' Nutty cooed. 'Don't you remember me? I was admitted to the hospital a few days ago.'

'You are a cadet.' It was a statement, not a question. 'How did you get my number?' The sternness was unmistakable.

'You gave it to me, doc.'

'I am not in the habit of sharing my number with all and sundry, especially my patients,' said the doc.

'Why are you getting annoyed?' Nutty persisted. 'I…'

Her words hung in the air as the captain disconnected the call.

'So much for your efforts,' taunted Billi. 'The doctor is clearly not interested in you.'

'He may have a girlfriend already,' suggested Lucky.

'All he has to do is to inform the CoCo that an LC had the cheek to procure his number and call him,' said Shiny, her forehead creasing with worry. 'And heaven will fall.'

True to her words, the entire lot of LCs belonging to both Zojila and Phillora Companies were ordered for a fall-in the very next morning. There was a flurry as 40 girls lined up before a grim-faced CoCo, four flinty-eyed *paltus* and two mean-looking CSMs. Thankfully, the Phillora CoCo was missing.

Something was seriously wrong. All the LCs could sense the brewing of a storm. It had to be something very serious for all of them to have been summoned.

Feeling like condemned captives facing a firing squad, they waited for execution.

'Which of you had the cheek to call Captain Iyer last night?' asked the CoCo, his sharp voice cutting the morning air like a sword. 'I expect the guilty cadet to confess.'

There was a shocked silence as the LCs grappled with the question. No one, except the gang of four, was aware of the call.

He subjected them to a penetrating look. There was total silence. No one confessed. 'Well! I don't have the time, so I will leave the matter to your Platoon Commanders. But, I expect a confession within an hour.'

Throwing another scathing look at the girls, he left them at the mercy of their respective *paltus*.

'Own up!' roared Major Sherawat.

No one spoke.

'I will give you a break of five minutes,' said Major Preeti Singhal, who was the Phillora *paltu*. 'The Phillora LCs can come and confess to me in private. Major Sherawat will be available for the Zojila cadets. Your time starts now.'

Confused and anxious, the LCs dispersed. Soon, clusters of girls could be seen discussing the matter in low voices.

'You must own up,' Billi told Nutty, as the gang of four gathered in her room. 'Not owning up will lead to punishments for the entire lot of LCs.'

'Are you crazy?' Nutty exploded. 'I can't bloody confess. It's better to be punished in a group than individually. Besides, what if they bloody relegate me?'

‘Shouldn’t you have thought about that before carrying out such an idiotic act?’ Shiny charged.

‘Not for a minute did I imagine that the bloody captain would call up the CoCo and tell him about the call. It’s not such a big deal. I am already out of love with such a stuck-up guy. Now I wonder why I fell for him in the first place.’

‘You are capable of falling in love with a chimpanzee,’ Billi remarked scornfully.

Five minutes passed, but no one owned up. So, a fall-in was announced.

‘Since no one has the courage to own up, all the first-termers will be punished for the guilty LC’s cowardice,’ declared Major Sherawat.

‘Let’s give them one last chance,’ suggested Major Singhal. ‘Remember, cowards don’t belong in the Indian Army. One of you has committed a blunder. She shouldn’t commit another blunder by being a coward. Now step forward and confess.’

There was silence.

‘Well! I gave you a chance. Major Sherawat, please take over.’

One hand went up hesitantly. It was Nutty. ‘Ma’am, why only the first-termers? Can’t it be a senior LC?’

A heavy silence greeted her question. It was blasphemy to involve the seniors.

Minutes later, the 40 girls were front rolling all around the ground. This was followed by 50 push-ups. Not just that, everyone got extra drill orders.

‘Welcome to Reichsführer Sherawat’s domain,’ grumbled Lucky.

'What's a Reichsführer?' Nutty asked, bewildered.

'Reichsführer was the highest rank in Hitler's SS,' Lucky said under her breath.

Reichsführer! That day, Shera was catapulted to a new rank. She was now at par with the likes of Herr Himmler.

Nutty was awarded 20 extra push-ups, and three extra drills for questioning the *paltus*. The wicked CSM added a few more push-ups to the list, after the *paltus* had left.

The upshot of the punishments was that the LCs spent all their free time stamping their feet on the parade ground. It was an act of releasing their frustration and anger, but it made the ground reverberate and brought great joy to the drill ustad. Pleased with their performance, Sappy was so moved that he said, '*Shabaash,* cadets.' It was rather uncharacteristic for the nitpicking ustad to compliment the first-termers.

Hours of practice brought with them happy tidings. A few LCs, who had failed the DST in the first attempt, managed to clear it, but some still remained at the bottom of the list. Among the failures was Nutty, who had developed sore feet from all the stamping, and Lucky, who still couldn't manage to stamp her feet hard enough.

Sappy declared that the LCs who had failed would be given one last chance if they wanted to proceed for the midterm break. Stamping began all over again, this time with additional zest. No one wanted to miss the midterm break, least of all Nutty and Lucky.

Hope prevailed.

PLANS AND PLOYS

It was essential now to clear the DST.

'The two of you have to clear the DST,' Billi warned her friends. 'I won't let you fail this time.'

The warning was repeated by Lucky's overstudy. Generosity being her second nature, she took both Lucky and Nutty under her wing. 'I will ensure that the two of you pass the DST this time, even if I have to keep you marching through the night,' declared the Wall. She harangued and bullied the girls into practicing till every little muscle in their bodies began protesting.

Confident after the gruelling practice session, the LCs pestered Sappy for a retest.

'Ustad, last time I failed because my foot had blisters,' Nutty wailed in a pathetic voice. Ever the drama queen, she spared no dramatics.

'I was unwell,' pleaded Lucky, joining Nutty's pleas for another try at the drill test.

Soon, a few others joined them with their own excuses for having failed the drill test.

To their delight, the instructor decided to give them one more chance to clear the DST. This time the drill ustad could find no fault with the two LCs. Their performance pleased the adjutant as well.

'You have passed this time,' he declared grudgingly. 'Next time, I will ensure that you go through a more difficult test.'

Delighted, the girls sprinted back to share the news with the rest of the gang.

Midterm break plans, which had been put on hold, were now placed on the fast-track. Thrilled by the thought of four days of fun and freedom, the first-termers spent every moment of their free time planning the break. There was a tangible buzz of excitement all around the campus.

The only ones who didn't add to the buzz, and went around with long faces and jealous serpents twined around their hearts, were the ones who had failed. Debarred from going on the midterm break, they had been ordered to attend extra classes.

'Thank god for Nutty,' said Lucky. 'Look at the bright side. Had she not called the doctor, we would not have been punished with extra drills and we would not have cleared the DST.'

'And so we would not have done the extra practice and not gone for midterm break,' sang the Jalna girl. 'Thanks to me, some of the LCs managed to clear the DST.'

The fortunate LCs who belonged to Chennai and the adjoining areas were planning to spend the midterm break by sleeping for the full four days. It was a luxury no one could afford while in the campus. Those who had to travel far, lamented the long journey which would eat into the four precious days they had. Only those with deep pockets could buy air tickets for the few days they would spend at home. Many of them abandoned the thought of going home, and planned on travelling to nearby places for a couple of days.

Lucky, Billi and Nutty belonged to the latter category.

'I am not telling my folks about the break, or my mother will embark on a matchmaking spree. The long journey will take away more than half of the break, and the rest will be spent decking myself to be inspected by prospective grooms and their families,' said Nutty. Thoughts of romance and a love marriage made her determined to resist an arranged one. 'In fact, I have no intention of going home till after the POP.'

'I am not telling my parents about the break, either,' declared Billi. Despite having changed the sim card on her phone and warning her parents not to share her new number with Banwari, she knew that going home would mean confronting the chap. She had no intention of allowing the fellow to upset her. 'If I go home, Banwari will pester me for a wedding date, and my father will demand to know how far I have progressed in bagging the Sword.'

'As far as I am concerned, going home is out of the question,' lamented Lucky. 'It's too far and too expensive to travel for a break of four days.'

'Let's go somewhere near Chennai,' suggested Nutty. Turning to Shiny, she asked, 'You will come with us, I hope.'

'I have no choice in the matter. Aaron, ever the ideal son, has already gabbed about the break,' fumed Shiny. 'That guy doesn't know when to keep his trap shut. We could have spent some quality time together, at a nearby destination, but then he had to prove his stupidity.'

'That's too bad,' Lucky commiserated with her friend. 'It would have been fun to go together.'

'Can't you tell them you failed the DST, so you have not been allowed to go home?' asked Nutty, who always had an answer.

'I can't do that. My parents won't believe me. Besides, what if the great Aaron goes and tells them the truth? No, I will have to go home with him.' Shiny shook her head sadly. 'You guys go ahead and enjoy yourselves.'

'We can all go to Puducherry. I believe it's a beautiful place with lots of French food,' said Nutty.

'If it's a beach you are seeking, what's wrong with Chennai?' We might as well stay here,' Billi pointed out.

'I think you should go to Puducherry,' Shiny suggested.

'Have you been there?' asked Lucky.

'Yes, I went with my parents a few years back. Puducherry was once a French colony, designed in a grid system. The streets have retained their French names, and the cops still wear the French kepi, which is a funny red cap,' Shiny informed them. 'I loved the place.'

'In that case, let's go there,' Lucky urged.

'I was thinking of going to Mahabalipuram,' said Billi. 'It has both beaches and historical temples. We can stay there for a day and then go to Puducherry. That way, we cover a lot of places.'

'Won't it be bloody expensive?' Nutty's brows creased anxiously.

'Why don't you make a budget,' suggested Shiny. 'You don't have to stay in expensive places, and you can travel by bus.'

'That's true,' said Lucky. 'Besides, we don't have to do fine dining. With a bit of planning, we can manage the finances. Mamallapuram, here we come.' She pumped her fists.

'Let's leave it flexible,' Nutty put forth her idea. 'If we like Mallupuram, we continue to stay there, and if we don't then we bloody move to Puducherry. That way, we won't feel rushed.'

'I think that's a good idea,' endorsed Shiny. 'By the way, my dear Coconut, it's not Mallupuram but Mamallapuram or Mahabalipuram.'

Destination decided, the girls started discussing the details. There was the budget and necessary arrangements to be made. Thoughts of a relaxing holiday kept the girls on their toes. Nutty dreamt of casanovas and romance, while Billi had plans of swimming and running as well as sleeping. With her easy-going attitude, Lucky decided to enjoy the events as they unfolded.

The break began with a bang. Not willing to let a single moment of the break flit past, the cadets were up early on the much-awaited morning. There was a flurry of activity as everyone rushed for breakfast. Decked up and eager, they began pouring out of the academy in groups, much like a flock of birds flying away. It was the long-awaited flight to freedom.

Cabs could be spotted entering and leaving the campus at regular intervals. Once out of the campus, the cabs fanned out in different directions, carrying their loads of boisterous cadets.

Having planned their moves in advance, the trio bid farewell to Shiny, who was leaving with Aaron in a few minutes. 'Enjoy yourselves!' she responded.

'Don't forget to bring back banana chips,' Lucky reminded her.

'I won't,' promised Shiny, hugging each of her three friends.

It was almost midday by the time the gang, minus one, reached Mahabs as they had decided to call Mahabalipuram. By now, Nutty was not the only one whose innards were raising flags of discontent. In a bid to maximise the vacation, the girls had started very early in the morning and the hurried breakfast had long been digested. Valiantly, they had soldiered on without protesting, but now their hunger pangs could no longer be ignored.

'I am hungry. It's time we found a place to eat,' said Nutty.

'Shouldn't we find a hotel and dump our bags there and then go in search of a restaurant?' asked Lucky, who was in no mood to lug her bag around. 'We could freshen up and then go for food.' She extended a bag of chips towards her friends.

'No, we will eat first,' the Jalna girl rejected Lucky's suggestion. 'We can hunt for a hotel afterward. In fact, we can ask the restaurant guy to suggest an affordable place.'

'That seems like a good idea,' agreed Billi. In the distance, they spotted a line of small restaurants. 'Let's first look for an affordable eatery.'

Nutty halted and sniffed around like a hound as they crossed a glitzy restaurant. 'I can smell tandoori chicken,' she remarked, her nose twitching excitedly. 'Let's go in. I am famished.'

'Don't be stupid, a meal here will cost us more than three meals elsewhere,' said Billi, steering the girl away from the restaurant. The Haryanvi girl had been chosen to handle the finances for the trip. 'We will have to skip dinner as well as breakfast if you eat there.'

'You are a bloody Hitler,' muttered the sullen Nutty.

'Patience, dear Doughnut,' consoled Lucky. 'Trust me! With so many eateries in this area, it will take just a couple of minutes to find the right one.'

Ten minutes later, having washed their hands in a cracked and stained washbasin of an average dhaba, the girls settled down at a rickety table. After shooting down Nutty's requests for the extravagant dishes, Billi ordered chicken biryani, which turned out to be surprisingly delicious. Perhaps it was hunger that added to the taste.

On being asked about an inexpensive hotel, the helpful owner pointed towards a nearby one. Although the room was too cramped after an additional bed had been placed in it, the girls were happy with the affordable tariff. The best part of the room was a view of the distant sea. They kicked off their shoes and went to sleep.

It was evening when Billi got up and shook her friends awake. 'Hey, we didn't come all the way here to sleep through four days,' she yelled. 'Get up, lazy bums.'

'You go ahead, I will join you later,' mumbled Nutty, refusing to get up.

'We are all going together,' Billi began tickling the girl. She threatened, 'If you don't get up in the next two minutes, I am going to pour a bucket of water on you.'

Stretching herself, Nutty sat up and yawned. 'You are a bloody cruel woman, worse than the CSM. We are on a holiday, in case you forgot.'

'I have forgotten nothing,' retorted Billi. 'Weren't you the one who wanted to walk around a beach? Now you want to snore like an overfed hog.'

'Pigs don't snore, do they?' Lucky giggled at the thought of a snoring pig.

'It's immaterial whether they snore or not. Let's go to the beach before it gets too dark,' spurred Billi, the self-appointed leader of the group.

A few minutes later, armed with packets of chips and a bottle of beer (Lucky's idea), they made their way to the beach. There were not too many people on the beach. The girls frolicked in the waves and ran along the edge of the water, the wind whipping their faces. With the sting of the salty air in their eyes and the soft sand under their feet, they ran close to the sea, dodging the waves that surged and ebbed in a rhythmic manner.

Wet and exhausted, they finally threw themselves on the sand to watch the waves frolicking and kissing the shores, and the sun spreading its red-golden rays. The sky was a palette of rainbow colours, and the sea reflected the brilliant colours of the sky.

Mesmerized, the trio watch the magical phenomenon. Lucky drew a sharp breath and whispered, 'It's beautiful!'

'It's bloody hypnotizing,' agreed Nutty. 'What about sunset? I am waiting for the sun to set.'

'Dear Doughnut, you won't be able to see the sunset from here. If you leave your bed early, you can catch the sunrise.'

'What the fuck! I don't want to get up early on a holiday. I will see the sunrise some other time.'

'Let's have the beer,' said Lucky, opening the bottle. She took a swig and passed it to Nutty.

'This bloody stuff tastes like piss and stinks like rotten fruit,' winced the girl after a small sip.

'You have to develop the taste for it,' said Lucky, who liked beer. She had been craving it for a while.

Billi dared a few sips before handing the bottle back to Lucky. 'Look at those girls,' she pointed at two young girls who were gambolling in the waves. They were jumping in and out of the water, their salwars rolled up till their calves.

'Watch me in action,' commanded Nutty. Pressing the end of her index finger and thumb together to form a ring, she let out a prolonged whistle, surprising her friends. The two girls looked over their shoulders and Nutty raised the beer bottle. Then she winked at them and let out another wolf whistle.

Indignant, the girls walked out of the water and ran toward a cop, who was posted at the beach to control eve-teasing. Swinging his baton importantly, the chap walked towards the three friends with the two complainants in tow.

'Ha!' he yelled over the roar of the waves. Spotting the beer bottle and the chips, he barked, 'Drinking and eve-teasing. Section 294 IPC. Stand up, all three of you.'

He picked up the bottle and sniffed. 'Drinking beer? You rascals, come with me to the police station.'

Billi drew herself to her full height and glared down at the tubby fellow, who was a full six inches shorter than her. 'Who are you calling rascals?' she shouted.

It was now evident to the complainants as well as the cops that these were not boys but girls with zero cuts. The three had looked like adolescent boys from a distance, but now they realized that they were mistaken. Clad in shorts and T-shirts, tanned and sinewy, the OTA trainees looked far from feminine.

'We are from the OTA,' Nutty got up and informed the cop.

'OTA girls? Why are you drinking and whistling at girls?' he asked, unwilling to back down.

'You want to see our identity cards?' asked Billi in a threatening tone.

The swarthy guy hesitated. Not only had he mistaken them for boys, he had accused OTA girls of eve-teasing. It would be embarrassing if his colleagues learned of his mistake.

'Okay, okay!' he held up his hand. 'No need to get angry. I am just doing my duty, madam.'

'Yes, of course. You must do your duty,' Lucky stepped forward to soothe the man's ruffled feathers. There was no point in antagonizing the fellow, if they were to stay at Mahabs for another day or two. Besides, it was not the cop's fault. Tanned, sinewy and crop-haired, they looked more like boys than girls, Lucky had realized. 'It's just a misunderstanding.'

'Yes, yes, misunderstanding. Very short haircut, dress and low light, so the mistake. Sorry, madam. I respect army. You are doing very good duty for country,' he bleated. To their utter surprise, he followed up the statement with a smart salute.

Turning to the two girls, he scolded them in Tamil and ended his sermon with, '*Po. Sheegram po.*'

The cop had barely retreated when Nutty broke into loud laughter. 'Imagine being mistaken for bloody eve-teasers. This is really funny.'

'It's been a great start to our vacation,' remarked Lucky. 'Hope the fun and adventure continues for the next few days.'

Darkness had fallen around them like a heavy cloak as the girls made their way towards the dhaba for dinner.

The next morning, Billi got up early and went for a run along the beach. Nutty and Lucky were snoring when she left the room.

A couple of hours later, the girls went out to explore the ancient temples of Mahabalipuram. Dozens of photographs and selfies later, they sighed with satisfaction.

'I didn't realize we were so close to the beach and temples. We can come here whenever we have a holiday,' said Lucky, taking a sip of the tender coconut water they had bought from a vendor. She had discarded the idea of beer in favour of a healthy drink. 'I would love to bring my parents here.'

'We must have seafood,' insisted Nutty. Her mind constantly on food, she could see little beyond the eateries and their menus. 'I spotted a bloody nice place with fried fish yesterday and asked the waiter about the menu. They allow you to choose the one that you want to be fried.'

'Let's keep that for the last day,' suggested Billi, who was keeping a check on the expenses. She also knew that Nutty would not be satisfied with one serving of the fried fish.

'You are such a bloody Uncle Scrooge, watching every penny,' cursed Nutty. 'We are here for a good time, and you won't loosen the bloody purse strings.'

'My dear Doughnut, don't be so angry,' Lucky soothed the girl. 'Billi is doing the right thing. None of us have that much money. If we blow the entire amount on the very second day, we will have to cut short our vacation. Besides, I think the biryani was delicious.'

The midday sun was beating down as the girls dragged themselves to a nearby eatery. Despite all their warnings, Nutty could not withhold the temptation of ordering fried fish. The food was served on fresh banana leaves and was delicious and affordable.

Back in the room, Nutty sighed with satisfaction. 'This is a bloody good place. I like it,' she said, linking her hands under her head and staring at the ceiling fan. 'The fish was delicious. No need to go to Puducherry. We can stay here.'

'So, it's the fish that decided the course of your actions,' Lucky teased her friend.

'I was thinking the same,' Billi hoisted herself on the bed and plumped up the pillow behind her. 'The hotel is reasonably clean and comfortable, the beach is not too far and the food is inexpensive. Why travel anywhere else? We can visit Puducherry the next time.'

'Besides, now we know the local cop,' Lucky laughed.

'The only problem is that there are no good-looking men,' lamented Nutty, who had been dreaming of romance. 'Just think of it. What a lovely time we could have had if there were some hunks around.'

'What about the cop? Will he do?' Billi joked, and Nutty threw a pillow at her.

The Adventure Continues

Certain incidents have a habit of repeating themselves, just as problems and history repeat themselves. The very next morning, Lucky decided to inaugurate the dress her mother had packed for her. It was a royal blue knee-length dress with spaghetti straps.

Nutty let out a wolf whistle as Lucky accessorized it with the floppy sunhat she had bought from a shop the previous day. 'You look like a film star,' she said. 'The sunhat adds a

stylish touch to your lovely dress.'

The compliment made Lucky preen with delight, and she brought out a pair of sunglasses that complemented her oval-shaped face. 'And now?' she asked, striking a pose.

'Just perfect!' said Nutty, who prided herself on being a know-it-all as far as fashion was concerned. 'I will borrow the dress and sunglasses for a photo shoot on the beach.'

'You are welcome!' said her generous friend and picked up the tote in which she was carrying a novel, a packet of chips and sunscreen. 'Let's go to the beach now.'

'Why don't you go ahead, we will join you shortly,' said Billi. 'Nutty and I will pick up some onion pakoras from the nearby shack.'

'That's an excellent idea. Please get some tender coconut also. See you at the same spot,' Lucky waved at her friends.

They had found a spot on Pallava Beach. It was close to their hotel and not crowded.

Ten minutes later, having slathered herself with the sunscreen lotion, Lucky settled on the sand and took out her novel. It was a breezy romance that she had picked up in the airport on the way to the OTA but had not found the time to read.

Lost in the book, she didn't notice the two boys who had plonked themselves near her. It was only after one of them whistled at her that she looked up at the rough-looking guys.

'Hi, beautiful!' said one of them. 'All alone?'

'Want our company?' asked another one.

There weren't many people on the beach at that time of the morning. Lucky decided to ignore the guys, but they crept closer. 'What's your problem?' she asked, exasperated by the pests.

'We want to make friends,' replied one of them.

'Get lost!' Lucky hissed. She gathered her things and stood up, but they blocked her way. 'Let me pass,' she said in an icy voice.

'No, darling! We don't allow pretty girls to pass without a kiss.' One of the guys inched closer.

Desperate, Lucky glanced out of the corner of her eyes. The hotel was a distance away and the closest group of beach bums were at least a 100 metres away. She swung her bag and hit one of the guys on his face, while shouting for help. In the meantime, a blast of wind sent her sun hat flying into the sea.

Enraged, the two men pounced on her. One of them caught her hands and began twisting them, while the other snatched her bag. She struggled, trying to kick them in the groin.

Suddenly, she felt the grip on her loosening. There was commotion as blows began raining down on the two hoodlums. Billi and Nutty had arrived. They clobbered the chaps and kicked them hard, bringing them to their knees.

'Bloody jackass! Bloody dust mites!' shouted the ever inventive Nutty as she used her hands and feet on the guys. Enthused with the support, Lucky joined in.

Picking up a stick lying nearby, Billi lashed out at the men. Unfortunately, the sea-worn stick crumbled after the third blow. Undeterred, the triumvirate began raining blows upon the two guys, who cowered before them.

Suddenly, a whistle sounded and a cop arrived. It was the same cop they had met the previous evening.

'Rascals!' he joined the girls and began beating the chaps with his baton. 'Madam, you leave them to me. I will take them to the police station,' said the policeman.

'No way!' Billi yelled, continuing to kick the rogues. 'We will teach them a lesson they will never forget.'

The commotion had attracted the attention of other beach bums, and soon there was a small crowd around the girls. A few onlookers joined them in beating the fellows, while some of them took photographs and made videos.

The two scoundrels finally fell at the cop's feet and begged him to rescue them.

Saluting the girls, the policeman remarked, 'Very brave, madam. You are good fighters and the country is proud of you. I am Constable Muthu. If you need help, ask for me at the police station.'

There was jeering and clapping as the constable led the two culprits away. It was the first time the crowd had seen OTA girls in action. Till now, their experience of action had been restricted to the big screen, but this was a live show. One of the women handed the girls a bottle of water, another offered them snacks, while their menfolk wanted to know about their training. There were several requests for selfies. Feeling like VIPs, the three friends posed with their admirers.

'They must be teaching you judo and karate, madam,' said a middle-aged man. 'I saw the way you were hitting. It was like karate chops.'

'It is good to see women fighting back,' commented an elderly lady. 'These goondas are making life miserable for young girls. They need to be taught a lesson.'

'How can I join the OTA?' asked a young girl.

The next few minutes were spent in dealing with dozens of questions that came forth from all directions.

'Whew! What a morning!' Nutty drew a deep breath after the crowd had dispersed. Suddenly she remembered the reason they had left Lucky alone at the beach. 'Where are the bloody pakoras?'

The pakoras, mangled, trampled and sand-coated, were now being gobbled by a couple of mongrels. 'Never mind, we will get some more,' consoled Billi. 'Let the dogs have their day.'

'Think about it!' remarked Nutty as they sat enjoying a celebratory meal at a shack a while later. For once, Billi didn't object to her choice of dishes. 'What an adventurous vacation this has been!'

'Truly adventurous,' agreed Lucky, digging into the fish fry. 'I am glad we dropped the idea of going to Puducherry.'

'That's true!' said Billi, as she forked out the money for the meal, and they began walking back to the hotel.

'It's an interesting vacation with three firsts,' Nutty counted them on her fingers. 'It's the first time we have been accused of eve-teasing, the first time we have beaten ruffians…'

'Most importantly, it's the first time we have been saluted,' laughed Lucky.

'Oh, yes! I had forgotten the bloody salute from Muthu. After all, not every OTA cadet is fortunate to be saluted by a police constable.'

'Not just that, being saluted even before being commissioned as officers is truly an achievement,' added Lucky.

'Wait till we narrate these incidents to Shiny,' exclaimed Billi. 'She will regret missing out on all the fun.'

~

All good things come to an end and so did the midterm break. The girls were reluctant to get back to the academy. Entering the gates of the OTA would mean the end of midterm break, so they loitered around.

'Let's enjoy one last meal outside the campus,' announced Lucky.

'I am craving a pizza,' declared the foodie in the group. She had been searching for eateries near the OTA on her phone. 'I don't mind a vegetarian pizza, if you want to save money, but I must have a pizza before the bloody academy kills me with its routine.'

'You and your food cravings,' snorted Billi. 'One would think you are pregnant.'

'Look, there is an inexpensive place called Hot Breads nearby.' Nutty pointed at the map on her phone screen. 'I remember Kale was talking about it. They have some good burgers and pizzas. Let's go there. PLEASE, Billi.'

'Let her satisfy her cravings, or we won't hear the end of it,' urged Lucky.

'Alright! Let me warn you that we have very little money left in the kitty, so no extravagant orders,' warned the accounts-in-charge.

'No extravagant orders, I promise,' Nutty threw a disarming smile at Billi.

It was a satisfied trio that entered the portals of the academy an hour later. By the time the sun began vanishing below the horizon, almost all the first-termers were back at the OTA. The Zojila Company was buzzing like a beehive, with the first-termers on a high. Everyone had a story to share, and an experience to narrate.

Those who had gone home for the break had brought back a lot of food, and soon the aroma of home-made food spilled out of the rooms into the corridors along with loud chatter from the rooms. Overstudies and understudies shared their goodies with each other and their course-mates. Bonhomie and banter was evident everywhere.

That night, no one wanted to hurry to the mess for dinner.

'When is Shiny returning?' Nutty asked. The three of them were lolling on the bed in her room, going through the photographs and videos of their vacation on her phone.

'She's supposed to reach by dinner time,' Lucky informed her friends, and passed a packet of chips around. 'Should we wait for her or proceed for dinner?'

'Let's go for dinner,' Nutty piped up. 'I am feeling hungry.'

'When are you not hungry?' chided Billi.

It was past nine when Shiny returned, excited and loaded with all kinds of goodies. She opened the packages as soon as the gang was back from the mess. Despite the food Nutty had loaded into her stomach, she pounced on the home-baked cake like a starving baboon and the party continued. The girls updated their friend about their adventures in Mahabalipuram.

'I am feeling so jealous. You guys had a rollicking time, while I was at home. Next time, I am joining the three of you,' announced Shiny.

It was past 9.30 p.m., but no one was in the mood to end the celebrations. It was at this time that Shera decided to spring a surprise on the first-termers. The break was over, as far as she was concerned.

Wearing sneakers, so her footsteps couldn't be heard, she stole into the Zojila Company to catch the cadets off guard. She walked into the very first room on the first floor, which happened to be Billi's.

The room was in a total mess. Lucky and Nutty were sprawled on the bed with the latter's legs stretched over the other girl. Shiny was sitting on the table, while Billi was on the floor, loud music playing from her phone. A half-consumed cake, a packet of banana chips and a few *chaklis* lay on one side of the bed.

Major Sherawat was not surprised. This phenomenon repeated itself after every break.

'So, the party is still going on?' Her voice saccharine sweet, Paltu smiled evilly.

As though struck by a bolt of lightning, the girls jumped up and stood guiltily before her. There was pin-drop silence as the officer's eyes moved meaningfully around the room. Billi surreptitiously kicked some scattered stuff under her bed, while Nutty and Lucky tried to hide the food behind their backs. Only Shiny had the presence of mind to pick up the box of cake and offer it to Paltu.

'Please take a piece of the cake, ma'am,' she requested. 'My mother is very good at baking.'

Major Sherawat took a piece and commented, 'It's quite good.' She paused and looked at the beaming Shiny, then continued, 'You should assist her in baking cakes, instead of wasting your time in the academy.'

Shiny's smile shrivelled like a punctured balloon.

A first-termer who was passing through the corridor noticed the sudden silence from Billi's room. She peeped in and noticed Paltu giving gyan to the four girls. In a matter of seconds, news about Pitiless Paltu's presence spread all over the company. Parties that were taking place in every other room, ended immediately, and the girls crept back into their own rooms. There was a hushed silence everywhere.

Paltu glanced at her watch. It was 10 minutes past 10, and 10 minutes past the 'lights out' time. 'Where is the JUO?' she barked.

A couple of minutes later, a very nervous JUO stood before the furious officer.

'Why have the lights not been put off? Get all the first-termers out of their rooms.'

An announcement was made, and the girls lined up before Paltu.

'I want everyone down on their hands,' she shouted, 'Give me 50 and then start rolling down the corridor.'

'Welcome to the gulag,' said a muffled voice, as the girls began rolling.

'With Reichsführer Sherawat in command,' sniggered someone.

It was a disastrous end to an enjoyable vacation.

FIRING WOES

Every few days, a new subject was introduced into the curriculum. This time it was WT (Weapon Training). It was considered the most essential part of army training. This was the real stuff. This is what they had joined the army for – to handle weapons that could kill the enemy in battle.

The cadets were taken through the details of the basic weapons used by the infantry, and at the platoon and section levels. The thought that they would be allowed to handle weapons like 9MM carbines, rifles, and LMGs (Light Machine Guns), excited the LCs.

The girls had to dress in dungarees and wear their web equipment to class. The numerous *putti* parades, during which they had been made to wear all kinds of uniforms, came in handy now. It took them just minutes to don the belt, pouches and backpack. The cadets now realized the benefit of the exercise that they had assumed to be futile punishment.

Standing in front of the mirror, Billi felt a sense of pride coursing through her veins. The training had brought a sense of pride in the profession she had chosen for herself. There had been many moments of uncertainty, but now everything was falling in place. She wished she had a mobile, so she could click a selfie and send it Daddu.

It was easy to imagine his pride at her achievement. She made a mental note to tell him all about the weapon training. He would love that.

'Hey! We are getting late. Hurry up,' shouted Shiny, and the LCs rushed for the fall-in.

Minutes later, they were pedalling in squads towards the class where Ustad Bhairon Singh Rajawat awaited them.

Dressed impeccably in battle dress, the ustad began the mandatory dress inspection. Not a crease in his uniform, he scrutinized their outfits, and a couple of LCs found themselves earning his disapproval.

As usual, the instructor found dozens of faults in their rigs and haircuts, and singled out the offenders for punishment. Nutty ran around the class with a 7.62 SLR (Self Loading Rifle) held high above her head, along with four others who had not polished their buckles to the ustad's satisfaction.

'I wonder what polish has to do with WT,' she complained to her companions as they ran.

'Nonsense cadet, no talking only running,' reprimanded the ustad, who had heard her.

After the dress inspection and punishments, the class began in earnest. The ustad went about his job like a robot, his movements brisk and mechanical. He picked up a rifle, and explained its characteristics before proceeding to the next part of the lesson. Dismantling the rifle, he rattled out the name, location, type and function of each part.

The experienced instructor dismantled the weapon with so much flourish that it seemed like child's play. Slowly and efficiently, he assembled the parts once again, before explaining the process in a reverse order. The ustad knew his job. His explanation was clear and easy to understand.

He repeated the demonstration, this time dismantling the rifle in a couple of seconds. Not once did he glance at the rifle. His hands moved mechanically. It was a feat meant to draw appreciation. Resisting the urge to clap, Nutty concentrated on the ustad's lecture.

'Clear? Can you do it?'

There was no response. The LCs knew that he expected them to repeat the performance, but most of them were not confident. Some of them wanted him to repeat the demonstration. The stern expression on his face discouraged them from asking.

'Ustad, can you show us one more time?' Nutty finally found the courage to ask.

'Were you sleeping? Should I wake you up?

Punishments were an inevitable part of Nutty's life, so she steeled herself for another round of running. But noticing the doubt on several faces, the ustad decided to oblige the cadets with a repeat demo.

'Any more doubts?' he challenged.

The consequences of doubts and questions were known to all the LCs, and no one responded to the challenge.

'Who will dismantle and assemble the rifle?' he bellowed.

There were no volunteers.

As luck would have it, the instructor picked Nutty. After all, she was the one who had asked him to repeat the demonstration.

It was a total fiasco. A very nervous Nutty dropped the firing pin and then the breach block, making the ustad furious. Poor Nutty found herself front rolling, once again.

After a break, the class started once again. It was only when they began the process of dismantling and assembling the parts that the LCs realized the difficulty of the exercise. Soon, quite a few of them were rolling and running around the ground.

Back in their rooms that night, the gang of four was not pleased with their WT lessons.

'We did more muscle-building exercises than learning about rifles,' complained Nutty, massaging her arms. All that running around the class with a rifle held high above her head had taken a toll on her. 'Bhairon Singh is a devil,' she declared.

'It will do you a lot of good,' said Shiny, 'The ustad is strengthening your arms, so you can wring the enemy's neck if the rifle does not work.'

'I will have to report sick if he continues in the same manner. How can you assimilate anything when you are tired and sweating at the beginning of the class?' Nutty pointed out. 'I hope the ustad is posted out.' Almost all ustads would have to be posted out of the academy if she had her way.

The dress inspection and the string of punishments resulted in a marked improvement in the turnout of the LCs. As the days went by, the ustads focused more on lessons and less on punishments.

WT lessons continued, sometimes stretching over three to four periods continuously, till the LCs learnt to handle the dismantling and assembling of the rifles quite efficiently. They were taken through lessons on other infantry basic weapons, and loading, unloading and different firing positions. They were taught the details of firing in lying, sitting and kneeling positions, and were taught both standing with support and without. They were also instructed on aiming and firing the weapons.

In the last lesson before the actual firing, the ustad kept harping on about HAT (Holding, Aiming and Trigger Operation) till the information was coming out of their ears.

'Why is he obsessed with bloody hats?' whispered Nutty, who had not been paying attention.

Her whisper reached the ustad's sharp ears, and she found herself rolling, once again.

Over the next couple of weeks, they were taken through lessons on other basic weapons of the infantry, their characteristics, assembling, dismantling, loading, unloading and firing positions. They were also instructed on drills associated with aiming and firing the weapons. The LCs learnt to react swiftly to the ustad's orders. *Bhar* (Load), and *Khali kar* (Empty), became easy to follow.

Satisfied with their theoretical knowledge and handling of the rifles, Ustad Bumble Bee as Nutty had named Bhairon Singh Rajawat, announced that they were now competent enough to carry out live firing. None of the girls had ever fired an actual rifle, except for two LCs who had been in the NCC. Their excitement knew no bounds when the training programme was put up on the noticeboard. Firing was scheduled to take place at the firing range the next Monday.

Come Monday, and the excited LCs dressed in dungarees, with backpacks and pouches strapped firmly to their uniforms, cycled to the armoury to collect their rifles. In squads of sixes and eights in two rows, they proceeded to the firing range that was across the Adyar River.

The drills for firing the rifles had already been taught in the WT classes, and now they had to be put to practice. Although a couple of WT ustads were at the firing, CoCo and Shera had also decided to grace the occasion with their presence. Written on walls all along the range were slogans. *Shoot to Kill*, read one. *Ek Goli, Ek Dushman* read another, yet another one reminded them of HAT (Holding – Aiming – Trigger Operation), which was Bumble Bee's favourite acronym.

Six square targets, four feet by four feet, had been set up at the base of a mound, and the LCs were to fire at them from a raised platform at a distance of 100 meters. A tent, where live ammunition was kept and used for firing, had also been pitched. A placard in front of it read 'AMMUNITION POINT'. Another tent, a fancier one, had been pitched nearby and was furnished with a couple of chairs and tables with a few files placed on the tables. This was where the CoCo and Shera sat, enjoying a bird's eye view of the proceedings taking place at the ranges.

After the usual dress inspection by the ustads (that morning there were five ustads), CoCo gave them a pep talk to pump up their *josh*. 'How's the *josh*?' he asked in filmy style.

'High, sir!' they shouted in unison.

The first firing squad of six LCs were ordered to line up in front of their targets with their rifles.

'Lying position,' shouted the ustad. Instantly, the girls dived to take up the lying position as taught in the WT classes. Nutty, along with five others, was assigned the job of delivering magazines filled with live bullets to each of the six LCs lying in position.

'*Bhar,*' bellowed the ustad. Aware that CoCo, Paltu and the ustads were watching them, the firers attached the magazines to their rifles and cocked them smartly.

Soon, the Bumble Bee's obsession with HAT became clear.

Crisp and clear, they heard him roar, 'FIRE!' At the ustad's order, the LCs were to fire 10 single shots at their targets.

Moving softly, so as not to disturb the girls' concentration, CoCo and Paltu came over and stood behind the firers. The LCs continued to fire.

Bullets landed all over the mound, and the entire mound at the target end was soon covered in a cloud of dust. The firing continued for a couple of minutes, and then there was silence.

Once the 10 shots had been fired, and the *Khali kar* drill completed, one of the ustads along with the six firers doubled down to the target end to see the result of their efforts. They stood alongside their targets after examining the number of hits. CoCo and Paltu sauntered up to inspect the targets along with an ustad, who carried a pen and pad. They stood for a while in front of Shiny's target, quite pleased with the result. Of the 10 shots, she had managed to hit eight in the inner circle.

Kiran had five hits on the entire target, Meg had managed seven, and Sasha three. Lucky had the lowest score of two. Despite the large target area, it was a dismal performance. The hits were spread all over. None of the hits were on the bull.

It was when CoCo and his entourage reached the last target that their eyes widened with wonder. Cockroach's target displayed 12 hits. The counting was repeated, and the result turned out to be the same. Perplexed, the instructors stared at the target.

Back at the firing point, Paltu marched towards the six LCs of the firing squad. 'How did you manage to hit 12 shots on the target?' she shouted at Cockroach.

The girl looked puzzled. She had been a sergeant in the NCC and a good shot, but 12 hits from 10 bullets seemed surreal.

Nutty, who had doled out the magazine to her, shivered in her boots. 'Bloody hell!' she muttered. 'How the hell did I manage to give 12 bullets to the cockroach?'

CoCo, followed by the ustads, confronted the six girls. 'All of you will report to the MI Room for an eye test. It seems that some of you suffer from a severe squint,' he remarked with a straight face.

It was evident that he was referring to Cockroach's target. It was also evident that he had decoded the mystery of the extra hits.

'I am glad that you LCs are not joining the fighting arms,' he continued rather chauvinistically. 'With you on the battlefield, the enemy will have reasons to rejoice.'

A few LCs had the cheek to giggle, and found themselves rolling.

The secret of the extra hits on Cockroach's target soon became clear. Lucky, who was positioned on Cockroach's left, had managed to shoot her neighbour's target instead of her own. The dust around the target confused her and she had fired at the wrong target.

The ustads took over. They dinned the HAT drill into the ears of the cadets till the words were tumbling out of their ears. Bumble Bee warned of serious consequences if there was no visible improvement in their firing. Although the HAT drill led to some improvement, Lucky continued to draw a blank. Her target remained unblemished.

Dissatisfied by the overall performance, CoCo gave them an earful, but he reserved the most caustic comments for the unfortunate Lucky. 'I will have a bow and arrow issued to you. You could also carry some stones when you go to war.'

'A bit of rolling could have a better effect,' suggested Shera.

As a result, the six LCs did more rolling than firing at the ranges that day. The next squad of firers were summoned to display their firing skills. The result was equally bad. Almost every LC proved her lack of skill that morning.

Visibly disappointed with the result, CoCo walked to the LCs. 'I shall classify your firing results "TOP SECRET" and keep them safe in my custody,' he waved the sheaf of papers in his hand. 'Were Pakistan to get a hold of these firing results, they won't delay launching an attack on us.'

Paltu, who was standing next to him, found it difficult to maintain a straight face and tried to hide her smile. There was a suppressed chortle from one of the LCs.

'You find that amusing?' CoCo barked. There was pin drop silence. And then the rolling began.

Next, CoCo gave a piece of his mind to the ustads. They were not strict enough, he told them. They had failed in their duties.

As they cycled back to the mess, Nutty mimicked CoCo and sent the LCs of her bicycle squad roaring with laughter. Lucky, who was at her shakiest best, laughed the loudest before banging into Nutty. Of the six LCs, four lay on the ground, their bikes under them. They were still laughing as CoCo, who was right behind them, halted his vehicle and jumped out.

'It seems as though you have enjoyed the morning. I want you to reverse.'

The LCs, who had been pedalling towards the mess for lunch, turned the direction of their bicycles towards the firing ranges.

'Don't you understand English?' he barked. 'Instead of sitting on the bikes, I want you to lift your bikes over your heads and run to the mess.' Saying this, he jumped into his vehicle and vanished.

This was by far the most strenuous punishment doled out to the LCs. Ruing the few moments of fun, they sighed and picked up their bikes.

'Bloody CoCo,' Nutty cursed as she jogged with the bike held over her head. Breathing heavily, she continued, 'Is it a crime to laugh?'

Crafty Pursuits

The only time the pace of training slowed was during the hobby class. It was the only place where they remained safe from the clutches of the seniors as well as of the instructors.

Cadets were encouraged to opt for one out of the gamut of hobbies available in the academy. There were a host of outdoor hobbies like parasailing, rock climbing, boating and sailing, riding, shooting, tennis and archery. These were taken by the adventurous ones, who wanted to add another feather to their cap. The lazier ones, who wanted to escape drudgery, could choose from a range of indoor hobbies like creative writing, music and dramatics, et al.

Lucky, who sang and played guitar, opted for music classes, while Shiny and Billi chose to get adventurous by opting for parasailing and martial arts. Billi's reasons were clear. She wanted to equip herself with skills that would take her further in the profession. Shiny had always wanted to experience the joys of parasailing, and this was an opportunity she was not willing to miss.

Although the others in the gang had no difficulty choosing their hobby, Nutty continued to dither. She had no ear for music, nor was she interested in any of the outdoor activities.

'Why don't you opt for dramatics?' suggested Shiny. 'You are a good mimic.'

'Not to forget that you are the resident drama queen of OTA,' smirked Billi.

'Thank you for the suggestion, but I will only opt for a hobby class that has a few good-looking GCs.' Nutty's mind was made up.

'Smart boys are as rare as perfect fitting bras,' Lucky quipped. 'The OTA is no place to hunt for them. With their zero haircut, and tanned skin, all the GCs look the same. Can you tell the difference from one to the other?'

'That's true!' agreed Billi. 'Besides, they look so exhausted. Romance is far from their minds, I am sure.'

'Not just the GCs, we all look alike, too,' retorted Nutty. 'Skinny, tanned and unglamorous in our buzz cuts. I am also exhausted, but I always have romance on my mind. Besides, what about the testorone? They have that running through their bodies, just like we have oserzone.'

'The male hormone is called testosterone, Doughnut, not testorone,' Lucky informed her friend. 'The female hormone is known as oestrogen.'

'Whatever! As I was saying, I will go around the classes and see which one has some smart GCs.' Nutty stuck out her chin in a challenging manner.

'You can't take forever to decide,' Billi issued an ultimatum. 'I have to submit the names and choices to Shera this evening. Everyone, except you, has given their choice.'

'In that case, go ahead and submit the list. I will deal with Shera in my own manner.' Nutty shocked everyone with her reply.

'For heaven's sake, please be rational,' pleaded Lucky. 'Paltu will eat you alive. I suggest that you put your name under music or dramatics. We will see if it can be changed later. That's if you don't like the class.'

It seemed like a reasonable plan. And so, her name was put on the list. The final decision would rest with Paltu, everyone knew. She would ensure that the LCs were evenly distributed in the hobby classes.

On the very first day of her music class, the tone-deaf Nutty managed to break a guitar string by tightening it excessively. Fearing the instructor's wrath, she took to her heels and found refuge in the dramatics class. True to her expectations, the boy-crazy girl found a handful of handsome dudes chatting animatedly. The discussion hinged around a skit they wanted to rehearse.

Not a single LC could be spotted anywhere close to the class. She had no competition. Heaving a sigh of relief, Nutty stepped into the class and all eyes turned towards her. Preening importantly, she strutted in with a smile. The magic lasted for a full three minutes as the GCs made a beeline for her. And then disaster struck as another LC made a grand entry.

She sashayed in with the attitude of a consummate model walking on the ramp. Their mouths hanging, the GCs, who had been flocking around Nutty, stared at the entrant. It was none other than Urvashi, aka Urvi, the ex-beauty queen from Chandigarh. Instantly, the cadets made a beeline towards the beauty queen, their mouths salivating like dogs during a heat wave. Urvi smiled and they became her slaves.

There was no point in trying to challenge the woman's supremacy over the fluttering hearts of her knaves. Nutty knew they wouldn't look at her, even if she were to take off her clothes and do cartwheels before them. No sane woman competes with a beauty queen for male attention. The battle was lost even before it had begun, so she walked into the arts class to lick her wounds.

A lone GC, sitting before a sheet of paper, looked up at her. Bespectacled and puny, he seemed the epitome of a scholarly man. She smiled tentatively, and he responded with a shy smile. It was a perfect situation. No competition, whatsoever. Nutty made an instant decision. She would take up arts for a hobby. It was better to have one admirer than none at all.

The switch from music to dramatics to arts was not difficult, and Nutty began attending the class. The girl had not a single strand of art in her DNA. She couldn't draw to save her life. Determined to impress the GC called Swapan Bose, who was not too artistic either, she worked very hard at drawing a horse.

The two of them got on like a house on fire. He had taken up the hobby due to his mother's insistence. 'You are a Bengali and Bengalis have art in them,' she had ordered. 'The army may be your profession, but art could also be a part of you.' The poor chap had no say in the matter. He was forced to enrol in the OTA because his father wanted him to be an army officer, and now he was drawing trees because his mother wanted him to be an artistic officer.

The art instructor was disappointed that he had only two students and both had not an iota of art in them. He kept them engaged in trees and flowers, while he did his own paintings.

It was Nutty's secret desire to draw horses. Although she had no talent, the girl had been impressed by a painting that was hanging in the anteroom. It was a beautiful one of several horses running in green, undulating fields under a canopy of cerulean sky. Drawing horses was an ambitious project, especially for someone who had no art in her.

The arts instructor suppressed his laughter when she described the painting and her desire to replicate it. Her announcement drew titters from her friends.

'Why don't you start by painting the walls of our rooms? They need a fresh coat of paint,' they mocked her.

Undeterred by their caustic remarks, Nutty decided to go ahead. She studied the painting in the anteroom with great attention, and struggled to copy it on a piece of paper so she could take it to the art class. Instead of the five horses in the original, hers would have two, she decided.

Week after week, she worked in silence, keeping her work secret. She neither asked for the drawing instructor's assistance nor the GC's. GC Bose, in the meanwhile, worked diligently on the trees, his efforts as dismal as those of Nutty's.

While their drawings were not improving, the relationship between the two aspiring artists was definitely on an upswing. They whined about their hardships, exchanged notes on their academic progress, and discussed their parents and parental expectations. They praised each other's creative efforts and offered suggestions to improve each other's drawings. It felt good to be on the same page.

The running horses refused to desert the girl. One evening, she carried the drawing sheet back to her room. 'Take another look at the painting that inspired you to draw horses and try to improve your drawing,' her drawing instructor had ordered.

That night, after dinner, Nutty sat at the study table giving her horses finishing touches. When she didn't make an appearance in Lucky's room, the gang guessed she was unwell and decided to check on her. They were surprised to find her engrossed in her project.

'Nice drawing,' complimented Lucky. 'You have still to draw horns on the cows.' She pointed out.

'My dear, they are horses.' Nutty snorted with annoyance.

Just then, Billi walked into the room. 'Wow! What a nice set of dogs. Don't you think they are a bit too big in size?'

An exasperated Nutty was about to retort, when Shiny walked in. 'What's going on?' she asked.

'Ok, let's ask Shiny,' suggested the artist in the gang. She was peeved at her horses being called cows and dogs. 'Which animal do you think I have drawn?'

Shiny walked to the table and had a long look at the animals drawn on the paper, 'They are goats, I think.'

Billi and Lucky burst out laughing, while Nutty looked extremely annoyed. 'You call yourselves my friends? You are bloody traitors,' she declared. 'I will never again show my drawings to you.'

'Don't get angry, dear Doughnut,' soothed Lucky, suppressing a smile. 'We know nothing about art. We wouldn't know the difference if we were shown an M.F. Husain, S.H. Raza or a Jamini Roy.'

'Who knows, your horses may land up fetching a higher price than the M.F. Husain's horses,' smirked Shiny. 'The costliest paintings are the ones people don't understand.'

'Nutty's painting may win a prize, for all you know,' said Lucky, smiling.

No one could dream that her words would come true.

With just two paintings to show for the term, the drawing instructor was at his wit's end. While the LC's horses were a pathetic lot, the trees drawn by the GC were worse. After much deliberation, he decided to save face by working on the horses. Soon, the unidentifiable creatures took a definite shape and came to life under his brush. The final version looked nothing like the one Nutty had painted.

When the two paintings were exhibited, the observers were unanimous in the view that the LC's horses were as good as those of M.F. Husain's, and the painting deserved a prize.

Nutty had the last laugh.

SWEET REVENGE

'An eye for an eye leaves everybody blind,' said Mahatma Gandhi. That's old hat. Not many can swallow that philosophy, since there aren't any mahatmas remaining in the world today. Besides, revenge is too sweet to ignore. And so it was with Nutty.

She had been the butt of many jokes ever since the morning when the four LCs were on their way to the beauty parlour and were sent in the wrong direction by a mischievous GC. He had quickly become Nutty's enemy number one, with memories of the humiliation she had suffered buried in the small vault of her heart. Not one to forgive easily, she was bent upon getting her pound of flesh. Fortunately for all concerned, the guy hadn't crossed their paths in the past few months.

The universe, however, operates on a theory of natural justice. It provides ways and means of getting even. That's the only explanation one could assign to the events that took place on that fateful day.

The gang of four had successfully passed their DSTs and had earned liberty passes. After months of waiting, they were free to enjoy their day, without the fear of punishments and restrictions. Taking extra care over their make-up, they took off for the city. Although they were togged in muftis, and the non-existence of lush hair was a setback, the four friends were determined to wring every drop of joy from the day.

They sat right in the front of the coach that was ferrying the cadets to the city, wolfing down packets of wafers. They prattled continuously throughout the ride. For once, Nutty was not interested in wasting time over the GCs seated at the back of the bus. On her agenda was the latest movie and a feast fit for royalty.

Shiny was craving sizzlers, Nutty wanted Japanese and Billi insisted on wholesome Punjabi food. Lucky was the only one without preferences, other than that the food should be different from the food at Yoddha Cadets' Mess.

Since they were determined on restricting themselves to the Phoenix Market City, the options were clear.

'Punjabi food is served almost every second day in the mess,' Shiny tried to deter Billi from demanding *chhole bhature* and *rajma chawal*. 'We can try that the next time. We are never served sizzlers or pan-Asian food in the mess, so why not those?'

'Hey! Punjabi food is not just *chhole bhature* and *rajma chawal*,' protested the Haryanvi lass, whose choices were rather limited to stuffed parathas or *chhole* and *rajma*. 'I want to try out mutton *mughlai* or *karahi* chicken.'

'You seem to have forgotten that *karahi* chicken was served in the mess on Wednesday,' Lucky reminded her friend.

'Mess cooks can't cook Punjabi food,' Billi scoffed. 'It's a mish-mash of their limited creativity. You have to be in Delhi or Punjab to know the taste of authentic Punjabi dishes.'

'We will skip Punjabi food this time,' Nutty vetoed. 'Let's look for sizzlers.'

'I second the idea,' Lucky piped up. She hadn't developed a taste for the rich gravies of the Punjabi dishes served in the mess.

'I third it,' said Shiny, who had been the principal proposer of the idea. 'We could also look at pan-Asian stuff.'

The ensuing online search threw up a few options, and after a toss-up between Kobe Sizzler and Mamagato, the four of them finally agreed to try out the fare at Mamagato.

Once they arrived at the mall, the cadets branched off in different directions.

The gang of four were studying the layout of the mall, when Nutty's eyes fell on a GC standing near a bookstore.

'Let's go to the ladies washroom,' she nudged the others.

'You go ahead. We will wait here,' said Billi, who was still seething about their food choices.

'Alright! I will be back in a few minutes,' said Nutty, rushing off in the opposite direction.

Having located the stores they wanted to visit, the three girls were waiting for their friend, when they noticed a very pretty girl. Clad in a figure-hugging, electric blue dress, she bounced towards them, her thick curls tossing around with each step. Her appearance attracted the eyeballs of a few GCs, and one of them even whistled.

Unperturbed by their attention, the girl waved and smiled cheerfully at the lot.

'Hi!' the girl tapped Lucky on her shoulder. 'Are you girls from the OTA?'

'Isn't it obvious?' growled Billi, running a hand over her stubbly scalp.

'I wanted to join the academy, but my parents didn't agree.'

'Thank God!' muttered Shiny.

'It's lucky they didn't agree,' responded Billi scathingly. 'You wouldn't have fit into the academy culture.'

'What makes you say that?' the girl wanted to know. Her voice was tinged with indignation.

'The academy is very different from what most people think,' Lucky explained. Something about the girl disturbed her. Her pouting, brightly painted lips, kohl-lined eyes, and voice seemed familiar. 'I have seen you somewhere,' she said, after scrutinizing the girl's face.

'You might have,' came the flippant reply. 'I am a model. Quite a few magazines have carried my picture on their covers.'

'No wonder,' Shiny commented drily.

'Wait!' Lucky exclaimed. 'I know who you are.'

Shaking with laughter, she caught hold of the girl's arm and ordered her friends, 'Look at her carefully. Can't you recognize her?'

'Nutty!' Billi shouted. 'Bloody hell! I just didn't recognize you.'

'I knew there was something familiar about her,' Lucky smiled triumphantly. 'It took me a while because she looked so different.'

'It's the setting. When one doesn't expect to see a person in a particular setting, even the slightest change in hairstyle, makeup or outfit can make them difficult to recognize,' Shiny expounded.

'All that is fine, but why are you dressed like this?' asked Lucky, her eyes settling on Nutty's hair. 'Is that a wig?'

'To reply to your questions, yes this is a wig. I wanted to try out my disguise on you guys. It's evident that you didn't recognize me. If you can't recognize me, nor can others.'

'Why wouldn't you want others to recognize you?'

'I have spotted the GC who played a prank on us the day we were hunting for the beauty parlour. I have wanted to pay him back for it, and now is the time to do so. Here's what I will do.'

She went on to outline her plan to the three girls. 'I will lead him to Mamagoto. You will enter the place after about 15 minutes. It's 11 a.m., so be there at 11.15 a.m. to catch the action.'

'Listen, I don't think...'

'Don't think, just be there,' Nutty interrupted Lucky.

Air kissing her stumped friends, she sashayed towards the spot where she had spotted the GC. She positioned herself a few feet away and began tapping her foot impatiently.

'Hi handsome!' Nutty addressed the gobsmacked fellow after a couple of minutes. 'Are you from the OTA?'

The chap straightened himself and preened. 'Yes, I am.'

'So, you will soon be an officer. I have always been fascinated by army officers. There's something very different about them. Unlike the other men, they are smart, courteous and loyal.'

He preened a bit more and smiled warmly. 'That's true!'

'I am Sue, short for Sunanda,' Nutty introduced herself.

'I am GC Karan Kapoor.'

'It's such a pleasure to meet a gentleman,' she batted her mascara-ed eyelashes at him. 'By the way, are you waiting for someone?'

'My friends are inside the bookshop,' he looked anxiously in the direction of the store.

'Aren't you interested in books?'

'I am, but not that much. Besides, where is the time to read? We have such a gruelling routine.'

'I think my boyfriend has stood me up,' she took one look at her wristwatch and sighed. 'He was supposed to be here an hour ago.'

'That's no way to behave with a lady. It's absolutely unacceptable,' remarked GC Kapoor.

'Now you know why I admire army officers. An officer would never have done something like this.'

'Never!'

'Now I will have to cancel my plans of watching a movie and having a nice meal.'

The GC looked to be full of sympathy.

'I had already bought two tickets for the movie, and now they will go to waste,' Nutty drew a deep breath. She pretended to think for a minute, before snapping her fingers excitedly, 'I have a plan. Why don't you come with me for the movie? In exchange, you could pay for lunch.'

Kapoor hesitated. Should he accept her offer? Sue was an attractive girl. The girl's offer of a movie held many promises. Not just the movie, she planned to share a meal with him. Who knew, the incident could even become a precursor to romance. His imagination ran riot.

Will he or won't he bite the bait! Nutty's heart raced. The guy wasn't bad looking. If only he hadn't crossed her path and got into her bad books. She sighed.

'I will be delighted,' he responded with a dazzling smile. He would have to inform his pals before the girl led him away, Kapoor realized. 'You will have to wait here for a moment, while I run up to my friends and excuse myself.'

'That's no issue.'

'Don't disappear,' he requested.

'I won't.'

The GC ran to the bookshop and informed the others about the change in his plans.

'What's cooking?' asked one of them.

'Nothing! I have to rush back to the academy. Someone is coming to meet me there,' he lied.

Kapoor didn't want the whole horde following him into the theatre. He didn't want competition.

He raced back to Nutty, half expecting her to have vanished like a dream. But she was there, waiting for him. Heaving a sigh of relief, he took her arm and led her towards the escalator. 'Let's go,' he said.

'We have some time before the movie begins. Shall we have something to eat, first?' She smiled innocently. 'I didn't have breakfast this morning.'

'Sure!' He was willing to travel to the end of the world if she wanted him to do so.

'Have you been to Mamagoto? They serve delicious food.'

The GC had no idea about Mamagoto or any other restaurant. It was his first time at the mall. Having checked the location of the restaurant on the location map, Nutty knew exactly where it was. Confidently, she led Kapoor to the place.

Finding a corner table, she began scanning the menu and so did her companion. Everything was exorbitantly priced. Suppressing a chuckle, she summoned a waiter and ordered tom yum soup and spiced Asian barbecued chicken breast.

Kapoor's eyes widened as he looked at the price of the dishes ordered by the girl. His mental calculator began toting up the price and tallying it up with the contents of his wallet. He could just about manage the bill, if he didn't leave a tip for the waiter.

'What will you have?' He came down to earth with a bang at the girl's question.

'I…I had a large breakfast. I am not hungry,' he croaked.

'You could share the dessert with me,' she prodded. 'I am watching my weight, so it will keep me from stuffing myself.' She went ahead and ordered Mama's chocolate brownie.

Kapoor broke into a sweat. The girl was going overboard.

'I wanted to join the OTA,' Nutty toyed with a fork. 'Unfortunately, my parents didn't agree.'

'Oh!'

'I have a few friends there. Lady Cadets. It's been some time since I met them. In fact, I am planning to visit the academy next weekend.'

'Really!' Distracted, he managed a weak smile.

'Is something the matter?' the girl asked.

'No, no. I am alright.'

'You have suddenly turned very quiet, so I was wondering…'

'Sorry, I was a bit distracted.' What the hell! If he was to spend money, he might as well make the best of the situation, Kapoor decided.

Just then, he saw three LCs entering the restaurant. Nutty, who had her back towards the entrance, missed the entry of her friends.

Kapoor was surprised to see the LCs making a beeline towards their table. They halted behind his companion, and one of them thumped her on the shoulder.

'Hi Sue! Imagine bumping into you here,' said Lucky.

'Hey Lucky! What a surprise! I was telling GC Karan about the three of you, and you are here.' After introducing the LCs to Kapoor, she asked, 'Do you mind if they join us?'

'It will be a pleasure,' he bleated, breaking into a sweat.

'What will you girls have?' asked Nutty, passing the menu around.

'I will have some sushi, and asparagus tempura,' Lucky decided.

'I like their grilled fish,' Shiny tapped the item on the menu card.

'How about chicken katsu and shrimp with dried chilli for you?' Nutty asked Billi. The girl had been looking doubtfully at the menu. Having never encountered any of the dishes on it, she was finding it difficult to decide.

Kapoor was at his wit's end. His mental calculator quickly processed the total amount that would have to be paid. There was no way he could afford the bill. Running away was not an option. The LCs knew his name and company. Word would travel in the academy, and he would never hear the end of it. Being a gentleman, he couldn't ask them to pay for the meal. So, the only thing was to borrow some money from his friends.

'I will make a quick call while you ladies order,' he said, making his way towards the exit.

Once out of hearing, he called the other GCs. Five minutes later, he stood before them. 'I want some cash,' he said.

'You were supposed to have gone back to the academy to meet someone,' said his friend.

'Well, I didn't. Look guys, I am in trouble and need some cash quickly.'

'What happened?'

'It's a long story. I will get back in 10 minutes and tell you everything.'

No questions were asked. Camaraderie came to the fore. Their pal was in trouble and needed cash. They managed to cobble together the princely sum of Rs 3,500, which would cover the bill and leave some over.

His wallet loaded, Kapoor ran back to the restaurant. The table was already heaving under the weight of the orders placed by the LCs. They had not ordered any dessert, he noticed thankfully.

Apologizing, he occupied his seat, the smile back on his face.

'You must have something,' insisted the LCs, who had guessed his predicament.

'Not this time,' he said, picking up a piece of tempura from Lucky's plate. 'I will have to leave you now.'

'Oh no!' exclaimed Nutty. 'Why?'

'My friend from the OTA called just now. I have a visitor, he informed me.'

'Won't you leave your phone number, at least?'

Kapoor gave her a number, alright. But it was not his number. After that, he called the waiter and paid the amount, before rushing out of the restaurant.

The gang of four burst into laughter. For Nutty, it was the sweetest revenge ever. Sweeter than the chocolate brownie she had ordered.

The DLTGH (Days Left to go Home) were steadily decreasing, and now they were down to single digits. With each day being struck off, the excitement grew. For the seniors, the camps and final tests were over. They would be commissioned after the POP. As for the first-termers, their final tests over, excitement was building up because they were going to be seniors after the term break. Those who had done well were eagerly waiting for the appointments to be announced.

Counting Days

Marking DLTGH (Days Left to Go Home) was an obsession for all the cadets. Their dreams soared in inverse proportion to the days left for the four-week-long break.

While most of the LCs looked forward to the break, there were some like Billi who were apprehensive about going home. Aware that Banwari and her mother would spare no effort at renewing talks of the wedding, she dreaded the vacation. The only thing that could take her mind off her looming troubles was home-cooked food. It had been a long time since she had had home-cooked *sarson ka saag* and *makke ki roti* or *rajma chawal*.

For Lucky, the mere thought of a family reunion was an exciting one. Shillong was a green paradise compared to sweltering Chennai. With luck, she would meet her mentor and narrate stories of the academy. Her mother had sent her a list of things she wanted from Chennai, with Madras sambar powder topping it. The last liberty had been spent shopping, and many of the cadets had bought things to carry home.

Finally, it was time to go home.

The thought of parting from friends made their hearts heavy. In the past few months, the cadets had become family, and the academy had become their home. The bond they shared went beyond the uniform and routine they shared. The roots of their ties were deep and strong. Their ties had been watered with sweat and blood. It was a sisterhood nurtured by the common experience of being pulverized and reshaped, and being baptized by fire.

'I will miss you,' said Shiny, hugging her friends. Eyes moist, they took off for their destinations.

Four weeks later, they returned, eager and ready to face every obstacle in their path. They were now seniors. The stay at home had been a balm to their exhausted bodies, and home-cooked food a comfort to their starving souls. Not long after reaching home, the cadets realized that they missed the routine and the hardship that proved to be a constant challenge. Surprised, they realized how much they missed their friends and the academy. The days when they wanted to run away from training were long past.

Since they were appointments, Shiny and Billi were the first to arrive at the academy. Billi had not been appointed as a CSM, as she had desired. She had been appointed SUO (Senior Under Officer). The post of CSM had gone to her friend, Shiny, leaving Cockroach to wear the tabs of a JUO (Junior Under Officer). Cockroach was furious, of course.

With power came responsibility. Gone were the days of reckless acts and mischief. The two would now have to lead a disciplined life and enforce it on others, since the direction of the company now lay on their shoulders. They had to lead by example.

Save for the appointment holders, no one had arrived. Even the first-termers were expected to arrive the next day.

The rest of the second-termers would begin trickling in soon after. At the moment, the company looked haunted.

Before going for the term break, the first-termers had to bring down their possessions – and vacate the rooms they occupied. Those rooms, after being cleaned and fumigated, now housed the first-termers. The second- termers had been allocated rooms that had once belonged to their seniors. The girls helped each other carry their boxes to the rooms.

'You have put on weight,' commented Billi, holding her friend at an arm's distance.

'I wholeheartedly return the compliment, dear. You are carrying the baggage of extra kilos on you,' giggled Shiny.

'It's the result of all the laddoos I ate. My mother almost fainted when she saw my buzz cut. Her first comment, after she got over the shock, was "Don't they feed you?" This was followed by a comment about how my skin has become so dark. Worried no one would marry me, she proceeded to plump me up. She also smeared my face with home-made fairness potions and lotions every single day.'

'No wonder you look more like a human being than a starving chimpanzee. I hope you brought some laddoos for me.'

'Of course, I have brought back a box of them for the three of you.'

The two girls walked towards the rooms they had vacated, footsteps echoing in the deserted corridor.

'I miss this room. It holds so many memories,' Billi stared pensively at the room in which she had spent several months.

'True! We have shed tears of frustration and joy, shared unforgettable incidents, and held innumerable meetings in these rooms,' agreed Shiny.

'It's nice to be back,' Billi sighed. Although she had anticipated that Banwari would pester her a lot back home, it hadn't been so bad. They had had a showdown, and she had categorically told him that he should abandon all hopes of marrying her. He had ranted for a while, but she stood firm in her resolve. As for her mother, one look at the tanned and skinny girl, and the poor woman had dumped all hopes of Billi's marriage. 'Forget marrying, no man will look at you,' she had said. 'Not only do you walk and behave like a man, you look like one too.'

And that had been the end of the matter.

Daddu had landed up the very next day after Billi had arrived to support her against her father, who seemed very disappointed to find that his daughter wasn't carrying the Sword in her bag. It took a while for him to understand that the Sword would be given during the POP. A couple of days into the vacation, the family had gathered around to hear the umpteen stories of her days at the academy.

Shiny had returned with an engagement ring on her finger. 'Tell me all about it,' pleaded Billi, as they sat enjoying the laddoos. She was keen on knowing about the engagement ceremony.

'Later,' Shiny replied. 'I will narrate everything when Lucky and Nutty are back.'

The two other girls, who held no appointment, were expected to arrive after three days.

Although the first-termers had yet to arrive, life for the appointment holders had already revved up. CoCo and the *paltus* briefed the appointments and handed them the schedule for the juniors. They were cautioned to handle the newcomers with care in the initial days, and not to rough them up the very first day. The toughening up was to be carried out in a slow and gradual manner.

'You have a tough job,' said Shiny. Billi had been busy making copious notes after dinner. 'Let me know if you need any help.'

'Thanks, but this is something I have to do,' said Billi. 'The *jungoos* will be arriving tomorrow and I have a lot to do before they come.'

Shiny lay on the bed reading a book Aaron had gifted her. She burst into laughter at regular intervals. At one stage she almost fell off the bed, unable to control her fits of laughter.

'Hello! What are you reading?' Billi asked, glancing at the cover. '*Boots Belts Berets,*' she read out the name. 'It must be rather funny to make you laugh so much. What is it about?'

'It's a book about the life of four cadets at the NDA, written in a hilarious manner. Funnily, one of the characters called Maachh reminds me of Nutty. His mischievous antics are legendary. You must read this one.'

'No, thank you,' said Billi, who never read anything other than prescribed books. She found it funny that a book could make anyone laugh. 'Give it to Lucky. She is likely to enjoy it.'

The next day started off smoothly. After an early breakfast, the two girls went for a haircut and set their rooms. The first batch of GCs and LCs arrived at around 11 a.m., forcing them to get busy. Rooms were allotted, a few sermons issued, and then the *jungoos* were sent running for their haircut. There was still a lot of documentation to be completed.

Quite a few of the *jungoos* of the Zojila Company had arrived that morning. Shiny, who was reluctant to tear herself from her book, ordered them to report to her after lunch. She was intent on finishing the book before doling out strengthening exercises to the juniors.

At the mess, the first-termers from Zojila Company were surprised to see their counterparts from other companies. Unlike Shiny, the CSMs of other companies had not been kind to the first-termers. LCs from Phillora Company were drenched in perspiration, their dresses crumpled and dirty. There was a dazed look on their faces.

The cheerful *jungoos* from Zojila Company presented a contrasting picture. 'Were you not punished?' asked the Phillora Company girls. 'Our CSM is a sadist,' they reported.

The first-termers of Zojila Company thanked their stars. They must have done some good deeds to deserve such a good CSM.

The *paltu*, who was the duty officer, also noticed the difference when she visited the mess during lunchtime. *The CSM of Zojila Company is not doing her job,* she mused. *I will have to appoint a different LC as the CSM.*

After lunch, the Zojila first-termers returned to the company, only to be told to assemble in front of their CSM's room. Shiny, who was on the last chapter, decided to finish the last few pages before dealing with them.

Fear and apprehension flew out of the building and the *jungoos* began talking. Their conversation began in low volumes, but soon got louder. The CSM, in the meanwhile, having reached a funny episode, was laughing. Disturbed by the noise outside her room, smile still in place, she peeped out and told them to be silent.

'Our CSM is an angel,' said a first-termer. 'She has a sweet and smiling face.'

'We are truly lucky to have her as a CSM,' said another.

'Did you see the condition of the other LCs and GCs? Their CSMs must be devils.'

At that very moment, Shiny, who had finished reading her book, emerged from the room. Her smiling face had transformed into one like thunder.

'Do you think this is a fish market?' Shiny pounced at them. 'Can't you understand simple English? I had asked you to maintain silence. What's so funny? Why are you grinning like a Cheshire cat?' she roared.

Nonplussed, the first-termers stared at the CSM, who had changed from an angel to a devil.

'And you, what's wrong with you? Can't you stand straight, why are you dancing, is there an ant in your pants?'

There was utter silence as the girls realized what they were up against.

'Not an iota of discipline in you. Start rolling down the corridor,' Shiny bellowed.

Front rolling carried on for 10 minutes. It was followed by sit-ups for the next 10 minutes, and then piggy back running. In less than half an hour, the sweating *jungoos* came to realize that their condition was no better than their counterparts in the other companies.

The angel turned out to be a true devil. Just then, intent on finding out why the LCs of Zojila Company had escaped strengthening exercises, Paltu made her appearance.

Shiny, who was lolling near the end of the corridor, met the officer.

'Where are the first-termers?' demanded Paltu.

'They are all here, ma'am,' said Shiny.

'I mean the ones who were having lunch in the mess,' Paltu raised her voice. The sweating and dishevelled LCs looked nothing like the neat and well-dressed ones she had seen in the mess. These were looking as though they had just emerged from a deadly typhoon.

'These are the same LCs, ma'am,' explained Shiny. 'I made them do some strengthening exercises.'

Satisfied, Paltu smiled and patted her on the shoulder saying, 'Carry on the good work.'

Nutty Goes Missing

There was hubbub in the corridors as soon as the second-termers returned from their break. The party continued till lights out. Stories of the break were shared, as were the goodies everyone had brought back. The presence of the newcomers made them realize that they were seniors now. No longer would they have to bear the brunt of the punishment of their seniors. Instead, they had the first-termers to rag. They had been given the rooms their seniors had once occupied. It was strangely moving to find their overstudies gone. Never had the girls imagined that they would miss the seniors who had bullied and punished them.

It was almost dinner time, but Lucky and Nutty had yet to arrive.

'Wasn't Lucky's flight scheduled to land at four in the evening? She should have reached the academy by five,' said Shiny.

'Her flight might be delayed. Flights as well as trains from the North East are infamous for delays.'

'I tried to call but her mobile is switched off. I had checked the flight status. Her flight landed at 6 p.m. I am sure she missed the flight.'

'Well! As a Senior Under Officer, I will have to tick her off. She has to be more careful of her conduct,' quipped Billi, who took her duties seriously.

It was while the two girls were returning from the mess after dinner, that a cab came to a screeching halt near them, and Lucky jumped out. She looked pretty, decked in figure-hugging jeans, and a T-shirt, her eyes sparkling. The girls hugged each other like long lost friends.

'Where were you?' asked Shiny. 'Your flight landed hours ago. We thought you missed the flight.'

'I met someone at the airport,' Lucky replied flippantly. 'We chatted for a while and then had dinner.'

'Is it someone special?' teased Billi.

'Don't let your imagination fly. It's a friend's brother. He's working for a multinational company here in Chennai.'

'So, the two of you flew together?' asked Shiny.

'No, we didn't. He was returning from a business trip to Mumbai. The two of us met near the exit.'

'Will you be seeing each other more often, now that you are both in the same city?' Billi wanted to know.

'I don't think so. Just for your information, he's not my boyfriend. We know each other, and that's all,' Lucky responded tetchily. 'You guys are so silly. You forgot, Nutty is the romance queen.'

'Speaking of Nutty, wasn't she supposed to arrive by the afternoon?' Billi asked, helping Lucky with some of her bags. 'What are you carrying in your bag?' she asked her friend. 'It weighs a ton.'

'Guess?' Lucky smiled, as the three of them walked towards her room.

'Nutty is the most irresponsible person I have ever met,' responded Shiny. 'She's not learnt her lessons, yet.'

'Now that you are the CSM, she has no reason to fear,' Lucky chuckled. The girls dumped the bags on the floor and flopped onto the bed.

'I will not hesitate to punish her. In the meanwhile, I have to deal with a couple of *jungoos*.' Shiny walked to the door.

'Well, I have a lot of work to do. There are so many things I want to tell you guys, but unpacking, setting up the room and then preparing uniforms will take a long time. Shiny, please send a *jungoo* to help me,' Lucky's voice followed Shiny.

'I will be back after an hour,' said Billi, getting up to leave. 'In the meantime, you can finish your chores.'

A few minutes later, a nervous *jungoo* stood at Lucky's door.

Lucky subjected the girl to severe scrutiny before ordering her to unpack. Shiny had chosen well. The first-termer, Harleen aka Harry, was an obedient and efficient worker. Working together, the two of them quickly put everything in order.

'Anything else, ma'am?' Harry asked after they finished tidying the room.

'That will be all,' Lucky smiled at the anxious girl. She presented her with a huge bar of chocolate.

It was past 10 p.m. when the lights out announcement was made, and Shiny and Billi returned to Lucky's room. There was no news of Nutty.

'She'll buy it this time. Carrying things beyond a limit have consequences. The term begins tomorrow, and she's not reached the academy. I see no reason for the delay,' Billi remarked.

'Absolutely true! Neither Paltu nor CoCo will forgive her this time,' said Shiny. 'As a senior, she should behave in a more responsible manner.'

'Let's not worry about what will happen.' Lucky remarked in her usual unflappable way. '*Que sera sera*, whatever will be, will be,' she hummed under her breath, before remarking, 'The night is still young. Our happy-go-lucky friend has a few hours to get back. In the meantime, let's share snippets of our vacation.'

'Yes, let's do that,' agreed Billi. 'I asked Shiny to share interesting bits about her engagement, but she refused to do so till Nutty and you had returned to the academy.'

'You got engaged to Aaron?' Lucky squealed. 'Hearty congratulations!' She jumped from the bed and hugged Shiny, who was sitting on the study table. 'It's so beautiful,' she remarked, inspecting the ring on her friend's finger. It was a band of gold with a five tiny diamonds studded into it.

'Thank you, Lucky.'

'Are you supposed to be wearing a ring?' Billi asked. 'LCs are not allowed to wear any jewellery.'

'You are right. I just wore it to show you guys,' said Shiny, removing the ring. 'I will take it off right now, so I don't forget.'

They spoke about their vacations. Billi shared the story of her encounter with Banwari, and Lucky narrated a few funny incidents that happened in Shillong.

It was past midnight when they broke off. But Nutty hadn't arrived.

She stole into the company at 5 a.m., just after the main gate had been unlocked.

The CSM's Woes

The post of CSM was much coveted by the cadets. The CSM was a powerful and important person, who was expected to accompany the officers on their rounds, keep the first-termers on their toes and maintain strict discipline. Right from Billi to Cockroach to Nutty, everyone wanted to be the CSM. For Shiny, it was proving to be a big headache, since it added a lot of unpleasant chores to her busy schedule, allowing her little time for her studies.

'We are now a gang of three,' remarked Lucky, when the gang of four gathered one night. Turning to Shiny, she said, 'What with you making only guest appearances, once in a while.'

'I am quite fed up of being the CSM. I would rather be the JUO like Cockroach,' countered Shiny. 'It's a much more comfortable appointment.'

'I wouldn't have minded being the bloody CSM,' Nutty piped up. 'CoCo and Paltu have not realized my potential. I can be very effective in that post.'

'We will convey your thoughts to CoCo,' Shiny tittered. 'For all you know, they may consider replacing me.'

'That will be a day,' Billi rolled her eyes. 'I can't imagine what will happen to the company if Nutty were to become the CSM.'

Ignoring her remark, Shiny continued, 'The *jungoos* are such dopes. One of them addressed CoCo as "Uncle".'

'What?' Lucky was aghast. 'I can imagine what happened thereafter.'

'He lost his cool and told me to look for an aunty. I found it difficult to control my laughter. Not just that, he chided me for being too lenient and asked me to deal with the *jungoo*,' Shiny laughed.

'It's true!' commented Lucky. 'You are too lenient with them. Do you want me to handle this?' Just hand them over to me and see what I do to the stupid *jungoos*. I can start tonight if you want…'

'Thanks a ton! They are all yours,' said Shiny, heaving a sigh of relief. Exhausted by the tasks she was expected to perform as a CSM, she was happy to have some help. 'You can start right away,' she added.

Carrying her packet of wafers, Lucky vanished from the room. The next minute, her friends heard an announcement, which resulted in the sound of scurrying feet as the first-termers ran down the steps for a fall-in.

It was 11 p.m.

The *jungoos* were surprised to see Lucky instead of their CSM. Their surprise quickly turned into pleasure to find that a petite and smiling senior stood before them.

She waited patiently for the first-termers to shuffle into a line.

'Everybody here?' Lucky asked.

'Yes ma'am,' came the reply.

The *jungoos* smiled at Lucky, quite sure that the fall-in was not for punishments, but for a friendly chat. Their faces lit up with expectant smiles as the wafer-munching

Lucky smiled and announced that she was going to teach them a couple of new games. Some of them were excited enough to clap their hands, while others beamed happily.

'You will have to play it in pairs. So, choose your partners and stand together,' explained Lucky with a beguiling smile.

Excited, the first-termers quickly chose their partners and stood waiting for the next step.

'The first race will be a piggyback race.'

The *jungoos* looked puzzled. This was not a game they had expected to play so late at night.

Snapping her fingers, Lucky called two *jungoos* and asked them demonstrate the piggyback position and made them run along the corridor.

'I will be timing you to see which pair comes first,'
declared Lucky.

The first-termers who had been saddled with heavy partners were soon panting and lagging behind those with lighter burdens on their backs.

'Let's give them a big hand,' Lucky suggested after the race. Her words were followed by applause for the winning pair. The applause drew the attention of the seniors, and some of them joined Lucky to watch the fun.

Once the first lot of pairs had finished, she reversed the pair and the piggyback race continued. Their smiles now wiped away, the panting *jungoos* were wishing the CSM would take over.

'Next game,' Lucky announced. 'You will now play the game of wheelbarrow. Let's see which pair comes first in this one.'

She ordered two first-termers to demonstrate the wheelbarrow position and followed it up with a race. It was a tough act, with one LC balancing herself with her hands on the ground, while the other held her legs and pushed her forward.

The exhausted first-termers requested for some time to practice the game. The request was readily granted by Lucky.

A few minutes later, the game of wheelbarrow began once again. By this time, the *jungoos* were sweating and cursing under their breath. The exhausted girls pleaded for a break, but Lucky was in no mood to oblige. After three rounds of practice, the wheelbarrow competition commenced once again.

One of the wheelbarrows collapsed as the pair could not synchronize their movements. Another LC sat panting on the floor as her partner, who had twisted her ankle, lay groaning nearby.

It was time for a lecture, Lucky decided. She had not delivered any till date, but this was the time to begin. After having made them fall-in again, she stood in front of the first-termers with her hands on her hips. It was a replica of the Reichsführer's pose during the sermons Lucky had been privy to.

'When the going gets tough, only the tough get going.' Lucky began rattling out what she had heard her seniors say in her first term, imitating the same mannerisms and passion.

'*Jo dar gaya, so mar gaya*,' she began. Words began pouring out of her mouth, and she spoke like a seasoned orator. Patting herself mentally, she continued, 'The army is not just a profession. It is a commitment for life. You have to lead tough and rough men, and if you are not better than them, you have no right to lead them.' Lucky was in her element. She believed in every word that she uttered.

'I want each of you to give your best, not just in the academy but in whatever you do. These are not punishments as some of you may assume. They are exercises that will toughen your body and mind. They are known as strengthening exercises. We shall now begin our next set of exercises, which is known as *putti* parade. You have one minute to change into your games dresses. Scoot,' she shouted.

The girls now knew that the senior meant business. They vanished in a trice. One by one they began trickling in after two minutes.

'Your standards are very poor,' Lucky scolded. 'Your timings are poorer than the poorest and you need a lot of practice. Combat dress. One minute.'

The *putti* parade continued for a long time. It was interspersed with a heavy dose of front rolling. It was at 2.30 a.m. that Lucky finally let them free.

The regular fall-in at 4.00 a.m. in front of the CSM's room found six first-termers missing, three wanted to report sick, and three wanted to go back home.

TACTICS

Some of the classes were fun. Conducted by Directing Staff (DS), as the instructors are known, they provided the much required chance to catch up on sleep, and the LCs looked forward to them. Most of them had learnt the art of sleeping with their eyes open, and never missed an opportunity to use the theory classes for a nap.

That day, the theory class was on tactics. Colonel Deepak Dhar was the instructor. The DS was a handsome man with an impressive personality.

Unlike in other classes, the LCs remained wide awake when he spoke. Goggle-eyed, they soaked in the words raining from his mouth. Such a good-looking person can't be too strict, was the general consensus. It was not an accurate analysis, they were to realize quite soon.

'India has a border that runs through different kinds of terrain. The armed forces are its guardians. The army has to defend the borders, therefore we have to take up defences along the border, and when required, carry out attacks, raids across the border and even lay ambush. Right from the plains to mountains and deserts, we have them all. These operations are termed as "Ops of War".

'Today we shall discuss defence in the plains,' lectured the instructor. All the LCs nodded their heads devotedly.

Nutty, who was sitting in the second row, let out a deep sigh. 'I must report sick tomorrow,' she muttered. 'My bloody heart is beating too fast.'

'Perhaps you suffer from hypertension,' suggested Lucky.

A piece of chalk landed on Nutty's head. 'LC Patil, start rolling,' thundered Colonel Dhar. 'You can take your neighbour with you for company.' He had been unable to decipher Lucky's name on her nameplate.

'And to make it difficult for the enemy to break through our defences, we have to create obstacles. What do you think these obstacles could be?' the Colonel continued.

'Low wire entanglement, and minefields in front of the troops could act as deterrents,' said Cockroach, who had come prepared for the lesson.

'Any other suggestions?' asked the instructor.

'Construct a ditch-cum-bund,' came the reply from Kiran, who had also done her homework.

Ditch-cum-bund (DCB) is a man-made obstacle. It is like a canal with two banks, the one on the enemy side a bit lower than the one on the other side. It serves as an obstacle for vehicles, mainly battle tanks The cadets had been expected to study its details in the notes handed to them before the class.

'Very good!' said the colonel. 'Any other ideas?'

'A double ditch-cum-bund filled with water could be an effective obstacle,' suggested Cockroach, continuing to come up with the ideas provided in the notes.

'Very good! Let's have some out-of-the-box ideas, not the ones covered in the notes.'

There was pin-drop silence as the LCs struggled to come up with fresh ideas.

'Can you not come up with a single idea?' urged the instructor.

The silence remained unbroken. 'Alright, I think it's time to bring in the others to do some thinking.'

The Colonel ordered the LCs rolling outside to enter the room. 'Let's see if you can come up with any ideas about obstacles to stop the enemy from entering your territory?' he asked Nutty, who was pleased to be back in the room.

'Sir, we could put some huge crocodiles, like the ones they show in National Geographic, in canals dug along the border,' proposed the irrepressible girl.

'That's a real good idea. A really innovative one, I must say,' praised the colonel.

Beaming happily at the class, Nutty sat down.

'No, don't sit down,' ordered Colonel Dhar. 'I have not finished the discussion. 'So, how many huge crocodiles will you need?'

'We can put a dozen of them,' replied Nutty after a couple of minutes of hard thinking.

'What will be the approximate length of the canal, and will you be placing the crocodiles along the entire length?'

It was a trick question. Everyone except Nutty realized the instructor's game.

'Yes, sir,' she answered. 'I will place them along the entire length.'

'What if the length is around 600 kilometres, including the main and subsidiary canals?'

'No problem, sir. They can be placed at the most likely approaches.' Nutty waited for applause, which didn't come.

'Considering you have a dozen crocodiles, there will be around one crocodile every 50 kilometres of the canal. I think the density would be rather low.' A sly smile lurked on the instructor's lips.

'In that case we can put one crocodile every 100 meters,' said Nutty, after some thought. 'That will stop the enemy.'

'In that case you will need 6,000 crocodiles.'

'Yes, sir,' Nutty said doubtfully.

'Where do you think we will find so many huge crocodiles?'

'We could get 1,000 initially, and then the rest can be acquired.' Nutty dug her grave deeper.

'And how do you propose to transport 1,000 huge crocodiles to the canal at the border?'

'They can be shipped.'

'In the desert? And have you given a thought about who will keep a tab on them and feed them?' The colonel was openly smiling now.

'The ASC can do that, sir,' responded Nutty doggedly.

A few giggles were heard from the back benches. By now, the girl realized she had put her head in the noose and that the instructor was tightening it with each question.

'Fantastic! We shall not discuss this any further. You can write a paper on this and take your own time to submit it. Am I clear?' Colonel Dhar was no longer amused. The game had continued for too long.

'Sir, I think this plan will not work,' admitted Nutty in a low voice.

'I was wondering how long it would take for you to realize the stupidity of your plan,' the instructor rebuked the girl. 'I asked you to think of innovative ideas, not ridiculous ones.'

He continued his lecture and followed it up with the documentary *Defence in Plains*. Although a few LCs slept through the film, Nutty watched it attentively. She was fascinated by the different strategies shown in the film.

The exercise had outlined the importance of planning and execution. It gave the LCs several ideas, which they shared with the instructor during subsequent classes. They could now think more logically.

As the days passed, the LCs were introduced to elements of attack, raid, ambush and the so called 'Ops of War' in different types of terrain, by day as well as night. The manoeuvres they learnt were put to good use by a few cadets.

A couple of LCs used the tactics they learnt to steal out after dinner to meet newly made boyfriends and slip back into their respective companies before the 10 p.m. deadline. Their meetings took place on the P Hill, near Adyar River or behind the swimming pool.

Sand Model

The last of the theory classes on tactics was followed by the Sand Model Exercise (SME). It was time to apply everything they had learnt in the theory classes. The SME required an astute mind, the expertise of a strategist, and a good memory.

The SME was considered a big pain by most cadets. The mind-boggling possibilities of the SME posed a challenge even to the most intelligent cadets. For the lesser mortals like Nutty, the exercise was nothing short of a nightmare.
As a result, cheating was rampant.

The first SME caused a lot of tension and anxiety. The fortunate ones who had been briefed by their seniors also suffered from bouts of self-doubt and tension.

The fear of the unknown took its toll. The only fearless ones were the ones who possessed PCK (Previous Course Knowledge) or the solutions of the previous SMEs conducted in the OTA. Of course, if it happened to be a new exercise with a fresh setting, all PCKs would be rendered useless.

The SME was conducted in a special classroom called the Sand Model Room, which was essentially a huge hall with a sand model placed in the centre and seating arrangements on four sides. One side was reserved for instructors, and the other three sides were occupied by students who were divided into small groups called syndicates.

There was a defined procedure for the SME. Firstly, sand models always represented some border area with China or Pakistan. Secondly, the enemy always belonged to the Red Land, and the defenders were from the Blue Land. The setting of the exercise, which included a list of resources like troops, weapons, and equipment available for planning the solution, was provided to the LCs a day prior to the actual exercise.

'Beware of the SME,' they had been warned by the seniors. 'It is the most important facet of war planning. A bad performance in the SME can ruin your chances in the final reckoning. Many cadets have missed the Sword of Honour only because they didn't perform well in this exercise.'

As a result, many of the LCs spent a sleepless night going over the procedure to work out possible questions and solutions. Some of them were clearly nervous, and some curious, while a few like Nutty remained nonchalant.

That morning, the seniors' warnings ringing in their ears, Billi and Shiny exhibited signs of stress. The two of them had spent much time revising their lessons; Lucky had a good memory, which helped. As for Nutty, she had decided to relinquish the responsibility of the result to Dame Destiny.

'Come on girls, cheer up!' she urged, as they trooped into the Sand Model Room. 'It's not the end of the world.'

The girls spotted the dreaded sand model, covering an area of approximately 15 feet by 15 feet, sitting in the centre of the room. It was a colourful replica of a war zone.

Green sawdust was evenly spread over areas depicting plains, brown sawdust over the undulating ground that represented mountains, with white tops portraying snow covered peaks. Strips of blue sawdust outlined the location of rivers. These were interspersed with miniature huts and trees to show villages and forests. Small models of troops, artillery guns, tanks and houses were also placed to show deployments along the border, which was marked with a red tape.

The exercise always started with the introduction of the sand model. After the introduction, an LC was required to describe the deployment pattern of troops. After this, the actual exercise would begin. The situation was given and the syndicates were told to plan their attack of a particular feature and capture it. Once the task was handed out, the instructors left the room, giving the syndicates time to discuss.

The LCs had been divided into four syndicates of five each. The gang of four was grouped with Kiran to form Syndicate A.

Cockroach was lucky to have had an elder brother, who had passed out of the academy a couple of years back. She had managed to gather the PCKs on several past SMEs. Confident and cool, she was a part of Syndicate B.

Foreheads beaded with perspiration, hearts hammering with anxiety, the LCs waited for the stern-looking instructors to hand out the problems.

As expected, the instructor asked for volunteers to introduce the sand model. This was the only part of the exercise which saw many hands go up, since this was comparatively easy and the selected person could be sure of being spared subsequent grilling.

Saddie was chosen to do the honours. It was akin to winning a lottery, so she went about the introduction in a happy frame of mind. Deployment of the enemy troops, guns and tanks were given out and indicated on the sand model with the help of miniature wooden models. Since the SME was on 'Attack in Mountains', the syndicates had to come up with strategies of warfare one could use on mountains. Next, an LC was asked to give out the narrative.

Once the preliminaries had ended, the instructors exited. The syndicates had to describe their plan of attack on the designated hill feature and capture it.

There were excited discussions as the LCs settled down to discuss and mark their own deployment and plan of attack on the sketch provided to them. The four syndicates sat at different corners of the room discussing the solution in hushed tones, each group trying to keep their solution a secret.

Keen on keeping Nutty from mischief and disruption, Shiny allotted her the task of fetching snacks and refreshments for their syndicate, while they began the discussion. Not that Nutty minded. She was content with running the errand as it was an opportunity to eavesdrop on the conversation of the other syndicates. Cockroach and her syndicate were of special interest to her. Her efforts at prying did not go unnoticed.

'What the hell are you doing, running around the place and disturbing us,' reprimanded the general's daughter.

Disappointed, Nutty returned to her syndicate.

'Sit down, Peanut,' ordered Shiny. 'For heaven's sake, let us concentrate on the solution.'

'I am not disturbing you,' pouted Nutty. 'I was trying to listen to Cockroach's plan. They are planning to place the Bofors guns behind the mound, and attack from the right.'

'There is no need to pry. Just settle down,' said Lucky, taking out some papers from her satchel. It was the PCKs.

'Where did you find the PCKs?' screeched Nutty.

'Shut up!' scolded Shiny, giving Nutty a stern look. The girls studied the PCKs and proceeded to mark the locations on the given sketch.

'Mark the artillery guns here and the mortars there,' Shiny directed Billi, who was marking the details on the sketch. 'We will attack from the left, the slope is not very steep there. There is adequate cover of trees in that area. Besides, the guns will not be firing overhead. By attacking the enemy from the left, we will be attacking from a flank, thus catching the enemy by surprise,' she read from the papers.

'It's a logical solution,' agreed Billi, as she finished marking the sketch.

One by one, all the syndicates submitted their plans and waited for the next part of the exercise.

After the break ended, and all the syndicates had taken their place, the instructor asked Syndicate B to mark their solution on the sand model. While Cockroach and her syndicate were carrying out the task, a few other instructors and Company Commanders entered the hall and sat down in the visitors' gallery. Sand model discussions are considered a very important part of military training and they carry a lot of weightage in grading. It is for this reason that DSs often attend the discussion.

A flurry of activity could be heard as the Commandant arrived and took his seat to witness the proceedings.

'Syndicate B, give out your plan of attack,' ordered the instructor.

A very confident Cockroach volunteered to narrate the plan on behalf of her syndicate. Her narrative was followed by a barrage of questions from the instructor as well as the DSs in the visitors' gallery.

'Why have you placed your artillery at that location?' asked one DS.

'What made you plan the attack from the right side, instead of the left?' came a question from another DS.

'Why have you not incorporated the Air Force?' asked the instructor. More questions rained from all sides.

A bit flummoxed by the volley of questions, Cockroach fumbled with her replies. Bit by bit, her confidence drained away as she found herself unable to come up with satisfactory answers to some of the questions.

Finally the Commandant asked, 'Is there any other plan by which we can tackle the enemy?'

There was pin-drop silence. It was apparent that none of the syndicates wanted to volunteer an alternative solution. Syndicate A was the only one that had presented a plan that advocated attacking from the left. It was a moment of reckoning. Realizing that this was her last chance to beat Cockroach, Billi raised her hand.

'Yes, go ahead,' the Commandant granted permission.

Brimming with confidence, the footballer walked smartly to the sand model. Picking up the long wooden pointer, she began speaking. 'Our syndicate plans to attack from the left…' She indicated the route of attack.

'Why have you decided on a left-flanking attack? What are the advantages?' the Commandant wanted to know.

'Sir, the left approach is lined with many trees. The forest provides a covered approach, whereas the right flank is open and can be easily spotted by the enemy, so the element of surprise will be lost.'

'Good! Do you have any other reason for the left-flanking attack?' The Commandant was now leaning forward with interest.

'Yes sir, this route is much shorter, so the casualties are likely to be much less,' said Billi, recalling the points Shiny had read out from her PCK. Slowly and surely, she parroted all the points. Her narration was concise, crisp and to the point. The Commandant seemed impressed with her answer.

'What is your name?' he asked.

'Lady Cadet Bijli Bijarnia, sir.'

'Well done, Bijli!' With that the commandant left the venue.

There was jubilation in their syndicate. None of the LCs, least of all Cockroach, believed that the gang of four had won due to their intelligence. Everyone suspected that they had found a PCK to help them solve the problem. The gang was not about to admit that, of course.

As they trooped out of the hall, Cockroach confronted Nutty. 'You don't deserve to win,' she hissed. 'So, where did you guys find the PCK?'

For once, Nutty retained her sanity. She scratched her chin and feigned innocence. Lucky couldn't suppress a chuckle as she heard her friend asking, 'PCK, did you say? Well! What is that?'

Applied Tactics

It was Lucky's birthday, and the gang of four planned to go on liberty to celebrate. Apart from the gift they wanted to buy for the birthday girl, they had other agendas. Billi wanted to enjoy a good meal, Lucky wanted to shop and Nutty wanted to catch a movie. As luck would have it, Nutty was denied an outpass because she was caught taking a shortcut during the cross country run.

'Why the hell did you have to take a shortcut?' raged Billi, as the gang gathered to discuss the matter after dinner. 'Didn't you see the ustad hiding behind the bush?'

'How the bloody hell would I know that?' retorted Nutty. 'You guys go ahead and enjoy. I will stay back.'

Everyone was aware that the girl had spoken out of anger. She knew that they would not leave her behind.

'Grow up, my dear Doughnut,' Lucky urged the sulking girl. 'We are seniors now.'

Shiny began pacing around her room, while the other members of the gang sat in a pensive mood.

'It's a sad situation,' said Billi dejectedly.

'Let's cancel our plans,' suggested Shiny. 'We have two options. We can celebrate in the room with some music and snacks, or go to the cafeteria.'

'It will not be the same,' Lucky looked disappointed. 'Papa Ferdy's food sucks. I am quite sick of it.'

'We can postpone the celebrations till the next liberty,' Billi came up with the idea. 'And hope that our friend will not commit some blunder and be denied an outpass again.'

The suggestion didn't go down very well with the gang. There was silence as the girls tried to come up with a better idea.

'I have an idea,' Nutty suddenly announced.

'NO!' there was a cumulative protest.

'Please, Nutty, don't torture your pea-sized brain,' snapped Billi. 'We've had enough of your ideas.'

'Listen, this one is sure to work,' Nutty exclaimed. Eyes sparkling with excitement, she continued, 'You guys proceed as per the initial plan, and I shall join you at the mall by 11 a.m.'

Familiar with her madcap plans, Shiny threw Nutty a disparaging look. 'Forget it!'

'Please Doughnut, don't…' Lucky tried to intervene, but the daft girl cut her short.

'It's a bloody fantastic plan, which just can't fail,' Nutty continued. 'I know the exact spot from where I can jump over the perimeter wall. Once that obstacle is cleared, it's easy-peasy to reach the bloody mall.'

The girls looked aghast.

It was a risky proposition, one that could get Nutty relegated. One by one, everyone tried to dissuade the girl. Their attempt at persuading her against carrying out the foolhardy plan failed, and the girls gave up.

On Sunday morning, as planned, the three girls trotted out of the campus at 10 a.m. While they made their way towards the mall, Nutty headed for the perimeter wall.

Moving stealthily, she managed to reach an isolated spot and climbed the wall, unobserved by anyone. She heard something rip as she jumped down the other side of the wall. Horrified, she realized that the seams at the back of her trousers had come apart.

It would be impossible to proceed to town in her present condition. Determined to return to her room and change her trousers before heading for the mall, she clambered up the wall, once again. Jumping back into the campus, she realized that her escape route to the company could no longer be used. The ground through which she had come was now occupied by a few GCs who were practicing for the upcoming football match.

Desperate, Nutty looked around for some other route. There was none. Shrugging her shoulders, she decided to wait behind the bushes. The wait was a long one, as it took more than an hour for the GCs to leave the ground.

Once the ground was clear, she dashed back to the company and headed for her room on the first floor. The *putti* parades had been a great help, she realized, as she changed into a fresh pair of trousers within minutes and skipped down the stairs.

The next moment, she came to a screeching halt. The Reichsführer was in the lobby, barking at a few first-termers. Exhibiting her legendary foul mood, Shera had embarked on a punishing spree.

Swiftly reversing her steps, Nutty managed to evade the officer's eyes. There was nothing to do, but to abort her plan of joining the gang.

Meanwhile, the trio waited at the mall, the inordinate delay in Nutty's arrival worrying them.

'She must have been caught,' opined Billi. 'I had warned her against carrying out this stupid plan.'

'Does she ever heed good advice?' retorted Shiny. 'That girl is reckless beyond reason.'

'Not just reckless, she is an idiot.'

'Let's give her some more time,' suggested Lucky, ever patient. 'She might have had to delay her plan due to some reasons.'

'We will give her another hour, and then we are going for lunch,' decided Shiny. 'If she isn't here by then, she is not likely to make it.'

Dispirited, they roamed around the mall, peeping frequently into the bookstore, which was to be their meeting point.

Back at the academy, Nutty waited for the lobby to be cleared of the officer and the rolling first-termers. Minutes were ticking by. She had promised to reach the mall at 11 a.m. and now it was almost 1 p.m. Should she wait indefinitely for Shera to stop the punishments or go to the mess for lunch? Missing a meal was not in her plans.

She decided to wait a few more minutes.

At 1 p.m. sharp, Shera finally decided to let the exhausted LCs go. She ordered them to proceed to the mess for lunch, and took off on her bike. Grabbing the opportunity, Nutty sprinted back to the secluded spot, and clambered over the wall, this time taking care that her seams didn't rip. Jumping down the wall, she flagged down an autorickshaw and headed for the mall.

It was past 1.30 p.m.

At the bookstore in the mall, Nutty found no trace of her friends. Recalling that they had discussed going to a famous Thai restaurant for lunch, she headed there.

As she had expected, the gang was surprised to see her.

'Welcome!' greeted Lucky. 'Join us.'

'You are only a couple of hours late,' commented Billi sarcastically. 'It's quite a commendable feat for an aspiring army officer.'

'You won't bloody believe what happened,' Nutty grinned unapologetically.

'Well, we are waiting for your story,' remarked Billi. 'I am sure it's an interesting one.'

'It's a bloody long story, and I am starving. Let's order food before I start narrating it.'

Over mouthfuls of butter garlic prawn, Thai green curry and phad Thai noodles with crunchy peanuts, Nutty shared the story of her escapade.

The rest of the afternoon was an enjoyable one, as the gang moved from one floor to the other, shopping and joking with each other. Lucky decided to buy a packet of cigarettes to replenish her stash.

'It will be impossible to jump over the wall with all this food inside me,' Nutty rued when it was time to return to the campus.

'You are not going back the same way,' said Lucky. 'It was risky enough to escape from the campus, but jumping right into the arms of an alert DS or ustad will be worse.'

'I agree with Lucky,' seconded Shiny. 'You are coming with us.'

'You want me caught at the gate?' screeched Nutty.

'We will find a way to smuggle you in,' Lucky allayed her friend's fears.

Hailing a cab, they made their way back to the academy. As Lucky had promised, smuggling Nutty into the campus proved quite easy.

'Thanks to the lectures and film on tactics, we managed to hoodwink our way through the obstacles,' laughed Nutty, excited with the day's happenings. 'I wish I had returned by the same route. It would have been more adventurous.'

'There is always a next time,' consoled Lucky, who was satisfied with the way her birthday had been spent.

Cross-country competition

Of all the runs, it was the cross-country practice, a 12-kilometre run that turned out to be an unforgettable experience. It was considered a very important event.

Running long distance in a competition requires an immense amount of mental strength. It is the 'never say die' attitude which helps one win a cross-country run. While the LCs had built up a reasonable level of physical fitness, they lacked the mental endurance to push themselves beyond the limit.

The final competition was just a week away, and they were at their final practice before the competition, which was scheduled the very next Sunday. Zojila Company had come last in the previous term, which had greatly annoyed CoCo and Paltu. They were determined to push the girls to give a better performance.

CoCo and Reichsführer, along with the ustads, had turned up for the cross-country run practice on that Sunday morning. By 6 a.m., the entire company had assembled at the start line.

The girls knew it was a do or die situation. Performing below expectations was sure to land them in CoCo and Paltu's bad books.

The practice run was going fine. A satisfied smile lit up the faces of the two officers who were watching closely.

Unfortunately, the smile did not last long. Two LCs were caught taking a shortcut. Cheating was disgraceful and unacceptable, but getting caught was worse. CoCo was boiling mad, and the Reichsführer was steaming. A blistering heat emanated from the duo, and the situation began crackling.

The entire company knew it was going to be a long day of trouble. CoCo did not utter a single word, but called for a company fall-in at 9.30 a.m.

He arrived in the morning, riding a motorcycle instead of his jazzy car. Parking the bike on one side, he sat on its seat and watched the LCs, who were lined up before the building.

'All in?' he asked.

'Yes, sir,' the CSM replied in a loud and crackling voice.

'Everybody, down on your hands,' he barked. The moment, the LCs went down on their hands, he shouted, 'Start kissing the ground. Get started, and don't halt till I order.' Then, he took out a book and began reading.

Doing push-ups soon after breakfast is the worst kind of torture. Famished after the 12-kilometre run, many of the LCs had stuffed themselves with five to six aloo parathas and a huge amount of egg *bhurji*. They found the going tougher than ever.

'Now get into *murga* position,' he ordered them, after they had finished 50 push-ups.

This was a tough position to maintain. They were to squat and then loop their arms behind their knees to hold their ears. Their limbs ached terribly. It made little difference to CoCo, who was engrossed in his book, and seemed to have forgotten about the pathetic condition of the LCs.

The girls knew that he had trained in the NDA (National Defence Academy), where endurance is tested beyond one's limits. To expect the same from LCs, they felt, was unfair. While the boys at NDA had three years of training, the LCs had had just 11 months of training.

Unable to bear it any longer, the JUO got up after about 10 minutes. 'Sir, we ran well. Please have some mercy,' she pleaded.

'Get back to your position. I don't like arguments,' he snapped cruelly.

CoCo took out his mobile and asked his orderly to fetch tea from the officers' mess. The chap, used to his boss's whimsical ways, arrived within minutes. With him was a thermos full of tea, which he poured into a glass for the Major. He stood waiting for further orders.

With the sun beaming on them, the position had become agonizing and a few LCs began mumbling.

'Silence!' roared the CoCo. 'Don't disturb.'

The whispering, which halted for a few seconds, restarted and gradually increased in intensity. 'You girls don't seem to understand simple English.' He kept the book aside and shouted. 'Get up! You have two minutes. I want you back in riding breeches. Go!'

Relieved to be released from the *murga* position, the girls ran up to their rooms to carry out his bidding.

Not one of them made it back in two minutes. Looking meaningfully at his watch, CoCo snarled, 'Pathetic timing! Alright, I will give you some extra time.'

Wan faces lit up. The girls smiled, only to be let down.

'You have two minutes and 10 seconds to change into combat dress. Your time starts now.'

Again, there was a scramble. This time, only one of the LCs could make it in time, so the others were made to do front rolls.

'Your timings are very poor,' he barked. 'You need more practice.' Clambering down from his perch, he went down the line, checking their dresses. One of the LCs had not tied her shoelaces properly. Another one's belt had not been put through the loop. He ticked them off with severity, before issuing a fresh order. 'I don't want anyone to be late this time. You have two minutes twenty seconds to change into your PT rigs.'

By now, exhausted with the constant running up and down, the LCs were beginning to wilt. They were late again.

'You seem to be enjoying *putti* parade,' CoCo remarked.

'No, sir,' the LCs replied in unison.

'In that case, you have to be back on time. It is as simple as that. Let's see you do it this time. Ready?' He looked around. 'This time change into your drill rigs. You have three minutes. Go.'

Desperate to make the cut, the girls vanished.

Panting, puffing and sweating, the LCs trickled out of the building. They were not able to make it this time too.

'Sir, we do not deserve so much punishment,' said Nutty.

'Who said this is a punishment?' smirked CoCo. 'It is a part of the strengthening exercises. We have just finished warming up. Now, we will proceed to the next stage.'

He poured out some more tea from the thermos and took a leisurely sip. An hour had gone by.

'We shall now do strengthening exercises for the entire body. First, the legs and knees, and then the ankles and calves. We shall exercise all parts of the body one by one.' He paused for their reaction.

The LCs were too tired to protest and waited for the order.

'Down on your haunches. Now go round that tree over there,' he said pointing to a tree, which was about 200 metres away.

It was a difficult feat, what with the sun rising higher and the temperature going up.

'It was a pathetic effort,' he pronounced. 'You took too long.'

'But sir, you did not allocate time,' one of the LCs reminded him.

'Didn't I specify a time limit? Well, I give you five minutes to repeat the performance.'

The LCs were horrified. It would take them no less than 15 minutes. Sweating profusely, they followed his order. Not one of them could get back in the allocated time.

'Now, we shall do exercises for back strengthening. Front rolling is best for that.' CoCo was in an unrelenting mood.

Just then, an instructor drove up in his car, and relayed some message to him in a low voice. It must have been important, for CoCo kicked his bike into action and rode away in a hurry.

Relieved, the girl finally straightened their backs.

Girding up for Competitions

It was a Saturday night, and three members of the gang were waiting for Shiny to join them. As a CSM, she had to deal with the first-termers before the gossip-session. The recent debacle during the cross-country run was on everyone's mind. The dismal performance required an immediate corrective action.

'I think it is time to formulate a plan of action, and do well this time,' declared Billi, the moment Shiny joined them.

'Can't we do it later,' said Nutty. 'We still have plenty of time for planning and plotting.'

'You are an idiot,' Billi snapped at the fun-loving girl. 'This is the right time. Unless we have a goal, we cannot work towards it.'

'Not only that, we have to ensure that Zojila Company wins as many competitions as possible,' Shiny added.

'Spoken like a CSM,' remarked Nutty. 'You guys are always thinking of competitions and winning. Relax! There's life beyond those things. Anyway, there's time enough for those things. We will cross the bridge when we come to it.'

'Dear Doughnut, don't you remember the story of the ant and the grasshopper?' chided Lucky. 'Winning takes preparation, and it doesn't happen at the last moment. One has to work towards the goal.'

'Correct! We have performed terribly in the cross-country race. The first thing to do is to prepare the *jungoos* for the competitions,' suggested Shiny.

'So, how do you propose to do that?' asked Billi. 'Those LCs look lost all the time.'

'Give them some time, Billi. Don't you remember our conditions when we joined the academy?' asked Shiny. 'We behaved like robots for the first 30 days, unable to differentiate between day and night.'

'Look, I am aiming for the championship, so we have to strategize to beat Phillora Company in every competition. The only way we can beat our rivals is to put in combined and cohesive effort,' Billi argued.

Her words had a rousing effect on the three friends..

The rivalry between the two companies was legendary. It had existed ever since the induction of Lady Cadets into the academy.

'Our grades may have improved, but the overall performance of our company lags behind the Phillora Company,' said Billi, frowning with displeasure.

'That's true! Besides, CoCo has made it a prestige issue. According to him, this is the first time Zojila is lagging behind Phillora Company,' added Shiny. 'The Reichsführer is also furious with the results of the earlier competitions. The Phillora girls beat us hollow last term, and unless we pull up our socks this time, it's going to be a repeat of our past performance.'

'I don't think Cockroach will cooperate. She hates Billi's guts,' Lucky provided her two cents. 'In fact, she has enrolled the support of a few LCs, and none of them are likely to listen to us.'

'This is no time for individual preferences. We have to work together to beat the Phillora girls. We have to involve Cockroach and her gang in the discussion. In fact, we have to speak to all the LCs.'

'How do you intend on doing that?' asked Nutty, chomping busily on the chips she had taken from Lucky's packet.

'We will have to find a way.' Shiny got up and began pacing the floor.

'I have a suggestion,' said Lucky, her eyes shining with excitement. 'While you speak to Cockroach and her pals, I will train the *jungoos*. They are raw and obedient. Let's begin by training them for cross country. That's what our seniors did.'

'That's right!' agreed Billi. 'Cross country is the first hurdle. Once the *jungoos* have been strengthened to run long distance, they will perform better in the physical tests.'

'Good idea!' agreed Shiny. 'I suggest that you restrain yourself, and not push them too hard.'

'Lest they run away from the academy,' laughed Nutty.

'One thing to remember is that cross country is the most important competition and carries the maximum weightage for the championship,' Billi added.

'We have to watch out for good players during the games period,' Lucky said, excited with the possibilities. 'We can then select teams for all the competitions.'

'It will be better if we ask for volunteers for each game, and then select the best out of them. Once that is done, the most capable one can be made responsible for training the team,' Shiny came up with another idea.

'Not a bad idea,' agreed Billi, who was the most competitive of the four. 'Let's put it up on the noticeboard.

We have to beat the Phillora girls at any cost, and the preparations for that have to begin immediately.'

They went on to discuss the modalities and strategies for the company championship.

'I have a very simple strategy, one that is sure to succeed.' Lucky fetched a notepad and pencil from the desk and outlined her strategy. 'The first thing is to take them through a gruelling regimen of strengthening exercises geared to build up stamina. Not only will it take care of the cross-country runs, it will also help in winning other competitions. Once they are ready, I will start taking them on the cross-country runs.'

'Not a bad idea,' agreed Shiny.

'Cross-country runs require us to maintain a steady pace. This has to be understood by the *jungoos*. The trick is to find an effort level that can be maintained for a long duration. For that, one has to build up endurance.'

'You seem to have done some research on the subject,' Billi stared at the grid being drawn by Lucky. 'I am convinced you will be able to train the *jungoos* to perfection.'

Once the cross-country race was out of the way, they discussed the other competitions. One of the competitions was on interior economy, which was all about the cleanliness and layout of one's room.

'I will take on the interior economy stuff,' Nutty offered. 'I will get the *jungoos* to clean up and arrange their rooms better than the Phillora girls.'

'Some of the girls have been brought up in a pampered manner and think that cleaning is not their job. Many have always had someone to pick up after them,' opined Lucky. 'Your job will be to make them fall in line.'

'Don't you worry about that,' assured the Jalna girl. 'I know how to get them working.'

'I am sure the two of you will do a great job. Now that the training for those two competitions has been taken care of, we have to discuss the drill and obstacle run competitions,' Shiny smiled encouragingly at her two friends.

'*Jungoos* are easy to handle, the problems lies in getting our course-mates to put in their best,' Billi expressed her doubt.

'We have to appeal to their pride and sense of camaraderie. I have no doubt that they will cooperate.' Shiny was confident.

For the next couple of days, Billi and Shiny worked in tandem. Their carrot and stick approach won over their course-mates. Everyone agreed that the Phillora girls were too big for their boots and had to be defeated. It took a lot of effort to convince Cockroach, who was the most resistant of all, but the idea of belonging to the champion company found favour with her. What finally worked was a smart move by Billi.

'Koel, you are one of the best swimmers, and your drill is perfect. If you were to take the responsibility of training the *jungoos*, we could easily swing the balance in our favour.'

'Please take the responsibility, Koel,' Shiny added to Billi's plea. 'We need your help.'

A little flattery can draw enthusiasm from the most reluctant person, and so it happened in this case.

After dithering for a couple of moments, Cockroach fell into their trap. 'I will do it, only if I have a free hand. No interference from anyone. I will do it my way.'

'No one will interfere,' Billi hastened to reassure the girl. 'We will leave the field clear for you.'

Once Cockroach had agreed, Billi discussed their strategy with CoCo and Paltu, who were happy that the Zojila girls had finally woken up. The two of them promised to provide assistance as well as ideas.

A checklist was prepared and every aspect discussed. To form the winning teams for the games competitions, Shiny and Billi made a list of the athletic girls who had represented their schools or colleges in different games. Once the list was ready, they chose the best girls amongst the players as captains and gave them a free hand to select their respective teams. The captains were now responsible for training their teams to perfection. The system worked. It gave a sense of purpose and importance to the captains, who took a keen interest and forced their teams to practice hard before and after games period in the evenings.

'I am sure we will beat Phillora this time,' Nutty said when the gang of four settled down in Shiny's room after dinner one night.

'You can never be sure,' Billi said. 'I don't think the Phillora girls are sitting idle. They must have plans and strategies up their sleeves.'

'True! Phillora appointees are very aggressive in their approach,' Shiny interjected.

'No,' Nutty retorted. 'I have been spying on them. The Phillora girls are in a blissful zone. They are just doing KPS.'

'What is KPS?' Lucky wanted to know.

'*Khao, peeo aur so*. That's what they are doing after their daily routine training,' Nutty chuckled.

'They are overconfident, basking in their past glory,' declared Shiny.

'So, they have been having an easy time, while we have been training so hard that we have developed six packs,' Lucky tapped her belly.

'Yes,' agreed Nutty, looking ruefully at her own belly.

'You shut up! Look at your belly. What you have is one big bulging pack.' Billi knocked Nutty's protruding stomach. 'You eat as though there is no tomorrow.'

Everyone broke into laughter.

'It's because we had Chinese for dinner. It gives me gas.' Nutty was not amused by the joke. 'I will show you my six pack in the morning.'

Things had been moving as per their plan. Nutty made the first-termers slog. As a result, everything was spick and span, and ready for inspection. The noticeboard was done up with colourful ribbons and not a cobweb could be seen anywhere. There was a marked difference between the two companies.

In the meantime, Lucky had been keeping the *jungoos* on their toes. Having done well in their practice runs, they were now keen on beating the Phillora girls.

'Do you want to be the champion company?' Lucky had asked the girls, the very first day they assembled.

'Yes, ma'am,' they all had replied in unison.

'Pay attention to what I am saying. A company that comes first in the cross-country run is likely to be the champion company. I know that the competition is far away but one has to prepare well in advance to be a winner and so, we shall start today. I'll take two sessions of 10 minutes each, twice a day. They will be taken before games and after dinner. We shall do only two exercises; the first one is to hold the legs up in a lying position and the other is sit-ups.'

The girls wondered what their senior had in mind. Ten minutes was no issue. They hoped it wasn't going to lead to wheelbarrow and the other games she had made them play the last time.

'I don't want you to think of the exercises as punishment, or else the very purpose of doing them will be defeated,' Lucky continued. 'If you do the exercises diligently, I will keep my word and restrict them to 10 minutes. I will leave you to do the exercises on your own. No supervision. No cheating. Is that understood?'

There was a resounding response. Both sides kept their word.

One week had gone by, and all was well. Although they were taken through a taxing regimen, the first-termers didn't complain.

It was a Saturday. The Zojila Company first-termers had returned from the mess after dinner and had assembled in front of their company in PT uniforms as per the drill laid out by Lucky.

'Okay, ready?' Her hands on her hips, Lucky stood before the *jungoos*. 'Lie down on your backs and slowly lift both your legs to 30 degrees. Don't bend your knees. Steady. Hold. I want to see who brings down their legs first. The one who can hold the position till the end gets a treat from me.'

The girls could hold their legs up for a much longer time than they could a week ago. Regular practice had strengthened their core muscles as well as their willpower.

It was while the girls were doing their exercises that Reichsführer arrived for a surprise check. She parked her car and stole silently into the lobby. She was surprised to see the first-termers doing sit-ups. There was no senior around. She stood watching from a corner, as the girls performed sit-ups in perfect synchronization.

'What's going on? Who has punished you?' demanded Reichsführer, after they finished.

'Ma'am this is not a punishment. We are preparing for the cross country,' said one of the girls.

'What nonsense! Call the CSM.'

'What's going on? The cross-country competition is far away,' Reichsführer asked Shiny, who had come sprinting down the stairs.

'Ma'am, LC Lakme is responsible for training the first-termers for cross country, and it's her idea…'

'Ask her to come here,' Reichsführer roared like a wounded tigress. She subjected Lucky to a grilling as soon as the girl arrived. 'What's the meaning of all this?'

'Ma'am, I wanted them to build up their stamina. They have been doing these exercises for a week now. I intend on taking them for a cross-country run before breakfast, tomorrow. We will follow the actual cross-country route,' Lucky explained.

'Don't start till I am here,' said Reichsführer in a stern and unsmiling manner. Striding out, she drove away.

Next morning, the *jungoos* and seniors had assembled at 5.30 a.m. They spotted Reichsführer arriving.

'Let's go,' she commanded, and all the LCs took off for the starting point. A couple of ustads were already stationed all along the route.

'Today we shall have a competition between the first-termers and the second-termers. May the best team win,' Paltu announced, after the entire company had lined up at the starting point.

Turning to Lucky, she said, 'LC Lakme, come and stand with me. This is your test. I want to see if your method has worked.'

'Ustad, shuru kare.' She addressed the ustad who was manning the starting point.

Just as the ustad was getting ready with his whistle, Lucky requested Paltu to give her a couple of minutes to address the first-termers. She took the *jungoos* to a side and said, 'My reputation is at stake and so is yours. I want you to put in your best. Remember, when the going gets tough, the tough get going. You have to win the race. Don't give up till the very end. Victory!' she shouted.

'Victory!' echoed the *jungoos*.

It was an exemplary performance. Although the seniors had gone through the race several times and knew the terrain like the backs of their hands, the *jungoos* made up for their lack of experience with enthusiasm and determination.

It was a close fight. When the run ended, the seniors just about managed to retain their superiority over the first-termers.

Although a trifle disappointed, Lucky knew it was not easy to defeat the seniors, who had six months of training to back them up. Paltu, on the other hand, was impressed with the performance of the first-termers.

'We will see who wins the next run,' Reichsführer told the LCs, convinced that the *jungoos* would make all efforts to beat their seniors. This was turning out to be much better then she had expected. Lucky had worked wonders with the first-termers.

The seniors were disconcerted. The juniors had almost caught up with them. They would have to be on their toes. Lucky was determined to make the first-termers win the next time. As for the first-termers, they were on a high.

The strengthening exercises helped in the other physicals too. The DST saw nine LCs clearing the test, while Phillora had just five. In the Battle Physical Efficiency Test (BPET) test, 14 came in the 'excellent' category and none failed. Phillora was far behind. They had only four in the 'excellent' grade and three LCs who had failed. The triumph motivated everyone.

Planning & Plotting

Constantly prodding each other to better their act, the gang of four put up an impressive performance. Billi had performed very well, and was now one among the first three cadets in the merit list. After an excellent performance in the sand model exercise, she had raced far ahead of the LCs and most of the GCs too. More importantly, she was in the race for the Sword of Honour, which is awarded to the best overall cadet in the academy. Shiny lagged not far behind. Lucky was among the above average performers. Nutty was the only laggard, and the gang pushed her all the time. Although she had improved her grades, a lot remained to be done.

The first week had been hectic for both Billi and Shiny, who were the SUO and CSM. As a result, all four of them could meet only twice a week.

It was only a fortnight later that they could get back to their routine of sitting together more often. The timings were getting streamlined, the first-termers were also settling down. The *jungoos* were given a regular dose of lectures and punishments immediately after lunch and then again after dinner. Sometimes, the punishments lasted beyond midnight.

After the championship, the gang focused on individual performance. Now that the cross country hurdle had been successfully crossed, the other tests required their attention.

'The PCKs are essential if we want to beat Cockroach,' surmised Shiny. 'Having said that, let me confess that I don't want Nutty to repeat her dubious methods.'

'Nor do I,' Bill endorsed. 'We have a lot at stake. Being the SUO and CSM, we can't take risks. Can you imagine the humiliation if we are caught?'

'Aaron has passed a few PCKs to me, but we need many more,' remarked Shiny.

'Where does he get them from?' Nutty wanted to know.

'His overstudy gave them to him after passing out.'

'Aaron is a lucky guy. My bloody overstudy gave me nothing but trouble,' lamented Nutty.

'Don't worry, I will find a way to get the PCKs,' decided Lucky. Next weekend, while the others were busy, Lucky pedaled towards the photocopying shop. She wanted to know if any of the GCs were getting PCKs photocopied. To her delight, she ran into Mathur just as he was stepping out of the shop.

'What brings you here?' she asked the strutting chap.

'Nothing! I came to grab a sandwich at the café,' lied the idiot.

'Well! Let me not delay you,' Lucky threw him a winsome smile. She was convinced that the guy was there to get photocopies of PCKs. She was also aware of his weakness for her, and she was determined to use that weakness to her advantage.

A shy smile followed by a flutter of lashes à la Nutty did the trick. 'Why don't you join me?' offered the floored fellow. 'We can spend some time together.'

'Why not?' replied Lucky, surprising the chap. He had expected her to refuse.

Delighted, he led her into the café and pulled out a chair for her. After that, he proceeded to empty his wallet by ordering not just sandwiches but also cutlets and ice cream sundaes. Mathur wanted to keep the girl for as long as possible.

The stupid oaf was over the moon with the pretty girl's attention. He boasted of his achievements, while Lucky pondered over a plan to slip into the photocopy shop.

Once Mathur stopped crowing about his imaginary feats, she excused herself saying, 'I will be back in a jiffy, after picking up a few things from the canteen. In the meantime, you can finish your drink.'

'I will wait for you,' he said, the chivalrous side of his personality emerging after a long hibernation.

'I will take not more than five minutes,' she promised, rushing out of the café.

She dove into the photocopy shop, where Nutty's young friend was busy churning out copies of PCKs. Her eyes were attracted to a stack of photocopies on a table.

'Whose copies are those?' she asked the young Lothario. 'Do these belong to GC Mathur?'

'Yes, ma'am,' admitted the gullible fellow.

'I will take them,' she pulled out her wallet. Then, noticing the doubtful expression on the chap's face, she added, 'Mathur is speaking to a couple of friends at the café. He's asked me to pick them up for him.'

The young shopkeeper, who had noticed Mathur speaking to Lucky, winked suggestively. 'GCs requesting LCs to pick up their stuff is rather unexpected.'

Lucky decided to ignore the guy's comment. Counting out the money, she smiled at him, 'Can you make one extra copy for me, please? Either Mathur or I will pick it up.'

'My pleasure,' he basked in her attention. 'I am here to serve you, ma'am.'

She knew Mathur would pick up the lot after leaving the café, and hoped the shopkeeper would not mention the extra set. Even if he did, the braggart couldn't do much except curse her wily ways. She chuckled.

It took all of three minutes for Lucky to collect the full set of PCKs and exit the shop. With a wicked smile, she tucked the lot in her satchel and rushed to the canteen to buy chips. Ten minutes later, she was back at the café, a big smile pasted on her lips.

'You took a long time,' complained Mathur. 'That's no way to treat a guy. I have been swatting flies for the last 15 minutes.'

'So sorry, Mathur,' she grinned in a conciliatory manner. 'There was a long queue at the canteen, but I requested a GC to buy my stuff.'

'I am not surprised. With a smile like that, you could convince an eskimo to buy an air-conditioner.'

Little did he know of the wicked deeds she was capable of.

That night the gang was in a jubilant mood. The PCKs had taken them a step closer to success.

'Tell us how you managed to get the set,' insisted Shiny.

'I got them through a lot of lies,' laughed Lucky, and went on to narrate the entire story.

'Are you sure the shopkeeper will not tell Mathur about the extra set of photocopies that you carried away?' asked Nutty, envying her friend's quick wit.

'I don't think he will share the information with Mathur. If my judgement of people is correct, the shopkeeper hates the guts of that GC,' Lucky smiled.

A Valentine Surprise

Lucky was in a terrible mood that morning. It grew worse as the day progressed. By mid-morning, all she wanted to do was pack up and leave the academy. Valentine's Day had brought back hurtful memories. Feelings she had assumed were interred, reappeared. Emotions of grief, loss and anger resurfaced with a vengeance.

Three years ago, she had fallen in love with a classmate. They had been together for two full years when he suddenly ended the relationship. No reasons were offered, no apologies made. 'I am moving on' was all he said. He left Shillong without leaving an address, but she knew he had found someone else to love.

She was devastated. It took her many months to recover, but traces of bitterness remained. Without fail, they re-emerged every year on Valentine's Day because that was the day he had ended the relationship. It was a paradox. People declare love on that day. They don't end their relationships.

'Love is a bitch,' she cursed. 'Men are not worth wasting time on.'

Things were not going well on the Shiny and Aaron front, either. Their competitive streak had ruined their easy relationship. He resented the fact that she was racing ahead of him. Shiny, on the other hand, spared no opportunity to point out he was lagging behind. It was all said in good humour, but Aaron didn't take it lightly.

Cupid had been hard at work as far as Nutty was concerned. She basked in the knowledge that GC Bose was besotted with her. 'I don't love him, but it's flattering to know that someone finds you attractive,' she confided in her friends.

Billi was focused on winning the Sword of Honour and had no time for a man. Her days were spent in upping her physical and academic performance. Cockroach was her rival, and she had no intention of being beaten by the girl. Even if she didn't get the Sword, she would not go home without a medal.

That afternoon, when the girls went to fetch their bikes from the cycle stand, Lucky found a single red rose stuck on her handle bar.

'Who could have put that here?' she exclaimed, her eyes running around the place.

'It has to be some GC. Today is Valentine's Day, remember?' chirped Nutty excitedly. 'You are bloody lucky. GC Bose did not remember the day. Bloody bedbug could have got me some chocolates, at least.'

'He's not the only one. Aaron hasn't bothered, either,' said Shiny. She was rather disappointed by her fiancé's amnesia.

'That may be so, but I don't have much respect for a guy who sticks a rose and vanishes without leaving his name,' remarked Billi pragmatically. 'The whole thing reeks of cowardice.'

'Look, I have no intention of trying to find the name of the person who put this rose on my handlebar,' said Lucky.

'Frankly, I don't care.' She plucked out the rose and tossed it away.

'Hello! What's bloody wrong with you?' asked Nutty, picking up the flower from the ground. 'Why are you taking out your temper on the poor flower? I am taking it to my room.'

'My dear Peanut, it's meant for Lucky, not for you,' reminded Shiny.

'Lucky doesn't want it,' Nutty pointed out. 'I love bloody roses and so I am taking it to my room. I will place it in water, so it remains fresh for a few days.'

'It's alright, take it with you,' said Lucky. 'It might be GC Mathur's idea, for all you know, and I have no intention of leading him on.'

Back in Billi's room, they had just settled down for a gabbing session when Nutty unwrapped the silver foil draped around the rose stem. 'Hey, what's this?' she exclaimed, as she smoothed out a slip of paper that had been cleverly hidden inside the foil. Everyone craned their necks to look at the strip of paper. Written on it were a few words in beautiful handwriting. 'Meet me at 12 noon, in the café the coming Sunday. Your secret admirer.'

'Bloody hell!' cursed Nutty. 'The mystery man is asking you to meet him this Sunday.'

'It must be a hoax,' Lucky dampened her friend's excitement. 'Someone is trying to fool me.'

'I think it is GC Mathur,' remarked Shiny. 'I have noticed the way he looks at you.'

'So have I,' said Billi. 'One would think that a braggart like him would have the courage to declare his love in person.'

'He might not want to declare it in our presence, so he's called her to the café on Sunday,' opined Shiny.

'We bloody well will be there to watch his declaration,' said Nutty. 'What do you think?'

'I think it is a splendid idea,' Shiny rubbed her hands together.

'I am not going to the café,' announced Lucky. 'The three of you can go and meet that idiot. It would be embarrassing to have him declare his love for me. I can't stand the chap.'

'What if it is someone else?' Billi pointed out. 'We are just assuming it to be GC Mathur.'

'That's right! It could be another guy,' agreed Nutty. 'GC Kale, for example.'

'GC Kale!' Lucky laughed loudly. 'That glutton has just one love, and that's food.'

'The only way to find out is to be there. You will be there, even if I have to drag you in chains,' decided Billi.

And so, that Sunday, the four of them made their way to the café. Lucky sauntered into the place, a kaleidoscope of butterflies flying inside her stomach, while her three friends loitered near the rear door. There was no sign of GC Mathur. Nor was GC Kale around.

Taking a deep breath, she walked up to a vacant table. Once there, she opened a book and began reading, her eyes darting to the door every few minutes. Five more minutes passed, but no one approached her table. From the corner of her eyes, she spotted GC Vedant Verma sitting at another table. Surprisingly, his girlfriend, the beauty queen, was not with him. He was also reading a book.

A few more minutes passed. It was now 12.15 p.m., and Lucky decided to leave the place. Just as she got up to leave, GC Verma moseyed up to her table.

'Hi, waiting for someone?' he asked. His eyes were twinkling with mirth, she noticed.

'Yes, my friends will be coming in a few minutes,' replied Lucky. Her heart was beating faster than that of a hummingbird. He affected her in a manner she had thought impossible.

'May I have the honour of your company till they arrive?' he bowed gallantly, before dragging a chair and sitting across her. 'Shall I order a chocolate milkshake?'

Tongue-tied and nervous, Lucky found herself nodding. 'Weren't you waiting for your beautiful girlfriend?' she asked petulantly. Noticing the gleam of amusement in his eyes, she blushed and stammered, 'I mean, the two of you are generally together in the café.'

'Just for your information, Urvi is not my girlfriend,' he chuckled. 'She is my first cousin, and we get along very well. I don't have too many friends, neither does she, so we spend some time together on Sundays.'

Lucky heaved a sigh of relief and smiled.

'Should I feel flattered by the assumption that you are jealous of Urvi?' he teased.

'Don't be silly,' she felt herself blushing once again. 'I have no reason to be jealous.'

'I am glad to see that you enjoy reading,' he commented, glancing at the book on the table. 'Not many people read these days. *On the Double*,' he read out the title. 'From the cover, I assume it has something to do with the army. What's the book about?'

'It's a hilarious book about four cadets training at the Indian Military Academy,' she smiled. Nothing pleased her more than discussing books. 'Have you read it?'

'Not yet,' he replied. 'I am reading *The Tattooist of Auschwitz* by Heather Morris. I would like to read the one you are reading. We could exchange our books.'

'Isn't it a tragic book?' Lucky pointed at his book. 'I don't mind you taking my book, but I am not sure I will enjoy reading about the Holocaust. I like to read happy books.'

'It's a good one,' he insisted. 'Try reading a couple of pages. In case you don't like the book, you can give it back.'

Lucky noticed her friends gesturing frantically. Fortunately, the GC had his back towards the trio. She didn't want them to interrupt the tête-á-tête with GC Verma. She had wanted his attention for a long time.

It was impossible to ignore the three girls, who were getting impatient. Nutty strode towards the table, her eyes sparkling with interest. 'Hey, haven't you ordered any food?' she began.

'Have you met GC Vedant Verma?' asked Lucky, and proceeded to introduce everyone.

He was at his charming best. Right from dragging chairs for them, to asking if they wanted a drink, Verma tried his best to be courteous. It cut no ice with Billi, who scowled darkly. Shiny wore a bored look on her face, and Nutty simpered.

It was an awkward situation. Much as Lucky wanted to continue talking to GC Verma, the unyielding attitude of her friends had a discouraging effect on him. Carrying Lucky's book, he left without a backward glance.

'What made you behave so rudely?' Lucky turned to her friends. 'You literally forced him to leave.'

'We didn't say a thing,' retorted Billi. 'In any case, why were you encouraging him to loiter?'

'Firstly, I didn't encourage him. He came up and asked if he could sit here, and I saw no harm in exchanging pleasantries,' Lucky raised her voice.

'Ouch!' smiled Shiny. 'I know you are soft on him, but we came here to find out about your secret admirer.'

'Well! Mathur and Kale didn't turn up, and I don't know of any other GC who could be my secret admirer,' snapped Lucky.

'Could GC Verma be the culprit?' a sudden thought struck Billi.

'Don't be silly. He has a girlfriend,' reminded Nutty.

'Urvi is not his girlfriend,' Lucky warbled in a happy tone. 'She is his first cousin.'

'In that case, there is no roadblock in your path,' teased Shiny.

'Can we order some bloody food, before I faint?' yelled Nutty, trying to be heard over Billi and Shiny's laughter.

'Yes, let's order some bloody food,' laughed Lucky, happy to change the topic.

Back in her room, Lucky lay in her bed, turning the pages of *The Tattooist of Auschwitz*. She ran a finger over GC Verma's name inscribed on the first page, and began reading the book. And a piece of paper fell down. Curious, she opened the folded paper and began reading the note. It was written in the same handwriting as the note with the rose.

I don't know if I will find the courage to tell you the things I want to tell you, so the note. I am your secret admirer, just in case you haven't guessed already. When did I fall in love with you? It could be when I first saw you in the MI Room. I don't really know. But, I have thought of you, every single moment of the day. Your face remains embedded in my mind. It keeps me going when the training becomes unbearable. I don't expect you to reply, but it will be nice to receive one.

Lucky stared at the note, reading and re-reading it several times. It was too good to be true. Her day brightened. She began floating on cloud nine.

The Final Camp

The word 'camp' conjured images of a leisurely and enjoyable experience in Nutty's mind. It was only later that she realized it was foolish to harbour such expectations. During the camps in the first term, they had gone through several minor exercises that required them to practice many of the lessons taught in the theory classes. The final camp was different.

The final camp was a big pain for the LCs. Apart from all other routine drills, parades and exercises, this camp involved long and strenuous trekking through all kinds of terrains, while carrying all the kinds of equipment and accessories that the sadistic instructors could think of. Physically draining and mentally demanding, the camp was geared to take a toll on their already fatigued bodies.

The long treks and minor exercises they had undertaken earlier had taught them to find their way out of dense jungles, to make their way through impenetrable undergrowth, and complete their tasks within the tight deadlines laid out by the cruel DSs. Pitching tents within five minutes was no longer considered an achievement, but a routine affair. Map reading, long marches, night navigation, handling different kinds of weapons, night firing, nothing remained a challenge. Everything that had once been thrilling was now a pain. Most exercises were designed to test human endurance, but they failed to whip up enthusiasm in the cadets. Even the idea of living in tents failed to hold exciting possibilities for the LCs.

This particular exercise was supposed to be the toughest of all exercises. It was also the last one before their Passing out Parade. It was to be conducted in the undulating hills of the Western Ghats, away from human habitation, about 150 kilometres from the OTA campus. While everyone grumbled and complained, the only ones excited with the prospect of the camp were Cockroach and her *chamchi*.

The general's daughter had performed well in every sphere of the training and was confident of beating her closest rival, Billi. Like the Haryanvi lass, Cockroach was also aiming for the Sword of Honour. As of now, Billi was trailing by one mark. Elated with her success, Cockroach was bent upon retaining her edge.

The footballer knew how the dice were loaded, but she wasn't about to give up without a fight. She had been watching her rival closely and knew that the girl was excellent in theory, but when it came to practical application, she was not unbeatable. Surprisingly, Cockroach seemed to know all about the training and the things to come well in advance. This prepared her for every obstacle.

It was during the class 'Operations of War', that Billi realized the excellent knowledge of her rival. The girl knew everything about warfare in mountains, plains and deserts. She also knew all about attack, defence, raid, ambush and infiltration in all types of terrain, and there was no doubt that she had come well prepared and possessed all the PCKs. All the LCs and even the instructors were impressed with the knowledge the general's daughter revealed. Not just the theory, she had done well in the firing tests too.

Word had spread in their first term itself. Her father had served as an instructor at NDA, and he had done a good job of teaching her about the practical aspects of the so called 'Operations of War'. She met her Waterloo when it came to the practicals.

Billi had a definite edge in some aspects of the training. She had displayed an astute mind while introducing the sand model and given out orders for the attack with aplomb. With that, the battle lines had been drawn. The only way to beat Cockroach was to excel in the outdoor exercises.

That morning, things were busier than usual. Although they were accustomed to rising early, that day began a trifle too early for their liking. Dawn had yet to break when the LCs clambered into army trucks, which in all fairness, should have been retired a decade ago. Sighing, they settled down for a bumpy ride. The convoy left the main road and wound its way through mountainous terrain, with the loose parts of the vehicle making noise.

The journey to the campsite was long and bone-rattling. Most army drivers give a damn about the conditions of the road and the vehicle, their only goal is to reach the destination by the specified time. It was an agonizing experience to be bounced about like marionettes on a string. What had begun as a pleasure journey, with much singing and jesting, soon turned into a silent one. All one could hear was an occasional grunt or a curse as the vehicle lurched over a hurdle. A few gluttons like Nutty lay spread-eagled on the floorboard, their bellies burdened by dozens of aloo parathas. Some smart ones, who had mastered the art of sleeping on any turf, through a tsunami, nodded off, their bodies swaying in rhythm with the movement of the vehicle.

The cadets finally reached the exercise area around lunch time. They unloaded their equipment and began to toil. Tents had to be pitched, snake pits dug, equipment organized.

It was at this stage that the clouds began building up, and the sky darkened. This was followed by a welcome drizzle, as the atmosphere began to cool.

Harshali, who was known as the 'baby of the course', stood in the open and turned her face up to enjoy the drizzle. A few others joined her, while the rest ran for cover.

A strong blast of wind threatened to blow them away. The tents swayed and seemed to fold up. The LCs needed to work together to keep them from collapsing. It was a couple of hours before the wind died, but clouds continued to hover threateningly above them.

All hopes of having a good time vanished when the cadets were handed over the schedule. Everything they had learnt in their theory classes was to be translated into action. The tactics, battle plans, route marches, long runs, almost everything would be covered in the various exercises that would take place during the camp. The infiltration exercises, night raids, cordon and search exercises involved good planning and execution skills.

In spite of the bad weather, there was no change in the schedule. The cadets were ordered to march to the mock village that stood many kilometres away. The village was to be cordoned and searched. Orders were given, and the cadets lined up to march through the inhospitable terrain. Stumbling over brambles and uneven landscape, weighed down with the heavy equipment, they began trekking in the dark.

'This is a bloody nuisance,' complained Nutty, pausing to scratch her leg. 'Imagine marching through thorny areas, dressed in a bloody battle dress and weighed down with a heavy backpack.'

'Stop wasting your breath,' admonished Shiny. 'This is the last camp and we have to perform better than the others.'

'How can I bloody perform when I don't even know who's the fucking enemy?' Nutty shouted. Six of them were walking in a single file with Billi leading. Apart from the four friends, Kiran and Jyoti were in the group of girls. Somewhere on the way, thanks to their idea of taking a shortcut, their group had become separated from the rest of their course-mates. Now, they were trying to come up with a strategy of their own.

'We'll find out when we reach the mock village,' Billi shouted back at Nutty. 'Now, just concentrate on finding your way there. There will be a lot of trouble if we get lost. As it is, thanks to you, we have managed to lag behind the others.'

'It was not my fucking fault,' justified the obstinate girl. 'If I need to pee, I need to pee. It's the bloody uniform, which makes it difficult. Boys have it easy.'

'So, who wants to halt for biscuits?' asked Lucky.

'Yeah, I am bloody hungry. You guys didn't let me have enough food because you said it would slow me down.'

‘Four stuffed parathas and three boiled eggs,’ Lucky rolled her eyes in the dark. ‘Save your energy, Nutty.’

‘Do you think there are snakes in this area?’ Nutty suddenly halted in her tracks as the thought of a reptilian attack came to her mind.

‘Will you shut up?’ Shiny shouted in the dark. She hated snakes.

‘Silence!’ shouted Billi. ‘Hold the torch over the map. I think we are lost.’

That brought the group to a sudden halt. Getting lost was the last thing on their minds. Poring over the map, they argued over which direction to take. In the end, it was Shiny who decided the course of their trek. They continued tramping for another hour, wondering if they were on the correct route. Then, they sighted the temporary shacks of the mock village.

To their delight, none of the other teams had reached yet.

Cautiously and stealthily, they crept closer to the shacks, intent on startling the fellows inside. The fake terrorists hiding in the mock village would be ready and waiting for the raiders as instructed.

‘Remember what the DS taught us,’ Billi whispered to her group. ‘Stealth and surprise are the most important elements of an attack. Take the enemy by surprise, and don’t allow anyone to get away. Victory will be yours if you follow the lessons taught in the theory classes.’

‘Victory!’ shouted Nutty, pumping her fist with *josh*.

‘Be silent, you idiot,’ hissed Shiny. ‘Didn’t you hear a word of Billi’s order? Stealth and surprise are the keywords.’

'Since you are so full of *josh*, we will allow you to lead,' Billi pushed Nutty towards the shack. 'Remember, no one is to be allowed to get away. We are right behind you.'

Enthused with the prospect of leading for the first time, Nutty squared her shoulders and led the charge. Bursting into the first shack, she ran into a figure crouching in the darkness. Summoning all her power, she charged headlong and collided into the person. She was so enthused that she forgot it was a mock exercise with a mock terrorist. In her excitement, she imagined herself attacking a real terrorist hiding in a house in Kashmir. Letting loose a volley of abuses, she boxed and kicked the person who she had caught. From her vocabulary to her feet and hands, she used every arsenal in her kitty.

Instead of surrendering, the mock terrorist dodged her attacks skillfully.

'*Saala chhachhundar*,' she shouted, frustrated at being thwarted in her attempts. Spitting expletives, Nutty fought like a wildcat. She headbutted his stomach. The chap responded by landing a heavy blow that caused Nutty to fly across the room.

Refusing to give up, she got to her feet and attacked the fellow once more.

Jyoti, who had followed Nutty into the shack, joined forces with her. Together, they brought the terrorist on his knees.

'Hands up!' Nutty shouted triumphantly.

Minutes later, her rifle pressing against his back, she led the mock terrorist out of the shack. The rest of the group emerged from the other shacks and surrounded them.

'*Shabaash,* cadets!' shouted the captured terrorist, and removed the piece of black cloth tied around his face.

Aghast, they stared at him. The terrorist was none other than their WT Ustad. '*Shabaash,* cadets!' he repeated, rubbing his aching ribs.

The next morning, the story of Nutty's feat spread all over the camp, drawing praise from the DSs as well as ustads.

'I had realized it was WT Ustad, and so I was bent upon getting my bloody revenge,' she boasted.

It was a lie, of course.

Examination Time

Back in the OTA after the camp, life seemed to rev up. There was no time to relax. Exams were fast approaching and with only a week left, it was time to get down to serious studies. As the tests approached, all shamming came to a halt, and the LCs began slogging. Nutty was the only one who was not affected by the examination fever.

'I can't study through the night. In any case, how does it matter if I get less marks?' she philosophized. 'I am not aiming for the Sword of Honour. Besides, I have decided to carry a few chits on my body.'

So, while the rest of the gang mugged military history and geographical details, Nutty made notes on tiny pieces of paper, intending to conceal them in her pockets.

'Don't you dare,' Billi threatened the girl. 'Remember what happened when you tried to take a shortcut during the cross country? I will not allow you to shame our gang.'

'Everything is fair in love and war,' said Nutty blithely.

'This is neither love nor war,' Lucky reminded the girl.

'For me, it is nothing less than war. A battle, if you please,' came the rejoinder.

'Enough! I will ensure that she doesn't cheat,' Shiny assured everyone.

The threat seemed to work. Nutty stopped fooling around and began taking the tests seriously. She began poring over the notes, under the stern eyes of Billi and Shiny. 'We will not allow you to fail,' they promised. 'You have to burn the midnight oil. There is no alternative.'

The three LCs had planned every move and worked all through the term, so they were well prepared. They had studied the PCKs and had made their notes. Every night after dinner, they sat together in Billi's room, poring over the notes.

'I suggest that we break the gang into pairs,' suggested Lucky. 'That way, we will be able to concentrate and help each other.'

While Shiny took charge of Nutty, Billi and Lucky decided to study together.

'Let's test each other by turn,' proposed Lucky, after they settled down to study. 'It will be faster and more effective.'

'That's a good idea,' agreed Shiny. 'We can give marks after testing each other. That will help us judge our performance and provide motivation for improvement.'

Sitting at the study table, Billi opened the notes and began shooting questions at Lucky, who was lying on the bed, her eyes closed, her hands behind her head. One by one, she replied to the questions without faltering. She had prepared well.

Once Billi had finished grilling her friend, they reversed roles. This time, it was Lucky's turn to ask questions. Billi proved to be fairly stingy in her assessment. Regardless, the two of them performed quite well.

They outlined the parts they didn't know and began working on their weaknesses.

In the other room, Shiny struggled with a sleepy Nutty. Despite preparing for one whole week, the girl was faring miserably.

'You have to answer to the point, neatly and in a logical manner. You will be judged by the way you express yourself on paper and not by what you have in your head. Remember, this is the final test. It is the last sprint, so give it all you have.'

'I am trying my best,' grumbled Nutty. After a few seconds, she added brightly, 'It's past midnight. Let's sleep now. Tomorrow, I promise to perform better.'

'No one's sleeping till we have finished the targets we set for tonight.' Shiny picked up the notes and marked the parts she wanted her friend to study. 'I want you to take up my lessons, now.'

The grilling session continued despite Nutty's protests. Shiny was relentless and wanted to beat Aaron. As of now, she had some catching up to do.

It was much past the witching hour by the time the two of them went to bed.

In a matter of one week, the four of them had performed much better than expected. To the surprise of her three friends, Nutty didn't do too badly.

Finally, it was examination time. Confident of their performance, the gang tackled their papers without stress. From the theory to the practical, they fared much better than expected.

'Studying in pairs is a great idea,' admitted a beaming Nutty. She was happy with her performance in the tests. 'Thank you for pushing me. I couldn't have passed otherwise.'

'I don't have any right to take the credit. It's thanks to your hard work,' Shiny praised the beaming girl. 'It was you who had to cram the lessons.'

'Now that the exams are over, it's time to party and enjoy,' Nutty rubbed her hands gleefully. 'Let's go to the café and meet the boys. It will be nice to know how they have fared.'

Everyone agreed that they could let their hair down… oops…chill out. And so, the boys were informed, and they met at Papa Ferdy's for a chinwag. Aaron, Kale and Mathur were feasting on mutton biryani when the gang strode into the café. The place was brimming with cadets, their chatter creating a din. Everyone was in high spirits. The swords hanging over their heads had been taken away for a while, so it was a day to celebrate. The ordeal was not yet over, of course. It would end only after the POP.

They exchanged notes about the tests, and everyone except Kale seemed satisfied with how they had performed. Over glasses of milkshake and biryani, they swapped stories, some sad and some hilarious. They shared some bits about their dreams and ambitions.

'I am glad it's all over and done with,' declared Nutty, taking a huge sip of her milkshake. 'It has been a bloody stressful time. I have never bloody slogged so much.'

'My dear Nuts, it isn't over till the fat lady sings,' quipped Aaron.

'Fat lady? Who's the fat lady and why would she sing?' asked Kale, helping himself from Mathur's plate.

'Yes, where's she going to sing? And more importantly, will the cadets be allowed to attend the event?' Nutty wanted to know.

'Dear Doughnut, you really have a hole where your brain should be,' chided Lucky. 'It's just a proverb.'

'Have you guys given a thought to the allotment of arms and services?' Aaron asked.

'Why waste time over that?' asked Nutty in her typical couldn't-care-less attitude.

'Darling, the allotment of arms will decide what we will do for the rest of our lives in the army,' Lucky informed the girl.

'I will be happy with whatever I get,' replied Nutty. 'Army Service Corps (ASC) would be good, though.'

'Yes, my choice is also ASC,' declared Kale, putting up his hand for a high five. Nutty ignored his gesture. 'I have been told that ASC guys get the best cuts of mutton and rations.'

'Shame on you!' spat Mathur. 'You should be opting for the fighting arms. I want to join the infantry.'

'Kudos!' Aaron slapped his friend on the back. 'As far as I am concerned, I would like to be allotted the same arms as Shiny.'

'As an engineer, I expect to be allotted Engineers, EME or Signals. One is never sure, of course. It also depends on the vacancies. For all you know, I might draw ASC or ordnance,' replied his girlfriend.

'I wish we could exchange arms with each other,' Nutty mumbled, between mouthfuls of biryani. 'That way, everyone can get the arms of their choice.'

'Not really!' Billi entered the fray. So far, she had remained silent, listening to her friends. 'For instance, you or I can't get JAG (Judge Advocate General) branch. It can only go to a law graduate like Lucky. Similarly, we can't hope for EME or Engineers since we are not engineers.'

'Any arms are okay, as long as you get commissioned in the army,' said Nutty.

'I wish they would start taking LCs for the fighting arms,' said Billi. 'Women are as brave as men. There are enough instances in Indian history to prove that. If Rani Laxmibai could fight the British army, why can't we?'

'One can do justice in whichever arms one is allotted. All you need is to remain honest and sincere,' quipped Lucky.

'Well said!' clapped GC Verma, who had sauntered over to their table. 'I agree!'

The tell-tale blush on Lucky's face had an irritating effect on Mathur, who got up and confronted Verma. Unaware of Lucky's affection for the GC, Mathur was hoping to make his own inroads into her heart. 'What brings you here?' he asked belligerently.

'Not you, my dear pal,' Verma laughed, his eyes crinkling with mirth. Pushing Mathur back on the chair, he continued, 'It's Lucky I seek. Do you have any objection?'

That shut up Mathur.

Lucky accompanied Verma to another table, and the two sat chatting for a few minutes, while Mathur fumed.

'Give up, Mathur,' suggested Aaron. 'Can't you see the two are besotted with each other?'

'I will smash my fist into his arrogant face, even if it's the last thing I do,' seethed Mathur. 'Lucky is stupid to fall for that pig.'

'My dear chap, the heart knows no reason,' consoled Aaron. 'Besides, I see nothing wrong with Verma. As far as I know, he's a decent and intelligent guy.'

He didn't want to tell Mathur that Lucky considered him a boor and a bore, nor did he point out that Verma was a suave and well-bred guy.

A Ball and a Half

With just a few days left before the POP, things pepped up to a feverish pitch. Amidst the endless competitions and drill rehearsals came glad tidings of the much-awaited OTA Ball. Everyone greeted the announcement with relief, since it would bring a much desired pause to their sweating.

Things became even more hectic after the announcement about the event was made. The fact that senior cadets were allowed to invite their friends created much excitement. Quite a few GCs, like Aaron and Verma, had found girlfriends amongst the LCs. In fact, there were many couples amongst the senior cadets by this time.

The cadets who belonged to Chennai were in great demand. They were requested to invite their sisters and other female friends.

D Day arrived. Everyone was busy getting dressed for the event of the year.

'I am going to bloody freak out,' declared Nutty, as she combed her non-existent hair for the umpteenth time. Spraying herself liberally with Lucky's perfume, she scrutinized herself in the mirror. 'Do you think there's going to be alcohol?'

'Aren't you going overboard, dear Doughnut?' Lucky paused in the act of wearing her shoes to dart an amused look at her friend. 'Can you imagine the mayhem if the cadets were served alcohol?'

'What's the point of having a bloody ball if there's no alcohol?' Nutty spoke as though she drank frequently. The truth was, she never had more than a couple of sips of beer. She continued to examine herself from all angles, and let out an exasperated sigh. 'Damn! I hate this haircut. How can a girl look like a girl with a zero cut?'

'I have an idea,' Nutty snapped her fingers.

'No!' shouted Shiny and Billi, who had entered the room. 'Not another one of your brilliant ideas.'

'Look, I am not involving you in my idea,' demanded Nutty. Placing her hands on her hips, she asked, 'Why are you so worried? By the way, not all my ideas are silly. At least this one is not.'

'May we know something about your wonderful idea?'
Lucky placed her hands on her friend's shoulders and sat her down on the bed.

'I have decided to wear my skirt and the wig to the party.'

Nutty's announcement sounded like a bolt of lightning. As usual, it was a madcap idea bound to cause trouble.

'Don't be an idiot,' scolded Shiny, shaking the girl. 'Do you think you can get away with this stupid plan?'

'Right from the DSs to their wives, everyone will be at the ball,' Billi added. 'How do you propose to carry out your reckless plan?'

Everyone tried to discourage the foolish girl, who sat with her chin jutting out.

'I see nothing wrong with my plan,' she insisted. 'No one will notice me in the sea of people at the party. No sir, it is a foolproof idea.'

'It is a suicidal idea,' Lucky spoke up. She had been listening to the arguments and counter arguments without commenting. 'We are getting late. Let's carry her, if need be.'

Together the three girls dragged their struggling friend out of the room and down the stairs to join the other LCs on their way to the ball. Nutty was no match for the strong-built Billi and Shiny. 'You are bloody *chamgadars*,' she screamed. 'You don't want me to enjoy the party, but I won't let you have your way.'

'Stop being a nuisance,' Billi growled under her breath. 'Start behaving like a cadet.'

'My darling Doughnut,' Lucky intervened. Linking her arm through her friend's, she led her out of the lobby. 'This is just one of the parties you will be attending. There will be better and bigger ones when you pass out as an officer. In those parties, you will not have a zero cut to flaunt, so cool it now.'

At last, Nutty calmed down and everyone sighed with relief.

It was a warm evening with a clear sky that promised to brighten with the moon. The venue was decorated with lights and streamers and looked festive.

Food and drinks had been arranged in stalls on the adjacent grounds. A photo booth had also been set up. As desired by Nutty, there was a stall where alcohol was being served, strictly for the instructors. Cadets were not allowed anywhere near it.

The soft music wafting out of the giant speakers was drowned by the excited chatter of the youngsters. A huge dance floor, lit up by floodlights, stood in the centre.

The ambience was enough to brighten anyone's mood. The air was thick with the smell of cologne and perfume.

All the cadets were dressed smartly in their 6 Bravo uniform. Sprinkled amongst the milling cadets were a flock of well-dressed girls, who had been invited for the party as plus-ones. Nutty felt a stab of envy in her heart.

'Your admirer is sidling towards this side,' giggled Lucky, as GC Bose made a beeline for Nutty.

'I don't want to be stuck with that bloody GC,' muttered Nutty, pulling Lucky into the thick of the crowd. 'Let's do the disappearing act.'

'How rude is that?' Lucky was outraged. 'The poor chap must have been waiting for this party for a long time. You can't do this to him.'

'I can, and I will do whatever I want. As far as I am concerned, GC Bose has outlived his utility. We were never a couple, no matter what he bloody thinks.'

'Do what you like,' said Lucky. 'I am getting myself some snacks.' She turned to go and collided with GC Verma, who had been following the two girls.

'Whoa! What's the hurry?' GC Verma's eyes crinkled with amusement.

'It's too crowded here,' Lucky replied.

'So, it is,' he agreed, propelling her towards another part of the lawn. 'Let's go somewhere quiet.'

'Where is your friend, LC Lucky?' she heard GC Bose calling out. The poor guy was looking lost. 'I have been looking for her.'

'Hi, she's there in the thick of the action. You will have to fight your way to her,' Lucky chuckled as the flustered GC thanked her.

'Is your friend avoiding the poor guy?' Verma asked.

'Yes, she has no intention of spending the evening with him.'

'What about you? Are you willing to spend your time with me?' Verma asked.

'Here comes our CoCo,' Lucky pointed at the smart and handsome officer, who was accompanied by his elegant wife. 'Isn't he smart?'

'I am jealous,' declared Verma.

Soon, some more DSs arrived and the party warmed up. The emcee announced there would be a competition to declare a Mr and Ms OTA. Each company would have to put forth two contestants who would have to walk the ramp. This would be followed by a question and answer session.

The cadets of the respective companies huddled together to decide their contestants, talking animatedly. As anticipated, Phillora put up LC Urvashi and LC Ritika as their choices, while Zojila nominated LC Koel and LC Smita. The Zojila girls were no match for the Phillora contestants, and everyone knew that Urvashi would win the title.

The adjutant of the academy rolled a huge disco ball on the dance floor to announce the commencement of the officer's ball and announced the first dance. Waltz music echoed through the venue and several instructors went up to the dance floor with their wives. There was a rush as GCs looked around for girls to partner with for a dance. Only a few bashful GCs lagged behind.

Lucky found herself dancing with Verma, while Shiny was happily ensconced in Aaron's arms. Billi, who had refused to go to the floor, found herself cajoled to do so by a huge cadet from Tajikistan. As for Nutty, she was nowhere to be seen. Not that anyone had the time to look for a pin in the haystack.

The wily girl had stolen out of the venue and had made her way stealthily into the company. Once there, she bolted to her room and changed into the tight and short black dress that she had wanted to wear. It took her all of seven minutes to dress. A dash of lipstick, some mascara and eyeliner later, she was whistling happily. She strapped her feet into a pair of high-heeled sandals, and with the wig sitting firmly on her head, she stole out of the company.

Stealing back into the party was hardly a problem for the girl who had mastered the art of camouflage and infiltration. Once there, she parked herself at the edge of the dance floor, which was crowded with gyrating bodies.
Barely had the dance ended when several GCs lined up before her to beg for the next dance. Elated with the attention, Nutty chose the smartest among them and sashayed to the dance floor. As she walked to the floor, she chuckled at the sight of a deflated looking GC Bose standing in a corner with another GC.

GC Rahul Sabnis was the closest to the man of Nutty's dreams. Tall, smart and witty, he regaled his companion with stories about the training, not realizing she was an LC. Nutty, who had given her name as Seema Kulkarni, was over the moon with all the attention he heaped on her. She had also invented an entire background for the so called girl. Seema Kulkarni apparently studied in Chennai and lived in a women's hostel that was very strict and didn't allow male visitors.

The smitten GC swallowed her entire story hook, line and sinker. He refused to let her go after the first dance. Not that Nutty was complaining. They continued dancing together till someone tapped Sabnis on the shoulder. It was his CSM wanting to have a dance with Nutty. He let her go with a nod and watched from the sidelines, intent on grabbing her the moment the dance ended.

As they whirled together, Nutty found herself dancing close to Aaron and Shiny, who threw her a curious glance.

'That girl looks very familiar,' Shiny whispered into her fiancé's ears, and he turned to study the adjoining pair.

'You are right,' he declared after a few seconds. 'I feel the same. But where could I have met her?'

The music changed to a faster beat and everyone whirled away, dancing like crazy.

'Shall we sit out this dance?' Sabnis shouted above the din. He wanted to speak to the lovely girl in private and led her towards the fringes of the crowd.

Giddy after all the attention and dancing, Nutty was happy to step away from the dance floor and monopolize the cadet's attention. 'I am hungry,' she announced.

'Let me fetch you some food,' Sabnis offered gallantly. 'Don't walk away till I return.'

'I won't,' she promised solemnly. 'Will it be possible for you to bring me a bit of rum and cola?' Nutty asked.

A guy who is in love will promise the moon and the stars and try to get them too. She knew it was a risky proposition for a cadet to approach the alcohol counter, but it was also a test. She wanted to know if he could live up to her expectations.

Her request took him by surprise. What she was requesting for was akin to committing suicide. For a moment, the love-struck cadet floundered.

'It's okay if you can't get it,' Nutty added fuel to the fire. 'A cola will do.'

It was an irresistible challenge for one who is trained to do the impossible. This was the first request made by his new girlfriend, and he decided to try his best to fulfil it. Getting the cola was no big deal. It was the rum that proved challenging.

Getting down on all fours, Sabnis went under the soft drinks table. There he debated on the next step. Camouflaged by a body of cadets that had lined up for food and soft drinks, he crept to the next table without being detected by anyone. All he could see were legs and feet around him. From under one table to the other, he crept till he was directly under the table serving alcohol. In his hand was the glass of cola.

Once under that table, he looked at the waiter's legs to determine his position. When the guy moved to one side, he struck out one hand to touch the bottles. It was a guessing game. He didn't know which of the bottles contained rum. Then he hit upon a plan. A huge bin next to the table was filled with empty bottles. He rummaged through them and took out a few rum bottles. Slowly and patiently, Sabnis drained the leftovers of alcohol from each bottle into the drink, till he had topped up the cola.

Job done, he crept from one end to another till he detected a table that was meant for empty plates and glasses. It was at the end of the hall and isolated. Slowly, he stood up. Elated, he made his way back to Nutty.

The two then sat chatting like old friends, eating and drinking to their hearts' content. Woozy after the drink, Nutty flirted with the GC. 'I want to see you again,' he said, 'Let's keep in touch. Soon, I will be commissioned and there will be no restrictions on my movements.'

They exchanged phone numbers and posed in the photo booth. It was an unforgettable evening on many counts. She had executed her plan to perfection.

The party was reaching an end, but no one wanted the evening to end. Winners were announced. LC Urvashi won the crown and the sash of Ms OTA, while the Mr OTA crown went to GC Narula. Soon, the bigwigs and the DSs began trickling out of the party.

There was a sudden rush at the food counters, and Nutty was glad they had grabbed enough food for the evening.

'There will be fall-in at the end of the evening,' Sabnis informed her. 'I will not be able to see you once the fall-in is announced. But I will call you as soon as I find an opportunity.'

His words rang a warning bell in her ears. A fall-in would require her to be back in time, dressed in her uniform. She would have to leave without creating any suspicion.

'Will it be possible for you to fetch me some water?' Nutty requested, and Sabnis rushed to do her bidding. Putting down her plate, she hurried away as fast as her high heels would allow her to walk. No one noticed. Slipping into the darkness, she removed her shoes and ran under the cover of the bushes. Back in the room, she slipped into her 6 Bravo and sped out like a bolt of lightning.

Panting and sweating, she rushed back into the venue just in time for the fall-in. Her friends glanced curiously as she joined them. 'I know what you did,' hissed Lucky, who had noticed her slipping in.

'I did nothing but enjoy the ball, much more than you did,' Nutty hissed back and smiled. 'The first half I enjoyed wearing the uniform, but the next half was double fun without the uniform.'

Lucky stared at the crazy girl, aghast at her audacity.

The Race for the Sword

Three cadets were almost neck to neck in the final run for the Sword of Honour. The one who was chosen to command the POP parade would get the Sword. The three candidates were noticeably stressed as they waited for the announcement about who would be the parade commander.

There was a thunderous applause as Billi's name was announced. It was an incredible feat. She had managed to beat the two GCs who were in the race. GCs Ankit Thakur and Siddhant Chauhan, who were in the running for the Sword, went up and congratulated her, and so did the other GCs.

The entire fraternity of LCs was excited at the prospect of Billi being chosen for the honour. It would be a matter of pride for the entire lot. Envy and jealousy took a backseat as the girls celebrated her success.

As for Billi, it was a matter of proving a point to her father. He wanted the Sword and she would get it for him, she had decided. Winning the Sword had been her sole aim throughout the training. It wasn't a solo feat. Everyone, right from Reichsführer and CoCo, to ustads to the LCs, everyone had helped her in whatever way they could. Ignoring the hoarseness in her voice, she spent several hours practicing commands, while her friends came up with various remedies to deal with her sore throat. Endless rehearsals were carried out till her commands were perfect.

Once in control of her vocal cords, she could out-shout everyone. Her crisp and loud commands delighted the drill ustad, who was playing the mentor's role.

Billi led the parade during the umpteen rehearsals, while the others banged their feet and dug their heels with renewed energy. The ustads shouted and motivated the cadets, trying to get the best out of them, and the adjutant rode all over the ground on his white charger, inspecting and ticking them off.

Blistered feet, aching muscles, stretched-to-limit ligaments, nothing mattered. What mattered was a stellar performance that would amaze the audience.

Mercifully, they finished their last rehearsal before the
POP, and everyone heaved a sigh of relief.

Too excited to sleep, the gang gathered in Shiny's room for a gossip session.

'Now that Cockroach is out of the reckoning, you must be a happy woman,' Nutty remarked, foraging through Shiny's desk for something to eat. Discovering a packet of banana chips, she planted herself on the floor and began munching. 'When I look back, I can't bloody believe that we have come such a long way.'

'Nor can I,' agreed Lucky, snatching the packet of chips from her friend's hands. 'I remember the awkward girl who rolled in with a lot of baggage on her body as well as brain.'

'You are a bloody liar,' snorted Nutty. 'I am not fat. I never was.'

'I will never forget the strengthening exercises doled out by the CSM, Paltu, CoCo and the seniors,' said Lucky. 'They did everything to break us, but we survived.'

'Those were not meant to break us, Lucky. They were meant to push us to the limit of our capabilities. Can you remember the first day?' asked Billi. 'Most of us couldn't perform five sit-ups or run for more than two kilometres. Today, we can easily do 100 sit-ups, climb ropes, run endless kilometres fully loaded. I, for one, owe it to all the strengthening exercises we were made to do.'

'All of it seems like it was in the distant past. When I look at the bloody *jungoos*, I can't believe we were like them in the initial days.'

The atmosphere suddenly turned somber when Lucky declared, 'I will miss you guys, once we pass out. Despite all the hardship and punishment, it's been a fantastic phase of my life.' There was a wistful look in her eyes.

'I will miss the midnight parties and pranks,' Shiny agreed. 'It was good fun.'

'Just imagine, we have been together for 340 bloody days, but it feels like a lifetime. I wonder how many minutes and seconds that works out to.' Sobered by the thought of being separated from each other, probably never to meet again, Nutty grew sentimental. 'You are right, buddy. I will miss you all. It's never going to be the same again.'

'You will soon be married and grow fat after a dozen kids,' Billi chuckled.

'I am not getting bloody married so soon. There's a lot to be done before one thinks of a husband and children. By the way, I am not planning to have a dozen kids,' Nutty snorted at the idea. 'Nor am I going to get fat.'

'As per my reading, Shiny will be the first one to marry,' predicted Lucky. 'I am in no hurry to tie the knot.'

'The next one will be Billi,' exclaimed Nutty, continuing the guessing game. 'Her mother will ensure she is tied in bloody knots as soon as she is commissioned. I won't be surprised if the policeman lands up with a bloody ring during the POP. Won't it be so romantic?'

'No way! With Daddu on my side, no one can force me into matrimony. As far as the policeman is concerned, he can hop for all I care.'

'All I am waiting for is for all the money to come in. We will be rich, you know,' Nutty changed the topic. 'With all the arrears and our salaries, the amount should be a big one. What do you aim to do with the money?'

'I haven't given it a thought.' Billi walked across the room and picked up a piece of paper and a pen from the table. 'Let's make a rough estimate of the amount,' she proposed.

'Not now, Bills,' Shiny snatched away the paper and pen. 'We can do that later. Don't you realize that soon the four of us will be going different ways? I am feeling terrible about that.'

'So am I. Frankly, I wouldn't have bloody made it through the training without your support. I love you guys.' Getting emotional, Nutty hugged each one of them by turn. There were tears in her eyes. 'You will keep in touch, won't you?'

'That doesn't need telling, my dear Peanut,' Shiny hugged her back. 'We have not bonded because we are in the same company. It's much deeper than that. We have suffered bruises, blisters, and broken egos by sticking together. One doesn't forget that.'

Her words brought back many memories of nights they spent motivating and helping each other, and wiping each other's tears. They had laughed, wept and raged together for 49 weeks, and that's a long time, especially when life is no party. It was their will to survive and help the others survive that kept them going.

The most important thing that the academy teaches a cadet is that it is not individual glory but team glory that matters in the end. A war is never won by an individual, but by the collective effort of each and every one. It's a lesson one never forgets.

It was team spirit that kept cadets from snitching even when they had to endure endless punishments meant to break them. The lessons learned were many, and these were the lessons that had won many wars and produced innumerable heroes.

'Here's an idea. Why don't we plan to meet somewhere next year, to celebrate the first anniversary of our commissioning?' Lucky sat up with excitement. 'We could all meet in Shillong for a week-long bash. I will host you.'

'Isn't that a fantastic idea?' Shiny looked at her friends. 'It could be Kerala, if you want.'

'What about Alakhpura?' Billi proposed, her eyes shining excitedly. 'We can organize a friendly match and participate in it, too.'

'I would have proposed Jalna, but I am not sure you girls will like the place.' Nutty looked doubtfully at them. 'I wouldn't blame you, though. It's a bloody dull place.'

'It's not the place that matters, it's the company.' Lucky hugged her friend.

In the end, the girls decided on neutral ground and voted for Goa.

It was late by the time they went back to their rooms, but sleep remained far from them.

The Final Step

The campus had been given a fresh coat of paint, and the mood was celebratory. Parents of senior cadets had begun trickling into the city, a couple of days before the POP. Most of the hotels around the academy were populated by eager parents, some of whom had arrived a few days before the event to visit the nearby attractions.

Entertainment programs, competitions and other events had been organized for the guests, and the campus buzzed with activity.

For the senior cadets, who were passing out, the day indicated the culmination of training. It was a day when they would finally earn their stars, an achievement they had waited for for too long. They had endured endless hours of torture for the stars on their shoulders. The juniors were no less excited, as they conjured images of a similar event for their own POP.

Billi, who had spent a restless night tossing stressfully on the bed, jumped up at the crack of dawn. Her stomach was a pit of butterflies. Commanding the parade meant being responsible for the way it went. Her parents, accompanied by Daddu, had arrived the previous day and were staying close to the campus. To her surprise, Banwari had also accompanied them. The lovestruck guy insisted on congratulating her after the commissioning.

'He is very repentant,' Daddu informed her. 'And very proud of you.'

'He's not given up hope,' said her mother, 'but he has promised not to pester you and wait for your final decision.'

Billi refrained from telling them that her decision would not change. It was a happy occasion, and she had no desire to ruin it with arguments. The pride in their eyes didn't escape her. She was in line for the Sword of Honour and this pleased her father no end. Not in his wildest dreams had he imagined his daughter would, one day, bring laurels to the family and the village. For Billi's mother, who had been the most vociferous critic of her daughter's decision, it was nothing short of an epiphany. As for the ever supportive Daddu, it was a vindication of everything he had done for the girl. She had proved herself invincible.

Lucky's parents and sister, who had arrived two days before the POP, were bursting with excitement at the thought of the commissioning. Having taken in the Chennai sights, they went around the campus preening with pride, clicking dozens of pictures, and sharing stories of her success with the other parents. Her younger sister, crazy about selfies and social media, had a collection of unique ones to show off to her friends. She posted dozens of pictures on her social media pages, earning her hundreds of new followers.

The Patils, who had taken the trouble to travel all the way from Jalna, were impressed not only by the magnificent campus, but also by the discipline and cleanliness in the campus. They had not been able to come to terms with the idea of their movie-struck daughter being an army officer. It seemed too good to be true. The unassuming couple were content in maintaining a dignified silence, save for the constant updates they sent back to the large joint family back in the village.

Joseph Chacko, Shiny's father, had a lot to tell everyone around him. A garrulous man, he boasted about his daughter's academic and athletic feats through her school and college life. Sarah Chacko was happy to take a backseat and enjoy the events along with Aaron's parents.

In her room, Lucky jumped out of bed, ready to embrace the day. Togged in her smart uniform, not a hair out of place, she stood before the mirror adjusting her peaked cap that added a special touch to one's personality. Tightening the belt, she admired herself for a few seconds. A resolute and muscular girl with determination stared back at her. Gone was the naïve and starry-eyed girl from Shillong. 'I have come a long way,' she sighed. Her dream had come true.

As she stepped towards the door to make an exit, Shiny paused for a couple of minutes to look around her room. It held countless memories, both good and bad. She ran loving fingers over her desk. It had seen her stooped for hours over her lessons, many of them frustrating. At the centre of the room was the bed on which the four girls had spent hours complaining and planning, and the closet that held so many secrets.

Nutty stood near the door, staring back at her room, strange emotions tugging her heart. This was the room where the gang had gathered many times to celebrate successes or mourn failures. Cheering and consoling each other, the friends had been the crutches that helped her walk the long and tough path. In a short while, she would have to leave this room forever. Another young girl would occupy it, dreaming the same dreams, sometimes crying with frustration, sometimes laughing with elation. Would she be mischievous, would she be daring or would she be ambitious, wondered the girl from Jalna. Drawing a deep breath, she turned. It was time to go.

A little later, having collected their rifles from the armoury, the cadets waited behind a wall at the Parameshwaran drill square, the ground where they had banged and stamped their blistered feet for hours on end. It was the same parade ground, the same cadets, the same ustads, the same rifles, but the day was special.

The parade was scheduled to begin at 9 a.m., just after the arrival of the chief guest. Billi's heart was palpitating. She held the Sword determinedly, waiting for the cue to lead the parade. The rows of sofas and chairs under the awning were occupied by officers in ceremonial uniforms studded with medals, and many distinguished guests.

She knew her father was sitting in the special enclosure waiting to see her lead the parade. In fact, every cadet passing out that day knew their parents waited to see them put their best foot forward. It was only a couple of hours till the coveted stars would decorate their shoulder tabs.

The Chief of Army Staff, who was the chief guest, arrived. An awed silence covered the ground as the spectators watched him going around in an open jeep, inspecting the cadets, after which the parade began in earnest.

Drums rolled, and the band struck up. Billi issued a command in a high-pitched voice, and the cadets marched past the spectators' gallery with a synchronized swing of their arms, their feet thundering. They saluted the guest of honour and carried out the drill of a lifetime. The sound of hundreds of marching heels hit the ground like an avalanche, much to the satisfaction of the drill ustads.

No one faltered, no one missed a move. Not a single cadet was out of step as they marched smartly with their weapons, determined to give their best. There were tears in many eyes as they watched the young cadets marching. There was a roar of appreciation and applause from the crowd. Cameras flashed and the moment was captured for posterity.

Then came the moment when the chief guest would give away the Sword of Honour and medals to the best cadets. Watched by thousands of eyes, some present during the ceremony, others over video and televisions, Billi was awarded the Sword of Honour. It had not come easy. She had triumphed over more than 300 cadets to head the merit list. GC Ankit Thakur, who was the Academy Cadet Adjutant (ACA), was awarded the gold medal. GC Vedant Verma bagged the silver medal.

After an inspiring address by the army chief, marching slowly to the tune of 'Auld Lang Syne', the cadets took their final steps towards a glorious future, the one they had spent many moments dreaming of. Eyes shining, they marched through the final phase of the parade, each one of them ready to lay their life in supreme sacrifice for the nation, ready to face the extreme risks and hardships the job involved. One thing was for sure; no one would shy away from the immense responsibility laid on their shoulders.

Once the parade was over, parents rushed towards their children. Each of them had one thing in common, they were bursting with pride at their offspring's performance. Soon, it was time for the Pipping Ceremony.

Billi's grandfather pinned the stars on her shoulder tabs and hugged her, tears flowing freely down his cheeks. Moved, she bent down and touched his feet and then the feet of her parents. Banwari hovered around with a sheepish smile on his face.

A visibly moved Baburao Patil did the honours for Nutty, while Shiny bent down so that her mother could pin the stars on her tabs. Ever dramatic, Lucky's father kissed the stars before putting them on his daughter's lapels. There was much hugging and dancing as families and cadets posed for pictures that would be posted on social media and treasured in albums. Dozens of newspaper and television reporters and cameramen were busy capturing the highlights of the event.

They took their oaths under a tricolour fluttering atop a 100-foot mast. It was a solemn affair. Unwavering and strong, the cadets pronounced their loyalty to the country.

'I will, as in duty bound, honestly and faithfully serve in the regular army of the Union of India and go wherever ordered by land, sea or air and that I will observe and obey all commands of the President of the Union of India and the command of any officer set over me even to the peril of my life.'

There was jubilation as the cadets threw their worries aside and celebrated the realization of their dreams. They broke rank, some of them breaking down with emotion and other breaking into cheers. They tossed their friends into the air, amidst shouts and cheers. They sang, danced and executed push-ups together, vowing never to forget each other. The truth was, they would not forget anything, neither the academy, instructors, ustads, or the lessons they had learnt. Billi and the medal winners found themselves at the forefront, with the flash of cameras dazzling their eyes. Feted and interviewed, they were the cynosure of all eyes.

'I owe it all to my grandfather,' Billi responded, when asked who had inspired her to join the army. As for the secret of success, she said, 'I am just an ordinary girl from a village, who dared to dream big.'

That statement was destined to become a headline the next morning. 'I am ready to live my dream.'

EPILOGUE

Life doesn't end with the completion of training. It begins, in fact. A roller coaster of events followed the four newly commissioned lady officers as they took up their responsibilitics in different units. Some hilarious, some excruciating. There was no let-up in excitement or adventure as they adjusted to their units and the men they had to lead.

The army is a conservative and male-dominated organization, in which the acceptance of women as army officers is difficult to come by. The lady officers had to compete physically, emotionally and mentally to gain respect.

While some of the male officers and men were derisive and hostile, others turned out to be tolerant or dismissive. Only a few displayed unconditional acceptance.

Erasing every synonym of the word 'fear', the lady officers struggled hard to keep up with the men, proving themselves time and again. Poised precariously on the tiny perch they had created, they continued to fight scepticism to earn the respect they deserved.

Acknowledgements

The journey from manuscript to the shelves is long and arduous. It requires the combined effort of many people. I am grateful to Bloomsbury and Prerna Vohra for converting a dream into a book.

To Anish Chandy, for representing the book to the publishers.

I am extremely grateful to my mother, Bharati Choudhury, who introduced me to the wonderful world of reading and inspired me to express myself in words. She was the one who set me on the path to become an author.

Writing a book on the military is challenging, and I am indebted to my husband, Ajoy Podder, for filling the gaps in information. He was also my beta reader who never minced words while criticizing my errors.

Work on a book, however, doesn't end after it is written. Editing, cover design, marketing and many other factors come into play before it hits the shelves. A big round of thanks goes to the Tara Khandelwal for going through the text and helping me iron out the creases. I am grateful to Gavin Morris for the excellent cover design.

I am grateful to all my readers for their faith in me. I couldn't have continued the writing journey without your love and support.

Author Bio

Born in New Delhi, Tanushree worked in the corporate sector for eight long years before she quit the rat race to write. Over the years, she has penned eleven novels including *Nurjahan's Daughter, Boots Belts Berets, On the Double, Escape from Harem, A Closetful of Skeletons, Before You Breathe, No Margin for Error, The Teenage Diary of Laxmibai* and *Decoding the Feronia Files*, which is the first Indian Cli Fi thriller. Two of her books, *Boots Belts Berets* and *The Girls in Green* are soon going to be adapted into web series.

She lives with her husband in Pune.